I0721216

The Cerberus File

By

Martin Fraser

Copyright © 2025 Martin Fraser

All rights reserved.

The characters and events portrayed in this book are fictitious. Any similarity to real persons, living or dead, is coincidental and not intended by the author.

No part of this book may be reproduced, or stored in a retrieval system, or transmitted in any form or by any means, electronic, mechanical, photocopying, recording, or otherwise, without express written permission of the publisher.

ISBN : 978-1-911761-30-3

Dedication

In Loving Memory of My Partner, Elaine Travers

On Christmas Day 2022, I presented Elaine with a cardboard golden box containing the manuscript for *The Shadow of the Albatross.* She spent the Christmas period reading the novel and found it irresistible. She became my biggest cheerleader. Elaine regularly asked when I was going to start the follow-up. The answer came soon enough. I began work on the *Cerberus File* in February 2023. She revelled in receiving each new chapter to proofread, seeing the story and character arcs develop.

Sadly, ill health dogged her in the second half of 2024. While we hoped and expected her to make a full recovery, fate cruelly intervened. She sadly passed away at the end of March 2025. *The Shadow of the Albatross* was published worldwide on 29th September 2025, on what would have been her 66th birthday. The *Cerberus File* is dedicated with love to her and the more than twenty years we shared.

Acknowledgements

No man is an island, and as Arnold Schwarzenegger pointed out in his book *Be Useful,* in reality, there is no such thing as a self-made man because everyone, regardless of their position in life, needs help somewhere along their journey.

There are many people to whom I owe a debt of gratitude. People who have kindly given their support, encouragement or expertise during the process of writing this book.

To my beloved and much-missed partner of over twenty years, **Elaine**, for her love, steadfast support, and the invaluable proofreading of my manuscript. I am devastated that she didn't live to witness the successful publication of *The Shadow of the Albatross* and now the *Cerberus File*

My Brother, **Grenville**. A man who has probably read more thrillers than I've had hot dinners. For his constant support and advice throughout this exciting journey.

To **Dr Tessa Hartmann CBE**, founder and CEO of Hartman House in Jersey, for her local knowledge and advice.

To my brilliant editor, **Zainab Adil,** for her expertise, support, and encouragement.

To my Publishing Director, **Elliot Alderson**, for his patience, understanding and relentless enthusiasm to drive this project forward.

And finally, to **Oscar** for his loyal companionship during long writing hours.

About The Author

After nearly 38 years working for Barclays Bank International Ltd, subsequently Barclays Bank Plc, one of the largest banks in the world, Martin Fraser took his chance and the opportunity to follow his dream.

Born in 1961, his mother taught music, while his father worked for the Signals Research and Development Establishment, the Military Research Centre in Christchurch, developing Military communications satellites.

From a young age, he developed a lifelong passion for history, reading, films, music, photography, the natural world and sport, which helped to fuel Martin's imagination and fill his inquiring mind with possibilities. With both parents, older brother Grenville and uncle, all writers or musicians, it was inevitable that Martin should harbour an artistic seed waiting to germinate and burst onto the world.

On countless occasions, Martin would sit at his desk and dream of leaving the bank and unleashing his creative talents, but personal circumstances wouldn't allow it. Eventually, though, when the chance came, Martin didn't hesitate.

In 2022, that dream was realised with the completion of his first novel, The Shadow of the Albatross, a fast-moving international thriller set around the millionaire's playground of Sandbanks in Dorset, Central London, and Wimbledon Village, featuring nefarious billionaire Olga Devereux. In 2023, Martin finished the first follow-up novel entitled The Cerberus File, set in London, Poole, and Jersey. Plans are already well advanced for the as-yet-untitled third novel to feature MI5 Intelligence Officer Greg Travers.

Martin lives in Poole with his beloved Rescue dog, Oscar. Martin eschews the current TV trend for grim, dour, dreary and confusing thrillers that leave one feeling distinctly un-thrilled and more often than not end with an unsatisfyingly damp squib. As Martin says, *"The clues in the title, a thriller should thrill, if it doesn't, what's the point?"*

Prologue

Greg Travers was a man in his element, with an enviable ability to see through the fog of war, to turn scraps of information into extrapolated facts. After several years of undemanding paper-pushing in the Home Office, the move to MI5 had provided him with the perfect platform for his unique set of skills. Married to the beautiful Cassandra, life was undeniably good. All that was about to change.

Within 48 hours, his life and everything he held dear had gone. A medical emergency had claimed the life of his wife and unborn twins. For four months, Travers' life descended into an abyss of alcohol and gambling as he sought solace from his grief in the nocturnal world of London's casinos and nightclubs.

Fate intervened during lunch in a Covent Garden restaurant when a man suffered a medical episode and collapsed in the arms of Travers' companion. The following day, he learned from the Police that the man, who had been seconded to MI5 and had died, was poisoned. Later that day, he found the woman he had lunched with brutally murdered.

Following several incidents, Travers was persuaded to return to work to help track down the perpetrators. The trail led to the door of ruthless billionaire businesswoman and philanthropist Olga Devereux, who was using her global philanthropic public image to mask her criminal activities of strip mining the mineral wealth of developing countries.

As the investigation deepened, Travers uncovered a plot to assassinate a prominent German politician, the grandson of the SS Colonel who murdered Olga's Grandparents and raped her mother during World War Two and on whom Olga had sworn vengeance.

The plot was foiled when the former Mossad assassin contracted by Devereux was apprehended and killed at the top of Portsmouth's Spinnaker Tower. Travers is forced to face his physical fears when attempting to save the life of his kidnapped partner from the clutches of Olga's vicious son, Hector, on the world-famous cliffs at Durdle Door, before a final showdown with Olga at her island retreat in the millionaire's playground of Sandbanks in Dorset.

With Olga arrested and the investigation closed, Travers reflects on his time, his loss, and what the future now holds. The investigation has opened his eyes to new opportunities. He feels it's time for a change, to move forward. So begins months of training and of shadowing experienced Intelligence Officers, learning the skills needed to transition from the office to working in the field.

As inexperienced as he is, he enjoys the challenge, combining the skills of the old and the new. However, the past will soon come back to haunt him with a vengeance when he learns of the Cerberus File.

Table of Contents

Chapter 1 2

Chapter 2 18

Chapter 3 33

Chapter 4 45

Chapter 5 58

Chapter 6 64

Chapter 7 80

Chapter 8 95

Chapter 9 105

Chapter 10 116

Chapter 11 132

Chapter 12 143

Chapter 13 155

Chapter 14 165

Chapter 15 176

Chapter 16 187

Chapter 17 198

Chapter 18 209

Chapter 19 222

Chapter 20 235

Chapter 21 246

Chapter 22 256

Chapter 23 270

Chapter 24 282

Chapter 25 284

Chapter 26 298

Chapter 27 306

Chapter 1

Greg Travers stood in the shadow of the bronze sculptured Freedom Tree in St Helier, the monument raised to mark the 60th anniversary of Jersey's liberation from the German occupation. He looked across St Aubin's Bay. The tide was out. To his left, he watched a steady stream of people walking across the sand and the concrete causeway, making their way towards Elizabeth Castle half a mile in the distance.

Children were splashing in the puddles left behind by the retreating water, four dogs were dashing across the vast stretch of newly exposed beach, tumbling after balls and scampering in playful pursuit of each other. A slight but perceptible chill was in the air, with a gentle breeze coming off the water. The last vestiges of summer were slowly but inexorably giving way to the first real signs of autumn.

Travers cast his eyes around the large sunlit bay before pausing to reflect momentarily. It had been an extraordinary year— one that had begun with the unimaginable. His wife, Cassandra, and their unborn twins had been taken from him when the year was still anew, which had cast him into a maelstrom of complete and utter despair. As Dickens eloquently put it, *"It was the best of times, it was the worst of times"*. Nothing had mattered, least of all his own well-being, including his liver.

Then fate intervened. The murder of Treasury accountant William Constable, who had been seconded to MI5, had set a chain of events in motion that not only dragged him back from the edge of an abyss of alcohol and oblivion but also catapulted him towards a new and quite unexpected future. That was several months ago. The catalyst responsible was the billionaire philanthropist, blackmailer, and murderer, Olga Devereux, who was now safely under lock and key. Travers' bruises had healed, and now, he looked forward to the future with renewed confidence.

He turned and looked at his watch; his connection was late. He had spent the last twenty minutes loitering, waving a copy of the Racing Post like a semaphore flag at anyone who looked remotely like his anticipated contact. Every time someone walked towards him, the paper would be produced and overtly displayed.

Five minutes ago, a well-dressed man had approached him. Travers got off the low stone wall he was sitting on, as the man drew nearer, Travers unfurled the paper. The man looked him in the eye, smiled, nodded, said good afternoon, and then proceeded to walk past him without any further interaction.

With no one else in sight and a growing sense of frustration, he folded up his paper once more and returned to his impromptu seat. For a moment, he considered popping across to the nearby Radisson Blu Hotel for a drink, before thinking better of it and resuming his watch-and-wait routine.

He didn't have to wait long before he heard the sound of rapid footsteps. He looked around to see a young man with shoulder-length black hair, and what looked like a week's worth of stubble, sporting an ill-fitting white T-shirt, ripped jeans and a black baseball cap loping towards him.

'Alright mate,' said the young man as he glanced down at Travers' paper now lying on the wall. 'Could you tell who won the 2.20 at Kempton Park yesterday?'

Travers stared at the man, taken aback, as much by the young man's dishevelled appearance as by the fact that he was using the recognition code that had been arranged and must therefore be his overdue contact. He reached for the paper, then turned to his new acquaintance.

'The 2.20 at Kempton? Who have you put your money on then?' Asked Travers, being careful to follow the scripted wording precisely.

'Stanley's Boy,' came the reply from the young man as he took off his cap for a moment and allowed the breeze to ruffle his hair, before running his hand through the thick shock of dark hair.

The horse's name was a nod to his former boss, Charles Stanley, who was known to be a keen follower of horses and, on occasion, a betting man. No such horse of that name was running at Kempton Park or anywhere else.

'Sorry, Stanley's Boy was a non-runner. Better luck next time,' said Travers as he looked the young man in the eye. The two men smiled knowingly, shook hands, and introduced themselves. Travers suggested they adjourn to the nearby hotel. It took barely a minute to walk the short distance to the Radisson, where they picked out an isolated table outside.

A few minutes later, a waiter arrived and took their order, re-emerging after a short while with their refreshments, then disappearing as quickly as he had arrived. Travers looked at the unshaven younger man sitting next to him, who could have easily passed for a university dropout, with his ensemble suggesting carelessness and a casual disregard for appearances.

'If I'd known MI5 had mufti days, I'd have dropped the suit,' said an amused Travers.

'Oh, this? Sorry, well, it helps me to blend in. If I wore my Tom Ford where I've been hanging out, I'd stick out like a camel in Hyde Park,' said Darius Hussain as he removed his baseball cap. His pronounced Mediterranean lilt now replaced by perfectly Received Pronunciation.

'I was sorry to hear about Stanley. I met him in Cairo about six years ago; he had just been promoted. I liked him a lot. He got me my first job here, and I've been here ever since. Anyway, Greg, what can I do for you?'

Travers took a large swig of his Gin and Bitter Lemon. He had asked for Hendricks but had to make do with Gordons; still, he was not complaining. It hit just the right spot. Replacing his glass on the square wicker table, he looked out across the bay before turning his head slightly towards Hussain.

'I presume you heard about the foiled bomb plot in London last week. The Counter Terrorist Command managed to grab one of the cell. No brains, just a bag carrier, but they did find evidence that at least one of the high flyers may have come through the Channel Islands and cleared the usual security checks. Anyhow, after a few hours of daytime television and other forms of sensory deprivation, he gave us a name, Ali Abadi. A specialist in chemical and biological agents. If the stuff he's handling is truly nasty, then he's probably used it. He's been on the West's wanted list for years. According to SO15, he was in London recently, but now they don't know where the hell he is; he's just dropped off the radar, vanished.'

Hussain looked across at Travers. Abadi was a name that most people in well-informed circles in the Middle East had heard of. A ruthless Syrian man of few principles, as likely to kill you for money as for faith.

'Do you have any leads?' Asked Hussain.

'Not really, Darius. We do know that we will not find these people hiding inside a truck or coming ashore in a rubber dinghy. There is a sophisticated and well-run operation smuggling these high-value targets in and out of the UK via the back door, helping to build up a network of Islamic militant cells. That kind of setup takes money, a lot of money. They have all the necessary documents and a network of safe houses. Abadi is the latest, but there have been others. They are walking in with a new identity, bold as brass, and disappearing off our radar. We need to find the pipeline and plug it.'

'That's... something. By the way, how are you getting on with your new boss?' asked Hussain.

'Like ships passing in the night. Since I left my old job, it's been non-stop training and shadowing. She joined last month, and they have been bouncing her around the country, meeting the teams. We seem to be in different orbits. From what I've heard, she has a pretty impressive CV. A retired RAF Wing Commander, who flew Tornado GR4 fast jets in the Iraq war and the F-35 Lightning over Syria,' commented Travers.

'I know her brother, George, he works for the police here, they are a talented family,' said Hussain.

Travers looked at his watch. He was due to check in with his mentor, who was following up another line of enquiry. 'Darius, I need to go. Look, has Special Branch got anyone on their watch list that might be involved in high-value people smuggling on the islands?'

'Well, we get the usual boat traffic that comes across from France, of course, I spend a lot of my time trying to pick up chatter from the immigrant community about the traffickers, hence my less formal attire. I've heard some unsubstantiated whispers about organised crime being involved, but nothing credible. I'll speak to the Force Intelligence Bureau; they may have a few names. Where are you staying?'

'We're at the Grand, here's my number, call me if you get anything.' With that, Travers rose from his seat, shook hands, then parted.

In the far corner of the bar at the 5-star Grand Hotel in St Helier, MI5 Intelligence Officer Claire Powell sat by the window overlooking the Esplanade and the bay. Having earlier delegated Travers to meet Darius Hussain, she had returned from a productive meeting with the local Head of Intelligence, Detective Inspector David Beckett. He had provided her with a list of names, persons of "particular interest", as he put it. It wasn't a long list, but those on it had the resources, the connections, and the disposition to warrant closer investigation. Powell slowly stirred a fresh cup of cappuccino as she pondered the names in front of her. Top of the list was the Spanish entrepreneur, Osvaldo Phoenix.

At that point, Greg Travers walked into the well-populated bar and briefly looked around until he saw Powell. He threaded his way around the tables until he reached the far left-hand corner of the room.

'Good afternoon, Claire.'

'Hello Greg, grab a drink,' said Powell as she waved the paper containing the list. 'The games afoot, DI Beckett has come up with some names we need to check. He currently has them under surveillance. I've passed them on to ops at Digital Intelligence. How did you get on with Darius?'

'Nothing definite, he's been spending a lot of time undercover around the immigrant communities, but so far, no one's talking. He's going back to the F I B to double-check a few things before getting back to me.'

Travers, reached across and took the notepaper from Powell and looked at the names. Instinctively slipping into analyst mode, he took his phone out of the breast pocket of his suit jacket, logged into an MI5 database, and began typing the first name on the list. Powell watched him, intrigued. She was well aware of his reputation as someone who had the capacity for original, outside the box thinking, and could imagine his analytical cogs spinning away as he began to smile with self-satisfaction.

'Phoenix is an interesting chap, very interesting,' said Travers, who proceeded to provide Powell with his immediate first instinctive impressions. 'Is he top of the list for a reason?'

'Beckett says Phoenix is a slippery customer, but they have never been able to prove anything. They're pretty sure he's involved in organised crime, but despite their best efforts, he always seems to come up smelling of roses.'

Travers thought for a moment and looked at the list again. 'Well, I suspect if we dig a little deeper into Mr Phoenix's life, we may find his sweet-smelling roses have benefited from some very unsavoury manure.'

Powell smiled. 'I can see how you earned your reputation. You have an aptitude for that side of the job. What made you switch to fieldwork?' Asked Powell.

'Logic, reasoning, the ability to extrapolate facts, that's just how my brain works, Claire, and that's all I'd done in the service. Then the Devereux case happened, I presume you have read the file? I'd been on compassionate leave, well, officially I'd been on leave. Actually, I'd spent most of it in a permanent alcohol-induced state of semi-consciousness. Then, I found myself in the middle of a multiple murder case. People were dying all around me, and I didn't want to wait around to be the next statistic. I wanted to help, to do what I do best. Somehow, Stanley managed to get the DG to approve it. However, as the investigation progressed, I ended up working in the field with Alicia

Downes. It was quite an experience, and after what happened to Cassandra, I needed a change, a new direction, something to focus on.

'How is Alicia now? Have you heard from her recently? We worked together several times many years ago. I was so shocked when I heard what had happened.'

'I spoke to her last week. She's okay, she's had several operations and some reconstructive surgery on her face. She's still convalescing,' replied Travers, 'but she can't wait to get back, and I don't think it will be long.'

Travers had been sitting in his room trawling through the other names on Powell's list, cross-checking them on MI5 databases whilst liaising with the Digital Intelligence team. A cold, half-drunk cup of tea sat on his desk, left abandoned, a casualty of his single-minded concentration. His absorption was broken by a knock on the door. Travers closed his laptop before walking across the plush, patterned carpet to open it. It was Powell; she breezed past him into the centre of the room, clearly motivated by a sudden sense of urgency. Travers closed the door.

'What is it?' Asked Travers.

'I've had a call from David Beckett, we may have a break. Akbar Hassan, a known close associate of Ali Abadi, has been spotted in St Helier. One of Beckett's men is tailing him,' said Powell.

'That's intriguing. I wonder what he is doing here. Where was he picked up?

'At the Ferry terminal. He's come in on the Condor. Jersey Customs and Immigration identified him. They were under instructions to let him through. The Police have had him on a long leash.'

'Marvellous, let's go and see where he sniffs then,' added Travers as he reached for his coat.

Powell and Travers promptly left the hotel and walked across to where their hire car was parked. They proceeded on a short journey to the Pier Street car park and left the vehicle there. Hassan was reported as just passing Liberation Square, heading southeast in the general direction of Fort Regent. They walked through an alley with the Royal Yacht Hotel on their right. It shouldn't be long before he comes into view. With his picture on their phone and a running commentary from Hassan's police tail, it was only a matter of minutes before they spotted him. A short, heavy-set man in his fifties, balding with a full, greying beard. He walked quickly with a rolling, almost exaggerated gait towards Pier Road.

Powell and Travers watched from a discreet distance as Hassan approached the new Fort Regent complex. He was heading for Langtree Hall, part of the new multi-purpose conference and exhibition centre. He paused briefly, appearing to use his phone before continuing his journey into the building. They watched as the detective assigned to follow him moved into the central lobby. Powell and Travers arrived moments later. There was a throng of people milling around, some looking at advertising hoardings of future events, others just looking around and admiring the new building. As they moved towards the auditorium, Travers suddenly realised that their target had disappeared. He looked across anxiously at Powell. A moment ago, there had been three pairs of eyes trained on the portly man; now there were none. In just a few seconds, he had vanished and given them all the slip.

Powell instructed the detective to remain in the lobby area and maintain a watching brief in case Hassan slipped back out. Accompanied by Travers, she stepped through the double doors into the medium-sized amphitheatre-style auditorium. Inside, the BSO and Symphony Chorus were rehearsing Verdi's Requiem in preparation for the gala opening night. Travers looked across the length and breadth of the arena, but Hassan was not to be found amongst the smattering of people. Some were officials listening to the rehearsal, whilst others were making final preparations for the glittering event. Travers noticed several doors leading off from the outer aisles on both sides of the theatre. With no sight of Hassan, they split up with Powell moving left and Travers to the right.

Travers opened the first of the doors on his side of the hall. It revealed a narrow white washed corridor, leading to what appeared to be nothing more than a storage room. He found a variety of props, spare chairs and some cleaning materials. Having checked all the cupboards and discovering no other exits, he returned to the theatre, walking down the steps until he reached the second door. On opening it, he found another corridor, much longer than the first. He looked around to see Powell emerging from her first doorway. Travers waved an acknowledgement before disappearing through his doorway and out of view.

Powell opened the second door and walked cautiously down a corridor. Several long tables stood against the wall, some cluttered with electrical equipment. Ahead, she could hear voices, indistinct but definitely voices. With a degree of circumspection, she edged her way towards the sound. Passing a closed door on her left, she moved slowly ahead, her attention fixed on the voices ahead, each word sharpening as she drew closer. As she reached the corner of the corridor and peered around the white plastered wall, she could see the backs of two men sitting at a table in the room. A third man was standing to one side, just out of view, but she could hear his voice; it had an Arabic intonation. The figure turned slightly, enough for Powell to be able to identify the man; it was Hassan.

Of the two men at the table, one suddenly stood, crossed to a wooden bench, retrieved a can from a rucksack, and returned, each movement measured, deliberate. Powell froze as she saw who the man was. One of the world's most wanted and ruthless terrorists, Ali Abadi, was no more than twenty feet away.

Slowly and as quietly as she could, Powell backed away. Then, turning, she retraced her steps along the corridor towards the auditorium's exit. As she quickened her pace, she heard raised voices behind her. She stopped and turned. The voices were not getting any nearer. Turning back, she was met by the sudden, jarring fist in the face that sent her sprawling onto the floor. Momentarily stunned, she scrambled to her feet. Barring her way was a tall, slim man, dressed entirely in black. Despite having what she considered to be handsome features, his piercing blue eyes betrayed a malevolence and a total ambivalence towards her. He stretched out his arm, directing her back towards the room.

Grabbing his arm with both hands, she drove the reinforced heel of her boot forcefully down on his kneecap and rolled him over her left shoulder before applying what she hoped would be a decisive final kick to his jaw. Seizing the moment, she ran towards the exit door, intent on finding safety. But within sight of the exit, her black-clad assailant grabbed her roughly by the neck, his large tattooed hand clamped tightly over her mouth and nose.

Travers emerged from the second door, having found nothing of interest. He paused to scan the hall's floor. There was no sign of Powell. He moved towards a gangway and walked across the wooden floor to the opposite side. As he strode, a sudden silence fell. The orchestra had stopped playing. The conductor had put his baton down and was speaking to the first violin about tempo. Travers reached the first door, opened it and peered down the corridor. There were no discernible noises. Closing the door, he walked towards the second. Before he opened it, his earpiece crackled, followed by the voice of the detective waiting in the lobby. As Travers tried to respond, the orchestra and chorus burst into life with Verdi's dramatic Dies Irae.

'What? Who? I'm sorry, detective, I can't hear you, there's too much noise in here, hang on a minute, I'm coming out,' said a frustrated Travers as he moved away from the door.

In a matter of seconds, Travers reached the lobby, where he was met by an agitated Detective Grady.

'What is it, Detective?' said Travers.

'We've lost Powell's signal, it just went dead,' said Brady.

'Right, come on, follow me,' said Travers anxiously as he turned and ran back into the auditorium with the Jersey detective following close behind.

As the requiem's dramatic strains filled the hall, the conductor cast an irritated glance over his left shoulder while the two men ran noisily across the floor toward the far-side aisle, reaching the second door. Travers opened it and looked down the corridor as far as he could see. All was quiet. Travers and Brady walked down the passageway to its end. The rooms they found were empty. Detective Brady opened an exterior door which led to a small car park. He looked around the parked cars, turned to Travers, shrugged his shoulders, then shut the door. The two men looked at each other. Brady alerted the command centre of Powell's disappearance while Travers began walking back up the corridor. Spotting something under a table, he stopped, bent over and picked it up, examining the crushed plastic.

'Brady! Look, it's Powell's earwig,'

It was now certain that Powell had been taken. It seemed highly improbable to Travers that Akbar Hassan alone could have been responsible; Powell was a capable and experienced operator, perfectly capable of defending herself against the likes of Hassan.

Within twenty minutes, the area was swarming with police. Blue lights carved through the darkness like surgical blades. The rehearsal died instantly—cast members herded away like cattle as officers tore through every corner of the venue. The corridor became ground zero, police flooding the adjoining rooms and car park with military precision.

Then a constable exploded through the entrance, his face chalk-white, eyes wild with horror.

Powell's body had been found. Crammed into a commercial wheelie bin like discarded rubbish.

The words hit Travers like a physical blow, buckling his knees. The world tilted. The brilliant, irreplaceable Powell—reduced to this. After two hours of brutal questioning with the local detectives, their voices hammering at him through a fog of disbelief, Travers stumbled back to the Grand Hotel, where he had the sad responsibility of informing Thames House about her passing. The call felt like signing her death certificate all over again.

After a whisky in the cocktail bar, which did nothing to lift his spirits, Travers walked the short distance round the corner to Casa Mia, his favourite Italian restaurant. He'd thoroughly enjoyed several meals there with Powell since their arrival. Despite it being autumn, the restaurant was still buzzing. As he sat mulling over the day's events, his thoughts were nearly drowned out by the endless chatter of the other diners. Much as he enjoyed the convivial atmosphere the restaurant usually provided, he hadn't any appetite for food now—his heart simply wasn't in it. He made his excuses and left without ordering.

In the Grand's cosy ground-floor bar, Travers made himself comfortable with a double Hendricks and Bitter Lemon. There were several groups of revellers there, warming up for the evening's entertainment with a few drinks before moving on to other venues. He glanced up at a muted, large-screen TV, which provided rolling news coverage. The main news of the day concerned the upcoming German federal elections, which were scheduled to take place in a few weeks. The candidates were out and about pressing the flesh, smiling and promising the earth with everybody else's money. Amongst the more prominent contenders was Otto Graf. He had narrowly avoided an assassination attempt in Portsmouth during the summer. The prevention of which had cost Travers, then boss Charles Stanley, his life. One of the favourites to be the next Chancellor, Graf, was on the campaign trail. Tonight, he was in Frankfurt, and the news media were all over it like a rash with wall-to-wall coverage.

Travers had never met Graf personally, but he had been at the heart of the investigation that uncovered Olga Devereux's vengeful plot to kill the German politician, and it gave Travers great satisfaction to have been the one to bring her to justice. He glanced around the bar, it was quieter now. Picking up his phone, he rang Detective Brady. Powell's death was now the responsibility of the States of Jersey Police. The investigation was ongoing, CCTV footage was being gathered, along with DNA evidence, but so far, nothing significant had turned up. Powell's death would probably impact their ongoing operation; he would speak to DI Beckett tomorrow.

He glanced up once more at the TV screen as the camera zoomed in on the stage where Graf was about to speak. Travers drained his glass, got up and wandered over to the convex bar and chatted with the Polish barman. As the man reached up for the bottle of gin, Travers heard a gasp behind him. Turning around, he saw a woman standing and staring at the TV screen. The picture was filled with smoke. Flames were shooting up into the German night sky. Travers snatched the TV remote from the bar and unmuted the sound. There was general panic, people screaming and running in all directions across the camera position. Police sirens soon replaced the frantic and distressed cries. It was pandemonium. Travers drained his glass and, with a final look across at the disturbing images on the television, he returned to his room.

Travers sat on his bed watching the rolling news coverage as the horrifying drama unfolded in front of him. It wasn't long before it was announced that Graf had been pronounced dead at the scene. The Federal Police and the GSG9 der Bundespolizei anti-terrorist unit had been fully mobilised as the desperate search began for the perpetrators. Travers' phone rang. He stretched across the luxurious white duvet to reach for it.

'Greg Travers.'

'Good evening, Travers, this is Wing Commander Le Sueur. Have you seen the news about Otto Graf?'

'Good evening, Wing Commander, yes, I've been watching it.'

'Pack your bags, I am sending a helicopter for you.'

'A helicopter, ma'am, I don't understand?'

'You need to get back here on the double. I'll explain everything when I see you,' said Le Sueur.

'What about Claire Powell, ma'am? I think I should stay here.'

'The Jersey Police are handling it, it's their jurisdiction. They will keep us informed of any developments. Just get back here, I'll advise your ETD shortly.'

'Very good, ma'am, said Travers.

Travers was not completely surprised to hear from his office following the death of Graf. The German was a man of considerable international standing, and there would undoubtedly be serious repercussions following his death. However, he was surprised to receive an immediate summons to London from his recently installed boss, a person he had not yet met in person or spoken to previously. What could be so important that it would necessitate sending a helicopter to pick him up?

Chapter 2

It was a somewhat chilly start to the day as Travers travelled to Thames House. It had been weeks since he had to negotiate the usual morning rush hour in London. Jersey had much to recommend it, a slower and less frenetic pace than the rat race he had been accustomed to in the capital. After saying hello to his former colleagues, he walked up the stairs to his old boss, Charles Stanley's office. As he approached the office, he was met by his friend and former colleague Nicky Andrew.

'Hello Nicky, how are you?'

'Hi Greg, Great, thanks. How are things with you? How's the new job going?'

'Much like the old job ended up; with people dying. I suppose you heard about the assassination of Otto Graf last night,' said Travers. 'I am afraid we lost Claire Powell yesterday too, in Jersey.'

'Oh my god no! I only had lunch with her last month, what happened?' said Andrew, visibly shaken by the news.

'We were following up a lead, searching a building, when we lost contact with her; she just vanished. Police later found her body in a commercial bin, she'd been strangled and dumped. The guys at the recycling centre would have had a hell of a shock in the morning,' said Travers.

'Are you going in there?' said Andrew, pointing to Le Sueur's office.

'Yes, she pulled me out of Jersey last night. She actually sent a helicopter for me. It can't be just the assassination. Do you know anything about it, Nicky?'

'No, but I'd hazard a guess it has got something to do with it. Oh, and I had better warn you, mind your P's and Q's in there, she's not as soft and fluffy as Stanley,' said Andrew with a mischievous grin as she turned and disappeared down the stairs.

Travers knocked twice on the door, and there was an immediate clipped response of "Come". As the door swung open, the Wing Commander stood up and walked around her desk towards him. Dressed in a smart navy blue two-piece suit. Travers could almost visualise her in uniform, barking out orders; there was something about former military personnel, especially officers, a bearing that sets them apart from their civilian counterparts. Travers estimated that she was probably in her early forties, with a figure that suggested that she still enjoyed the demanding fitness regime she would have been accustomed to in the services.

'Come in, Travers,' said the Wing Commander. 'I'm Steph Le Sueur.'

The couple shook hands warmly as she formally introduced herself and gestured towards the chair in front of her desk. Travers glanced around the office. It was far less austere than the previous occupants' preferred taste. There were several framed photographs of RAF jets hanging on the walls. The old and well-worn wooden desk, favoured by Stanley, had been replaced by a smart curved Beech cantilever desk, with drawer pedestals at each end. On it, a model aircraft, a Tornado, alongside a family portrait, showing Le Sueur in uniform with presumably her husband and two children.

'Would you care for a Tea or Coffee?'

'Thank you, ma'am, a cup of tea would be lovely,' said Travers as he took his seat and looked across at the woman that he would now be reporting to.

Travers was intrigued. Apart from last night's phone call, it was the first time he had had any contact with his new superior. The retired RAF officer was a world away from the previous incumbent, the well-built if overweight, straight-talking Yorkshireman Charles Stanley. Steph Le Sueur cut a slender figure, probably not more than five feet six, shoulder-length dark blonde hair with an educated, polished diction well suited to Officer training at Cranwell. Still, anyone who could fly a Tornado at Mach 2 under fire in the Middle East and rise to the rank of Wing Commander was deserving of respect.

'I'm sorry that we have not had a chance to meet before, Travers. The Director has had me on a whistle-stop tour around the country, and my feet have barely touched the ground since I took over. I am also sorry to have to pull you out of Jersey at such short notice, especially after what happened to Powell. The authorities there will keep us in the loop, don't worry, we'll get whoever killed her and bring them to justice, but there is a more immediate problem to deal with,' said Le Sueur.

'I presume you are referring to Otto Graf, ma'am?'

The Wing Commander glanced down at an open folder in front of her, turning over a sheet of A4 paper, and she glanced superficially at the contents.

'I've been reading your file. It makes for interesting reading, particularly the last twelve months.'

'Yes, I was afraid you might have noticed that.'

'Don't worry, I admire a man who can cut cards with the devil and, by his own strength of character, walk away with a full deck. I see you read Classics at University,' said Le Sueur.

'Yes, I did, it's always been a subject that interested me. Is there any particular reason for your interest, ma'am?'

'Tell me about Cerberus?'

'Cerberus, ma'am? In Greek myth, Cerberus was the three-headed dog that guarded the gates to the underworld; he stopped the souls of the dead from escaping,' explained Travers.

Le Sueur reached for her phone, picked up the receiver, and put her phone on call forward, then closed the folder in front of her.

'Cerberus is the reason you are here. Are you familiar with Project Cerberus, Travers?' Le Sueur's tone of voice changed and was noticeably more serious.

Puzzled, Travers thought for a moment, rifling through his memory. Was this something he had somehow overlooked or forgotten during his hectic months of training?

'Cerberus Project? No, ma'am, I'm sorry, should I?

'I hope not. If you had, the Director General would probably have suspended you and put you under immediate investigation. The Cerberus file is classified as top secret. I didn't even know of its existence until this morning. I was only read into it as a result of the assassination.'

She reached across to her safe, opened it, and recovered a folder.

'This is for your eyes only, unless you want to be put on a plane and sent to our centre in the Falklands as the new cleaner. Do I make myself plain?'

'Abundantly, ma'am.'

Travers was well aware of the restrictions of the Official Secrets Act, which he had signed many years ago.

'Travers, the assassination of Otto Graf has opened a massive can of worms that the Government hoped it had buried, and it could have far-reaching repercussions. A lot of people would be looking over their shoulders if this file were to enter the public domain. Heads would certainly roll, and swiftly. The government would collapse, and it may not just be ours; others could follow like dominoes.'

'I'm sorry, ma'am, I don't wish to appear obtuse, but how could the Graf assassination bring down the government, what's the connection, and what does all this have to do with me?' Travers asked, confused. 'We didn't do it, did we?'

'It concerns Olga Devereux. The Director General has been on the phone with the head of the Federal Intelligence Service in Berlin. They know all about the plot to kill Graf in the summer, and they know who was behind it. They want to interview her,' said Le Sueur.

'So, what's the problem, ma'am? They can send someone over or set up a secure video link and talk to her from Germany.'

'Travers …the problem is, we don't have her.'

There was no disguising the edge in her voice. As a decorated former fighter pilot, she found it intolerable that high-profile criminals with money or influence could still wheedle their way out of justice. What angered her most was not only the failure of the system but the frailty of the people who served it.

'What! Why not? Where is she?' said Travers. It was news that Travers could scarcely believe. Devereux was a ruthless and unscrupulous woman who had made a fortune through the corruption and manipulation of others, and had been complicit in lord knows how many murders and other acts of brutality. He had handed her over to the police himself, expecting that she would spend the rest of her rotten life in prison.

'She walked. She did a deal with the former Home Secretary, and she walked. In return for her freedom, she provided a list of prominent names; some were just corrupt, but for others, she provided irrefutable evidence that they were colluding full-time or part-time with foreign powers. Governmental, Civil Service, Diplomatic, Military, Financial, Industrial, the names are all there. Eventually, our investigation implicated the Home Secretary himself. The PM was furious and gave him the choice of facing prosecution on a charge of treason or falling on his sword. He chose the latter. Officially, he is suffering from nervous exhaustion and is going to spend more time with his family, under our watchful eyes. You can remove one rotten apple from a tree and no one will notice, but if you have dozens, people will start to believe the tree is rotten. The Cerberus file contains the names, evidence, and protocols for keeping all these people under our control. This is beyond top secret, Travers. If the contents of this file became public, even our closest friends and allies wouldn't trust us, we would become an international pariah.'

Travers stood up and walked over to a window overlooking the river. Given her crimes, it was difficult to imagine any circumstances that would have allowed Devereux her freedom. Her threats of vengeance for the death of her son, Hector, as she was led away by the police, which he had dismissed, were now becoming manifestly and frighteningly tangible. He turned around and looked directly at his new boss.

'Olga Devereux instructed her son, Hector, to kill Alicia Downes. Is she going to be told that Devereux is free?'

Le Sueur looked down at a police file on her desk and flicked through several pages before she found the particular passage she was looking for. Pausing, she pursed her lips as she scanned the page for a few moments, then, with a puzzled expression, looked up at Travers.

'Hector's Devereux's body, minus his right hand, was recovered from the water at Durdle Door and pronounced dead at the scene. His missing appendage was found over twenty miles away, when police searched Devereux's island home in Poole Harbour, would you care to enlighten me?'

Travers suspected that she would not have approved of his unorthodox actions, but there was little point in evading the question when, if she didn't already know, it would take no more than a phone call for her to resolve the anomaly herself.

'Well, ma'am, after Hector had gone over the cliff, and Alicia was safely heading to the hospital, I rang Devereux; she was on her island in Poole Harbour getting ready to run. I went there with Detective Roberts to bring her in.

'And the hand?' enquired Le Sueur.

'It was a spur-of-the-moment thing, ma'am. I was angry about what had happened to Alicia. I wanted to shock Devereux into realising that it was all over. It was bagged up in Roberts's car, and well, I thought it might come in...' Travers cut short his sentence.

'I see,' said Le Sueur. 'Well, don't make a habit of it, turning a blind eye is one thing, removing someone's hand, even if they no longer need it, is pushing my boundaries, ok?'

'Yes, ma'am. Ma'am, Devereux has a motive and a score to settle. Alicia was beaten and raped by her during her abduction, I think she has a right to know,' said an insistent Travers.

'That woman has almost unlimited resources and influential contacts all over the world. She could be anywhere,' said Travers.

'Travers, you found her once before. She may have the resources, but so do you. This instruction has come right from the top, the very top; that's why you were recalled. The PM is rattled; he thinks she's involved. He has given this department carte blanche, a free hand to do whatever it takes to bring her to justice. Unofficially, nothing is off the table,' said Le Sueur.

'Yes, ma'am, I understand.'

'You can bring in anyone you need. The Director, the Home Secretary or even the Prime Minister, if need be, will sign it off. You can tell them whatever you like, but the Cerberus file is strictly classified unless the Director clears them. Now, have you got somewhere to stay? I understand you sold your house in Wimbledon?'

'Yes, ma'am, too many bad memories, I bought a place in Lilliput in Dorset. With my change of duties, it didn't seem so essential to be based in the capital,' said Travers.

'Very nice, well, we'll find you somewhere to stay tonight and then sort something out while this is going on. The Communications team have set up a room for you, you'll have access to everything from there.'

'And Alicia, ma'am?'

'Yes, very well, you can tell her about Devereux, but not Cerberus for the time being, unless the Director authorises it. I'll speak to her myself to discuss the situation.'

Osvaldo Phoenix sipped his champagne as he walked across the grounds of his luxury home in Jersey. Beside him stood Ali Abadi, a tall, gaunt man with short, dark, thinning hair and a long scar on his right cheek, the result of a chemical splash during an experiment many years ago. He was smoking a Bolivar Royal Corona cigar that seemed almost too big for his narrow mouth. Forty-two-year-old Phoenix was cultured and well-dressed, even in his own garden. Originally from Spain, he was a man who had always craved success and habitually lived beyond his legitimate means.

Now, after years of black market deals and dubious associations, he had the rewards he yearned for, and the fruits of his success could be seen everywhere. He imported everything from exotic building materials, alcohol, food, tobacco, including Cuban cigars and perhaps most lucrative of all, people. There was a never-ending demand, and he catered for both ends of the market. Abadi had been particularly lucrative; he was wanted by everyone, the risks were greater, and so was the price.

Abadi sat under the shelter of a large green awning as he picked up a tumbler containing a large measure of Macallan ten-year-old single malt whisky.

'Excellent, really excellent. You have a remarkable facility here,' said Abadi, who enjoyed another mouthful of the vintage whisky before putting down the heavy Waterford crystal glass and picking up his smouldering cigar. He took an extravagant inhalation before an equally exaggerated exhale, slowly blowing an enormous cloud of billowing smoke into the air.

'How did you find this place?'

'When I came here, I wanted more than just somewhere to live; I needed a base for my operations, away from prying eyes. The owner of the land didn't know what was here. It had long been forgotten. I came across an old historical article with all the details and coordinates. It was perfect; I made him an offer he could not refuse. The planning permission for the house covered all the extra building work. I replaced the electrics, plumbing, and ventilation, then continued developing it. It is right under the authorities' noses, and they still have no idea,' said Phoenix.

Abadi took a final extended draw on what remained of his cigar, savouring the last remnants of the sublime Cuban tobacco with its exotic, spicy and woody notes before stubbing it out on the ashtray. He looked around at the villa and the extensive grounds leading to the winery beyond.

'This is not the usual smugglers' haunt; it must have cost a small fortune.'

There was a pause as Phoenix looked across at the willowy man sitting opposite him, whose sunken hollow eyes made him feel uncomfortable as they stared unblinkingly at him.

'You know the answer to that as well as I do,' replied Phoenix.

'And what are your plans? You know that the police are searching for you. British Intelligence, the CIA, it will be difficult to move around as freely in the West,' said Phoenix.

'My instructions were very simple. She gave me a list of targets. I gave her a list of my own. I understand that you have been shopping for me; some of the items are difficult to obtain, even on the black market, but with your connections...' said Abadi.

'The flasks arrived three days ago. They are refrigerated in a secure area of the complex. Mr Abadi, I have dealt with a lot of things in the past, and I don't have many scruples, but I won't be sorry when that stuff is off the island,' said Phoenix. 'Why can't you just blow something up?'

'It is not just death and destruction, it is to instil fear, to cause panic. Your boss is truly remarkable. I thought I was ruthless and without conscience. She is extraordinary, I presume, given your relationship that you also know her, shall we say…intimately?'

Before Phoenix had a chance to answer, a man came out of the house, tipped his head towards Abadi, and then approached Phoenix, stooping and whispering into his ear, to which Phoenix nodded in acknowledgement.

'Thank you, Hades.'

'Mr Abadi, it seems that your associate, Mr Hassan, has disobeyed your instructions and become the subject of a police investigation. I cannot risk attracting any unnecessary attention from the police, especially after we had to deal with that woman at the auditorium. Hades will look after him, he is very experienced and efficient in these matters.'

Abadi nodded in acquiescence, showing little interest in the fate of his comrade.

The two men continued to talk for a further thirty minutes before eventually moving into the house as the chilly autumn breeze scoured Phoenix's expansive grounds.

Alicia Downes took one last look across Holland Park before turning away and closing the French Doors. The grass, parched by a long, hot summer, was turning lush green again, thanks to the many weeks of unsettled weather. She walked across to her comfortable black high-backed leather sofa and turned on the television. After several minutes of channel hopping and finding nothing worthy of her attention, she turned it off and tossed the remote control to the other end of the sofa. It seemed to her that every passing day was becoming longer and longer, more and more tedious.

Downes was desperate to return to work. Picking up her diary, she thumbed through the pages until she found the crucial date. The appointment with the medical team would determine whether she could be cleared to return to duty. Pouring herself a glass of wine, she stood and stared into the large mirror hanging on the wall opposite the French Doors. The surgeon had done a good job; she'd never been that keen on her old nose anyway. As she looked at the results of her facial reconstruction, her study was interrupted by a phone call.

'Hello, Alicia Downes.'

'Alicia, hi it's Greg, how are you? I hope this isn't an inconvenient time?'

'Greg, hello, no, not at all.'

'Alicia, I'm in London, I need to see you, it's important,' said Greg.

'London? I thought you were working in Jersey?'

'I was, I've been recalled. Can I pop round?'

'Yes, of course, it would be lovely to see you,' said Downes.

'OK, I'll see you in an hour.'

Travers parked his car and walked the short distance to Downes' apartment. He had visited her on several occasions during her convalescence when he wasn't being ushered to another training exercise. As he reached the top of the third floor, he saw her waiting at the door. After exchanging greetings and a warm embrace, they went inside and sat on the sofa. Two glasses of Prosecco were perched on a small ornate mahogany table beside them. Greg reached for one of the glasses.

'Cheers. You are looking great, no scars or bruising anymore. How are you feeling?'

'Physically, fine. I'm just really bored; it's so frustrating. I can't wait to get back to work,' said Downes. 'I just hope I'm cleared by medical. Now, what's up?'

'As you know, I was working in Jersey on this people smuggling issue. I presume you heard about the assassination of Otto Graf in Frankfurt. Well, before the smoke cleared, I got a call from Wing Commander Le Sueur to report back at once. She didn't say why, but she sent a helicopter for me! So it was obviously pretty important.'

'How's Claire?' interjected Downes.

'I'm sorry, Alicia, but I am afraid she was murdered yesterday. The Jersey Police are in charge of the case, but they are keeping us updated. I am hoping that I will be able to go back and help with the investigation, but I think our new boss has other plans for me.'

Travers then went into more detail about the circumstances of Powell's death. The news had upset Downes. The pair had joined the service together, become close friends, then, later, drifted apart, not helped by several overseas postings. She had always regretted that she hadn't made more effort to keep in touch. Now the matter had sadly been taken out of her hands. It was a painful reminder that life is transitory and not to be taken for granted.

'Listen, Alicia, there is a serious issue brewing. The German Government are under intense pressure to find out who murdered Graf. If no terrorist group claims responsibility, then there is a short list of contract killers that are known to be active. We, and everyone else, are trying to locate them, if only to eliminate them, figuratively speaking. There is one obvious suspect at the top of everyone's list, who has previously tried to kill him, Olga Devereux. The Germans already know about her from last summer, and they want to talk to her, but there is a problem, and it's a big one.'

'What's that?' asked Downes.

'We don't know where she is.'

'What do you mean, we don't know where she is. She is supposed to be in prison.'

'That's what I thought. There has been dirty work at the crossroads. Some grubby deal with the former Home Secretary, he let her go. Now, they have no idea where she is or what she is up to, she may be involved with Graf's murder, or she may not' said Travers, trying to conceal his anger.

'Shit! So what happens now?' asked Downes.

'We have to find her before it really does hit the fan.'

'We also have to help find Graf's assassin. Le Sueur told me this morning that the Germans are sending one of their top investigators over here. When they find out that their prime suspect, who we are supposed to have under lock and key, has been released, someone is going to have a lot of sauerkraut on their face, and a lot of explaining to do,' said Travers, draining his glass.

Downes's physical scars from her encounters with the Devereux family had healed, but the psychological wounds were deep. The very mention of her name had sent shivers through her body. The news that she was at large was a terrifying thought.

'Where are you going to start looking for her?' Asked Downes.

'The first time around, she was a public figure, hiding in plain sight. Once we suspected her involvement, we knew where to find her; we just had to prove it. Today…she could be on the dark side of the moon for all I know. However, if you accept the premise that she is behind it as a starting point, and we switch our focus to finding Graf's assassin. That could lead back to Devereux.'

It was another two hours before Travers eventually left Downes' apartment, replete, after Downes had provided him with the most divine dish of Garlic-Butter Steak Bites. It had been a stressful return to London with the spectral shadow of Olga Devereux hovering over them once more. Despite the unsettling news, any time in Alicia's company was always time well spent. He felt better knowing that she knew, despite the anxiety it had caused. Tomorrow, he would speak to the Wing Commander and ask for the Director General's authority to read her fully into the Cerberus file.

Chapter 3

Dark, acrid smoke rose slowly from the King Henry VIII School building in South East London. No warning had been given, just a thunderous bang as though an almighty clap of thunder had sounded overhead. Flames could be seen emanating from the shattered windows, with thick black smoke beginning to engulf the wounded structure. Children ran screaming from the building into the school grounds, some with flaming clothes, others bloodied by broken glass or falling debris, as desperate passers-by ran in to help, oblivious to the danger.

Before long, the emergency services sirens could be heard getting closer and closer. In a matter of minutes, the Fire Service, the Police and several ambulances had arrived on the scene. Civilians were calmly ushered from the area as the fire crews attempted to guide those still inside the burning school out to safety. Teachers offered comfort and support to those children who did not require any immediate medical attention. At the same time, police secured the area and began taking witness statements.

Twenty-five children and three teachers had been killed by the blast, and many more were injured, some seriously. After five hours, the flames had been extinguished and the Fire Service had begun their investigation. It would be a while before the full report would be made available, but one thing had been established very quickly: it was not an accident. At MI5 Headquarters at Thames House, Millbank, there had already been an emergency meeting with Counter Terrorist Command (CTC).

The charred and shattered remains of an improvised explosive device had been found in the school building, which had been detonated remotely. Whilst no organisation or group had come forward to claim responsibility officially, a letter had been received by MI5 stating that this was to be the first of several indiscriminate reprisals that would occur. No reason or timetable was given, nor were any demands made; it was a simple statement of murderous intent.

Senior Intelligence Officer Steph Le Sueur looked through the initial report and the letter. There would be further meetings with the Joint Terrorism Analysis Centre before advice would be given to the government as to the appropriate response. Le Sueur put the report down on her desk and turned to look out of her office window. As she cast her eyes down onto the busy street below, she watched as a continuous stream of pedestrians passed by beneath her office. Male, female, young and old all going about their daily business, totally unaware of the fact that somewhere in the city, a madman was threatening death and destruction, apparently for no other purpose than a desire to kill innocent people.

As she turned again to face her desk, her landline phone rang. It was the main reception. She had a visitor. The man tasked with investigating the school bombing, Detective Chief Inspector John Deery, had arrived for a briefing. After a few minutes, there was a knock at her door. As she opened it, the burly frame of John Deery stepped towards her.

'Wing Commander Le Sueur?' he enquired.

'Wing Commander Stephanie Jane De Vinchelez Le Sueur…retired. Do come in Detective Chief Inspector Deery.' She said with a welcoming smile.

'Crikey, that's a name and a half. Good morning, Wing Commander Le Sueur, it's a pleasure to meet you.'

She led the Inspector into her office and motioned towards a chair beside her desk. Deery took a moment to look around the office. He had not been in it since his last meeting with Charles Stanley. That was several months ago now, so much had happened since then.

'Can I offer you a cup of tea, Inspector?' asked Le Sueur.

'Thank you, well, I never say no to a fresh brew, I've not been in here since your predecessor's time. Such a shame what happened to Charles.'

'Detective Chief Inspector…'

Before Le Sueur could continue her sentence, Deery interjected.

'Wing Commander, since we are going to be working closely together on this, please just call me John, or Deery if you prefer, I understand that the lads at the office call me one or two other names but I'll not embarrass you or myself with those, having only just met,' said Deery with his usual London bluntness.

'Alright then, John, well, I'll not be the one to throw titles at you either. Just call me Steph. Now, what's the latest on the School?'

'We are still trying to pull all the available CCTV footage we can get our hands on, to see if we can get a shot of whoever planted it. As far as the IED is concerned, it wasn't that sophisticated. A basic exothermic device with an electronic trigger. They probably set it off by phone. The lack of serious technology is going to make tracing the perpetrator more difficult at this stage; almost anyone could have put it together, well, perhaps not my mother-in-law, but it's a pretty open field. The boys in the lab are going over the bomb fragments now.'

Le Sueur then showed the letter they had received from the bomber to Detective Deery, who frowned as he read through the brief text.

'Is that it?' he said. 'It's not much to go on. We don't even know what the motive is, perhaps there isn't one. He could just be a nutter. Apart from the forensic analysis, we are doing all the usual checks, including people who might have a personal grudge against the school, one of the staff or pupils. If anything comes up, I'll let you know.'

'Alright, John, unless this note is some sort of sadistic hoax, we had better be prepared for more incidents,' said Le Sueur.

With that, Deery got to his feet and shook the Wing Commander's hand before leaving her office.

As he walked down the stairs, making his way out of Thames House to return to Metropolitan Police Headquarters, he bumped into his old friend Greg Travers.

'Hello Greg,' said Deery, shaking Travers' hand warmly.

'Hi John, what brings you to these parts?' said Travers.

'I've just been having a chat with your new CO, Wing Commander Le Sueur, quite a change from Charles Stanley. How are you two getting along?' asked Deery.

'Ok. It's a bit early to say, I've only just met her myself. I've been in Jersey. When Otto Graf was assassinated, I was immediately recalled. There's a bit of a flap on. They've roped me into the search for potential suspects. What about you?'

'I'm heading up the investigation into the school bombing, and your new boss thinks there may be more to come. Anyway, I must dash. Good to see you again, Greg. We'll catch up soon,' Deery put a friendly hand on Travers' arm as he turned and walked briskly away towards the entrance.

Travers sat alone in his small makeshift office with nothing other than a fresh and still steaming mug of tea for company, and the remains of a cheese and onion sandwich. In front of him, a wall of monitors linked him to other departments and agencies. Le Sueur had given him a list of possible suspects to evaluate and hopefully eliminate. As he worked through the names in front of him, the one name that kept coming back was the black widow lurking in his subconscious, Olga Devereux.

According to the Cerberus file, she had given up a lot of names and thrown them to the wolves to save her own skin. Then, there was the former Home Secretary, how much did he really know? Would he be willing to talk? If Devereux was still in the UK, then someone was shielding her. She was far too well-known not to be spotted. Much more likely was that she had run and left the country, making her much harder to track down.

Osvaldo Phoenix sat in a deckchair on his lawn. On his laptop, he watched the continuing rolling news coverage of the school bombing on the mainland. Although cultivated, he was, nonetheless, a ruthless businessman who was not in the least bit bothered about bending the law when it suited him and was not above breaking it completely, as he had done on many occasions.

Whilst he was perfectly willing to employ the services of "Hades" to eliminate troublesome business rivals or anyone who threatened the success or security of his ventures, he felt uneasy at the thought of murdering innocent people, particularly children. As he watched the endless speculation pour from the mouths of the seemingly endless conveyor belt of fresh-faced reporters, his mistress Penelope approached him.

Her long, dark, wavy hair bouncing across her shoulders. A Greek beauty in the classic tradition, she had been a successful model before being seduced by Phoenix on one of his business trips; since then, she had never left his side despite his dubious activities.

Penelope put her arms around Phoenix's neck and hugged him. He responded by stroking her arm, before taking her hand and kissing it, looking up into her eyes.

'That man Abadi, I don't like him, how long is he going to stay here?' she asked.

'Not long, my dear. His travel documents have been prepared. He will be gone soon. Happily, he has work to do elsewhere,' said Phoenix.

'What does he do?' asked the curious woman.

'It is better that you do not know, stay away from him…please darling.'

Penelope looked at the screen sitting on the table beside them. It was showing the earlier news footage of the burning school.

'How could anyone do that? It's monstrous,' said Penelope, gripping Phoenix's arms so hard that her finger marks were clearly visible after she had removed her hands.

'We all have blood on our hands, even you mi amor,' said Phoenix.

Before she had time to question his comment further, his phone rang. It was Abadi.

'I'm sorry, I must go, business.'

Phoenix finished his glass of champagne, closed and picked up his laptop, then kissed his mistress before leaving her and walking back to the house. From there, it was a short walk through a concealed entrance to his multi-million-pound underground complex. A massive subterranean lair with living quarters, a kitchen, a generating station with renewable energy, and a state-of-the-art communications room. It was here that he accommodated many of his unofficial house guests, including Ali Abadi and the late Akbar Hassan.

Phoenix entered one of the guest suites where Abadi was waiting for him.

'Mr Phoenix, I understand you have my documents.'

Phoenix reached into his pocket, where he produced an envelope, which he handed to Abadi.

'Here, travel documents, new identification and passport, everything you requested.'

The Syrian opened the envelope and examined the contents carefully.

'Most excellent, the passport, I have used many forgeries, this looks as good as the real thing,' said Abadi.

'It should be; we have a contact in the Pimlico Passport Office in London. We arranged to send your details to their Central Printing centre in Durham. What you are holding is not a forgery, it's a genuine UK passport, as is the biometric data, with certain changes, of course. You will leave tonight, flying direct to London Heathrow. Your special luggage will be sent on to you by our courier tomorrow.'

'Thank you, your reputation is well deserved. Now, if you will excuse me, I have a few things to do before I leave,' said Abadi.

Phoenix stood on his bedroom balcony looking out across the green vista and the sea beyond. Despite a general economic downturn following the Coronavirus pandemic and the war in Ukraine, his business was booming. People always want to be somewhere else, whether they are refugees, economic migrants or people wanted by the authorities. It was all money to him. He poured himself another Brandy. After more than twenty years, it was far too late to search his conscience for any long-lost sense of morality. He enjoyed the good living his business ventures provided, and he wasn't going to give it up despite his dislike for some of those he had been helping.

At the States of Jersey Police Headquarters at 5 La Route du Fort, Saint-Helier the pursuit of MI5 officer Claire Powell's killer was all-consuming. DI Dave Beckett was leading the hunt. Powell had been strangled with the C4-C5 Cervical Vertebrae broken, and her body dumped in an industrial waste bin. CCTV had shown four figures leaving the rear car park close to where the body was found, but identification had been proving difficult. Only one man had been positively identified, Akbar Hassan. However, things changed when his body was discovered floating in the sea off Plemont Beach on the North West coast. Detective Grady handed the Pathologist's report to DI Beckett, who immediately opened it and, after a few minutes smiled.

'He didn't drown then?' said Beckett, looking up at his colleague.

'No, sir, death by asphyxiation and finished off by a broken neck. He was dead long before he went into the water,' said Grady.

'Alright then, I want to know where he's been and who he's seen since Powell died. I want everything. There's a connection. Someone killed him, and I want to know why?'

It only took a matter of hours before word came through that someone had remembered seeing Hassan in a St Helier bar, and he had not been alone. The head barman remembered seeing him with a tall, lean man, with dark hair, dressed smartly in black or dark clothing. The witness described him as "a good-looking bloke". This was what Beckett had been hoping. Detective Grady was immediately dispatched to see what else he could be persuaded to remember.

The Up and Down Bar on Queen Street was a small popular sports bar, frequented year-round by the locals. Grady walked in and made straight for the counter, showing his credentials to the man behind it.

'Are you Thomas?' he asked.

'Yes, sir,' answered the man respectfully.

The Detective showed Thomas the photo of Hassan, whom he had previously acknowledged as having seen at the bar.

'I understand that when you saw him yesterday, he was with a man. I believe you described him as tall, slim, with dark hair and wearing dark clothing, is that correct? Have you seen this man here before? Is he a regular?

'Yes, sir, he comes here quite often, good looking guy, he usually has a girl on his arm. Spends a lot too,'

'Do you know his name?' asked Grady.

'No, sorry,' said Thomas, 'but, well, he doesn't look like your regular punter. He's really tall, elegantly dressed and has a distant, almost detached manner about him. He's a bit strange, if I'm totally honest.'

'Do you have CCTV in here?'

'No, we don't.

'Alright, Thomas. You say he might be in tonight?'

'Yes, that's what he said, but well, you never know. It's a bit like "see you later".'

'Thanks again, Thomas, if you see him again, give me a call, please,' said Grady as he handed the barman his card before leaving.

It was a long shot, but it was just possible that the man would return, particularly if he didn't know the police were actively looking for him. Grady advised DI Beckett of the situation and requested a female detective in plain clothes to join him at the venue as soon as possible. If they were lucky, they would pass for an anonymous couple enjoying a night out. Then, it was just a question of watching and waiting.

For more than three hours, Grady and 28-year-old DS Amanda Willis had sat at a table in the corner of the bar. Up to this point, no one matching the rough description of their man had appeared. Grady looked across the crowded room until he caught the eye of the barman, Thomas, who was still on duty. He shook his head.

Just as Grady was beginning to think it was going to be a wasted evening, an imposing figure wearing black trousers and a matching jacket over a black round-neck T-shirt walked in, accompanied by a young woman. Grady nudged his colleague and nodded towards the man as he strode gracefully across the bustling floor towards the small bar. It must be him. Grady looked at Thomas, who nodded.

Grady and Willis watched the couple closely as they sat at the bar and conversed with the bar staff.

'I'm sure I know that girl,' said Willis, staring intently at the figure in front of her. 'Yes, now I know where I've seen her. She goes to my gym; I've seen her several times.'

'Really? That's the play then. If she goes off to the ladies, follow her, a bit of girl chat and then find out what you can about him,' said Grady, who now felt much happier. They didn't have to wait long before the chance came. The couple under surveillance had been in close conversation for about an hour when the woman climbed off her stool and walked towards the toilets. Willis picked up her handbag, got up from the table and followed.

As she approached the entrance, the door burst open as a pair of giggling girls came out and returned to the bar. Willis advanced to the wash basins where she began to ferret about in her bag before eventually producing her lipstick. She looked across at the reflection of the other woman now standing next to her before catching her eye.

'I'm sure I've seen you at my gym. Hi, my name's Amanda.'

'Oh, hi Amanda, I'm Susan. Yes, I go as often as I can,' she said as she applied another coat of eyeliner.

'It's busy here tonight,' added Willis. 'I saw you come in earlier, is that your boyfriend with you? He's pretty hot!'

'Oh, Hades? No, he's not my boyfriend. We've been on a few dates, though.'

'Hades?' Willis echoed, raising an eyebrow.

'Yeah,' Susan laughed. 'His real name's Andreas Drakos. I think the nickname comes from him being Greek and always wearing black.' said Susan, laughing.

'Greek? Does he work here then?'

'Yes, he works at the Phoenix winery,' Susan said as she flicked at her hair with her fingers before turning towards Willis. 'Well, I should get back to him. Enjoy your evening.'

With that, she walked out of the toilet and back to the bar where Drakos sat with his phone in his hand, having just finished a call. After a few minutes, Willis also left and returned to her table, where she advised Grady of the details that had been revealed to her by Susan.

Thirty minutes later, Grady and Willis watched as Drakos and Susan rose from their stools by the bar. He acknowledged the staff with a cursory wave of his hand as they walked through the crowded room onto Queen Street. The detectives decided not to follow them. The information Detective Willis had gleaned had been verified by headquarters. For the present, Drakos remained a person of interest rather than a suspect.

Chapter 4

Three days had passed since the assassination of Otto Graf, many people's favourite to be the future Chancellor of Germany and one of the most powerful men in Europe. The German media were still giving the event blanket coverage. As far as the public was concerned, there had been no significant developments and no suspects named beyond the usual wild and ill-informed media speculation. The German Domestic Intelligence Agency, the Bundesamt für Verfassungsschutz (BfV), were investigating all known political activists, the anti-capitalists, as well as all those who had been publicly critical of Graf in the run-up to the elections.

On the German domestic front, progress seemed to be grinding to a premature halt. Such was not the case overseas, where the German Foreign Intelligence Agency was co-ordinating with its allies. Western intelligence agencies had a number of international contract killers on their radar. Some had been crossed off the list as they were known to be "busy elsewhere" at the time of the killing. Those that remained unaccounted for were now the subject of an intensive international multi-agency search.

Deery returned to his office, feeling somewhat chastened after a short but animated meeting with the Chief Constable, who was himself still irritated after fending off the Vice President of the BND, the German Foreign Intelligence Service. He had found it increasingly difficult to disguise his criticism of the apparent lack of progress the police were making in pursuit of the possible Graf suspects. Deery reached for his mug of tea, took a swig, and then grimaced with disgust when he discovered that it was barely lukewarm. It seemed to be one of those days.

It was just before midday that Deery's door burst open, and one of his junior colleagues rushed in, much to his superior's consternation and displeasure.

'What the fuck! Can't you bloody well knock before you barge in? I need to have a chat with your mother, sunshine. Well, what is it?' barked the exasperated Detective Chief Inspector.

'Sir, I've got Detective Adams from Charing Cross on the phone, he thinks something is brewing there. Do you want to have a word with him?' asked the young officer, still smarting from his boss's scolding.

'Alright, son, put him through. What's his name…Adams?' said a conciliatory Deery, who realised that it wasn't the young detective's fault that he was in such a bad mood. It was just a short fuse day.

A few moments later, the phone on Deery's desk rang; it was Adams. A pub landlord in Covent Garden had reported two men acting suspiciously and carrying a large rucksack, which they then left tucked under a table at the bar next door before walking away. A few minutes later, two uniformed officers on patrol went to investigate. They found the bag.

'Did they examine the bag, Detective Adams?' asked Deery.

'Yes, sir, briefly, very briefly. It's a job for the bomb squad, I'm afraid.'

Deery strode out of his office, slamming the door behind him. Adams had passed on a description of the two suspected bombers, and all available units were on the lookout for them. The incident room was a hive of activity, as officers studied CCTV monitors of the London streets around the Covent Garden area. The two suspects had been spotted in the Strand heading southwest. Officers had been dispatched to intercept them. Deery knew full well how difficult it would be to keep tabs on them in the busy London streets, but if they disappeared into the Underground, it would be almost impossible. British Transport Police had been notified and were on full alert.

A patrol car pulled up in Duncannon Street just beyond the entrance of the Charing Cross Underground Station. Having left their car, the two officers walked back towards the busy station entrance. As they did so, they caught sight of the two young men walking towards them about ten yards away. The two couples stood and stared momentarily at each other as though transfixed. Then, like athletes responding to the starter's gun, the suspects turned and sprinted away, bursting through the throng of people and down the stairway leading to the Underground station. The two policemen followed, one clutching his radio as he reported the active pursuit and requested backup. The other bounded down the steps two at a time, his eyes trained firmly on the fleeing men.

As he approached the bottom of the steps, two burly BTP officers were already grappling with the struggling men. One of the two men was lying prostrate on the floor, shouting and screaming obscenities as the officer sat on his legs, trying to hold the man's hands behind his back with one hand, while reaching for his handcuffs with the other. The other, a powerful man of over six feet, was flaying about in a frantic attempt to avoid the grasping hands of the other officer. Seconds before the pursuing Metropolitan police officers arrived to assist, he had managed to push the policeman to the ground and make his escape by leaping over the barrier to lose himself amongst the thousands of commuters.

With the arrival of reinforcements, the still belligerent prisoner was led away handcuffed with an officer on each arm, while other officers continued the pursuit of the missing suspected terrorist inside the subterranean station. The corridors were packed with commuters of all shapes and sizes jostling their way through the throng as they made their way down to their intended platforms. Two lines served the station, the Northern Line and the Bakerloo Line, each with a northbound and southbound platform. With trains arriving every two to three minutes, it would be almost impossible to prevent someone from making good their escape.

British Transport Police, accompanied by MET officers, headed straight for the platforms in the hope that they might catch sight of the elusive suspected bomber. It was a next-to-impossible task, with the platforms crowded with people awaiting the next train. As the police officers stood on the platform, nothing seemed out of place. Then came the familiar rush of cold air, followed by a low rumble and the flashing of sparks from the wheels against the black background of the tunnel, along with the screeching of brakes, signalling the arrival of the next train at the platform.

As the train slowed to a stop, the police moved quickly to the doors. Impatient passengers surged forward. When the doors opened, travellers poured out like water from a breached dam, sweeping aside anyone in their path. Once the rush subsided, those on the platform pushed onto the train. A few snagged recently vacated seats, most grabbed handholds before the train pulled away. The officers watched the chaos, knowing their presence at the doors was the best deterrent they could offer. Soon the doors slid shut and the train pulled away, leaving the brightly lit platform behind and disappearing into the black tunnel. The officers looked at one another and shrugged.

DCI Deery had joined the officers on the Northern Line Southbound platform, but there had been no sign of their suspect. The thought that he might have slipped through their fingers was a cause of immense frustration for Deery. Checking in with the other teams did nothing to improve his demeanour. The bastard might be miles away by now, or he might be skulking around the station waiting for things to quieten down. At least the eight station street exits were covered, so they had a chance of picking him up there if he tried to slip away.

Deery had all but resigned himself to admitting defeat when an urgent call came in for backup on the police radio. There had been an incident on platform 2 of the Southbound Bakerloo platform. One of the original arresting officers had spotted their suspect, who, seeing the policeman approach him, had panicked and run, knocking an elderly man to the ground in the process. Deery and the TFL police contingent raced to the scene.

At least with a positive sighting, the police could now focus their resources. There were hundreds, if not thousands, of people milling around. Deery glanced down at his phone at the CCTV photograph of today's fox which had been proving so elusive. Officers were again covering the platform while others were mingling with the travelling public. As Deery scanned the constantly moving faces around him, more police officers joined the search, the net was closing.

As he moved through the arched corridor leading to the Bakerloo Southbound platform, Deery caught sight of something carelessly stuffed into a nearby bin, some of the coloured material still protruding from the lid. He opened it and pulled out the garment. It was a burnt orange coat. He reached for his cell phone again, the CCTV image showed one of the two fleeing suspects wearing a coat of a similar colour. If the perpetrator hadn't escaped already, then he was here, somewhere. The Detective Chief Inspector signalled the other members of the team to his discovery before moving on towards the platform. A moment later, he heard screams ahead of him and the sounds of panic.

On the platform, passengers were rushing in all directions, like startled rabbits. Deery fought his way through the tunnel against the flood tide of panic-stricken commuters trying to get away from the scene. When he reached the platform, he saw the sickening sight of a young constable lying prone on the floor, a growing pool of blood forming a crimson corona around the stricken man's head. The stab-proof vest he had been wearing was no defence against a vicious slash across his throat. Two officers had tried to provide emergency first aid in a vain but unsuccessful attempt to prolong the young man's life. Other officers were clearing the area and keeping the prurient onlookers at bay.

'What the fuck happened?' bellowed Deery as he ran towards two Transport Police Officers standing at the far end of the platform. 'Where did that fucking wanker go?'

'In there, sir,' said the Sergeant, pointing to the tunnel.

'What are you doing standing around here then? Go in and get the bastard.'

'Sorry, sir, we can't, health and safety regulations, the trains are still running.'

'Fuck health and safety, I want that little shit. If he gets away, you'll be directing traffic around Trafalgar Square for the rest of your career, Sergeant,' said Deery.

Before the embattled officer could respond, a blood-curdling scream could be heard coming from inside the tunnel, followed seconds later by the squealing of brakes as the train came to an abrupt halt just beyond the entrance of the station. Deery and the Sergeant gingerly jumped off the platform onto the track and ran towards the stationary train, being careful to avoid the two live rails and the 750-volt DC flowing through them. The battered and bloody body of the man they had been pursuing was now lying outstretched across the rails immediately in front of the train. His severed head rested several yards further down the track. The Sergeant turned away in horror.

'Well, I don't think we need to worry about a cause of death,' said Deery as he looked at the now-smoking head propped up against one of the live rails. 'Sergeant, get hold of the Duty Manager of the Emergency Response Unit.'

Greg Travers yawned and ran his fingers through his hair as he stared at the array of computer monitors in front of him. He was tired. Steph Le Sueur had given him six names, names of people who could conceivably have been responsible for the assassination. Some, whose movements he had successfully tracked over the last week, were eliminated. Others were proving to be more resistant to his forensic search. Yet despite his relentless and unstinting efforts, he couldn't get out of his mind the one missing name that should have been at the very top of the list.

Wherever she was, Olga Devereux would be savouring this moment. He needed some fresh air. Travers left his office, grabbed a cup of tea, and walked across Millbank until he reached the bank of the Thames. There he stood, watching the water flow gently in front of him for a few minutes. Spotting a bench nearby, Travers sauntered across and sat down. Stretching out his legs, he leaned back until he felt the support of the bench against his back. He closed his eyes while the warm autumn sunshine bathed his face.

The moment of peaceful tranquillity was suddenly broken by a tap on his shoulder. For an instant, he was annoyed that his few minutes of peace had been interrupted. Then his half-engaged scowl broke into a broad smile when he saw that it was Alicia Downes. Travers jumped up and embraced her warmly.

'What are you doing here?'

'I have a meeting with Le Sueur', said Downes.

'Did she say what it's about?'

'No, but it could be about my medical, I suppose. Anyway, how are you, any developments?'

'No, not really. I'm just going round in circles investigating this list of Graf suspects. It's true they're all experienced wet workers and not particular about who they kill, but I keep coming back to Devereux. It's just too much of a coincidence.'

After a few minutes, Downes checked her watch; it was nearly time for her meeting. It had been an all-too-brief interlude, but it had made a difference. Travers felt better, at least temporarily. Seeing Downes again had given him a jolt of much-needed energy. He escorted her back the short distance to Thames House. The Wing Commander had been to see her at her Holland Park home whilst she was convalescing, so introductions would not be necessary.

Travers returned to his veritable bunker, where he continued to brood; Le Sueur would expect an update from him soon, and he would need to have answers. He picked up the paper containing the department's list of suspects. Three he had crossed out as they were out of the country, the other three would have to wait. Travers reached across his desk for a beige folder marked classified, the Devereux case file, which was a heavily redacted version of the top-secret

Cerberus file. It contained all the relevant information held on the Olga Devereux investigation; perhaps there was something here that had been overlooked.

Included in the file were details of Devereux's family, her three surviving children who still controlled the Albatross Corporation, a vast international conglomerate worth billions. They also retained ownership of the Albatross Foundation, the charitable institution created by her late husband. Olga had expanded the foundation and later used it as a cover for the illegal strip-mining of mineral and precious metal deposits worldwide, generating millions in illicit, untaxed income. The foundation was now under government oversight through the overseas aid department.

As Travers thumbed through the broad strokes of the Devereux family history, he noted that Olga had two siblings, both older, who had very much stayed out of the public eye. One was Alexander, a highly respected surgeon, now living and working in America. The other was Maria, ten years older than Olga, according to the file, she was living in the Channel Islands. It was at this point that Travers recalled an interview Olga had given to a local writer, Ryan Jones, for a business magazine article some months ago. Jones told him that it was wide-ranging and had discussed her family at length.

Travers reached for his phone and quickly scanned his contacts until he found the J's. Almost as soon as the phone began ringing, Jones picked up. After exchanging the usual pleasantries, Travers asked him just how much Olga had revealed about her immediate family members during the interview. Jones confided that she had initially been reticent about discussing her older sister. Eventually, after some cajoling, she had been persuaded to open up. According to Jones, the two sisters had had a major falling out many years ago over Olga's much-publicised lifestyle, something which many of the senior members of the family disapproved of. Travers thanked Jones for the information. The germ of an idea had come into his head; all he needed now was to get his new team leader to go along with it.

Wing Commander Le Sueur sat at her desk and stared at the model Tornado GR4 displayed proudly in front of her. Her thoughts harked back to an earlier time, when all she had to do was fly a multi-million-pound fast jet at Mach 2 over enemy territory, accomplish her sortie and return to base without getting shot down. Today, she was flying a desk and taking flak from the Deputy Director General of MI5 and the Home Secretary, then fending off awkward questions from the German Foreign Intelligence Agency. They all wanted answers, but so far, she didn't have many.

There was a knock on her door. Travers walked in and stood in front of her desk.

Le Sueur tossed the file she had been reading back into her overflowing in-tray. Despite having only recently met Greg Travers, she was aware of his reputation for thinking outside the box and creating a reliable narrative from fragments of apparently incongruous information.

'Good morning, Travers, well, I hope you have some good news for me.'

'Good morning, ma'am. I've been looking at Olga Devereux's file. I don't have any proof, but my instinct tells me that she is behind the assassination. I'd stake my reputation on it. Did you know she has an older sister living in Jersey? Apparently, they fell out some years ago. I'd like to go and see her. It's possible they may have been in touch since Olga's fall from grace, or she may know where she is. I would also like a tap on her phone and to check her phone records, just in case.'

'Alright, I'll sort out the surveillance and records request with the Jersey Police. I'm not sure how much you will get out of her. Whatever bad blood has passed between them, when push comes to shove, remember blood is thicker than water. I doubt she'll give her up, but I suppose it's worth a try. Just be careful.'

'Yes, ma'am, thank you,' said Travers.

With his request approved, Travers returned to his office. He didn't know quite what to expect from his contact with Maria, whose husband, film producer Michael Scholefield, had died during the coronavirus pandemic. Given the situation, he needed a lucky break, and he didn't much care where it came from. He had to explore every possible avenue.

It did not take long to locate the contact details of Olga's sister. Travers had spoken to her on the phone, posing as writer James Flynn; he had persuaded her to talk to him as a follow-up to the earlier interview given by Olga to Ryan Jones during the summer. The hour-long flight from London Heathrow had been smooth and straightforward, and it was only a few minutes from Jersey's airport to the large and imposing house overlooking St Aubin Village where he was to meet another member of the Devereux family. He took with him a copy of the original article written by Jones, which he had re-read during the flight.

Knocking on the front door, he waited for several minutes. Stepping back a few feet, he looked around at the beautifully landscaped gardens. It was certainly an impressive house. Travers turned back towards the building just as the front door opened. The unmistakable countenance and manner of a household's trusted butler stood in front of him. Travers introduced himself as James Flynn and said that Mrs Scholefield was expecting him. The butler invited him over the threshold and led him into the Drawing room, advising that Mrs Scholefield would be with him shortly.

Travers looked around the beautifully decorated room. Mrs Scholefield was a woman of exquisite taste. On the walls hung several family photographs, including one of the two sisters together, which had obviously been taken some years ago, but there was an unmistakable family resemblance. As Travers stepped forward for a closer look, the drawing room door opened, and Maria walked in. Slender and elegant with an hourglass figure, with shoulder-length grey hair, tied back, and pale blue eyes, though perhaps not as lustrous or seductive as her younger sisters. She extended her hand and introduced herself before inviting Travers to sit down.

'Well, Mr Flynn, how can I help you?'

'Mrs Scholefield, firstly, thank you for seeing me, particularly at short notice. As I mentioned, I am following up on the last interview your sister, Olga, gave a few months ago. The article she was featured in concerned her business empire and charity work. However, she commented a great deal about the importance of family, and yet I understand that there has been a major falling out between Olga and other members of the family, including yourself.'

Travers wasn't sure how candid Scholefield would be, if at all. He had no reason to expect her to reveal any intimate details of family rifts. Nevertheless, she did make it very clear that many members of the family were not at all happy about Olga's extravagant and much-publicised social life. Maria and Olga had not spoken for ten years and scarcely seen one another in the ten years before that. It seemed clear to Travers that the estrangement between the two was a cause of much distress, at least to Maria, who fidgeted nervously while talking.

Other than her apparent agitation when discussing her younger sibling, Travers found Scholefield to be charming and surprisingly candid; she had even been happy to show him around her magnificent house and grounds. She maintained that she had had no contact with her sister and would certainly not entertain the thought after her arrest in the summer, which had brought such disgrace on the family.

After an hour or so, Travers thanked her for her time and left the house to drive the short distance to the airport for his return flight to London. Scholefield stood at the front door and watched as Travers' car disappeared out of sight, then turned, flicking the edge of the door behind her with her fingers until it clicked shut. She walked slowly back to the drawing room, where a figure of a woman stood in the window, staring out at the drive. Hearing a noise, she turned away from the glass, and with a contented smile, walked towards Scholefield as she entered the room.

'So that's the man you spoke about?' asked Scholefield.

'Yes, Maria, that's the man, Mr Gregory Travers. A member of MI5 and the man responsible for Hector's death. I'm looking forward to meeting him again, face to face,' said Olga Devereux. 'He won't be nearly so happy to see me next time.'

Devereux reached across and picked up a banana from the nearby fruit bowl and slowly peeled it, exposing the soft, pale yellow flesh of the fruit. Delicately, she caressed the tip of the banana with her tongue before biting off the end.

'No, not happy at all.'

Chapter 5

Greg Travers walked out of the bar at the famous Dog and Fox pub in Wimbledon Village, carrying a large glass of Babich Headwaters Sauvignon Blanc and an Aperol Spritz. Despite the inexorable passage of time, the autumn sun was still pleasantly warm. There was a stillness in the air with no discernible breeze to further subdue the sun's weakening rays. Travers put the drinks on the wooden table by the outside wall and took his seat. Without a moment's hesitation, Alicia Downes reached across for her glass of New Zealand wine.

'Cheers,' said Downes as she brought the glass to her lips and took a large, satisfying sip before returning it to the table. 'I don't think I've had that one before, it's rather nice.'

Travers did not attempt to disguise his pleasure at seeing Downes again. She looked well, the facial scars had healed, and her blue eyes were sparkling again. When he had seen her last, she was still officially convalescing and consumed by the monotony of her enforced inactivity.

'Well, Alicia, how are things with you? You're looking very chipper today, anything you'd care to share?'

'I had a really good meeting with Steph the other day. She wants me on her team, provided I'm cleared by medical,' said Downes, whose beaming smile evidenced just how thrilled she was about the prospect of returning back to work.

'Great. When is your medical?' asked Travers.

'Monday, I'm so bored now, I can't wait to get back to work. Oh, and life at home has taken an interesting turn, too. I think I'm being watched.'

'What! Are you sure?' said a concerned Travers.

'Of course I'm sure, Greg. It's my business. The good news though, is whoever they are, they're not very good at it. They are just skulking around Holland Park opposite my apartment with a pair of binoculars, looking more like a Peeping Tom. Usually there is just one; occasionally another one joins. I did think of going over to introduce myself and offer them a mug of tea laced with either a laxative or a sedative. It would have been so much fun.'

The news that Downes was under surveillance worried him. Travers was convinced that Olga Devereux was somehow involved in the Graf assassination. He was also acutely aware that she would exact bloody revenge for the death of her son Hector. Alicia had been at the scene that day and a party to the desperate events that unfolded. Devereux was a woman now devoid of conscience or compassion. There was no telling what she was capable of, but if she was behind having Alicia watched, it could only spell serious trouble.

Although from her demeanour, Alicia didn't seem particularly perturbed at the new attention she was enjoying. Downes could see by Travers' furrowed brow and the subtle change in the inflexion in his voice that he was concerned by the revelation and moved to reassure him.

'Greg, I've been followed by the Russians, the Chinese and even the Americans, and they know their business. Whoever is keeping an eye on me, they are not professionals.'

'All the same, I think we should have them picked up,' said Travers. 'At least we might find out who they are working for. I'll speak to Le Sueur.'

Only a few months had passed since the William Constable case. It didn't take much for Travers to recall all too clearly, the anxiety he felt when Deery told him that it was possible he might be targeted by the same people who brutally murdered his friend Lisa Scott, who had witnessed Constable's poisoning in Covent Garden. Despite all his reasoning, he began seeing killers everywhere. Every time he caught the eye of someone staring at him, his imagination ambushed him. Could it be the face of a ruthless killer, or just another passer-by? He vividly remembered finding the butchered, blood-soaked body of Lisa in her bedroom. The full horror of that moment haunted him. If somebody was watching Alicia, it was likely that they were watching him too.

Instinctively or perhaps subconsciously, Travers looked around at his fellow drinkers, then beyond the low perimeter wall at the passing pedestrians going about their business. It was too early in his fledgling career in the field to feel comfortable about being followed. Turning back to the table, he picked out a slice of orange from his glass of Aperol Spritz with his fingers and chewed it mercilessly down to the rind before dropping the remnants into an ashtray.

'Has there been any update on Claire?' asked Downes.

'No, not really. The Jersey police are still investigating. I was in Jersey yesterday as it happens, and spoke to DI Beckett of Special Branch, who's in charge of the investigation. They have their eyes on a Greek character who goes by the name of Hades. He sounds a bit of an oddball, but he's an associate of the person we were following when Claire disappeared. At the moment, they don't have anything to link him to her murder.'

'And how is the Graf investigation going? Any developments?'

'Developments? Well, speaking of Jersey, I went to see Olga Devereux's older sister, Maria. She has an incredible house, boy, money really does flow through that family. They apparently had a major falling out some years ago. I thought she might be able to give me some personal insight into Olga's whereabouts, but she says she hasn't seen her in ten years. I've ruled out some of the suspects on Le Sueur's list. I still have two or three to look into, but my gut still says Devereux is behind it. It's just too much of a coincidence to be ignored.'

Their conversation was interrupted by the clatter of hooves behind them. The horses from the Wimbledon Stables next door were gearing up for their outing through the village street and onto Wimbledon Common for their regular exercise. Despite the daily occurrence, it was always an event that turned heads and caused many of the passing shoppers to pause and watch the parade of horse flesh, which was always followed by one of the staff carrying a bucket and a very large shovel, which invariably caused a degree of amusement. Travers turned to Downes, who was particularly tickled at the sight of one of the stable girls hurriedly pursuing a large chestnut horse that had chosen that moment to discharge a bountiful quantity of "manure" along the road as it walked down towards the common.

'That's why they grow such fine roses in the village,' explained Travers.

Half an hour later, the fading sun had all but disappeared behind a swirling bank of livid grey clouds. There was now a chill in the air, with maybe rain to follow. Travers and Downes retired inside to the comfort of a vacant pair of two-seater gold velour sofas in front of a tall, rough stone chimney breast surrounding an open fireplace. Downes stared at the welcoming and warming flames for a few seconds before removing the yellow Cashmere scarf that had adorned her Charcoal grey crewneck sweater. She glanced up at the tall mirror hanging directly above the open fire before turning and sitting down on a sofa.

Travers, returned from the bar with fresh drinks, sat on the sofa opposite to Downes. He looked across the oblong wooden coffee table at Alicia as she leaned forward and grasped her fresh glass of wine. He cast his mind back to the summer when his late boss, Charles Stanley, first introduced them, then working together to bring Olga Devereux in. He greatly admired and respected her as an intelligence officer, but even more so as a woman.

'How are your parents, Greg? What did they say when you told them about your change of duties?'

'Honestly? I think they were ok about it. After what happened to you, I didn't labour the potential on-the-job risks, but the important thing is that we are talking again. As I told you down in Sandbanks, when Cassandra died, I just pulled the emergency cord, stopped the world and got off. Nothing seemed to matter anymore. The people I needed the most, the people who would have understood, the people I should have asked for help from, I blindsided. After we wrapped up the Devereux matter, I decided to visit them, tell them how I really felt after Cass died, and tell them everything…I told them all about you, too. Perhaps not quite everything, even though Mum did give me the third degree. They send their best, by the way and hope to meet you before too long.'

'Oh no! Really? Said Alicia with wide-eyed, exaggerated horror.

'Don't worry, you needn't blush, it was nothing too embarrassing. Well, apart from my mother asking if she would need to buy a new hat!'

Alicia Downes was one of those people who had the gift of making whoever she was speaking to feel as though they were the most important person in the world. Well-educated, well-travelled, and an easy and natural conversationalist, she was the perfect companion. Having already exchanged more intimate confidences than many long-standing married couples, their relationship had given Travers the emotional fulfilment and support he had needed after the events of the previous nine months. Notwithstanding the near-death experience they shared at Durdle Door when Hector Devereux met his timely end, an experience that would bind the two of them together forever.

The conversation flowed smoothly and uninterrupted for another hour. It was as though the many months of Downes' tortuous recuperation had never happened. She was optimistic, full of life and energy, with her captivating smile and sparkling eyes, it seemed to Travers that she was back to her old self. Having crossed the insidious shadow of the Albatross organisation once before, now, with Alicia back by his side, he was ready to begin the hunt for their nemesis, Olga Devereux, again.

It had been a lovely few hours, a chance to relax, unwind and catch up. Tomorrow was going to be a demanding day for both of them. Travers called a taxi; it would probably take the best part of an hour, depending on the traffic, to cover the almost eight miles to Holland Park. His offer to travel with her to Holland Park was gracefully declined despite the prospect of her recently acquired but unsolicited stalker waiting in the wings for her.

Chapter 6

It was going to be a very busy Monday morning for Travers. Early starts just didn't agree with him, with a sausage roll in one hand and a strong cup of tea in the other, he had entered his "bunker", admittedly not fully awake. A midday appointment, marked of high importance, with Steph Le Sueur had appeared on his calendar. Top of the agenda was an update on the remaining names on her list of potential Graf suspects.

Also attending the meeting was his friend, DCI John Deery. He would need to work fast if he were to gather enough information on the outstanding candidates to placate his new boss' urgent need for answers, at least enough for him to make an educated and informed guess. As he waited for his system to boot up, he sent Alicia a text message of good luck before her medical today. Having seen her yesterday, he was pretty confident that it should be a formality.

At midday, he knocked on the Wing Commander's door. After a moment's delay, Travers walked in. In front of him was Le Sueur, sitting behind her beech desk. The burly figure of Detective Chief Inspector John Deery rose from his chair, stepped forward and greeted Travers with his usual whole-hearted firm handshake. The two men sat down as Le Sueur picked up and opened a beige folder with a large "Classified" stamp emblazoned on the front. She glanced at the topmost sheet before addressing the two men.

'Good afternoon, gentleman. Before you arrived, I received a call from the Deputy Director General. This morning, he had a video conference call with the Vice President of the German BND, the Executive Director of

Europol and a Vice President of Interpol. There was only one item on the agenda, and you can guess what it was.'

At which point she tossed the file onto her desk and turned first to Greg Travers.

'Well, ma'am. I have been reviewing the list of possible suspects you provided. If they stick to their modus operandi, I think we can eliminate five of them. Four were definitely not in Germany at the time of the assassination, and the fifth was arrested on a job by the Mexican Police last month.'

'And the last one?' pressed Le Sueur.

'Ayesha Emara, an Egyptian National, known in Intelligence circles as the Asp, on account of her penchant for using snake venom. I don't think I'd be popping round to her place for dinner. The last confirmed sighting was in Turkey last year. Since then, nothing, she's completely vanished,' said Travers with a shrug of his shoulders.

Le Sueur pursed her lips as she scribbled a note down on a piece of paper.

'Do we have a photograph and a description of this character, Emara?'

'Yes, ma'am, albeit several years old,' said Travers as he thumbed through his file.

'Alright, have it sent out to all agencies, including the CIA and NSA. Anything else?'

'Yes, ma'am. Olga Devereux. I spoke to her older sister, Maria, last week. She insists she has no idea where she could be and has had no contact with her since her arrest.'

'Do you believe her?' asked Le Sueur.

'Well, I have no reason not to at this point. Reports suggest there has been bad blood between them for many years now. There is just one more thing, and I would like to bring the Inspector in on this. I spoke to Alicia Downes yesterday. Someone has her under surveillance at her home. You know my thoughts on Devereux, ma'am. I think there might be a connection.'

Le Sueur considered the matter for a moment before turning to Deery for his thoughts.

'I'll pop round with a couple of my boys and pick him up. Whatever else they may be doing, I am sure we can pull them in for questioning for something, stalking, or just being a public nuisance.

'Thanks, Inspector, I appreciate it,' said Travers.

Le Sueur then called on the DCI to provide her with an update on the two recent bomb incidents. As Deery had previously indicated, the initial school bombing was, by modern standards, fairly primitive with a basic C4 RDX compound and a timer which had been activated remotely. Unfortunately, as no one had claimed responsibility, the very simplicity of the device made tracing the originator difficult, for those moving in those circles, C4 was readily available.

The Covent Garden device was much more interesting, though. Due to the vigilance of a local publican, the device had been spotted soon after it was planted, and the police, subsequently, the bomb squad, were called in to defuse it. Even better was the fact that one of the bombers had been arrested trying to evade capture and was still being interrogated.

'We arrested one of the fuckers, I beg your pardon, Wing Commander, suspects, outside the station. Screaming like a randy fox, he was. The other one got over the barrier and away into the station. We sealed off the exits and flooded the area with men, and eventually, we flushed him out. When he saw us closing in he must have lost his head, panicked and run into the tunnel. Unfortunately, moments later, he met the incoming train head-on on so to speak. The next thing I saw was his bonce bouncing down the track like an overripe melon,' said Deery.

'Yes, thank you, Chief Inspector, you need not have been quite so graphic in your description. At least you have one of the suspects in custody. What has he had to say for himself?' questioned Le Sueur. 'And what of the bomb itself, any clues?'

The Chief Inspector provided Le Sueur and Travers with a progress report on the interrogation, which to date had actually yielded little new information of real value.

'What of the explosive device, Chief Inspector? Have you got any further with discovering who is behind this murderous campaign?

Deery reached into his pocket for a black notebook, skipping through several pages until he found the details he wanted.

'PLX, otherwise known as Picatinny Liquid Explosive, developed by the Americans during the Second World War,' began Deery.

'We've come across it once or twice, ma'am. It's a liquid binary explosive, mostly Nitromethane with a dash of Ethylene Diamine,' added Travers 'It's pretty volatile stuff. It just requires mixing and then detonating. It's what they call a thermobaric or fuel-air explosive,' continued Travers.

'Chief Inspector, this is clearly a step up from C4. You need to get to the bottom of this, and quickly. We were lucky this time. That man you are holding knows something. I am not going to wait until we have another incident with hundreds of fatalities. If the Met can't persuade him to talk, in the interests of national security, we'll take him off your hands. I have no doubt that we have the facilities to provide him with the additional motivation necessary.

After further discussion regarding the direction of the investigation, Le Sueur closed the meeting, with Deery promising to provide her with a full update and evaluation of the suspect's interrogation tomorrow. As the two men rose to leave the office, Le Sueur called Travers back. Travers and Deery shook hands before the Chief Inspector turned away, opened the door and left. Travers turned and resumed his seat, waiting for the Wing Commander to elaborate.

'The German Foreign Intelligence Agency are sending two of their operatives over here tomorrow, in part, to assist us, as they put it, with our investigation, but also to follow up some leads of their own. I have assigned Heidi Buchan from personnel to be their liaison, do you know her?'

'Dark auburn hair, dimples, dark red lipstick? I have bumped into her a couple of times,' said Travers. 'What exactly are her instructions apart from babysitting duties?'

'She will introduce them to the right people, show them around and generally keep an eye on them. We don't want them talking to anyone or going anywhere they shouldn't.'

'I presume neither Heidi nor our German friends know anything about Cerberus?'

'No, and it has to stay that way. They have their own file on Olga Devereux, and they are looking for her too. We just have to make sure we find her first.'

Travers returned to his makeshift office. He stared at one of his blank computer monitors for a few moments, just as a writer might look at a blank Word document or a sheet of paper, waiting for the spark of inspiration —the moment of magic that sets everything in motion. All he saw was fog, bits of a disjointed puzzle with as yet nothing tangible to connect the dots. He sat back in his leather reclining chair and put his hands behind his head. He had built an enviable reputation as someone who could see through the murk that confounded everybody else. There was a knock at the door, his friend Nicky Andrew stood in the doorway holding a fresh cup of tea.

'Bless you, Nicky, that's just what I need right now,' said Travers as he leant towards her and took the large black mug from her hand. 'My head's going round and round with this Graf business. The Director General wants answers, the Wing Commander wants answers, and now we have a couple of German agents from the BND coming over, and they are going to demand answers.'

Andrew stayed for about twenty minutes listening patiently as Travers expounded his thoughts, theories and frustrations. She had always been a good sounding board, and it was an ability that he appreciated enormously. Travers glanced at his watch; it was after two. Alicia should have completed her medical by now. When he spoke to her over the weekend, she hadn't indicated what her plans were for today following her examination. He dialled her mobile number. She picked up almost immediately. Her voice sounded upbeat and buoyant. She had gone to lunch after leaving the Thames House Medical Centre and had just returned home. The medical had gone without a hitch, and the psych evaluation seemed to go well. She would have to wait until tomorrow to find out if she was deemed fit to return to work, even though the Winger Commander was keen to have her back as soon as possible.

Travers informed her of his meeting with Le Sueur and John Deery earlier, and that the Chief Inspector would deal with her unwelcome voyeur, who was now hiding in the trees opposite her windows.

Having received the reassuringly good news from Downes concerning her medical, Travers rang John Deery. Following the meeting with Steph Le Sueur, Deery had returned to continue the interrogation of the surviving suspected Covent Garden bomber. Travers was keen to glean as much information as possible, especially with the impending arrival of the Germans, knowing how thorough they were likely to be.

'Greg, I do have some news for you, I am not sure if it is good or bad, though. The good news is, I don't think this is Islamic terrorism, even though the guy is clearly of Middle Eastern origin. I've dealt with several members of Al Qa'ida and Harakat Mujahideen, and this guy just doesn't fit the profile. He's not a fundamentalist, but he is a junkie. I'll bet someone picked him up and offered him a regular fix and a wodge of cash and got him to carry the bag,' said Deery.

The news that the two bombing incidents were not due to Islamic terrorism created another disturbing problem. If not them, then who, and what was their endgame?

'John, if this chap is not a true believer, we should be able to break him down and find out where he has been living and who his contacts are. We were dead lucky this time that they were spotted, and we got to the device before it detonated. We don't have time to sit around and wait for the next one to go off.'

'You're right, Greg, leave it to me. I'll offer him a carrot first. If he doesn't have a nibble, I 'll get my wife's rolling pin out and start on his fingers! I am sure we can persuade him to share whatever he knows. I'll get back to you if I have any news.'

Travers chuckled to himself as he put the phone down. Deery was all bluff and bluster, but as a man, he was the salt of the earth. However, he would certainly put the fear of god into someone who wasn't accustomed to his roguish London humour.

It had been a long day, apart from conversations with Alicia Downs and John Deery, Travers had also spoke at length to Interpol and the Jersey Police. Tomorrow was going to be another lengthy day. Le Sueur had already warned him that he would need to be available for their German visitors, who would, no doubt, want to talk to him, given his unique understanding of Olga Devereux. Travers was determined to enjoy a relaxing evening before the rigours of the morning. His temporary digs in Churchill Gardens were nothing to write home about, but they were comfortable and only a short trip from Millbank, and they had the advantage that he didn't have to share them with anyone. Le Sueur had given him the option of sharing a safe house, but since the death of his wife, he had become used to his own company. He poured himself a long Bombay Sapphire Gin, topped up with a Britvic Bitter Lemon, and sank back onto a large black faux leather sofa as he listened to the news on television, as his bath slowly filled with a mixture of hot water and relaxing mineral salts.

Travers awoke with a start. It must have been the effects of the gin and the long soak. He had slept deeply, perhaps too deeply. He stretched a reluctant arm across the soft grey duvet, to the edge of the double bed to reach his old Omega Seamaster wristwatch sitting on the bedside table. Squinting uncomfortably, then slowly blinking, he attempted to focus on the blue watch face. Slowly, the hands came into sharper focus. It was late. He turned on the radio;

the 8 o'clock news had started. He checked the alarm on his phone, it had chimed, snoozed three times and been cancelled. Travers cursed softly, swept aside the duvet and hurriedly washed, shaved and dressed. It was going to be another breakfast on the hoof. At least, it was an easy twenty-minute walk to Thames House, and on a sunny day, a pleasant stroll along the bank of the Thames.

On arrival, Travers headed straight for the canteen before returning to his small but well-equipped room, now armed with a large cup of strong tea and a bacon roll. Logging on to his system, he first checked his emails. Thankfully, there was nothing that required his immediate attention and most importantly, nothing from his boss, Steph Le Sueur, to indicate the imminent arrival of Fraulein Koehler and Herr Hoffman from the Fatherland.

Travers sat back in his seat, breathed a sign of muted relief and took a sip of his steaming hot tea, quickly followed by a large bite of his crusty roll. This had the unfortunate effect of sending a sizable squirt of brown sauce out of the opposite side of the roll, narrowly missing his clean white shirt before landing with a plop on his desk. In the solitude of his present surroundings, the normally restrained Travers allowed himself a few choice words of "industrial" language as he cleaned his desk before finishing off his bacon roll without further mishap.

Just before 10 o'clock, the mobile phone on his desk rang; it was Alicia. She had just received a phone call from Le Sueur confirming that she had passed her medical and that she was to report the following day to discuss her return to work. She was ecstatic. No sooner had Travers put his mobile phone down, his landline rang. This time it was the Wing Commander. He was to report to her office immediately to meet the two German intelligence officers who had just arrived. Travers put on his suit jacket and made his way out of the small room and up the stairs to his superior's office.

On entering the office, he saw her standing in front of her desk, chatting with the two visitors. Also in the room was Heidi Buchan, the Leith-born Scot who had been brought in to look after them; in reality, her role was to keep an eye on them. Travers walked across the room and greeted his intelligence cousins. Christina Koehler was striking, slim, average height with long, straight red hair, green eyes and more freckles on her tanned face than he'd had hot dinners. Franz Hoffman was the very antithesis of a classic German stereotype, rather short, almost stocky, with receding dark, slightly curly hair and dark brown eyes. He shuffled forward, extending his hand to meet Travers. They both greeted him warmly with a firm handshake.

With the introductions and formalities completed, the four took their seats. Le Sueur brought the visitors up to speed with the latest information currently available, avoiding any references pertaining to the Cerberus file and Olga Devereux's murky "get out of jail free" deal with the former Home Secretary. As Travers listened intently to the discourse, he was surprised and slightly perturbed by the amount of intelligence the Germans had already accrued on Devereux's criminal activities.

They had also been made aware at an early stage by the Director General herself that Devereux was no longer in custody, which had not gone down well, given the previous assassination attempt on Otto Graf. Koehler and Hoffman were anxious to follow up several lines of enquiry relating specifically to Devereux, starting with her office in Poole and private island in neighbouring Sandbanks. Today, they would receive a full update from various MI5 departments as well as briefings with other UK agencies.

Tomorrow, Travers would escort Christina Koehler to Poole to question senior management still working at Albatross House and visit Olga's island retreat and the nerve centre of her criminal empire. Whilst Buchan would remain in London with Franz Hoffman, who had received a tip-off from a German informant that a former employee of Devereux's had information to sell regarding her illegal activities. Whilst Travers had been to Poole and Sandbanks during the summer with Alicia, he had not previously visited the Albatross building himself which had been part of her brief. Following some persuasion, he had managed to convince Le Sueur to allow Downes to accompany them to Poole by virtue of her knowledge of the building and having spoken to a number of the staff there during the previous police investigation. Despite some reservations, Le Sueur had agreed to Travers' suggestion.

The following morning, Travers, Downes and Koehler set off from Waterloo Train Station on the approximately 2-hour 20-minute direct trip to Poole. In this instance, it was far more convenient than driving, which Travers normally would have preferred. Albatross House was a little more than a five-minute walk from Poole Station.

The carriage was less than a third full, and the absence of children running up and down the aisle, creating mayhem, was not lost on the travellers. Travers sat in the window seat next to Downes, directly opposite Koehler, with a narrow table separating them. It was the first time that the German had visited the south coast. Travers watched her as she stared out of the window at the passing countryside. Her long flame-red hair cascaded across her shoulders against the jet-black background of her Hugo Boss jacket. Catching sight of his attentiveness through the reflection of his face in the glass, she turned her head slightly until her green eyes met his, holding his gaze, she smiled coyly before turning away. Travers' lips, oblivious to any hostile witnesses, quivered with marked satisfaction. Suddenly, he felt a sharp pain in his right ankle. He looked sharply around at Downes, who smiled back at him, but it was a look that could have only one possible interpretation. She then re-crossed her legs and continued to read her magazine.

It was a short walk from the Railway Station along Serpentine Road to their destination. The huge granite-clad Albatross House dominated the skyline with its three massive interlinked heptagon towers, each containing eight floors. Travers, Downes and Christina Koehler walked around to the front of the building, pausing for a moment in front of the seven wide stone steps leading up to the entrance. They looked up at the formidable structure towering over them. Travers glanced across at Downes, who appeared hesitant.

'You ok, Alicia? Christina and I can do this,' said Greg.

'Yes, I'm fine, Greg, thanks, let's crack on,' Downes replied.

'Is there something I should know?' said a puzzled Koehler, who knew nothing of the significance of the moment.

Travers did not answer but looked across at Downes, it was not his place to make public the sordid details of what took place on the seventh floor and left it to Downes's discretion.

Downes thought for a moment, but only for a moment. After all, this was both woman to woman, an ally and a fellow professional, and she wasn't someone given to hiding her thoughts.

'I broke into Devereux's office during the summer and cracked her safe. Unfortunately, I was caught getting out, and they didn't like it. She and that bastard son of hers tortured me, up there.'

The three then walked up the steps to the glass and stainless steel entrance and through the double doors to the reception area. The long wooden desk on the left, in front of the security window, was just as Downes remembered it. Travers walked up to the counter, where he spoke to a polite young man in a dark blue uniform. Shortly afterwards, he returned to the waiting ladies and informed them that someone would be down in a few minutes to take them up to the Albatross offices.

Five minutes passed, and then a young, well-dressed man approached them. He introduced himself as Maxwell Jarvis. He would take them up to meet the chief executive. With a nod to security, one of the electric turnstiles was opened, and they followed Jarvis across the stone flooring to the lifts. As they ascended in the mirrored lift, Jarvis told them that he had worked there for ten years and been Mrs Devereux's personal secretary for five until she was forced to relinquish control in the summer.

On reaching the seventh floor, they walked across the foyer to C block, where Jarvis released the electro-magnetic doors. They walked around to the left, where there were several glass-fronted offices. Jarvis knocked on the second door and entered the room. He spoke briefly to the man sitting behind a large, light wooden desk before bidding the three visitors to enter. The man stood up and introduced himself as Nicholas Woodford. He explained that he had been appointed by the Government to oversee the Foundation, the charitable wing of the Albatross organisation, since the removal of its founder, Olga Devereux.

Woodford escorted the trio across to B block and Devereux's office suite. Having unlocked the heavy wooden door, the four walked in, across the plush carpet towards the centre of the room. Koehler wandered across to the large windows and looked out across the harbour towards the Purbecks. Downes looked around the room. It was unchanged since the last time she saw it. On one side of the suite were the same two white Italian leather sofas where she had been held down by Devereux's thugs, beaten, drugged, and violated. Despite her best efforts, she couldn't free her subconscious from the dreadful memory of what had happened to her that night. All the psychological training she had received was swept aside by what that woman had done to her. The physical scars had faded, but the sight of the sofas had brought the remembrance and horror flooding back.

'Mr Woodford, is there any reason why this room has not been reused or repurposed?' asked Travers, who had noticed that Downes was still clearly affected by the place.

'The building is still owned by the Devereux family. This is still technically her office,' replied Woodford.

'Mr Woodford, I presume she has not been back,' asked Koehler.

'Not to my knowledge,' he replied.

'Could she come back without your knowledge?' added Travers.

'Mr Travers, this is her building,'

Downes turned away from the sofas, her fists clenched and face drained of colour.

'Would you mind if I had some air?' said Downes.

Woodford picked up a phone and called his secretary who appeared a few minutes later.

'Max, would you take Miss Downes upstairs to the roof garden please?'

Travers and Koehler remained in the suite for another ten minutes. The large oil painting of Olga's grandparents had been removed from the wall and still sat on the floor nearby. The wall safe behind it was open but long since emptied.

Koehler continued to question Woodford and several other key members of staff who were present during Devereux's residency there. Travers was anxious to join Alicia. Her undercover experience and confidence had fooled most, but to those who had sharp eyes and a willingness to see, the papered cracks were there. Jarvis led Travers up the A block stair to the eighth floor, which housed one of two restaurants. Passing through a small bar, Travers was directed through a sliding door which led to the patio and roof terrace, where he found Downes sitting at a table with a glass of water.

'Hi there. How are you feeling now?' enquired Travers as he sat down beside her and put a reassuring hand on her forearm.

'Better now, thanks. I'm sorry, I really was okay going into the building, but seeing those sofas brought it all flooding back, I guess I'm not quite as tough as I thought I was.'

'I'm sorry, Alicia, it's my fault. I shouldn't have asked you to come, it was too soon.'

'No, it was my choice, Greg. Besides, who knows what might have happened between you and Fraulein Koehler on the train if I hadn't been here?' said Downes knowingly.

'Well, I wouldn't have a bloody great bruise on my
ankle for one thing,' said Travers with a disarming smile

.

Chapter 7

The Limehouse area of East London was steeped in history, although the Blitz of the Second World War and late twentieth-century redevelopment had changed the area greatly. Gone were many of the old Victorian buildings, replaced with modern apartment blocks. It was here that Franz Hoffman was to meet Ernest Lazlo, a man of dubious reputation and formally employed by Olga Devereux as one of her hatchet men, until his services were dispensed with. It was a half-hour drive from Millbank, crossing Lambeth Bridge, passing through several districts south of the Thames, including Walworth and Bermondsey, before re-emerging on the north side of the river via the Rotherhithe Tunnel.

Buchan picked up a vehicle from the car pool, then began the drive to Limehouse with Hoffman beside her. Hoffman was a garrulous, ebullient character, and like his colleague, his English was excellent even though he had never visited or worked in the UK. He was aware of many cultural references through his love of British television. He was even able to quote from the likes of Dad's Army and Fawlty Towers.

As her black BMW approached the Limehouse Basin, Buchan pulled over and parked on a side road. Lazlo had insisted that he would only talk to Hoffman alone; if he saw anyone else, the deal was off, he didn't trust the British police. Buchan handed the German an AN/PRC 148 transceiver; should he need assistance; she wouldn't be far away. Hoffman got out of the car and began walking towards the marina and the apartments where his contact was waiting. Buchan, meanwhile, remained in her car with her handset resting on the dashboard in front of her. As Hoffman continued walking into the distance, he paused for a moment as though suddenly uncertain, and looked back at Buchan, who acknowledged his glance with a confident wave of her right hand whilst continuing with a call on her mobile in her left.

After twenty-five minutes, there was an unexpected and urgent request from the German for assistance. Having finished his conversation and left Lazlo's apartment, he had caught sight of someone watching the proceedings from the corner of a nearby building. Hoffman recognised him instantly. Andreas Vasilakis had been on the German Intelligence Agency's watch list for several years and was suspected of involvement in several terror-related incidents in Germany. It would be quite a feather in his cap if he were able to bring him in.

Buchan listened intently as Hoffman gave a running commentary over his radio as he followed the Greek national towards the Limehouse Ship Lock. As he turned the sharp corner leading to the lock, Hoffman stopped in his tracks. Vasilakis had disappeared from view; he was nowhere to be seen. The German stood for a few seconds, perplexed, shaking his head in a mixture of disbelief and anger at having such an important target within reach and then losing him. He picked up his AN/PRC radio and took a few steps forward as he continued to scour the area, then swore loudly in German before composing himself and advising Buchan in English that he had lost him.

He continued to walk past several houses as he drew closer to the lock itself. Checking the grounds of each building, he found nothing! Having reached the end of the lock, Hoffman stood for a moment, peering in each direction, then turned around and scratched his head. Had his target given him the slip? Had he somehow doubled back? As he wondered, he heard a noise behind him. He spun round. The towering and menacing figure of Andreas Vasilakis loomed over him like an emissary of death. Hoffman knew his adversary's ruthless reputation meant that his life might now be counted in seconds. He pulled the radio to his mouth but only had time for one desperate and heartfelt cry.

'Buchan!'

A clubbing blow to the head brought the much smaller man to his knees. Hoffman struggled to get to his feet, but he was no match for the overpowering strength of his assailant, whose arms were quickly around his neck like a python squeezing the life out of him. He couldn't get away, and there was no sign of help. Franz Hoffman gave one last strangled gasp of life before it was snuffed out, and he collapsed to the ground. Vasilakis, not content with his deadly work, grasped the unconscious man's neck and head in his hands and with a grisly crack twisted it sharply to the right.

Then, picking up the lifeless body dropped it without ceremony into the lock. He retrieved the radio that the German had dropped during the brief altercation. Buchan was calling Hoffman's name, again and again. The only reply she received was from the Greek.

'He's dead.'

It was a further ten minutes before the police arrived. They found Buchan's car with the driver's door open, but there was no sign of the MI5 officer. Her German colleague was also unaccounted for. The area was immediately sealed off while the police conducted an exhaustive search, including house-to-house enquiries. Within an hour, and to their immense relief, they found her, handcuffed, gagged and locked in an outbuilding close to the lock. Buchan advised the police that Hoffman told her that he was heading towards the Limehouse Ship Lock, following up on a lead from Lazlo when they lost contact. When no trace of Hoffman could be found, divers were called in to search the basin and drain the lock.

News quickly reached Steph Le Sueur at Thames House. It was more bad news and would necessitate a difficult phone call to advise Christina Koehler of her missing colleague and then potentially, depending on the results of the search, another call for the Director General to the Head of the German Foreign Intelligence Agency to explain how one of their agents was killed during a combined operation on UK soil. It wasn't long before Heidi Buchan returned to Headquarters, having been cleared by the medical staff and providing a full statement to the police. As requested, she reported straight to Le Sueur to be debriefed. The Wing Commander wanted the full facts before she contacted Koehler.

'How are you? Without waiting for a reply, Le Sueur briskly continued 'Well, Buchan, what the hell happened? You were supposed to look after him. It is bad enough when we lose our own people, let alone one of our allies,' said Le Sueur curtly.

'I'm sorry, ma'am, but he insisted on going alone. When he came out, he said he thought he was being followed and went to investigate. When he didn't return, I went to find him. I got as far as the ship lock, and that's all I remember. I woke trussed up, gagged and blindfolded in an outbuilding,' said Buchan. 'Have they found Hoffman yet?'

'No, the police are draining the lock as we speak. Did he say who he thought was following him, or any clues?

'No ma'am.'

'Alright, Buchan, that's all for now.'

Travers, Downes and Koehler were making their way to Poole Harbour where a police launch was standing by to take them across the water to Parkson, Olga Devereux's private island, when the call came in. Travers took it and listened intently without interrupting as Le Sueur laid out the disturbing details of Koehler's partner's disappearance. Travers had found out only recently just how dangerous life could be "in the field". Downes, for her part, had played down the risks, although they all knew and accepted there was an inherent danger and risk to life involved in the intelligence community. Koehler sensed something was wrong, very wrong. Despite Travers' silence as he noted the details relayed to him over the phone, his expression told the story.

'Alright, ma'am, I understand. I'll tell Christina. We'll get back as soon as we can.'

'What is it, Greg?' said Downes, gripping his arm anxiously.

Travers turned to Koehler, who stared back at him, her green eyes narrowing; she knew instinctively that it was bad news.

'I'm sorry, Chris, but Franz is missing. Things are a bit sketchy at the moment. He went to meet a contact, someone called Lazlo. Do you know him? He then told Buchan that he thought he was being watched and went to investigate. After that, nothing.'

'What about Heidi?' said Downes. 'Is she alright?'

'It seems so, she was tied up and left in someone's outbuilding, the police found her during the search. I'm really sorry, Chris. We need to get back to London; the police are still looking for him.'

'Yes, I have heard Franz talk about him. He is an informant; he used to work for Devereux, mainly in Europe as an enforcer until he outstayed his welcome. She tried to, I think the expression is, cancel his contract, you understand this meaning? However, he managed to get out of the country. Franz heard that he was back in London, but ready to make a deal.'

It was early evening by the time Travers and his female companions arrived back in London. Darkness had fallen, and there was a chill coming off the river as they entered Thames House, where the lights were still burning brightly. There was little time to gather their thoughts as they hurried up the stairs where Le Sueur was waiting for them with news of the search. A double tap on the door by Travers was greeted with the usual one-word response, "come". The three walked in. Three chairs were positioned in front of the Wing Commander, who sat behind her desk, on it an in-tray that was still seemingly overflowing.

She introduced the man beside her as Chief Inspector Leslie, who was in charge of the Limehouse search. She gestured to the three to take their seats. Le Sueur turned and looked up at the tall, tanned, Chief Inspector briefly before focusing her attention on the German woman sitting anxiously in front of her.

'Officer Koehler, I very much regret to inform you that the body of Franz Hoffman has been found. He has been murdered. Your office has been informed. I'm very sorry.'

'Do you know how he was killed?' asked the shaken Koehler.

'The post-mortem has not been conducted yet, but the Pathologist at the scene says that he was strangled and his neck was broken. His body was discovered when they drained the Limehouse Ship Lock.'

'Chief Inspector, have you found any evidence of the perpetrator, any clues?' asked Travers.

'Not as yet, just Mr Hoffman's radio. We are still searching the area,' said the Policeman.

Travers sat back in his chair as Le Sueur continued talking, but his mind was now elsewhere; something about Hoffman's death was nagging him, something familiar. He stared blankly into space as his brain desperately tried to recall the information he wanted. His apparent lack of attention caught Le Sueur's roving and disapproving eye.

'Am I boring you, Travers?' she asked.

'I'm sorry, ma'am, but something has just struck me,' said Travers.

'I assumed as much, what is it?'

'You said that Hoffman was strangled and then his neck broken?'

'That's right, the initial report suggests the fracture was mid-neck, why?' asked Le Sueur.

'Ma'am, Claire Powell was strangled and then her C4-C5 cervical vertebrae were broken post-mortem before her body was dumped. Powell and Hoffman were both well-trained and experienced. Whoever did this knew what they were doing.'

Without any further discussion, Le Sueur picked up her phone and rang Forensic Pathology. She had one question and she wanted an immediate answer. After a few moments, she had it: Hoffman's C4 cervical vertebrae had been snapped.

With the victims already dead. The breaking of the neck was gratuitous and suggested the killer harboured a particularly sadistic and unnecessarily cruel personality. The information that the Pathologist had given Le Sueur confirmed Travers' suspicion that the murders were almost certainly committed by the same individual. However, with no physical evidence or eyewitnesses, there was very little to go on. The Wing Commander turned to Travers.

'Get on to DI Beckett in Jersey in the morning. I want the latest information on their investigation into Powell's murder, including their list of possible suspects, persons of interest, everything, and tell him that there may be a connection with Hoffman's death. Oh, and get hold of a copy of the Pathologist's report. I want to know if they managed to obtain any trace evidence or DNA from the body.'

'Miss Koehler, you had better check in with your superiors for further instructions. The police are still searching the Limehouse area, so there is nothing we can do for the moment. You three had better get some rest, tomorrow is going to be a busy day.'

With that, Travers, Downes, and Koehler rose to their feet, paid their respects, and left the office.

After the long day travelling, followed by the news of the death of their colleague, Travers felt that they could all do with a drink, especially Chris Koehler, and some time to process what had transpired today. With Koehler staying at the Westminster London Hotel, just around the corner in John Islip Street, it seemed sensible to escort their companion there and avail themselves of the excellent bar.

As they walked through the bar and the renowned Steakhouse, Travers' eye was caught by a waiter carrying an enormous and fabulous-looking Aberdeen Angus Tomahawk Steak. He watched it pass under his nose, which flared with subconscious desire. It was in marked contrast to the rather limp ham sandwich he had chewed his way through earlier in the day, which was several hours past its best even then. The prospect of making himself a toasted cheese sandwich back at his flat in an hour or two was rapidly losing its appeal.

They sat at a table within easy reach of the chic bar, which was surprisingly quiet given it was the middle of the evening, although the Steakhouse itself was busy. An empty bottle of Chablis sat between them, with a second half-empty bottle sitting comfortably in a bed of crushed ice within an ice bucket. Travers looked across at the two women who were deep in conversation, talking shop and swapping stories. As women and experienced Intelligence Officers, albeit for different but allied countries, they had quickly formed an easy rapport.

Travers listened-in half-heartedly to their conversation, politely nodding occasionally as one does when feeling like an unexpected interloper in the presence of a private conversation. He drained his glass and cast an envious glance around the restaurant. He looked at his watch, it was getting late, too late now to order a large Tomahawk Steak. He resigned himself to the inevitable homemade sandwich; at least it would be fresh. His thoughts were broken by a sudden burst of uncontrolled laughter. It was good to see Christina laugh; she hadn't given much away, but it had been a tough day for her, experienced or not.

There was time for one last drink, Travers and Downes still had to get home, and who knew what tomorrow would bring? Three small shot glasses of Schnapps were called for to toast the memory of their fallen colleague. The three rose to their feet as Koehler proposed a short but moving salute.

'Mein gefallener Kamerad. Schlaf gut, Franz.'

The three raised their glasses before downing the shots in one. After a moment's respectful pause, they left their table and walked towards the bar exit. Travers and

Downes embraced their German counterpart and strode out of the hotel and back onto John Islip Street for the short return walk to Thames House.

As they proceeded along the pavement, Travers could no longer contain himself.

'Well?'

'Well, what?' replied Downes as she playfully ignored Travers' very obvious curiosity.

'Don't give me that "well what" routine. What did you find out about her? You were getting on like a house on fire. I felt like a proper gooseberry in there.'

'Is that green aura you are displaying the result of that dodgy ham sandwich you had, or do I detect a hint of frustrated envy, Greg?' Recalling his flirting with Koehler on the train, she was going to play this out.

'Envy? Of course not. It's professional curiosity that's all,' Travers said in as casual a manner as he could manage.

'She comes from Aschaffenburg, worked in Frankfurt for a few years with the local Police there before being recruited by the BND. She trained in Berlin and has been with them for nine years, likes dogs, sports, and oh, did I mention that she's married, well separated.'

Having returned to Thames House, Travers immediately called a taxi for Downes' half-hour journey back to Holland Park. She offered to share the taxi and drop him off. For a moment, he considered it, but despite the chill in the air, it was only a brisk twenty-minute walk alongside the river to Churchill Gardens, and anyway, it would help to clear his head of Chablis. As the taxi pulled up, the pair embraced before Downes climbed into the back seat of the black cab and drove off into the night. Travers followed the car's taillights until they were out of sight. There was still a steady stream of traffic passing along Millbank in both directions. Travers quickly crossed the road and began his short journey home. He was glad of his heavy navy blue woollen greatcoat, which offered a measure of protection against the chilly breeze coming off the water. The cold air was a reminder that autumn was now in full swing and winter was coming.

Pimlico Gardens seemed very different to Travers in the darkness than the open leafy area that he had so often walked through to work during the day. Perhaps it was just his troubled state of mind. He hadn't walked this way at night before. Like most woodland areas, the darkness often lends an unnatural sense of unease. Nothing had changed, the trees were the same, the shrubs just where they were during the daylight hours, and the William Huskisson statue was still in its place. Yet the rustling of the leaves and the constantly shifting shadows caused by the moon, played unwelcome tricks on his mind. He kept as close as he could to the main road, although several of the streetlights were out. As he approached the mid-point of the gardens, he saw a man standing some distance away, close to one of the trees. Travers slowed his pace. His eyes strained in the gloom as he tried to get a better look at the shadowy figure in front of him. As he drew closer, the figure suddenly moved and began walking closer. Travers could feel his heart beating faster, his anxiety increasing, the adrenaline coursing through his body.

Travers looked around. The road was quiet with fewer cars now passing by. He could feel the hair bristle on his arms as his muscles tensed. The effects of the evening's Chablis were gone, overwhelmed by the mounting tension he felt as the large unidentified man drew nearer. The man pulled his right hand out of his coat pocket. Travers could just make out something silver between his fingers, glinting in the moonlight. Suddenly, the man stopped. Travers prepared himself and continued slowly walking along the pavement towards the darkened figure, his fists now tightly clenched, hidden under the cuffs of his long coat. The man raised his arm; the glinting silver Travers had spotted was now a mobile phone pressed to the man's right ear.

As the two men crossed, the stranger looked at him, acknowledged him with a nod, then walked on in the opposite direction. Travers gathered up his shredded nerves. With a sigh, he relaxed and exhaled a stream of expended air, made more prominent by the bright moonlight emerging from a thick cloud.

Travers stopped and looked over his left shoulder. The man with the phone was still walking away from him, now almost out of sight. Travers turned once more and carried on. In a few minutes, he would be in Churchill Gardens and close to home. He felt slightly embarrassed at his nervous reaction to what had just occurred. The stranger had been doing no more than he was, walking and minding his own business. He needed to get a grip. Hoffman's murder, compounded by the fact that Alicia was being watched, had rattled him. Perhaps he should have shared Downes' taxi after all.

After about 20 minutes, he finally turned into the Gardens and reached the terraced house that was his temporary home. He cast off his heavy coat onto the back of an armchair and his house keys onto the sideboard. After finding something quick and simple to eat, he sat down on the sofa in front of the television with a large glass of Vodka. He closed his eyes as he savoured the moment. Finally, he could just kick back for a while and relax.

Just before midnight, he awoke. He looked around. His tall glass of vodka and Lemonade remained mostly untouched, standing where he had left it on the tallest of the nest of tables beside the sofa, the ice long since melted. He had no idea how long he had been asleep, but it must have been at least an hour. He swung his legs off the sofa and rose to his feet. He wasn't sure if he felt better or worse for his unexpected nap. He picked up his mobile phone, turned off the TV and the lights, and then slowly ascended the stained wooden stairs to the first floor, stopping off first at the bathroom before finally entering his bedroom.

Turning on the bedroom light, he saw a medium-sized grey ceramic pot on his bedside table containing a plant with a large number of green ovate leaves of varying size and bell-shaped flowers with a purple and yellow tinge to them. Standing up against the pot was a white envelope with his name handwritten on the front. Travers sat on the bed and picked up the envelope. After examining it carefully, he gently opened it. Inside was a small white card with just four words written on it. "See you soon, Greg". He put the card down and immediately checked that all the external doors and windows were securely locked; they were, but that hadn't stopped somebody from gaining entry and leaving a plant in his bedroom, and why a plant?

Picking up his mobile phone, he dialled Alicia Downes' number. After about twenty seconds, she answered.

'I'm sorry to disturb you, Alicia. Were you asleep?'

'No, I was just doing some reading. What's up?'

'Whilst we've been away, someone paid me a visit. The house was secure when I left, and everything is still locked. They left a plant in my bedroom.'

'What? A plant? What kind of plant is it? Describe it to me.'

'I don't know, well it's got oval green leaves, bell-shaped purple flowers and a very faint scent, it's a plant, what more can I say?' said Travers.

'I don't like it, Greg and I don't like the fact that they got into your house. Why don't you come over and stay here for the night?'

It was a tempting offer. Especially after his nerves were stretched during his walk home earlier, and then having had an unauthorised visitor bearing gifts. However, ultimately, he decided against her generous offer. Choosing instead to taxi back to Thames House and sleep in his office. Downes suggested taking the note and the plant with him, where they could both be examined and identified.

The following morning, he was summoned to Le Sueur's office. Both the note and the plant had been inspected.

'Good morning, Travers, sleep well?'

'Frankly, no, ma'am,' said Travers, whose current makeshift office was barely big enough for his desk, chair, and monitors, and certainly not conducive to sleeping in with any degree of comfort at all.

'Alright, first things first, we are going to move you out of your current digs, we'll sort out the details later. Secondly, I'm afraid the note is clean; there are no prints on the card or the envelope apart from yours.

'And the handwriting?' asked Travers.

'We've drawn a blank there, but if it makes you feel any better, I can tell you who it doesn't match, your friend…Olga Devereux.'

'However, we do know what the plant is, and if someone is looking to send you a message, it couldn't be clearer.'

'What is it then, ma'am?' said Travers.

'Atropa Belladonna.'

'Deadly Nightshade.' Interjected Downes.

'I prefer roses myself,' said Travers with a sardonic air of disdain. However, the symbolism of sending him such a deadly plant was not lost on him; regardless of who wrote the card, he'd bet a pound to a penny that Devereux was behind it.

Chapter 8

Olga Devereux sat in the exotic orangery at her sister Maria's home in Jersey, surrounded by tropical palms and looked out over St Aubin's Harbour. It was a fine day, and the sun was streaming in. She watched as the gentle breeze tested the resilience of the surviving hardy annuals in the borders of Maria's beautiful and well-maintained garden. In front of her, on a circular Rosewood table, stood a glass of Prosecco and a copy of one of today's daily papers.

She leant forward and took a sip of the chilled sparkling Italian wine as she continued to stare out into the distance, lost in her thoughts and her memories. A day did not go by that she did not think about her beloved son Hector. Every waking hour, she was consumed with a growing, festering hatred, both for the man she held responsible for his death, but also for the establishment and country that spawned him.

Devereux's self-absorption was interrupted when her mobile phone rang. For a few moments, she ignored the call, then stretched out her well-manicured hand and picked up the receiver. It was Osvaldo Phoenix.

'Mr Phoenix, good morning.'

'Mrs Devereux, I thought you would like to know that my former house guest has made the necessary preparations for London as you requested. They will be conveyed tomorrow and the authorities notified accordingly,' said Phoenix.

'Excellent, and the other matter?'

'The letter has been delivered today, properly Mailmark franked. Hades will remain in London and will report back to me if there are any developments. Our friend from Palmyra will be returning to Jersey within 24 hours. All the required arrangements have been made here, I take it the timetable has not changed?'

'No, there is no change. The conference is scheduled at the castle in ten days, my source tells me preparations and local vetting are being finalised. If there are any late changes, I will let you know,' Devereux put the phone down on the table and picked up her Prosecco and took a contented sip.

Devereux's sister walked into the orangery. Her blonde hair, streaked with grey, glistened in the sunshine. Olga turned and greeted her older sibling, who sat beside her, with a smile. There had always been a close bond between them. Younger by ten years, Olga had always looked up to her for her wisdom and poise. When their mother died, Maria had been there to comfort and support Olga, who had found the loss particularly difficult. Whilst Maria did not approve of Olga's illegal activities and had made her feelings known in no uncertain terms, theirs was still a relationship that had stayed the course despite all the adversity that had come their way; there was no sibling rivalry.

After Olga's arrest and subsequent release, who else should Olga turn to than her sister? Someone who understood and shared the horror of their family history. She did not condone Olga's desire for revenge, but neither did she oppose it. She could shed no tears for any descendant of former SS Colonel Wolfgang Dietrich, the man who had their grandparents shot and then raped their mother all those years ago.

Maria topped up Olga's glass of Prosecco and then poured a glass for herself.

'Well, Olga, did Phoenix have anything interesting to say? I gather that obnoxious man Abadi is returning to the

Island. I really don't know why you had to use him of all people. There must be a dozen others you could have used.'

'Maria, you know perfectly well that this is not a job for amateurs. He is the best, he knows what he is doing, and he has no love for the British Government. With Phoenix on the payroll, we also have someone adept in smuggling, particularly people smuggling. When Abadi has done his job in London and here, he will be gone, Phoenix will make him disappear,' said Olga.

'And you, Olga, what will you do? You know the authorities will come looking for you.'

Olga knew that, despite her almost unlimited wealth and resources, whilst she remained in Jersey, she was vulnerable. She looked away for a moment, into the distance as though in a daze, before returning to the present and looking directly into her elder sister's pale blue eyes.

'I shall go abroad, out of their reach, but the British will atone for what they did. Blood is thicker than water, Maria, and I will not stop until their blood flows like water from a wellspring. For as long as I live, they will pay.' There was no doubting Olga's sincerity.

The two women raised their glasses of Prosecco and toasted their family before rising and slowly walking past the ornate fountain in the centre of the orangery and then into the extensive gardens as they continued to talk.

Detective Chief Inspector Deery, accompanied by three other plainclothes detectives and a second car with two additional men, approached Holland Park, a fifty-four-acre area of Kensington woodland and formal gardens just to the west of central London. Deery's orders were simple: locate and detain individuals suspected of maintaining an illegal surveillance of Alicia Downes' flat.

Downes had told him that she had been aware of someone at the front of the building for several days, usually sitting in a car or hovering around further down the pavement on the other side of the road. This morning, she reported that she thought she saw the reflection of a lens or possibly binoculars at the rear of the house. From Deery's point of view, nabbing the one in the front would be far easier, given that the rear backed onto the semi-wild woodland of Holland Park. With one car stationed at the far end of the road, Deery's car approached Downes' Victorian town house, pulling into a nearby space not far from the building, where he waited and watched the suspect who was parked close by.

Twenty minutes later, Downes drove down Holland Park towards her flat as pre-arranged with Deery. As the detective had hoped, a camera lens emerged from the suspect's open driver's window and followed her as she approached her home. Downes walked up the half-dozen white stone steps to the front door and let herself into the building, and quickly disappeared from sight. Deery and one of his men got out of their car and casually walked along the pavement towards the man's vehicle. When they reached the silver Audi A4, Deery dangled his warrant card through the open window and under the nose of the startled driver.

As he leant against the driver's door, he looked down at his feet for a moment, noticing a pile of at least a dozen used cigarette stubs which he disturbed with the toe of his boot.

'Good morning, sir. Gosh, that's a really nasty habit you have there. Would you mind stepping out of the car, please,' said Deery as he opened the car door to encourage the occupant to come quietly. The bearded man, whom Deery estimated to be in his early thirties, reluctantly did as he was requested following a second prompt and, escorted by the other detective, followed Deery to the detective's car. The man sat in the back seat, as Deery put on a pair of protective gloves before examining the camera. As he flipped through the digital images, he shook his head and turned to his colleague.

'Looks like we've got another guest for lunch today, Bill.' Then, turning back to the suspect. 'We'll what's your story, bird watching? You've been looking at the wrong kind of birds. Where you're going mate, you won't be seeing any of either variety for a while, but you had better start singing like one when we chat later, or you won't be on the streets before next year's nesting season.'

Having read the man his rights, Deery instructed two of his men to take the suspect in and book him. As the car pulled away, Deery and his remaining colleague walked across towards the building containing Downes' apartment. She had been watching the proceedings from her third-floor window and came downstairs and opened the front door, where she met the two detectives.

Before Deery had a chance to provide her with an update, she interrupted him and asked that he accompany her back upstairs to her apartment. Leaving his colleague on the doorstep, Deery followed Downes up the stairs and into her flat. He paused for a moment after entering her apartment as he gathered his breath after climbing the six flights of stairs. After composing himself, he looked around the hallway leading into the drawing room.

'Out of breath, Chief Inspector?'

'It's alright for you, you're used to it, and besides, there is a lot more of me to shift.'

Downes walked across to a beautiful small octagonal walnut table on which was an alabaster figurine of the Greek Goddess Aphrodite and a small pile of today's post.

Downes picked up the small collection of letters and handed the top one to Deery.

'It came today; I've not opened it for obvious reasons.'

Deery took hold of the letter. It was addressed to Miss Alicia Downes, stamped and franked. He ran his fingers along all four edges of the envelope and could feel two small wires on one side of the letter. There was a small smear on the other. He slowly raised the envelope and sniffed it, there was a slight, if unmistakable, odour of marzipan. He looked intently at Downes. It was a letter bomb. As he held it in the palm of his hand, he could feel the slightly uneven weight distribution. Carefully, he replaced it on the table. He immediately put in a request for the bomb squad to attend and for the other residents in the building to be evacuated until the suspect package had been removed. The other letters on the table were bona fide and had been accounted for.

Before going downstairs to wait for the bomb squad, Deery asked Downes if he could see the view from the rear windows overlooking the semi-wild Holland Park woodland. Looking out of the third-floor drawing room window, it was next to impossible to tell if there was someone in the woods or not. He had planned to search the woodland area adjacent to her property. That plan had been derailed somewhat as a result of her unexpected postal delivery. As they walked out of the flat, they stopped again at the hall table, where Deery made an admiring comment about the ornament adorning it.

'Why, Inspector, you do surprise me. I wouldn't have taken you for a "classics" kind of man,' said Downes with a wry smile.

'Well, I wouldn't go quite that far, but I've seen Spartacus a few times, you know, the one with that fellow, what's his name… Kirk Douglas.'

'It's Aphrodite, the Greek Goddess of love, amongst other things. Greg gave it to me during my convalescence. It's beautiful, isn't it?'

The bomb squad arrived and, after examining the letter carefully, removed it from Downes' apartment using a containment chamber. With luck, they would be able to defuse the device without the need to blow it up using a controlled explosion, thereby providing the forensic team with a great deal of valuable evidence. With additional police units now on site, a thorough search could be made of the extensive woodland grounds surrounding the house. Whilst this was in progress, Deery drove Downes back to Thames House, where Wing Commander Le Sueur and Greg Travers were waiting.

'Well, Detective Chief Inspector, I hear you've had a busy morning. Have you started interrogating the man yet?' she enquired.

'One of my colleagues has started softening him up. I checked in with him a few minutes ago. Miss Downes' analysis was right, he's certainly not a pro. I don't think we'll get much out of him. My guess is he's a low-level felon whose been paid some cash to stooge around and keep an eye on her. He probably only knows the person who paid him,' said the Chief Inspector.

At that moment, Le Sueur's phone rang; it was Captain Turner from the Explosive Ordnance Disposal Unit. The news was both intriguing and perplexing. The IED had been simple to deactivate, and the components were being examined to try and determine their origin. Le Sueur thanked the Captain for the information, put her phone down and turned to Travers and Downes, who were standing together on one side of the desk.

'Travers, this is a conundrum for you to chew on. The letter bomb's been defused. It had a very thin layer of plastic explosive material in it. Only dangerous, if you had a heart condition, not enough to be lethal, it would certainly have given Downes a very nasty shock if she had been careless, but as IED's go it was very primitive and shouldn't have got past anyone with even a basic awareness,' said Le Sueur.

'Someone's playing games, ma'am. That's the only explanation. My plant, Alicia's letter. They're telling us that they can get to us, it's a message.'

'From?'

'You know my thoughts, ma'am. Who is the common denominator? Alicia and I were both there when Hector Devereux took his nosedive off the deep end. I think this is all part of Olga's twisted plan to even the score. She has caught up with Otto Graf, and now I think we are next on her list of things to do,' said Travers.

'Chief Inspector, what about these bombings, do you think they are connected?

'I don't know, ma'am, we are still questioning the bomber we apprehended at the tube station,' said Deery. 'There seems to be a bit of a pattern forming. The blokes at the tube were anything but committed; they ran like startled rabbits when they saw us, and the man following Miss Downes was about as amateurish as it gets. I don't think we'll get a lot out of them.'

Le Sueur picked up the report on the break-in of Travers' lodgings. She read out the findings to the group. It didn't make for good reading. The door and window locks had not been tampered with. Whoever left the plant in

Travers' bedroom gained access with a key and was then able to disable the monitored alarm system using the correct code, deposit the plant then reactivate the alarm before leaving.

'When were the locks last changed, Wing Commander?' asked the Chief Inspector.

'They were changed last month,' replied Le Sueur.

'And who has access to the keys and the alarm combination?'

'Myself, Personnel, and of course the occupant,'

'And the alarm code, how often is it changed?'

'Every time there is a change of occupant.'

Deery looked across at Travers. He didn't need to be Sherlock Holmes to know what the Detective was thinking. What were the chances of someone outside having a key to his house and also being able to disable their sophisticated alarm system?

'Wing Commander, in my professional opinion…you need a plumber,' said the Chief Inspector. 'Sorry, but it looks like an inside job to me.'

'Christ, a leak, that's all we need. I'll need to speak to the Deputy Director General about this. We have one or two properties off the official register. We'll discuss this again later today. Chief Inspector, it's always a pleasure. Keep me abreast of developments, please.'

Travers and Downes acknowledged their superior and joined Deery as he walked out of the Wing Commander's office.

As they reached the building's entrance, Deery, who had preceded the other two, stopped and turned. Travers expected one of his friend's customary spontaneous, if slightly sarcastic, but light-hearted quips. He didn't get one; instead, it was a more sobering reflection on the circumstances of their meeting.

'Do you really think Devereux is behind all of this, Greg?'

'Yes, John, I do. If you had seen her face when she was arrested after Hector's death, you would too. She was ruthless and unprincipled before; now you can add twisted and malevolent. She made a promise to me when I last saw her in Poole, the day she was arrested. I expected her to be locked away permanently and dismissed her threats, but now…I believe she intends to keep it.'

Chapter 9

Detective Chief Inspector Deery had barely finished his routine morning briefing when he got a call from his boss, Superintendent Wakefield. It was not the usual request for an update on a particular ongoing investigation; this was urgent, and the Assistant Commissioner wanted to see him straight away. Deery put the phone down; it certainly wasn't usual to be summoned to see the AC, and he wondered whether it related to a complaint or disciplinary matter. It couldn't be denied that his style of policing was colourful. He had probably upset a lot more than his fair share of people, including his superiors. Had someone complained? Whatever it was, he would soon find out. As he rose to his feet, his door opened, and a young officer on the tea run had a fresh mug for the detective.

'Thanks, leave it on the desk, Mike, the AC wants to see me,' said Deery as he walked past the young man, continued through the office and out into the corridor.

'Come in, DCI Deery. I'm sorry to spring this on you, but I understand you are the officer running with these London bombings. Are we making any headway?' asked Wakefield.

'We're still working on it, sir. We are questioning the surviving suspect from the Covent Garden package, but I think they were basically couriers rather than the bombers themselves. I am not sure how much he will be able to tell us. The School bomb was so basic that they could probably have put something like it together in their own Chemistry lab. It makes tracing the bomb makers near impossible.'

'I see, well, I think that is about to change,' Wakefield picked up a letter on his desk and handed it to

Deery. 'That was received by the Times today, read it. Fortunately, they passed it on to us, rather than run a story.'

Deery took the paper from the Assistant Commissioner and read the contents in full.

'Shit! Have we found it?' said Deery.

'They found a small container in Waterloo Train Station. Police sealed off the area and removed the suspect package, which went straight down to the Ministry of Defence's Science and Technology Laboratory at Porton Down. When they opened it, they found a vial, test tube size. They are testing it now. We've issued an immediate DSMA 3 notice to muzzle the press, but they know very well the panic this would cause, so they are happy to cooperate, we are reporting it as just another suspect package, and we'll issue another statement shortly that it was a hoax,' said the Assistant Commissioner.

Deery looked down at the sheet of A4 paper that was in his hand and re-read the short letter written on it. Blowing up a school or trying to explode a bomb in a busy Covent Garden was bad enough, but if the Porton Down boffins confirmed what was in the vial, it could be catastrophic and bring London to a standstill.

Deery returned to his office grim-faced. The stakes had been raised, and he still had no real leads to work on apart from the spotty-faced young man languishing in his interview room, who still professed to know nothing. The AC had promised to call him as soon as the scientists had confirmed what they were dealing with. Never one to be constrained by red tape, Deery rang through to Dr Rachel Stewart at the Pathology lab for a favour.

Forty minutes later, Deery walked through the door of the interview room where he met the Duty Solicitor, and to date, his one and only suspect, twenty-three-year-old student Jamal Akeem.

Other than admitting to taking money to deliver a package, Akeem had so far admitted nothing. After twenty minutes, Deery's patience finally wore out. He didn't have time to play with. The young man was nervous, fidgeting constantly. He was reluctant to make direct eye contact. Deery knew the man was hiding something, he wasn't sure what, but just needed to find the right key to "unlock" him.

'Jamal, have you ever heard the name Olga Devereux? Was it ever mentioned by someone else, someone visiting the flat? The person who paid you for this job, what were they like? Were they British or foreign? Were there more jobs you could do in the future? Was this the first of several you would be paid for?'

Akeem continued to look down at the table and declined to answer any of the detective's questions. Exasperated, Deery reached into his pocket for a small box which he put on the table in front of the man.

'Do you know what's in this box, Jamal? Your associates were going to expose the population of London to this. These are the same people who paid you to deliver the package, Jamal.'

Deery then opened the box containing a small sealed test tube on a bed of cotton wool. Inside the tube was a small quantity of white powder. The detective took out the test tube and laid it on the table in front of Akeem, who stared nervously at it.

'Well, Jamal, will you help us, or do you want to see a lot of your friends die?'

Deery rolled the tube towards the man, who became extremely agitated.

'Ok, ok.'

Deery walked out of the interview room, feeling pleased with himself. It was a small victory, but it was a victory nonetheless. The psychology of his plan had worked perfectly. At least he now had the address last used by the two men before they carried out their abortive plan at Covent Garden. Shortly afterwards, Deery led his team to the address that had been provided. It was empty, as he suspected it would be, but hopefully, it would still yield invaluable clues. The room was photographed, dusted for prints and everything that wasn't nailed down was documented, bagged up and taken away for forensic examination. In the rubbish bin, all the scraps of paper were carefully checked.

In his office, Deery picked at a crumpled piece of notepaper that had been recovered from the suspect's accommodation; on it was a list of initials. He looked at the letters again, KH, CG, WTS and PM, but the more he looked at the list, the less sense it made. It was just initials, with no context or details.

Deery's telephone rang; it was the AC again, wanting answers. Deery picked up his notepad and walked once more up the stairs to the Assistant Commissioner's office. As he stood outside Wakefield's office, he felt as though he were standing outside the Headmaster's study. He knocked twice and then opened the door. On this occasion, the stern-faced AC did look like a Headmaster who was about to reprimand him for misbehaving in class. Deery stepped forward towards the desk, ready to receive his metaphorical six of the best.

'DCI Deery, I have just had to fend off a very annoyed Solicitor who claims you endangered both himself and his client by your reckless antics earlier during your interview.'

'Yes, sir,' replied the non-committal Detective.

'Well? Did you intimidate the suspect and endanger everyone in the room with an extremely hazardous material?'

'Not exactly, sir,' replied Deery, who could barely contain his self-satisfaction.

'What do you mean, not exactly, did you or didn't you?'

'I borrowed a spare Test Tube from Pathology and some extra fine-grain flour from the kitchen. It is true I may have led Akeem to think that it was dangerous, though.'

'Flour!' said the incredulous Assistant Commissioner.

'Well, it did the trick, sir,' said Deery, with just a hint of a self-congratulatory smile.

Deery briefed the Assistant Commissioner on the raid, outlining the key points and mentioning the list of initials found in the waste bin. As he spoke, he sensed growing impatience in his superior. Wakefield's replies were short; his usual follow-up questions absent.

When Deery finished, the Assistant Commissioner cut in. He thanked the detective, his expression shifting from the severity it had worn when Deery entered to faint amusement at the success of methods he could never publicly approve of. A moment later, his face hardened again, all humour gone.

'We have had word back from Porton Down. The substance in the vial recovered from Waterloo has been identified. It's Balamuthia Encephalitis. It has a 98% mortality rate. If you become infected, you have pretty much bought it. If this were to be introduced into a major air conditioning or ventilation system, the results would be devastating. The Home Secretary and the Prime Minister have been informed. Whatever else you are dealing with, drop it; this has unconditional priority. Whoever this maniac is, they have to be stopped. Whatever resources you need will be made available. Obviously, the news blackout will be extended until further notice. Keep me informed, Chief Inspector.'

Deery, having assured the Assistant Commissioner of his best efforts, left and returned to his office. The only clues he had were a scrap of initialled rubbish, a young man who was probably nothing more than a courier, and the knowledge that there were only a limited number of people known to be capable of obtaining and handling such a dangerous substance.

While Deery's team scoured through the files for specialists in bioterrorism, he drove the short distance from the Embankment to Millbank. Experience had taught him that if there was one person who could find a needle in a haystack, it was his friend Travers. The pair shook hands warmly. Travers invited him to join him in his small and rather cramped room, stopping off first to grab a cup of tea.

'Alright, John, what brings you over here in such a hurry? It couldn't be a spot of bioterrorism, could it?'

'Bad news travels fast,' said Deery.

'We had a meeting with Wing Commander Le Sueur earlier. We are already working on it. We have open links with allied agencies, trying to identify and locate everyone we know who has a history of using biological agents.'

Deery then produced the crumpled paper containing the initials found in the suspect bomber's flat. Travers looked at the paper, then at his friend. Deery could almost see the cogs working, Travers smiled, and then the answer was revealed in all its observable simplicity.

'What was the school where the first bombing took place?' asked Travers as he tried to lead Deery to see what had quickly become clear to him.

Deery thought for a moment, then replied, 'It was the King Henry VIII School.'

'The second was Covent Garden,' chipped in Travers, 'and the third?

Deery looked again at the paper and swore under his breath in irritation. How could he not have seen it, of course; they were the targets. The first three sets of initials were the sites that had already been targeted. Which just left one, PM. As Deery continued to mutter obscenities, Travers was already searching his database for London landmarks or buildings featuring those letters.

'The only one listed is the Petrie Museum of Egyptian Archaeology in Malet Place. I don't know why it should be targeted, but there it is, it's the only PM listed by the tourist board, I've also checked the Land Registry within London.'

'Bugger! It was staring me in the face all the time. Thanks, Greg. This case is beginning to give me a serious pain in the arse. I am getting stick from everyone above me in the food chain, and that's a bloody impressive list, right up to the Home Secretary and the Prime Minister,' said the irascible Chief Inspector.

'Well, John, if it's any consolation, I don't think we are getting very far either. The Deputy DG blew a fuse when Le Sueur suggested there might be a mole in MI5.'

The two men sat at the desk searching for something positive to lighten the unremitting sense of despondency. They needed a break.

Osvaldo Phoenix opened the door to his palatial villa and greeted the man in his doorway, Detective Inspector David Beckett. The two men had met several times before, usually at social events on the Island, where prominent citizens would often cross paths, given the island's size.

'Good afternoon, Detective Inspector, what brings you to this part of the Island? I take it this is not a social call?'

'Good day to you, it's just routine, we are trying to speak to one of your employees, Mr Andreas Drakos, and I understand he works in your winery?'

'That's correct. May I ask why you want to speak to him? Is he in trouble?'

'As I said, it's routine really, we are investigating a missing person who was later washed up on Plemont beach, a witness in a local bar reported seeing him with Mr Drakos. We would just like to ask him a few questions. Do you know where he is, sir?'

'I am sorry, Detective, but I don't know where he is. I believe he took some time off, something about a sick relative, I think.'

Sensing that the detective's inquiring mind had not yet been fully satisfied, Phoenix invited him inside. They walked into a large and very tastefully furnished living room bathed in light. In front of them, a wall of floor-to-ceiling glass panels through which could be seen an enormous grass lawn. Beckett walked around the room. There was an abundance of fine art on display.

'Now, Inspector, what is it that you want to know?' Phoenix asked. There followed a succession of standard police questions regarding Drakos' employment history, how long he had worked for Phoenix, his lifestyle and how he came to be on the Island. Providing new identities and backgrounds for people that he had smuggled into Jersey or the UK was his "stock in trade" and something he took great pride in, so he was not going to be caught out by this flatfoot.

'Now, you said he had taken some time off to visit a relative,' said Beckett.

'No, I said he mentioned something about a sick relative.'

'So you do not know who or where this relative might be?'

'Sorry, not at all, Inspector,' insisted Phoenix

Before Beckett had time to ask another question, Phoenix's phone rang. He listened to the call for a few seconds, then paused, turning to his visitor and explaining to the Detective that it was an important business call that he had to take, and could they continue this conversation another time. Beckett acquiesced, thanked his host, and said that he would make his own way out. He rose to his feet and walked back the way he had come towards the front door.

As he reached the hallway, he was greeted by Phoenix's mistress, Penelope Papandreou, wearing nothing more than a short Dior bathrobe, her long, damp, dark hair falling across her shoulders, a large towel in her hand.

'Oh, excuse me, Miss Papandreou isn't it? I'm DI Beckett. You have probably forgotten, but I think we've met before, although it was quite a while ago.' Despite having no reason to be embarrassed, he could not disguise his feeling slightly awkward, as the near-naked woman approached him.

'Hi, yes, sorry, I've just come out of the pool,' said Papandreou as she mopped her wet jet black hair with the towel.

'I've just been having a nice chat with Mr Phoenix about Andreas Drakos. Do you know him? I understand he is away visiting a sick relative.'

'Oh, I'm sorry to hear that. Ozy did tell me that he was away in London for a few days.'

'London? Really? I see, I must have misheard,' said Beckett 'Tell me, does Mr Drakos come here at all?'

'Yes, he pops in all the time to see Ozy'

'Thank you, I think you had better go and take care of that wet hair of yours,' said Beckett, who now had some of the answers he came for.

Twenty minutes later, Papandreou returned, dried and now fully dressed. Her lover, Osvaldo Phoenix, having finished his telephone call, sat in his extended conservatory with a large glass of Courvoisier VS Cognac in his hand and a freshly lit Bolivar Cigar resting in a lead crystal ashtray. Papandreou walked into the conservatory, wrapped her arms around his neck and kissed Phoenix gently on the lips.

'What did that policeman want, Ozy?'

'Hades,' said Phoenix curtly. 'It's nothing for you to worry about.'

'Why does he want to talk to him?' she said.

'The police are investigating the death of Akbar Hassan. Hades was spotted talking to him in a bar, and they think he may know something which could help them; that's all. By the way, Ali Abadi will be returning later today for a couple of weeks or so. He'll be staying in the complex, so you shouldn't see him, and if our inquisitive policeman should visit again, you know nothing…understand?'

Papandreou had known Phoenix for over five years since they met at the Casino de Monte-Carlo; he was cultured, rich, successful and well-travelled, and she was a successful model. Back then, she only saw the dashing entrepreneur, the image he wanted her to see. By the time she became aware of his other activities, it was too late. However much her conscience troubled her, and it did from time to time, it didn't trouble her enough to give up the trappings and the lifestyle she had become so accustomed to and dependent on.

Phoenix didn't share all his dirty secrets with her, but she knew enough. She had been repulsed by the recent school bombing and the thought that the man responsible, that malignant purveyor of death, Ali Abadi, was once again staying close by sickened her to her stomach. She could turn a blind eye to the usual smuggling of contraband and even the high-value people trafficking that had made his reputation on the dark web, but all that had changed since the appearance of "that woman".

Chapter 10

There was a knock at the door of the Cabinet Room. A moment later, the Prime Minister's Principal Private Secretary walked in. Sitting on his Mahogany chair midway along the cabinet table, the Prime Minister placed a thin folder that he had been reviewing back into Old Stripey, his confidential blue box, closed the lid, locked it and put it to one side. He then stirred his freshly made cup of tea as he looked out of the window at the rain streaming down the glass. As his PPS reached the table, the Prime Minister took a brief sip of his still-steaming cup before looking up and greeting his senior official.

'Good morning, Godfrey. Well, I hope you have some good news for me. I don't know what's worse, facing the opposition or my backbenchers. Actually, I think I do, at least you can see the opposition daggers glinting in front of you rather than standing there waiting for the stabbing pains in the back from one's villainous colleagues behind me,' said the Prime Minister with a heavy slice of sarcasm.

Godfrey Williamson was a man who appeared to have been born to be a civil servant. Tall, with angular, chiselled features, short dark hair with an upright, almost military bearing. A consummate professional who had risen swiftly through the civil service ranks. He had been Private Secretary to several ministers, as well as the previous Prime Minister, before his downfall.

However, such was Williamson's unsullied reputation and integrity that following the election of the new Prime Minister, he was happy to accept the role as Principal Private Secretary to the new incumbent. With increasing international tensions and so many domestic issues snapping at the Prime Minister's heels, Godfrey

Williamson's clear and measured thinking was a constant source of reassurance for the embattled man in Number Ten, as he fought off attacks from all sides of the political spectrum, including his own.

Williamson handed a small number of official letters to the Prime Minister, who looked through them before noticing that his PPS had retained the last one.

'...And that one Godfrey?'

'Prime Minister, this one arrived today, it's a letter addressed to you. It wasn't marked "personal or confidential". It's been screened, so I took the liberty of opening it. I think you had better read it.'

Williamson handed the letter to the Prime Minister, who took it out of its brown envelope and began to read the contents. His expression changed immediately from one of jovial repartee to grim-faced reality. He looked up, stone-faced, towards Williamson.

'You've read this, Godfrey?'

'Yes, Prime Minister,' replied the Civil Servant who understood the gravity and significance of the contents of the note.

'Godfrey, cancel today's meetings, all of them. Get hold of the Home Secretary, the Director General of the Security Service, the Chief of the Secret Intelligence Service and the Commissioner of the Metropolitan Police as quickly as possible. Godfrey, this is not a COBRA meeting. I don't want the usual hangers-on. Just those four, they are to come here, Number Ten, and Godfrey, if anyone asks, this is just a routine security briefing.'

'Yes, sir, I'll see to it at once,'

With that, Williamson turned and left the Cabinet Meeting room. The Prime Minister held the devastating note in his hand, slowly shaking his head as he ruminated.

Steph Le Sueur had only just returned from an urgent meeting with the Director General, which had been prompted by his Prime Ministerial invitation, when her phone rang. It was DI Beckett from Jersey Police providing her with one of his diarised updates on the Claire Powell murder investigation. In truth, the search for the MI5 Officer's killer had been proving problematic. The one definite lead, Hassan, had washed up dead on a local beach.

However, now there had been a development. Powell and the man she had been following were both dead, and the modus operandi was identical: strangulation and a fracture of a cervical vertebrae post mortem. Beckett's investigation had received a further boost when Travers revealed to him the details of Franz Hoffman's death in London. All the available evidence suggested the same as yet unknown perpetrator, but all that was about to change.

'Ma'am, we have three people killed by the same method; it's too much of a coincidence to consider that these are not related. One of the people we've been keeping an eye on here is a Greek chap called Andreas Drakos, who was a known associate of Akbar Hassan. He works for a local businessman, Osvaldo Phoenix, who, as it happens, was on our list of persons of interest, which we gave to Claire Powell when she came here with Greg Travers to look into the people smuggling issue.'

'I see, Detective Inspector, have you questioned him? Do we know where he is now?'

'Well, ma'am, this is where things get really interesting. When I questioned Phoenix, he didn't know where Drakos was; he suggested he might have gone to see a sick relative, but was pretty non-committal. Later, I spoke to Phoenix's mistress, she said that he had told her that he had gone to London,' said Beckett.

'DI Beckett, I'd like to see everything you have on this man, Drakos, and I want a picture if you have one. It sounds like we're looking for the same man. Well done.'

It was the first bit of actual good news Le Sueur had received in days, at least now they had a name to investigate, or two, if you included Phoenix.

In the Number Ten Cabinet Room, the Prime Minister sat grim-faced in front of the fireplace over which hung the famous portrait of Sir Robert Walpole. Sitting on his right was the Home Secretary, Deborah Roberts, a highly capable and well-regarded woman, and unusually for the time, respected by both sides of the house. Across the famous green baize-covered Cabinet table sat the guardians of Britain's security, the Metropolitan Police Commissioner and the heads of the Security Service and Secret Intelligence Service. Also in attendance was the Prime Minister's Principal Private Secretary, Godfrey Williamson.

The Prime Minister picked up the envelope containing the letter that had arrived that morning. He glanced down at the contents and then up at the people facing him. He paused, searching for the right words to begin with, as the others around the table looked on.

'Ladies and gentlemen, I received this letter today, which I believe is from the person responsible for the terrorist activity we have been facing. You will be aware that the latest incident involved the delivery of a sample of the deadly bacteria, Balamuthia Encephalitis, in a package left at Waterloo Station. The perpetrator of this nightmare is now threatening to disseminate weaponised versions of this throughout the capital if their demands are not met,' said the Prime Minister.

'What are their demands?' asked the Home Secretary.

The ashen-faced Prime Minister turned to his colleague.

'Our heads…in a basket. All of us. Cerberus to be made public, full disclosure, followed by our immediate resignation, and prosecution on charges of treason.'

'Treason? That's ridiculous, Prime Minister,' said the shocked Commissioner.

'Commissioner, the Cerberus file contains a lot of names, domestic and international, many of them very well known to the general public. Some of them are guilty of corruption, backhanders, and insider trading, which is bad enough, but the others have been actively consorting with foreign powers against the interests of this country and we have been covering it up, because to publicly admit what has been going on and the widespread level of corruption would cause a catastrophic crisis of confidence in this country, never mind the international repercussions. It would be disastrous.'

There was a moment of stunned silence as those present absorbed the implications of what the Prime Minister had just said. The only piece of remotely good news was that the letter contained no deadline. At least for the present, they still had time to act, but time was running out.

Greg Travers returned to Thames House after an early lunch with Alicia Downes when his mobile phone rang. It was Le Sueur, and there was an anxiety in her voice that he hadn't heard before. She informed him that she had had a conference with the Director General, where she had discussed the earlier meeting with the Prime Minister. Travers was to report to her immediately, though there was no indication as to the exact nature of the emergency.

When Travers knocked and entered the Wing Commander's office, he was shocked and surprised to see the MI5 Director General sitting next to her. It was rare for internal meetings to take place outside her own office. Le Sueur gestured Travers towards the empty chair in front of her. Once he had taken his seat, she deferred to the Director, who proceeded to recount the earlier events at Downing Street. She acknowledged that the stakes had been dramatically raised. However, the Prime Minister had made it clear at the meeting that they would not be intimidated by threats and that Government policy remained unchanged. Travers shook his head as he thought about the consequences of multiple biological attacks on the capital. The search for Devereux was still floundering, with no definite leads, only circumstantial evidence, speculation, and Travers' gut instinct.

Le Sueur then provided them both with the new information that DI Beckett had given her that morning. Perhaps this would inject some much-needed impetus into the investigation.

'Ma'am, Drakos' employer, Osvaldo Phoenix, that name was on the list of suspects given to Claire Powell by DI Beckett when we were investigating the people smuggling ring in Jersey. After what Beckett has said today, I think we should follow that up,' said Travers.

Turning to the Director, Travers requested that, given the urgency of the situation, DCI John Deery, who was already leading the hunt for the bombers, and Alicia Downes, who had been targeted, be brought on board and briefed on the Cerberus file, considering their previous experience. The Director agreed to Travers' request.

'Alright, Travers, you had better go and pack. The Wing Commander will arrange your flight to Jersey. Hook up with DI Beckett and find out what Phoenix is up to, and if he is mixed up with this mess, put a stop to it, and stay in touch, Travers. I want to know what's going on,' said the Director General as she rose to his feet and walked to the door.

Travers finally zipped up his black Samsonite Upscape suitcase and propped it up by the door of his lodgings. He still had thirty minutes before the car that was to take him to Heathrow was due to arrive. Travers poured himself a modest two fingers of Stolichnaya Vodka, topped up with a dash of Lemonade.

He then sat back on the sofa and looked around the rather uninspiring lounge that had been his temporary home since he was summoned back from Jersey. He couldn't wait to get back to his new home at Lilliput in Poole as soon as this business was cleared up. He and Alicia had spent some time in and around the area in the summer during their investigation of Olga Devereux, and it had made a most favourable impression. With his Wimbledon Village home irreparably compromised, he had decided to sell and move to the south coast, where he bought a lovely property overlooking the harbour.

It had not been a good night for Alicia Downes; she had tossed and turned and lost count of the number of times she had looked at her watch. Nothing was as disheartening as imagining one had been asleep for hours only to find that just a few minutes had lapsed. The arrival of a letter bomb on her Holland Park doorstep, addressed to her by name, had prompted Le Sueur to move Downes temporarily to a safe house under the watchful eye of a fellow intelligence officer.

The move had jarred with Downes's sense of independence. She had worked on her own during overseas assignments without the need for such "parental oversight". Downes woke suddenly from a deep slumber when her "chaperone" shook her arm and called her name. She had no idea what time she had finally fallen asleep, apart from the fact that it was sometime after 4 a.m., but now, abruptly awake, she felt worse. The last thing she wanted was an early morning briefing.

'Good morning, Downes, take a seat and help yourself to a tea or coffee,' said Le Sueur, whose lively demeanour suggested that she had clearly had a lot more sleep last night than her subordinate. Downes walked across to a trolley and poured herself a strong black coffee. As she did so, there was a knock on the door and a familiar face breezed in, DCI John Deery. The two exchanged pleasantries. The bleary-eyed intelligence officer watched as Deery poured himself a cup of tea, followed by several heaped teaspoons of sugar, before joining Le Sueur at her desk.

Over the course of the next hour, the Wing Commander read them into the Cerberus file and its full repercussions. She also updated them on yesterday's meeting with the Director General. There had been no new developments overnight or this morning, but the Prime Minister needed answers, and he needed them fast. He was standing on the trap door with the gallows hanging over his head. If they could not apprehend the perpetrator, who then made good on their threats, thousands of innocent people could die. If they caved into the demands, the government would certainly fall, and as for the country, disaster beckoned.

It was a beautiful late autumn day in St Helier. Travers had enjoyed a 30-minute swim in the opulent indoor pool at the Grand Hotel before breakfast, followed by his 09.30 meeting with DI Beckett. He had spoken to Alicia and heard all about her sleepless night, for which he had some sympathy. His small room in Thames House was barely big enough to house a camp bed. It was quite cramped, that he had been on the point of acquiescing to Le Sueur's offer of an alternative safe house in the interim. He smiled as he imagined Alicia's irritation as he described the comfort of his double room at the five-star hotel on the seafront at St Helier.

The Police Headquarters at 5 La Route du Fort were only a short twenty-minute walk away. Travers had briefly considered taking a taxi but decided against it. As he walked along the Esplanade, past Liberation Square and the famous Pomme d'Or Hotel—which had housed many senior Nazi officers during the occupation—he glanced up at Fort Regent. The last time he had come this way was with Claire Powell during their ill-fated pursuit of Akbar Hassan as he climbed the hill toward the fort complex.

Travers continued through the La Route du Fort tunnel, which ran beneath Fort Regent. A short distance beyond stood the Police Headquarters, his destination. Completed in 2016, the building's vernacular stone façade and wide expanses of glass filled the interior with natural light. As Travers entered the station foyer, he was met by DI Beckett, who had been expecting him. After a brief greeting, Beckett led him up several flights of grey, patterned, carpeted stairs to his glass-panelled office on the third floor.

Beckett opened the file on his desk, which contained photographs, reports and all the relevant material pertaining to the Powell murder investigation. Travers had maintained contact with Beckett since his return to the UK, speaking to him on several occasions. Now, two aspects of the investigation had piqued his interest, particularly following the murder of the German Franz Hoffman. Andreas Drakos and his boss, Osvaldo Phoenix. Travers looked at the post-mortem report for Powell; it was the first time he had seen it in detail. It couldn't be a coincidence that Powell, Hassan and Hoffman were all strangled and had their cervical vertebrae snapped.

'Do you know where this man Drakos is now, Inspector?'

'No, his picture has been issued to all units on the Island. If we find him, we will bring him in for questioning. I've also passed it on to Wing Commander Le Sueur along with all the information we have on him.'

Travers continued to look through the file, then came across the black and white A4 photograph of Andreas Drakos. He held it up, staring at the grainy image.

'Well, I'd take a heavy bet that he's been in London recently. The MO on Hoffman was identical, you don't break a man's neck that easily without training. Can you check your CCTV at the ferry terminal and the airport? It's possible you might get lucky, especially if he doesn't know we are looking for him. I'll ask Wing Commander Le Sueur to contact the UK Border Force to monitor departures.'

Travers put the photograph back in the file and handed it to DI Beckett.

'Now, Inspector, what about Osvaldo Phoenix, how much do you know about him?'

'He arrived in Jersey about twenty years ago, he's a very successful entrepreneur, mostly importing; a generous patron of the arts on the Island, enjoys gambling, chess, fine wine and being seen in the right places with people that matter,' said Beckett.

'So how does such an upright person end up top of your list of people of interest?'

Beckett rose from his seat and looked out of the window for a moment before turning back to face Travers.

'Phoenix has a lot of very influential friends here, but some of his other contacts are not the people you would want to invite to dinner, at least not a polite dinner. We've nothing on him, we've no evidence, nothing at all. Just rumours and hearsay, but as I said, some of his associates are regular visitors downstairs.'

'However, this man Drakos works for him, you say,' enquired Travers.

'Yes, he turned up six years ago. Phoenix took him on to work at his winery, but he seems to be more of a personal assistant than a grape trader.'

'I'd like to meet this man, Phoenix Inspector, socially, do you think you can engineer it?'

Beckett thought for a moment and looked at his watch 'Do you play chess, Mr Travers?'

An hour later, the two men walked up the wide stone steps which led to a large, elongated patio area. Two curved stone staircases, one on either side of the patio, then ran up to and met at the first-floor entrance to the Olympus Club. Travers paused after reaching the patio and looked up at the impressive traditional French chateau façade with four columns supporting the portico.

'Don't tell me you are a member here, Inspector?'

'No, a Chief Inspector's salary wouldn't be enough to get me through the door; however, this is police business, and no doors are closed to me. It's a private members' club for the well-heeled. I know that Phoenix is a member here, though, and he's here most days. He comes in for lunch, a few drinks, a game of chess and talks business with some of his cronies.'

Beckett and Travers walked through a large and luxurious lounge area. There were a number of members standing at the bar, some waiting to be served whilst others were busy talking. Travers looked around the room. Designer dresses, tailored suits, expensive watches and jewellery everywhere and nothing that looked like it had ever come off a peg.

It was another half hour before Beckett nudged Travers' arm. A tall, slim middle-aged man wearing a light grey pinstriped suit strode into the room with the confident air of someone who believed they belonged there. He waved to two men at the bar before moving away towards an empty table by a window. As a waiter collected some empty glasses, the man snapped his fingers twice until the young man responded and walked towards him. After some hesitation, he took the man's order and quickly left. Travers watched the interaction intently. It hadn't taken him long to make his own assessment; he didn't like him. He had an aversion to arrogance, and this man had it in spades; every gesture and glance had "Do you know who I am" written all over it. A few minutes later, the young man returned with an ornate crystal Stephfe of white wine, which he set down on the table. Shortly after that, another member of staff appeared carrying a large wooden chessboard and pieces, which he dutifully set up before withdrawing.

Travers and Beckett watched as Phoenix poured himself a glass of wine and looked down at the chessboard in front of him before starting to set up the pieces.

'Well, Mr Travers, I hope you brought a good set of balls with you, there's your chance. Sometimes he has a prearranged opponent; other times, he waits to see if anyone has the bottle to challenge him. I made that mistake a few years ago. He signed me in for lunch. Well, I'd played a bit in my youth, so I accepted his challenge. It was all over before I'd finished my first drink.'

Travers picked up what remained of his Vodka and Lemonade and walked across the room to where Phoenix still sat alone.

'May I join you?'

'Do you play?' asked Phoenix condescendingly, in a manner that did nothing but reinforce Travers' first impressions of him, as he beckoned Travers to the seat opposite him.

'Now and again,' replied Travers.

'I'm sorry, I didn't catch your name.'

'It's Travers, Greg Travers.'

Phoenix took the black and white queens and concealed them in his hands, then offered Travers the choice. He picked the left hand. With a smug smile, Phoenix opened the palm of his left hand to reveal the black Queen.

'Let's play,' said Phoenix.

Phoenix opened with the expected Pawn to King four. Beckett had warned him that Phoenix was known to be an aggressive player and fond of opening gambits to catch his challengers cold. Travers generally favoured mirroring his opponent in the early development of pieces when playing black, but in this instance, he opted for the Sicilian Defence with Pawn to Queen three. Beckett watched intrigued as the game proceeded at a pace. Travers had made some early gains and was forcing the normally aggressive Phoenix on the defensive.

'My compliments, Mr Travers, you are an excellent player. I've not seen you here before.'

'No, I work in London, I'm only here for a few days. I came with Detective Inspector Beckett.'

'Really, so you are friends with the Inspector, are you, how interesting, and what brings you to Jersey?'

'I work for the British Government, we are helping the Jersey States Police investigate the recent murders,' said Travers. He had considered spinning a yarn, but the situation in London was so grave that if Phoenix was involved, he needed to provoke him into either giving himself away or prompting a later indiscretion that would implicate him.

Travers studied Phoenix's reaction to the news. The Spaniard didn't look up but remained focused on the game. Travers would have to rattle his cage a little harder. For the next thirty minutes, the two combatants fought for control of the board. After many exchanges of pieces, at last Travers had his opponent in check. Though not serious, it was a source of great annoyance for Phoenix that he had been outmanoeuvred. He ground his teeth and then muttered something in Spanish under his breath. By this time, several people had walked over to watch the two men slug it out. As the match reached the latter stages, the pressure began to tell on Phoenix. In previous games, he was rarely pushed, let alone threatened with defeat, but now the tension was etched on his face; he now dithered before each move lest a mistake prove fatal. Travers scented blood, his man was on the ropes, and it was time to strike.

'By the way, I believe you know a friend of mine, Olga Devereux,'

'Who?!' said Phoenix, who was becoming more agitated as the spectre of defeat loomed closer. Travers had him in check once again. Phoenix's options were narrowing.

There was a murmuring amongst the large crowd that now surrounded the table.

Phoenix frowned 'No… I don't think I know her,' as his fingers hovered over the prized Queen that he was now about to be forced to sacrifice.

'Really? I was sure you did, and I expect you know her sister Maria as well, since she lives here; in fact, I was talking to her only the other day, and your name came up.'

'I tell you I don't know her, or her sister,' said the increasingly annoyed and flustered Spaniard as he reached for his glass of wine and took a large gulp.

Travers had outthought his adversary and broken him down piece by piece until his arrogance crumbled. If his hunch was correct, and there was a connection with Devereux, Phoenix might now be forced into carelessness, and the police would be watching his every move. The game drew to its now inevitable conclusion, Phoenix's King was boxed in. The hunter moved in for the kill.

'Checkmate, Mr Phoenix,' said a deadpan Travers, who did his utmost not to gloat despite the enormous satisfaction it had given him.

It was the first time anyone at the club could remember him being beaten. The disconsolate red-faced Spaniard stood up, glared and reluctantly shook Travers' hand, thanking him for the game and left the arena, pushing past the crowd without further interaction. Whilst several of the enthused spectators went over to congratulate the victor.

As the throng of well-wishers slowly dispersed, Travers got up and walked across to the bar where a smiling Beckett was waiting to add his fulsome congratulations. It was time to leave the party. Neither Travers nor Beckett knew what the result of the lunchtime tussle would be.

Travers had moved the deadly game forward; the next move would be Phoenix's.

Chapter 11

Alicia Downes was exhausted; she tossed her Burberry Camel trench coat over the chair in the lounge. It had been another busy day, constantly on the go. In the morning, she was following up on the results of Travers' investigations regarding the prime suspects of the Graf assassination. After lunch, she accompanied Christina Koehler from the German Foreign Intelligence Agency as she continued her own enquiries and those of her late colleague, Franz Hoffman. There was no time to ease her way back. Le Sueur needed her, but her body and brain were not yet back up to speed; she was wilting, yet there was no let-up. She poured herself a glass of white wine, sat on the sofa, and glanced at her phone. There was a text from Travers. She read it and smiled, took another sip, then kicked off her shoes, put her feet up and closed her tired eyes.

Just as she reached the blissful point where her semi-conscious state crossed the boundary into the unconscious, she was rudely woken by the sound of Ron Jackson, with whom she was now temporarily cohabiting. He bustled his way in through the front door of the Vauxhall safe house, dropping his bag on the floor and throwing his keys onto the side table. Downes had reluctantly allowed herself to be persuaded by Le Sueur to move into a safe house for a few days until the current crisis had passed. Jackson was a bit of a rough diamond, but his heart was in the right place, and though she hated to admit it, she was glad of the company, at least for a while.

After a delicious Chinese takeaway, she retired to her room to read for a while before having an early night. She left Jackson watching football on the television downstairs.

Her room, as with the rest of the house, was comfortable and tastefully decorated, if a little mundane for her own taste. She undressed and slipped into one of the few luxuries she could bring with her, a silver cashmere dressing gown. Lying on the bed, she picked up the thriller she had brought with her and began reading a few pages. Her eyelids were so heavy that it was as much as she could do to keep them open. Downes reached across for her phone. There were no new messages. She re-read Travers' text and replied briefly, congratulating him on his chess victory before returning to try and finish the next chapter before she fell asleep.

Sometime later, Downes woke, still lying on her bed. Her bedside light shining brightly, the book that she had been reading, now on the floor, its pages splayed. She looked at her watch; it was approaching midnight. A noise had woken her up, or perhaps it was just her imagination? Every house has its own unique characteristics. She knew every creak and groan at Holland Park, but this wasn't her house. Then she heard another, perhaps a floorboard? Downes got off the bed and made her way to the bedroom door, and slowly opened it. Stepping out of the room and turning on the landing light, she looked along the passageway. All was quiet. She stood and listened and heard nothing. Walking to Jackson's room, she quietly opened the door and peered around it. The room was empty. His bed had not been slept in. Closing the door, she walked back along the oak-stained landing. He had probably fallen asleep watching television, much as she had done upstairs. Downes walked to the end of the landing and looked over the bannister.

The spill of the landing light partially illuminated the wooden staircase leading down to the ground floor; beyond that, there was darkness. Downes carefully edged her way down the flight of stairs, holding onto the bannister. All the downstairs lights appeared to be off, and she could hear no sound from the TV. As Downes entered the lounge, she felt for the light switch, which she remembered was just inside the door on the right. Stretching out her hand, she ran her fingers across the smooth plaster as she searched for the chrome dimmer switch she knew to be there. Eventually, and with some relief, she found it. The light did not come on. She called Jackson's name, but there was no response. The hair on the back of Downes' neck now stood tall as she felt the full flow of adrenaline and fear surge and course through her body. The kitchen was on the other side of the lounge. There, she would find a torch and the circuit breakers for the electrics. With her left hand running along the sideboard as a point of reference, she stepped forward towards the kitchen.

Almost immediately, she bumped into something and stumbled, sprawling onto her hands to break her fall. She spun around on her knees and stretched out an arm into the darkness, searching for the obstacle. As she crawled forward with both hands on the hardwood floor, her hands were wet and slightly tacky. She reached forward with both hands and, to her utter revulsion, in her grasp was the head of Ron Jackson, his prickly facial stubble drenched in his blood. Horrified, Downes drew a large intake of breath; she wanted to scream, but knew she mustn't. Desperately, she covered her lips with her blood-soaked hand to silence her despairing need to emote. Her phone and an emergency panic button were upstairs. Downes stepped over the lifeless body in front of her and retraced her steps back to the welcome sight of the still partially lit stairs to the first floor. Hitching up her blood-stained dressing gown, she ran up the stairs and into her bedroom, immediately pressed the wireless panic button on her bedside table, then picked up her phone and dialled 999.

As she waited for the emergency services to respond, she turned away from the bedside table and sat on the bed.

At the outer edge of her peripheral vision, she saw a shadow; there was movement, a dark figure. Downes wheeled around in shock. In front of her was a very tall, sinewy man. His black clothing was now embellished by the crimson spoils of his latest brutal killing.

'Who are you? What do you want?' demanded Downes, who knew that help was probably only minutes away. The longer she could keep him talking, the better her chances of survival until back-up arrived.

'Hades.'

'Really, and what does everyone else call you? How did you get in here? Who sent…'

'Shut the fuck up bitch! You ask too many questions, I don't like people who ask questions,' he said sharply.

'Why? What is this all about? Who has sent you?'

This time, Hades did not reply. He began moving towards Downes, who stepped back until she felt the bedside table pressing against her back. His soulless, dark eyes were staring menacingly at her. She had precious little to defend herself with as he drew closer.

As she backed away, her fingers glanced against what remained of a glass of water on her bedside cabinet. Picking up the glass in her left hand, she threw the water in his face, then broke the glass against the table and lunged at Hades with the fractured tumbler, cutting his face. Hades grabbed the hand holding the glass and shook it violently, forcing Downes to let it go. He then gripped her throat with one of his massive hands and began to squeeze the breath from her. Downes could feel her energy draining away. Her attempts to fight back proved futile against the overwhelming size and strength of her assailant. During the struggle, the top drawer of her cabinet opened slightly.

Downes could see her small pair of nail scissors, if she could only reach them. Feigning a loss of consciousness, she slumped slightly, giving her the chance to stretch her left hand into the narrow gap. Grasping the scissors, she slammed them into the hand that had been choking her, then into Hades' throat, causing copious amounts of blood to flow from the relatively small wound.

As Hades recoiled, Downes could hear the sound of multiple sirens approaching. Enraged, Hades slapped her fiercely across the face before flinging her across the bed and onto the floor beyond. Then, with one hand trying to stem the blood flowing from his neck, he fled. Downes scrambled to her feet, grabbed her phone and ran out of the bedroom and down the stairs towards the now-open front door, using the light from her phone to find her way. As she reached the gate, the police and emergency services arrived, but there was no sign of Hades. Returning to the house, the downstairs electricity was quickly restored, and the full horror of Jackson's murder was apparent. He was a burly, strong man and not someone to be easily overpowered. Evidently, Hades had surprised him from behind. The black sofa on which he had been sitting had been pulled over onto its back, with Jackson's body now lying prone on the floor beyond it, with a deep laceration to his throat. As Downes provided the police with her statement, two senior officers from MI5 arrived and introduced themselves to the police.

Thirty minutes later, Downes was driven back to Thames House. The crime scene at the Vauxhall safe house was now sealed off. She was escorted to the briefing room. To her surprise, given the lateness of the hour, she found both Wing Commander Le Sueur and the Deputy Director General waiting for her. She explained that she was notified at home as soon as the emergency was raised. When it became known that Jackson had been murdered, she alerted the Deputy Director. Downes repeated the details of the attack that she had previously imparted to the police. There was now no doubt that somebody in MI5 had tipped off the murderer. This man, Hades, had both the location of the Vauxhall safe house and details of the alarm system, which could only have come from in-house.

The Deputy Director General picked up his mobile phone, and a few moments later, he placed a call to the nearby Westminster Hotel. After speaking briefly to the Duty Night Manager, he informed Downes that a room at the hotel was being prepared for her.

'Alright, Miss Downes, you had better go and get some sleep. This is off the books; no one outside this room knows where you are staying tonight. Let's keep it that way. Report back here tomorrow. Wing Commander, I want that mole. Get your best people on it. I will update the Director.'

The following morning, it was only thanks to a wake-up call from the hotel that Downes finally emerged from her hotel room. She had slept very soundly in a comfortable bed. Despite the lateness of her arrival there, she felt secure. Emotionally and physically drained by the horrific events of the previous evening, she had tried with only partial success to keep her mind off the dreadful circumstances that had brought her to the hotel. She enjoyed a full English breakfast in the company of her German counterpart, Christina Koehler, who was still a resident there whilst her own investigations were ongoing. Despite their short association, Downes had found it valuable to be able to discuss the events with a person who had an innate empathy through her own experiences, rather than a well-meaning civilian.

After parting, Downes returned to her room. With very little to pack, she sat on her bed and surveyed the beautiful and stylish décor that the Queen Guest Room offered. If only Le Sueur would be willing to sign it off, she would be more than happy to stay here for a few days. As

Downes pondered how she might broach the subject of her future residency, her phone flashed; it was a text from Travers. No sooner had she replied, relaying to him the events of the evening, he rang. It was good to hear his voice, even if it was anxious and filled with concern. She did her best to reassure him that she was fine and that it was business as usual today. Though unconvinced, he accepted her word, knowing that in reality there was little he could do about it, sitting as he was in his hotel room in Jersey.

Osvaldo Phoenix sat in his comfortable wood-panelled office at the Phoenix Winery, not far from his villa. Business was booming, while the local maritime climate was not altogether conducive to viticulture. However, he was able to import considerable quantities of harvested grapes, primarily from France, Spain, and Italy, which were then put into huge stainless steel vats for fermentation and maceration. As one of the few wineries on the Island, he was able to produce white, rosé, red, and sparkling wines for local consumption; the rest he exported at prices that successfully undercut many of his more well-known competitors. He picked up a sample bottle and poured a small glass of white wine produced from the green-skinned Phoenix grape, a fact that was a constant source of amusement to him. With Elderflower and Herbaceous notes, it was an aromatic wine much to his liking. Draining his glass with a slurp of satisfaction, he picked up the bottle and left his office.

Passing several large storerooms containing either bottles or barrels of ageing wine, he reached a door marked private. After looking around to ensure he was not being observed, Phoenix unlocked the door and proceeded inside, then locked it again. At the opposite end of the small room were two large metal storage racks behind which was a heavy steel door, with two equidistant deadlocks on either side of a large steel handle. Phoenix produced two keys from his pocket and unlocked it. Despite the weight of the door, it opened easily to reveal a steep set of concrete steps descending downwards into the darkness. The flick of a light switch illuminated the passageway as far as the eye could see. Phoenix began his descent. At the bottom of the stairs was a short plastered corridor leading to another steel door. Phoenix unlocked and opened it.

The dark, shadowy world of Osvaldo Phoenix was alive with movement. Teams of illegal immigrants smuggled in under his direction worked tirelessly to process and pack a vast array of contraband—tobacco, alcohol, drugs, weapons, prescription medication, and stacks of cash and bullion. As Phoenix walked through the complex, he nodded approvingly at the organised chaos around him.

Branching off the main corridor was a warren of smaller rooms and passageways. Some served as extra storage; others were makeshift sleeping quarters for workers who had yet to be processed by his organisation or were still waiting for the forged identification that would let them move freely above ground.

At the far end of the complex, isolated from the rest, lay a series of luxury suites reserved for Phoenix's most valuable guests—prominent figures of the criminal underworld or fugitives wanted by international authorities for terrorism, such as the recently returned Ali Abadi.

Phoenix knocked at the door of the entrance to the last suite. The beech door swung open, and standing in the doorway was the tall, willowy figure of Ali Abadi. His gaunt, almost emaciated face was a testament to his preoccupation as a wholesaler and distributor of weapons of mass destruction. He invited Phoenix into his room. Although without windows, the suite was luxuriously furnished, bright and airy. The pair sat on opposite sides of an oblong wooden coffee table inlayed with gold leaf.

Phoenix, himself virtually without scruples, felt uncomfortable in the presence of a man who thought nothing of murdering hundreds of innocent people to satisfy his thirst for bloodshed and death. Since his last visit, he had blown up a school in London and but for the incompetence of the men selected, would have inflicted many more casualties in Covent Garden had the device exploded.

'Have you heard from Mrs Devereux?' asked Abadi.

'Yes, I spoke to her earlier today. Her informant in the British Security Services says that the Government doesn't know what to do. They cannot give in because they will be publicly humiliated and the government will collapse, but they have no answers; they are stumbling about in the dark. Tell me, if the British Prime Minister does not agree to her demands, is she really prepared to use those biological weapons?'

'Yes, London will understand the true meaning of terrorism, as will all those she holds responsible for her son's death.'

'I want you to avoid any unnecessary time in the open until this is finished and you are safely out of the country. We had a local detective sniffing around here a few days ago, making enquiries about Hades and the recent murders. I don't want to give the authorities any excuse to come back and start poking their noses around here,' said Phoenix as he stood up, still brandishing the bottle of wine he had brought with him from the winery. He continued

'This vindictive venture of hers is a needless threat to my organisation...'

Before Phoenix could finish his sentence, Abadi rose to his feet and stood directly in front of him.

'Your organisation? Mr Phoenix, be careful. You do not bite the hand that feeds you. I know more about your organisation than you think. All of this, I know she paid for. You were just a playboy and minor smuggler when you left Spain, now you are a multi-millionaire with a business empire. She could take it away tomorrow if she thought she couldn't trust you,' smirked Abadi.

Phoenix knew that every word Abadi had said was true. He had always had a talent for smuggling, but his expensive lifestyle required more money than his small-time black market operation could hope to deliver. When he met the ever-opportunist Olga Devereux at La Rascasse during the Monte Carlo Grand Prix weekend, he had been easily seduced by her charisma and wealth. The following morning, she offered to provide him with the financial backing he needed, for a price; she wanted a foothold in the Channel Islands. He had readily taken the bait and was now firmly on her hook. He was also acutely aware that if he displeased her, she could just as easily reel him in and cast him aside without a second thought. After a few passing words, Phoenix left Abadi's suite and made his way along a short wood-panelled companionway to the stairs leading to the concealed entrance at his villa.

At last, he could sit and enjoy his wine in peace. Selecting a Flamenco Crystal glass goblet from his mahogany drinks cabinet, Phoenix slowly poured a half glass of wine, took a sip and sat back, closing his eyes as he savoured the wonderful bouquet before slowly taking a second swallow. He thought about his conversation with the odious Abadi, he didn't like him or anything he stood for. The sooner he completed his task on the Island and was out of the country, the happier he would feel. Yet he couldn't deny the debt he owed Olga Devereux, he looked around the room adorned by expensive works of art and a lifestyle he could only dream of as a younger man. He had not seen Olga in person for several years, but she seemed to have changed since her son's death. She had always had a tremendous single-minded sense of purpose and a flexible approach to the rule of law, but there was now a malevolent, vengeful streak that went beyond simple avariciousness.

Chapter 12

Greg Travers looked out of his window at the five-star Grand Hotel overlooking St Aubin's Bay. The tide was on the turn; in a few hours, the vast swathes of open sand would be completely underwater. There were still some late-season tourists who chanced their arms and chose the open causeway leading to Elizabeth Castle. Although with the incoming tide, they may have to resort to Charming Betty or Charming Nancy, the amphibious buses known affectionately as Ducks, to convey them back across to the mainland once the rising waters had cut off their retreat.

With a half-hour swim and a full English breakfast behind him, Travers phoned Alicia Downes. She was a confident, strong, resourceful woman however, the last few months had knocked her back. Now this latest incident had shaken her once again. She would never show it, but Travers could tell from her voice that the hairline cracks were still there, and would probably remain so until they cleared up this case once and for all.

He finished dressing and proceeded down to the Champagne lounge, where he met DI Beckett. After exchanging small talk, the two men walked out of the hotel entrance through the revolving door and down the three steps leading to the deserted terrace in front of the hotel. The fine weather was holding with just a gentle breeze. Travers led Beckett to one of the wicker tables at the front of the terrace, where a glass screen acted as a windbreak.

Travers brought the Jersey detective up to speed with the previous night's news. Beckett shook his head as he was told that there was now no doubt that the man he had previously identified as Andreas Drakos, nicknamed Hades and categorised as "a person of interest", was now wanted for the murder of Ron Jackson and the attempted murder of Alicia Downes.

Before Beckett could reply, he was briefly interrupted by Carlos, a Spanish waiter, who put a tray down on the glass-covered wicker table containing two cups of tea.

'Do you have any idea where Drakos is now, Greg?' asked the Detective.

'No, Inspector, all I can say with certainty is that he was in central London last night. The police have put out an all-ports warning. Every agency has been alerted, but we don't know what his plans are; he might just go to ground or look to slip out of the country,' said Travers, who continued.

'I think you might have to re-evaluate your investigation, Inspector. This man, Drakos or Hades or whatever he calls himself, has definitely killed once in the UK. He was linked to that man Hassan, who turned up dead on your beach with a broken neck. He may have been involved with the murder of Claire Powell. Alicia said he was tall and immensely strong and nearly strangled her with one hand. You said he works for Osvaldo Phoenix?'

'Yes, when I spoke to him, he claimed he didn't know where he was, but his mistress said he was in London,'

'This mistress, what's she like, Inspector? Do you think she knows more than she's telling?'

Beckett removed his mobile phone from his jacket pocket. After a few moments of searching, he handed the device to Travers. He looked at several pictures of the beautiful former Grecian model and then scrolled through a brief biography before handing the phone back to the Inspector.

'Lucky man,' commented Travers. 'I wonder if she knows what a bastard he is?'

'I don't know, but she certainly enjoys the fringe benefits. She walks around like she's the Queen of Sheba. She hangs out with a group of well-heeled girlfriends at the Atlantic.'

'She doesn't work then?'

'Work? I doubt if she has the time nowadays. A few years ago, she used to be on the top rung of the modelling world; she could name her price. Then she met Phoenix, and now? Now, she's a lady who lunches.'

'Inspector, you say she is usually at the Atlantic?' questioned Travers.

'It's a luxury hotel on the west coast overlooking St Ouen's Bay. She's there for lunch most days, I believe. I don't know what Phoenix is up to, but she spends money like there's no tomorrow.'

'Well, Inspector, I am going to find out,' said a smiling Travers as he finished his cup of tea.

Travers left the Detective Inspector and returned to his hotel room. A plan was coalescing in his mind. Phoenix was now more than a person of interest. Apart from Travers' recently acquired dislike for him, he had links with the man Hades, who had attacked Alicia and murdered Ron Jackson and may also be connected to the murder of Claire Powell and possibly others. DI Beckett had suggested that Phoenix's mistress, Penelope Papandreou, may have unintentionally let slip the whereabouts of Hades. If this were true, perhaps she could be persuaded or induced to provide further vital information. She was a woman who enjoyed attention, and according to Beckett, revelled in flirtatious conversation.

With his course of action now clear, Travers rummaged through his suitcases for something suitable to wear.

The trip by car from the Grand to the Atlantic Hotel was a brisk twenty minutes or so around St Aubin's Bay and along the A13. The traffic was thankfully light, and Travers enjoyed the spectacular views out across St Ouen's Bay as he approached the hotel entrance. With the high season now past, Travers had no difficulty parking and walked in through the main entrance, its frame entwined with wisteria vines now bare of their heavy summer blossoms.

The foyer was a combination of traditional rough stone walls, stained wooden flooring, with an elegant white plaster ceiling with recessed lighting and moulded cornices. Modern artworks featured prominently throughout the room, with paintings and sculptures tastefully displayed. Travers strolled to the rear of the hotel, where he heard the sound of voices and laughter. Entering the terrace and pool area, he estimated around twenty people gathered there, enjoying the relaxing ambience and the now-weakening autumn sunshine.

Travers casually strolled around the pool, observing the residents as they chatted to one another. He couldn't see Papandreou there, although there was a group of very well-turned-out women who could have easily passed for the cast of one of the "Housewives of…" programmes. Travers was slightly disappointed; perhaps she just wasn't there today.

He slowly walked through the middle of the group, glancing left and right to ensure he had not missed her, then returned to the hotel and headed for the cocktail bar. It was busy a celebration of some kind was taking place. Several helium-filled balloons were bobbing around, seemingly with a life of their own and a noticeable degree of levity amongst the drinkers. Travers didn't recognise any of the faces. Then he noticed a woman with long dark hair sitting alone on a bar stool with her back to him, talking to the barman. Travers weaved his way through the partygoers until he reached the relative calm of the bar.

The bartender was still holding the half-empty bottle of Taittinger Champagne that he had used to refill the young woman's glass as Travers approached the bar. Taking the remaining stool, he rested his right arm and glanced at the woman beside him. There was no doubt in his mind; it was Penelope Papandreou. Despite many years away from the modelling circuit, she was still stunningly beautiful with not an ounce of surplus fat on her. In a fabulous black Erato dress stretching down to her ankles and with her pitch-black hair tumbling across her shoulders, she would still grace any catwalk today. Putting down her mobile phone, she picked up her glass, still frantic with effervescent bubbles and took a sip. Turning her head slightly, she caught Travers' eye, and he smiled.

'Good afternoon, that looks particularly nice, I am a Bollinger RD man myself; however, when in Rome,' said Travers as he signalled to catch the attention of the bartender.

'A glass of Taittinger, please,' said Travers.

The bartender reached over for the open bottle of Champagne and poured a fresh glass for Travers, who studied it for a few moments until the bubbles began to settle. He took the glass in his hand and turned to Papandreou.

'Yamas.'

She turned towards him, her mouth breaking into a warm smile as though renewing an old friendship. 'Have we met?' she said, looking him in the eye as she tried to recall a previous meeting.

'No, not exactly, Miss Papandreou. My late wife was a huge admirer of yours, she regularly attended the major fashion shows in Milan, Paris, London and on one occasion, New York. There must have been as many pictures of you around our house as there were of her own family, she was practically stalking you,' said Travers, smiling. 'My name's Travers, Greg Travers by the way. If you'll forgive me for saying so, for someone clearly enjoying retirement, you look amazing, Miss Papandreou. If the social whirl gets a bit tedious, you could step straight back into the business. I am sure the fashion houses would welcome you back.'

'Oh, please call me Penelope. Go back to that life? All that travelling, exercise routines, and constantly watching what I can eat. No, I don't think so.'

Papandreou took another sip of her champagne as the conversation continued. Travers found her easy to talk to. She was relaxed, certainly flirtatious and demonstrably tactile, constantly touching his hand or leg during their exchanges. As he listened to her chatter away, Travers' thoughts turned towards Phoenix. How could this lovely creature be involved with someone like him? He looked around the still full bar area.

'Are you on your own today? I'd hate to think that I am keeping you from your husband.'

'I'm not married. I love it here. I come most days, sometimes to catch up with my girlfriends, and sometimes, just to get away.'

'Get away? From what?' Travers said enquiringly.

Penelope hesitated, her fingers circling the rim of her glass. 'Ozy… I mean, my boyfriend. He's a successful businessman, but some of the people he deals with are not nice. To be honest, he scares me sometimes.'

'I am sorry to hear that. Wait… Ozy—do you mean Osvaldo Phoenix?'

'Yeah? You know him?'

'Oh yes, Mr Phoenix, we've met. We had a game of chess at his club.'

'Chess? He takes his chess very seriously, no one beats him,' said Papandreou.

'Well, I think I may have ruined his day then,' said Travers.

'Oh my god! Did you beat him? That's why he was in a dreadful mood when he got in yesterday.'

Papandreou was delightful company, but Travers was going to have to start probing a little deeper for more information about her boyfriend, the bad-tempered Mr Phoenix. Perhaps a few more glasses of champagne would help the process along, soften her up and make her a little more pliable. Having suggested another glass, she confided that Phoenix maintained a Suite at the hotel which he used for some of his more favoured clients. However, she was free to use it whenever she liked.

Without hesitation or waiting for Travers to comment, she called out to the bartender, who swiftly produced a fresh magnum of chilled Taittinger in an ice bucket. Travers looked at the enormous bottle now sitting on the bar. Never mind the bill that would, in itself, give Le Sueur palpitations when she saw his expenses, if he drank his share this afternoon, he would probably be flat out on the floor by teatime despite his reputation.

Hopping off their barstools, Papandreou and Travers left the cocktail bar. Travers, holding the ice bucket, watched enviously as the sylphlike Papandreou in front of him glided gracefully in her dress between the clientele still occupying the bar whilst he swivelled this way and that as he manoeuvred his way to the entrance, doing his best not to bump into anyone. It was a short distance to the luxury one-bedroom Atlantic suite. Papandreou unlocked the door and walked in, followed by Travers, who put the ice bucket on the coffee table in the lounge. Opening the full-length sliding glass doors, they walked out onto the private terrace, which offered views across the gardens and the Atlantic Ocean beyond. It was still pleasantly warm. Papandreou brought out two champagne glasses whilst Travers wrestled with the stubborn cork before it eventually shot out with a tremendous pop. The two sat at a small white table in the sun and looked out across the tranquil panorama. They enjoyed a relaxing hour's conversation as the champagne flowed before the sun's rays faded and they decided to adjourn indoors to escape the late afternoon chill.

Papandreou was certainly the life and soul of any company she was in. The abundant flow of champagne did nothing but amplify her vivacious and flirtatious nature to the point that Travers began to feel he was getting into dangerously deep water. She spoke at great length about her upbringing in Greece and rapid progression in the modelling industry to become the hottest property in the country, with her face on the front cover of every fashion magazine in Europe.

As they nonchalantly talked, Travers was careful to ensure that her glass was never empty. She didn't seem at all inhibited and appeared almost blissfully happy to describe the moment when she walked away from her stellar career after meeting and falling in love with Phoenix. At the time, she was tired of the constant travel and the demands of being one of the leading models around, and she needed a break. It came in the form of Osvaldo Phoenix, Ozy as she called him.

She had just completed a major fashion shoot in Monte Carlo, and to celebrate, the management took the girls to the fabled casino. There she met Phoenix, oozing charm and old-world sophistication, who fawned over her. She was flattered and drawn in with gifts and trips out on yachts that were moored in the harbour owned by his criminal associates. Before she realised what was happening, she stunned her agency by walking away from the world she loved, ignoring the pleas from her shocked friends and moved in with Phoenix. He showered her with everything that his growing black market enterprise could offer, including an introduction to class-A drugs, particularly cocaine.

By the time she realised what she had lost, she had a new master. The more she spoke about her new life, the more Travers resolved to bring this unsavoury man to justice. She was a trusting but now deeply troubled woman. He contemplated revealing his true identity to her, but would that encourage her to open up to him or frighten her off? After some thought, he decided against it.

Travers glanced at his watch; it had just turned 4 pm. He reached across to the low wooden coffee table next to his sofa and lifted the bottle of Taittinger out of the melted iced water beneath it. After shaking off the drips, he leant across to the pale blue sofa at right angles to his own, on which Papandreou was elegantly lying with her legs drawn up under her.

As he stretched out to reach her glass, her hand intercepted his and gently held it as he poured more champagne into the crystal goblet. He looked across at her as their eyes met in an ocular embrace. She reached down with her other hand and slightly pulled the hem of her black dress, exposing her light olive-toned legs. Travers could feel the hairs on his arms extend as he looked up at her beautiful features. Her eyes were mesmerising; it was now so easy to see how the world's cameras had loved her so much. The transitory spell was only broken when the champagne bubbles overflowed and began dribbling down the side of the glass. Travers quickly pulled his hand away, almost sheepishly. As Papandreou slowly ran her hand provocatively along the length of her thigh, Travers vainly tried to effect an air of nonchalant indifference.

Travers knew that he had to refocus and keep his mind on the job, at least for now. She was a free spirit, but like a beautiful moth fatally attracted to a flame, she was ensnared and unable to break free. Whatever his personal feelings towards Phoenix, he wanted to help her if he could. She had admitted that she often came to the Atlantic to "escape", but from what?

'Penelope, have you ever heard Ozy mention any names, visitors or people he's in business with? Has he brought anyone to the house that you have seen?'

'No, very few. He does most of his business away from the house, away from me. He did have this creepy guy around, an Arab, Ali something or other. He came to the house once. Ozy told me never to talk to him. I think he had something to do with that school bombing in London. I know Ozy is involved with something pretty shady, I don't see him much at the moment, and of course, there is Hades, he's always popping round to talk to him.'

'Penelope, this is really important, that man you mentioned, Ali, do you remember his second name? Can you describe him for me?' asked Travers, who was already fearing the worst if what she was saying was true.

Papandreou giggled as the effects of the champagne finally caught up with her. She stood up, hitched up her dress, then shuffled her way across to Travers' sofa and sat herself down at the far end, kicked off her Louboutins and raised her feet till they rested on Travers' lap.

'I'm sorry I can't. He was tall and thin, with almost hollow cheeks and dark receding hair, oh, and he had some kind of scar or injury on his face. That's all I can remember.'

'You're sure about that?' said Travers, turning to face her.

Papandreou had answered enough questions and now had other things on her mind as she casually moved her calves back and forth across Travers' groin. Ignoring her overtly suggestive flirtation and the blood surging to his loins, he waited for an answer, which, with a deep sigh, eventually came.

'Yes, he just appeared one day in the garden, Ozy told me to stay away from him. He was here for a few days, then left. Apparently, he is back on the island. Who is he?'

'Penelope, if you see this man again or Phoenix mentions him, I want you to call me as soon as you can. Will you do that for me?'

'Alright, are we done now with the twenty questions?' said Papandreou, with an unmistakable twinkle in her eyes.

Papandreou reached over to the coffee table and picked up Travers' half-empty glass. She took an extended sip, then leaned across with one hand resting on his thigh and held it up to Travers' mouth with the other. Holding the glass by her hand, he finished the last of the champagne, then kissed her gently on the cheek. With the glass now drained, Papandreou put it back on the ornate wooden coffee table. With an exaggerated yawn, she sat up, arched her back and stretched both arms over her head. The action had the intended effect of thrusting her perfectly formed breasts, which had been visible through her designer dress, outwards towards Travers. This 21st-century Aphrodite was now seducing every cell in his body, filling both his head and loins with an increasingly problematic and inconvenient truth that was becoming harder and harder to ignore.

Chapter 13

It was a little after six that Travers finally left the Atlantic Hotel. He stopped off at the bar and ordered a black coffee while waiting for the taxi to take him back to the Grand. He would return in the morning to pick up his hired car. Despite now suffering a slightly fuzzy head, it had been a productive afternoon. He had left Papandreou fast asleep, sprawled across her king-sized bed with what remained of her modesty obscured by a soft pink Egyptian cotton sheet.

As he sat in the bar, he reflected on what had transpired. Papandreou had given up a lucrative career, whisked off her feet by the charismatic Spaniard. However, the excitement soon faded. Now she felt no more than a chattel, an adornment to be displayed and controlled like so many of Phoenix's works of art. What troubled Travers more were the two names she had mentioned. The first was Ali, with the description she had been able to give, he was almost certain that it was Ali Abadi, top of the West's most wanted list, an expert in weapons of mass destruction, and just the man to be behind the biological threat in London. The second was Andreas Drakos, who called himself Hades. She had confirmed what DI Beckett had said to him earlier, that he was presently in London, something Phoenix had omitted during his talk with the Jersey detective.

Travers' train of thought was fleetingly interrupted by the waiter bringing his coffee. After a brief conversation, the courteous and jovial middle-aged man took the cup of coffee off the tray and placed it on the table. Travers thanked him, then added a spoonful of sugar and began stirring the black coffee. As he did so, he glanced around, there was no sign of the partygoers who had been noisily occupying the cocktail bar earlier. Several couples were scattered throughout the room, and half a dozen young women were occupying a table in the far corner, who Travers thought might have been some of the same group he had seen by the pool when he arrived. As he sipped his coffee, Travers sat back in his comfortable armchair. It would be another twenty minutes before his taxi arrived. He was tired. When he got back to the privacy of his hotel room, he would contact Le Sueur and bring her up to speed. He might even discuss what options were available as far as Penelope Papandreou was concerned, if any.

As he sat relaxing with his eyes half closed, Travers suddenly became acutely aware of a familiar voice close by. He sat up, the residual effects of the Taittinger abruptly supplanted by a spontaneous surge of adrenaline. He looked towards the open doorway, his pulse quickened, and his eyes focused intently on the entrance. The voice grew louder until Travers could see the faint shadow of a figure stretching across the frame. The arrogance in the tone of voice was unmistakable; it was Osvaldo Phoenix. Travers braced himself. Then he heard another voice, it was one of the management calling Phoenix. The sound of the voices then diminished. Travers swiftly walked over and looked round the corner of the room, just catching sight of Phoenix as he and the other man disappeared.

Travers' thoughts turned to the woman he had spent the afternoon with. What would Phoenix's reaction be if he went to the suite and found Papandreou there? There was nothing he could do; the last thing he wanted was for Phoenix to become suspicious of Papandreou or suspect any connection between the two of them. He walked towards the foyer where an elderly couple had just arrived and were checking in, fortunately, there was no sign of Phoenix. Travers' taxi arrived a few minutes early, and with just a swift backwards glance, he opened the rear door and got in.

Twenty minutes later, Travers arrived back at his hotel and walked up the steps, across the marble hallway past the concierge and up the magnificent grand staircase to his Ocean View room.

Once inside, Travers took off his shoes and flung himself onto the freshly remade king-size bed. As he luxuriated in the enveloping folds of the soft white duvet, he was conscious that he could still smell Papandreou's Christian Dior perfume. It was a reminder, as if he needed it, of the time they had enjoyed together but also of the rash promise he had made to help her leave Phoenix, but for a few moments at least, he tried to clear his mind of those cares that seemed to be mounting daily. After five minutes of unadulterated self-indulgence, Travers rolled over, climbed off the bed, took his clothes off, and headed for the shower.

Travers, now refreshed, sat in the window of his ocean-view room and looked out across the bay; the last rays of the sun were fast disappearing beneath the western horizon. For a moment, he considered raiding the mini bar for a shot of whiskey before thinking better of it. A cup of tea would suffice for the moment. There was no point in adding to the afternoon's alcohol intake. He picked up his mobile phone and spoke to Steph Le Sueur. The Home Secretary had been badgering the Director General for an update on their investigation, and she'd been getting it in the neck all day ever since. What Travers was going to tell her would only exacerbate matters. The Prime Minister was already rattled; the news that Ali Abadi was now almost certainly involved in the bombing campaign would only make things worse. MI5 and MI6 had been trying to bring him in for years. His pre-eminence in weapons of mass destruction was well deserved. As far as Hades was concerned, the Met were still trying to trace him, but so far, nothing.

Le Sueur was more definite regarding Phoenix's mistress, Penelope Papandreou. Travers could help her as long as it did not compromise MI5 or His Majesty's Government. She reminded Travers that the mission was simple: find out who was behind the London bombings and the threats to the government and stop it, but MI5 was not a charitable organisation for those who had made bad life choices. While he had tried to make a logical case for helping her, Le Sueur was adamant; his responsibility was clear. Travers put the phone down. He was disappointed at her stubbornness, but not entirely surprised; one doesn't get to that pay grade without understanding the necessity to toe the party line.

In the luxury suite at the Atlantic Hotel, Penelope Papandreou slowly opened her eyes; her head was still swimming and fuzzy with the effects of the champagne. She stretched out her arms and yawned extravagantly. Pushing the pink cotton top sheet aside, she looked around the room. She was alone, her companion now gone. She had enjoyed his company; he had been intelligent, funny, yet attentive and respectful, resisting her shameless attempts to seduce him. She stared intently at the diamond-encrusted white gold Cartier watch on her wrist, struggling to focus on the Roman numeral indices. After a few moments of frustration, she gave up, rolled over onto her tummy and grabbed the soft white pillow between her arms and buried her head in it. A few minutes later, she lifted her head as though coming up for air before yawning again, taking in a huge gulp of air. With a bleary eye, she reached for her mobile phone lying on the far side of the bedside cabinet, but only managed to send it tumbling to the floor, where it bounced just under the bed.

Papandreou made no attempt to disguise her irritation; the words may have been in Greek, but the meaning would have been universally understood. She leaned over the side of the bed and, with her right hand, tried to reach the phone. As her hand searched the thick pile carpet under the bed, she felt a sudden sting and hastily withdrew her hand. There was a tiny speck of blood on her finger. Papandreou wondered if she had been bitten by a spider. Now there was no question of staying in bed, if there was one thing that she was afraid of, it was an aggressive spider.

Casting the sheet to one side and swinging her naked legs across, she sat on the bed. Then, surmising that whatever it was that had bitten her was still in close attendance, she stood up and took a step away from the king-size bed, before kneeling down and peering under it. She immediately picked up the phone and put it on the bed before continuing her search for the condemned arachnid.

Something caught her eye nestling amongst the fibres of the carpet. Edging closer to the underside of the bed, she reached out for the object which still glinted even in the failing afternoon light. Returning to the bed, Papandreou studied the find as she held it between her fingers. It was a single white gold earring in the style of a letter J with a diamond stud at the top. Her heart began to beat faster and faster as she continued to gaze at the delicate piece of jewellery. How did it get there? Sometimes Ozy's business associates brought their girlfriends, but more often Ozy supplied female "companionship" to sweeten the deals, but he hadn't had clients in the suite for weeks. The more she thought about it, the more she brooded, and the more she brooded, the worse she felt.

Papandreou showered, dressed, straightened the bed and disposed of the empty bottle of Taittinger. Phoenix was due in the Atlantic early evening, where he was meeting the hotel manager about a new arrangement for leasing the suite. Before leaving, she hid the earring in her handbag. She would need to think carefully about what to do next. Ozy was not a man to question, but her agitated mind was racing. Who did the earring belong to? Who was J? What was it doing in their suite and under the bed? Papandreou walked down to the cocktail bar, her mind now so preoccupied, she scarcely noticed anybody else.

The afternoon crowd had gone, and the bar was largely deserted. She sauntered over and took her place on the same barstool that she had occupied earlier in the afternoon. The female bartender turned and smiled at Papandreou

'Hi Penny,' said the affable and glamorous young woman.

'Hi Juliet, expecting a busy night? You've not seen Ozy around, have you?'

'No, not since I've been in. Usual?' asked the bartender.

'No, not tonight, I had a full skin earlier. Just a cappuccino, please, Jules.'

Juliet smiled at Papandreou's back-to-front colloquialism, but she got the message.

Papandreou reached into her bag for her phone. As she did so, she felt the solitary earring in a small zipped pocket. Running her finger across the outline, she couldn't help but wonder again who it might belong to. As her mind whirled, Juliet presented her with her cup of coffee. Her concentration suddenly broken, Papandreou looked up and for a few moments stared back at the pretty auburn-haired woman across the bar before smiling and thanking her. Papandreou then sent a text message to Phoenix to let him know where she was. As she sat sipping her coffee and scrolling through her social media messages, she heard the sound of laughter. Turning her head, she saw a group of six women enter the bar and walk towards her. Three were close friends of hers. Squealing with delight, they broke away from their company and rushed over to greet her. The other women approached the bar more deliberately. Introductions followed. The group, dressed up to the nines, were on their way out for a meal to celebrate an engagement.

The group congregated around the bar, orders were placed, and the drinks began to flow. Papandreou chatted animatedly with her friends as over the next few minutes, other women arrived and joined the throng. As one of the girls began discussing her latest beau, Papandreou casually looked around at the chattering assemblage. Her eye was caught by one of the younger women who had arrived with the first group. She was tall, possibly five feet nine or ten, slender with short flaxen hair. Her fingers and wrists were festooned with jewellery. Her low-cut black dress barely covered her backside and left precious little to the imagination. Around her neck was a thin silver or white gold necklace, suspended beneath it a charm which nestled deep within her overflowing cleavage.

Papandreou leant over to one of her friends and whispered a question into her ear.

'That's Jessica Ashley, she's the only person I know who can have her head in the clouds and her fanny in the gutter at the same time.'

'Really?' said Papandreou.

'Don't let the jewellery fool you, Penny, she's no rough diamond, she's just rough. Jess believes the way to get ahead is to give one.'

Papandreou roared with laughter at the suggestion of such impropriety. Then, whilst trying to control the unexpected outburst noticed that she had caught the eye of Ashley, who began walking towards them.

'Oh no, she's coming over,' said Papandreou.

Jessica Ashley strode over, bold and confident, said hello to Sarah, Papandreou's friend and then introduced herself to Papandreou. As Ashley leant forward to shake hands, the charm at the base of her necklace broke free from its concealed anchorage and dangled freely in front of her chest like a pendulum. At the end of the long silver cable chain was a single letter, it was the letter J with a diamond stud at the top. Papandreou shook the limp hand; it was the epitome of shaking hands with a wet fish.

'I like your charm, Jessica, it suits you, all you need now are some matching earrings,' said Papandreou pointedly. The trap was set, and with Ashley's brains situated between her navel and the hem of her dress, she fully expected her to walk into it with both feet. It didn't take long.

'Thanks, I used to, but I lost one of them recently. I've been searching for it everywhere,' said Ashley.

'Oh dear,' said Papandreou with just a suspicion of sarcasm. 'Perhaps you lost it in bed?'

Ashley was either too clever or too stupid to pick up on Papandreou's comment, other than to admit that it was entirely possible, as she does like to "move around a lot in bed". The thought of which did nothing to alleviate the growing contempt she felt for this brash young socialite who clearly considered all men fair game in her quest for self-advancement.

Papandreou sat on her perch and watched Ashley as she held court, lording it over friends that the Greek had known for many years. Ozy had many failings, and he was certainly a ladies' man, but the more she thought about it, the more impossible it seemed that he could have stooped so low as to have shared a bed with this trollop, yet the proof was in her handbag. Papandreou looked down at the remains of her coffee. She was frustrated and she was angry. It was bad enough that she felt trapped and controlled by a man she thought she loved, but now she might be sharing him with this woman.

She pushed her coffee to one side; she didn't care that she was still feeling the effects of the Taittinger; she wanted something stronger. Papandreou called over to Juliet, who was busy opening a fresh bottle of Prosecco for one of her customers. A few moments later, she turned and walked over to where Papandreou was sitting.

'What can I get you?'

'Metaxa, please, Jules, a large one,' Papandreou knew she would probably suffer for it later, but right now she didn't care. She watched as the bartender produced the blue-topped bottle of 5-star Greek Brandy from under the counter; it was a taste of home. Perhaps it would calm her down and settle the butterflies nestling in her stomach. She observed the amber spirit with its warming golden hue for a moment before taking the glass in her hand and almost draining it at the first attempt. As the smooth, mellow spirit worked its way down her body, she puffed out her cheeks and then raised the glass once more, finishing off the remaining few drops.

Suddenly, she felt a hand on her shoulder; it was Phoenix. She jumped off the stool, put her arms around his neck and, stretching up, kissed him passionately. As they embraced, she could just see far enough over Phoenix's shoulder to discern Jessica Ashley observing them. She maintained eye contact with Ashley throughout the warm embrace until the younger woman finally turned away. Satisfied that her point had been made, Papandreou removed her arms from her lover's neck.

Declining the offer of a drink, Phoenix took her hand and the pair walked out of the bar. As they approached his scarlet Ferrari 296 in the car park, she paused as she opened the door, hesitating at the thought that that brazen hussy had been in there before her. As she took her seat, she looked across at Phoenix. Was this the final act of betrayal? Was the lifestyle she craved really worth the price she was paying? The twin-turbo V6 burst into life as Phoenix revved the engine, pulled away and headed for home.

Chapter 14

Travers peered out of the small port side window of the Airbus A319 as it crossed the Thames for the last time, descending towards London Heathrow. The early morning flight with British Airways had given him little chance for breakfast, and he was famished. The call from Le Sueur late last night was urgent. The Prime Minister was fretting and demanded answers from his beleaguered Home Secretary, the Home Secretary was flexing her muscles and pressuring the Director General, who in turn was badgering the Wing Commander, and at the bottom of the food chain was Travers, whom everyone now expected to come through and save the world — or, more particularly, the Prime Minister's job. Travers shifted his position in his seat slightly. It was only an hour's flight, but he felt cramped. On his right was a portly middle-aged gentleman who had been almost shoe-horned into his seat. Heaven help him if he had to get out in a hurry.

Travers looked again out of the small window; the sunny weather of Jersey had been replaced by a gloomy London squall. The Captain had tried to cheer everyone up by announcing that it was expected to clear by late morning, though judging by the look on many people's faces, they remained unconvinced. Travers sat back in his seat as he prepared for landing. The corpulent man next to him hurriedly tried to stuff the newspaper he had been reading into the webbing attached to the back of the seat in front of him but only succeeded in screwing it up like used fish and chip paper. Then, with a loud slam of the tray against the seat and a forceful lean back, he jolted the entire row. Travers didn't particularly enjoy flying, and he was always happy to get his feet back on terra firma. As such, he looked forward to the landing. He glanced at his fellow traveller, whose face exuded a reddish glow with a slight sheen as perspiration began to ooze from its pores. His hands now gripping both armrests with a vigour usually reserved for the dentist's chair.

The plane lined up for final approach on Heathrow's Southern runway 27L. Travers sat back and watched the undercarriage through the rain-covered window. He was feeling more relaxed now that the flight was almost over. A slightly jarring bump and the low rumble of rubber on asphalt confirmed what Travers' eyes told him: they had arrived. His body lurched forward before being restrained by his seat belt as the engine thrust was put into reverse and the plane rapidly decelerated under braking. The plane then taxied to its disembarkation point close to the Terminal 5 building before coming to a full stop.

Despite the usual request to remain in their seats until the engines stopped, as soon as the plane had come to a standstill, there was a general free-for-all as passengers unbuckled themselves, rose to their feet and tried to retrieve their bags and coats from the overhead lockers. Travers glanced momentarily to his right. The man in the seat next to him was still struggling to find the release catch to his seat belt. With some sympathy for the man's obvious frustration, Travers leant across and freed his travelling companion from his temporary confinement, then sat back in his seat and waited.

With only hand luggage, Travers swiftly passed through the arrivals and customs area. As he did so, a uniformed security officer approached him, identified herself and requested that he accompany her. The officer pushed open the office door and walked in. Travers followed her, where he was greeted by a familiar face.

'Alicia, this is a pleasant surprise. What are you doing here?'

'Good morning, Greg, Steph Le Sueur told me that you were coming back this morning, I didn't have anything on that couldn't wait an hour, so I said I'd pick you up,' said Downes. 'I see you are travelling light, come on, the car's outside.'

The traffic on the M4 and the Great West Road into Hammersmith was congested, much to Downes' frustration; she liked nothing better than to open the throttle on an open road and feel the wind in her hair, but crawling along behind a convoy of articulated lorries was no fun at all.

'How was your trip?' enquired Downes.

'It was ok apart from having to share my seat with King Kong, and I could do with a bite to eat, I'm famished.'

'Well, you'll need a hearty breakfast, you have a meeting with the Home Secretary and the DG this morning, they're getting nervous. The Prime Minister is running out of patience, and John Deery is running out of leads. The Director is sharpening her axe, and I think she might have to give the Home Secretary someone's head. I get the impression that Le Sueur is feeling the squeeze, and she's decided to pop your head above the parapet next to hers. That's why she's dragged you out of Jersey this morning. She needs someone who can convince the PM that they can crack this, alternatively they will become a sacrificial scapegoat. The Prime Minister and the Government have a biological sword of Damocles hanging over their heads. The next few days are going to be critical.'

With a large bacon sandwich and a mug of hot tea inside him, Travers felt better as he gathered his thoughts once more in the confines of his small room. Beside him, Alicia Downes, was always a good sounding board for him to bounce his theories and ideas off. He rang DI Beckett in Jersey in case there were any last-minute developments.

Travers was uncomfortable about leaving Jersey and had asked Beckett to keep an eye out for Penelope Papandreou. He had only met her once, but could tell that behind the confident and flirtatious exterior, she was vulnerable, and he was sure that she knew more about Phoenix and his business than she had let on. Travers jotted down bullet points on an A4 pad when Downes' mobile phone rang. It was Heidi Buchan. The two women enjoyed an animated conversation for several minutes, interrupted by sporadic bouts of laughter. Travers tried to focus on his notes despite the sometimes raucous hilarity coming from Alicia.

Once Downes had finished her call, Travers put down his pen and stared at her pointedly, questioning. She knew that expression. She maintained eye contact, tilted her head slightly and cocked an eyebrow as she teased him mercilessly.

'We shared a bottle of Rioja the other night and had a girlie chat,' said Downes.

'Really? I didn't know you knew each other.'

'She is still helping us out and looking after Christina Koehler. We'd had a really frustrating day, and she thought it would be nice. We shared tapas and a bottle, and listened to music. Did you know she plays the piano, cello, and saxophone? Oh, and naturally, we talked a lot about men. She wanted to know all about you, I think she fancies you, Greg,' said Downes, with an element of surprise in the tone of her voice.

'Very funny, you needn't sound so surprised,' replied Travers.

Downes smiled and laughed at Travers' embarrassment. He looked at his watch, it was almost time to go. It wouldn't do to keep the top brass waiting, especially if they were looking for someone to carry the can for an impending disaster.

The meeting went much as he had expected, present in the briefing room were the aforementioned Home Secretary and the Director General of MI5, together with Wing Commander Le Sueur. Representing the Police was the Assistant Commissioner of the MET, alongside Detective Chief Inspector John Deery. There was a general restating of the known facts before Deery was called to provide a Police update, of which there was precious little. Travers had some sympathy for his friend as he tried to put a positive spin on a wholly negative situation. Travers hadn't previously met the current Home Secretary, but Deborah Roberts was a formidable operator, widely respected, and despite a disarmingly decorous outward appearance, was not a woman to be trifled with. The Civil Service had a nickname for her, the "Rat Catcher".

He watched as the minister lambasted the detective for his apparent lack of progress, like a dog with a bone, she latched onto any perceived moment of indecision and wouldn't relent until she felt she had made her point. After several minutes of ministerial haranguing, Travers had had enough and, as respectfully as he could, interrupted the Home Secretary's political posturing. Travers noted the disapproving look that the Director General gave to Le Sueur as he continued speaking over the minister, and deflecting the withering criticism that had been directed towards his friend.

The increasingly irritated minister, unaccustomed to being backed up by anyone, let alone a civil servant, looked across reproachfully at the Director before sitting back into her chair as Travers continued. Travers' air of respectful but well-informed and articulate oratory mollified the angry and frustrated Home Secretary at least to some degree. However, it would be of little comfort to the already agitated Prime Minister that Travers had confirmed that one of the world's most dangerous terrorists was almost certainly behind the threats. The Home Secretary made copious notes as Travers explored several possible hypotheses, yet the problem remained the same, and time was against them. The minister's adviser leant across and reminded her of another imminent meeting. The Home Secretary quickly looked down at her watch before gathering up her papers and placing them in her briefcase. Thanking the attendees for their time, Roberts stood up and shook hands with the MI5 Director, then, with her adviser trailing in her slipstream, rushed out of the door.

Deery leant back and locked his hands behind his head. It had been a bruising encounter. He looked across at Travers, who smiled.

'Don't mention it,' said Travers, who could read the relief etched on his face.

Before Deery could reply, the Director turned towards Travers and interrupted them.

'Alright, Travers, now that political windbag has gone, where do we stand?'

'Well, ma'am, I believe the man harbouring Abadi is a shady local Jersey businessman called Oswaldo Phoenix. The man DCI Deery is chasing, Andreas Drakos, also works for him. I've managed to ingratiate myself with his mistress. I think we can use her. She's looking for a way out, and it would be really helpful if I could offer her a deal in return for information she has on Phoenix's black market activities,' said Travers.

Although Le Sueur had already poured cold water on the idea, given the urgency of the situation so vigorously expressed by the Home Secretary, he hoped the Director would be more amenable to the suggestion. She looked across at the Wing Commander and thought for a few moments.

'Ok, Travers, offer her whatever it takes to get her to talk. Afterwards, we'll see what we can do.'

'I take it that means afterwards, we'll drop her faster than a hot "jersey" potato!' said Travers cynically.

It was the answer that Travers had expected. If he was to help Papandreou in any meaningful way, he was going to have to do it himself. The meeting broke up, leaving just Travers, Le Sueur, and John Deery.

'Well, Travers, what's your next move? I think you had better get back to Jersey and start pumping Phoenix's mistress for information. If we don't start making something happen, we will either be poisoned in the next few days or seeking alternative employment,' said Le Sueur.

'Yes, ma'am. I do have a few thoughts. Miss Papandreou said she was sure that Drakos was staying somewhere in the Wimbledon area. Phoenix is a debenture holder at the club, so he probably has a house near there that he rents out. If we could find the house, we might find Drakos.'

'Alright. Inspector, I suggest you concentrate your search around the SW19 area to start with,' said Le Sueur. 'You've got his photo, haven't you?'

'Yes, Wing Commander, it's a copy of his passport photo sent by the States of Jersey Police. We also have the description provided by Miss Downes.'

'I don't want to be a wet blanket, Chief Inspector, but if this is our man, I expect the photo will be almost useless. Miss Papandreou says Phoenix has been smuggling people past Border Force, often in plain sight, for years. Abadi is on all the watch lists but he has been popping backwards and forwards between the Channel Islands and the mainland without a care in the world,' said Travers.

Travers walked out of Thames House with Inspector Deery, the two men wandered across Millbank as far as the river. There was a cool breeze in the air but at least the rain had stopped now. Travers leant over the wall, watching the mass of grey fast-flowing water rushing east towards Tilbury and the estuary beyond as the tide ebbed. Deery stood with his back to the water.

'Thank you for what you said earlier, Greg, the Home Sec's on thin ice and she's looking for someone to blame. It's true, though, we're not getting anywhere fast. We are charging the man we caught at the tube, but he's small fry.'

'We need to draw them out of their hideaway,' said Travers. 'You know that we still have a mole in MI5, the Director has been going ballistic, and they're vetting everyone, every level. Right down to the cleaners.'

There was a pause in the conversation. Then Travers suddenly gripped Deery's arm, who looked round at his friend.

'I've just had an idea, John. It's a bit chancy, but I think it can work as long as Alicia agrees to it. Come with me; we need to have another talk with the Wing Commander.'

Travers pulled out his mobile phone and called Downes. They spoke for several minutes, then he and Deery returned to Thames House and headed upstairs to the Wing Commander's office. Travers knocked on the door, and the pair walked in. Le Sueur was on the telephone. She looked up, sensing it was important and quickly told the caller that she would call her back.

'Well, gentlemen, what is it?'

'Ma'am, I would like you to assign Alicia Downes another safe house…and route it through the usual channels, make sure it goes through HR.'

'Why?'

'Somewhere in this building, there is a leak, both Alicia's and my safe house security was compromised, Alicia was attacked, and Ron Jackson was murdered. Someone disclosed that information, and the man we are after tried to kill her. The London investigation has stalled, ma'am. We need to jump-start it.'

'And you are prepared to risk Miss Downes' life?' said an incredulous Le Sueur.

'No ma'am, not at all. I have spoken with Alicia; there is a contract out on her. Until this is settled, she will always be at risk. She wants to do this. Detective Deery will have the property staked out. I believe the traitor will pass on the information, and someone will make another attempt to kill Alicia.'

Le Sueur shook her head; the idea frankly appalled her. The potential risk was unpardonable. Her career in the RAF was based on discipline, precision planning, and the mitigation of unnecessary risk.

'Have you considered the consequences if something goes wrong with this scheme?'

'I'm sorry, ma'am, but if we don't catch this man and his confederates, a lot more people are going to die soon. They have targeted Alicia once and failed. We have to tempt them out into the open, and doing this will give them another opportunity, but this time we'll be waiting for them.'

'Detective Chief Inspector, what's your opinion?' asked a highly sceptical Le Sueur.

'Wing Commander, I agree there is a risk, but in the light of what the Home Secretary said this morning, I don't think we have much option,' said Deery.

Le Sueur retrieved a folder from her desk drawer and began thumbing through the pages until she reached the list of London safe houses.

She ran her finger down the list of properties, ranging from small apartments in the city centre to detached homes in the leafy suburbs.

'Do you have an area in mind, Travers?' asked Le Sueur.

'Ideally, South West, but the area is really secondary, we need a house that is easily accessible with plenty of natural cover, and if you can arrange some broken street lighting, that would be perfect. Ma'am, think of it as a giant lobster pot. Nothing must deter them. We must make it as easy to get into as possible. Once they are in, we shut the trap,' said Travers assertively.

'And what of Miss Downes? She was lucky last time, are you sure you have thought this through Travers?'

'She won't be alone, ma'am, and we'll have the place under constant surveillance with night vision cameras,' Travers said with an air of confidence that belied his reservations, but he could see no other way.

'Alright, Travers, you and the Chief Inspector draw up your plans, let me know which property you want to use.

I will need to clear this with the Director, and I want to talk to Downes too.'

With that, the two men rose from their seats and left Le Sueur's office. Travers knew that the selection of the right house was crucial. For the sting to work, everyone had to believe that she was there and alone, but especially the traitor in Thames House.

Chapter 15

Penelope Papandreou's naked body lay motionless on the wooden table. Her eyes open, her body covered only by a white towel across her midsection. Her right arm pressed tight against her naked torso whilst the other, having slipped off the table, dangled with the first and second fingers pointing towards the floor. A few moments later, a young blonde-haired health professional emerged wearing a white uniform. Walking around the table, she noticed the stray arm hanging limply and took it by the wrist, held it for a moment, then replaced it onto the bench next to Papandreou's body.

The room was warm, with the unmistakable aroma of essential oils and incense, with subdued lighting adding to the relaxing ambience. The masseuse placed fresh warm towels over Papandreou's legs and then continued to work on her arms and shoulders, working her fingers deeply into the soft tissue. Then, turning Papandreou over, she leaned over her client, running her hands down the full length of her back, until reaching the base of the spine where her fingers briefly slid under the still warm towel covering her bottom. Papandreou moaned as the unceasing waves of relaxation washed over her. The bliss was unremitting. It was a fortnightly two-hour ocean massage at the Atlantic Hotel Spa that she regularly looked forward to.

Today was different. She was fraught, she was tense, she hadn't slept well, and she couldn't get the thought of that social-climbing bitch, Jessica Ashley, shagging with Ozy behind her back out of her mind. To compound her misery, she had had a row with him this morning. She needed a break, a chance to clear her head and a chance to think. When she told Ozy that she was going to visit a girlfriend in London, he had flown into a rage and made it abundantly clear that she wasn't to go. Despite his controlling nature, he had never been so insistent before. She felt stressed. However, after a two-hour full body massage with Orange, cloves, ginger, and Fucus Serratus seaweed, she felt better. At least for the moment, she was calm, relaxed and would sleep well later. As the session drew to a close, the masseuse asked Papandreou to roll over, where she finished with a head massage. The masseuse then covered Papandreou with more warm towels and let her rest for a while.

Twenty minutes later, Papandreou had dressed again in her tight-fitting black wrap leather dress and made her way out of the Spa area. As she entered the bar, she was surprised to see Phoenix sitting there, animatedly talking to the bartender.

'Hello, darling,' said Phoenix. 'I'm sorry about this morning, I knew you were having a session today, so I thought I would surprise you afterwards and take you to lunch.'

'Hello, Ozy. Lunch? Yes, that would be nice.' Papandreou wondered just how quickly the efficacious effects of her morning massage would now drain away, once his fragile temperament began to fray.

Phoenix waved at the bartender, who smiled warmly as she approached him.

'Two Proseccos, please, Juliet.'

As Juliet acknowledged the order, Papandreou waved and called out that she wanted a Cranberry Spritz instead.

'A Cranberry Spritz? I am buying you lunch, Penelope, I want you to have a proper drink,' insisted Phoenix, whose brittle temper was already beginning to show signs of breaking down.

'Ozy, I've just spent two hours and £165 detoxing, I don't want to waste it.'

Phoenix pursed his lips in irritation as she continued to ignore his wishes. He turned to the bartender and waved in acknowledgement of the change in order.

'Yes, Mr Phoenix,' replied the bartender as she turned away and reached across for an already open bottle and removed the stopper. She carefully poured the sparkling wine into a tall flute glass, then returned the stopper, placing the bottle to one side. After she had prepared the requested mocktail, Phoenix picked up the two glasses and took them over to a nearby table.

'I'm sorry about this morning, Penelope, but I don't want you going to London for a few weeks, I want you to stay on the Island.'

'Why? Does it have anything to do with that man you keep talking to, Abadi?'

'It doesn't concern you. Just do what I say, woman!' said Phoenix brusquely.

'Don't call me "woman", I have a name, or have you forgotten it?' Papandreou could feel her anxiety rising again as the tension increased. Phoenix was not a man to cross, but he was becoming more and more difficult. Notwithstanding her discovery of the earring, over the last few months, he had become increasingly detached. The arguments had become more frequent as his ability or desire to control his temper diminished. As she raised her glass for another sip of her non-alcoholic cocktail, she looked across the table at him. She could see the anger in his eyes as they narrowed. She was not going to provoke another outburst by accusing him of cheating on her. Not yet anyway.

It was an uncomfortable and short-lived get-together and not one that Papandreou was enjoying. She sat at the table for several minutes after Phoenix had abruptly left following another heated exchange of words. Her hands still gripped the arms of her chair to stop her fingers shaking. Her face flushed with the embarrassment of the whole episode, she dabbed her watering eyes with a handkerchief. Several curious onlookers, initially disturbed by the incident, now turned away, ignoring her sobs, leaving her to her own devices. The bartender walked over, put a consoling arm around Papandreou and offered a few words of comfort. Which she gratefully received.

'Thank you, Jules, I am sorry about the scene. I don't understand what's got into him these days. I can't stand it. I don't know what to do anymore. A fresh tear formed and began to trickle down her left cheek before she quickly rubbed it away with her forefinger's knuckle.

'Why don't you just leave him, Penny? You have many friends.'

'If only it were that easy. He is not someone that you walk away from. I know too much, too many of his dirty secrets.'

Papandreou smiled nervously as she reached across and grasped the cocktail glass containing what remained of her Cranberry cocktail. With one swallow, it was gone. She ran her fingers through her waves of shoulder-length pitch-black hair, stood up, straightened her dress and walked across to the bar where she exchanged a few words with Juliet, who furnished her with a small glass of Metaxa. Picking up the glass, she swirled the shot of amber liquid round and round before finally raising it to her lips and taking a single swallow, then returned it to the bar. After serving another customer, Juliet came to the end of the bar where Papandreou was sitting.

'How are you feeling now, Penny?'

'Ok, thanks, Jules.'

'That nice guy you met here the other day, why don't you speak to him? You said he wanted to help.'

Papandreou looked up at the bartender, as though a penny had dropped. She had been so self-absorbed with her anger over Phoenix's ranting that she had completely forgotten.

Rummaging through her handbag, she eventually found the card that Travers had given to her. She held it in her hand and gazed at the simple card. It was plain and unfussy with just his name and two phone numbers printed on it. Taking another sip of brandy, she looked across at Juliet as much for approval or reassurance.

The bartender walked across until she stood in front of the hesitant Papandreou. The two women looked at one another. Then, with the decision finally made, she took her mobile phone out of her bag and began dialling the mobile number on the card. The phone rang for thirty seconds before dropping to voicemail with a standard pre-recorded message. Papandreou left a very short message requesting Travers call her, but leaving no further information. Putting her phone down on the bar, she looked at Juliet. She was disappointed that she had not been able to speak to him.

'Why don't you try the other number then?' said Juliet, 'What do you have to lose?'

Papandreou picked up her phone again, looked at the card and began dialling the landline number. Almost immediately, someone picked up the call.

'Security Service MI5, how can I help you?'

Papandreou hung up immediately, shocked. Stunned, she stared at the bartender.

'Well? Who is it? What's wrong?'

'It's MI5!'

'You mean the man you were entertaining works for…'

Juliet didn't have time to finish her sentence. Papandreou knew what a precarious position she was now in. Her relationship with Oswaldo Phoenix was difficult enough as it was. If he were to suspect or find out that she had been talking to someone from the Security Services, her life would be worth very little.

'I'd better be going, thanks for the drink, Jules,' said Papandreou as she nervously fumbled trying to return her phone to her handbag.

Papandreou hurriedly slid off the bar stool and walked out of the bar. As she reached the large foyer, she saw several people coming in, amongst them Jessica Ashley, her arms draped around a man old enough to be her father, not that it seemed to bother her. She was not in the mood to tangle with her and did her best to ignore her.

To her dismay, Ashley spotted her. Uncoupling herself from her ageing escort, she walked across to talk to her with a beaming smile as false as everything else about her.

'Hi, babes, how nice to see you again. How are you? We must have a drink sometime,' gushed Ashley.

With everything that was going on at the moment, the last thing Papandreou wanted was to spend a minute longer with Ashley.

'By the way, Pen, guess what I found in my laundry basket last night? You'll never believe it. My missing earring! I'm so pleased, I thought I had lost it forever.'

Papandreou stood rooted to the spot and watched speechless as the scarlet woman turned away and re-joined her partner. The pair then headed off towards the bar. For what seemed like an eternity, Papandreou, her mind now a mass of jumbled emotions, slowly walked through the foyer as she headed towards the exit and the car park beyond. Ashley's revelation had confounded her assertion that it was her earring that she had found under Phoenix's bed.

Twenty minutes later, Papandreou, driving Phoenix's Lime green Lamborghini Huracan, pulled into his horseshoe drive. His bright red Ferrari was already there. Opening the large, heavy front door, she left the car keys on a silver tray on the hall table. She could hear voices, it was Phoenix. As she continued to listen, she soon realised that he was talking on the phone to Andreas Drakos. She paused, hovering just outside the drawing room but within earshot.

Usually, his business conversations didn't interest her, but circumstances had changed, and so had she. For years now, she had looked the other way and accepted the lifestyle she now enjoyed without the need to trouble her conscience. However, the discovery of the earring meant she was no longer the only game in town. As she stood silently behind the door, her mobile phone suddenly rang. She frantically scrambled to find it in her bag. With Phoenix now alerted to her presence, she walked casually into the room and waved at Phoenix, who was still engaged in conversation.

Papandreou looked at her phone; the number calling was unknown, though it did seem familiar. She felt uncomfortable and peculiarly vulnerable. Whilst Phoenix was still talking, she sensed his suspicious eyes following her every move as she walked through the room. She picked up the call and put the phone to her ear. It was Travers.

'Hello Claire, I was just thinking about you this afternoon,' replied a wary Papandreou.

'Hi, Penelope. Is Phoenix with you?' said Travers, who immediately realised she couldn't talk freely.

'Yes. That's right. Yes, I would love to catch up again as soon as you can fit me into your busy schedule.'

'Have you heard him mention Ali Abadi since we spoke?' asked Travers.

'No. I'm sorry I can't make that day.'

'What about Andreas Drakos?' asked Travers.

'Yes. That sounds ok, I'll need to get back to you though.'

'Listen, Penelope, I am working in London at the moment. Ring me when you can. If things get difficult for you, contact Detective Inspector Beckett, you know him, don't you?'

'Yes, ok, I'll get back to you, bye for now, Claire,' Papandreou ended the call.

Papandreou turned around and found herself face-to-face with her adulterous lover. He scrutinised her, studying every flicker of her increasingly nervous appearance.

'Who was that? Anyone I know?' asked Phoenix.

'No Ozy, just a girl I met down at the Atlantic, we had a few drinks and a chat,'

'You must introduce me sometime; you know how much I like to meet your friends.'

Papandreou resented his constant need for control; everyone she met became the subject of interrogation and suspicion. The more he stared, the guiltier she felt. It was an impossible situation; she could feel her face blush, and her hands felt clammy. The tiny hairs on her arms tingled as the nerves grew. She had to get out before things got out of hand and her composure failed her completely.

Phoenix turned away and walked across the floor to an ornate drinks cabinet, where he opened the door to a concealed fridge and removed a partially consumed bottle of white wine. He held up an empty glass towards her, but she declined to join him, turned and left the room. Phoenix topped up his glass and then returned the bottle.

Sitting on her luxurious super king-sized bed, Papandreou looked at the phone sitting on the bedside cabinet. She had been thinking about it all day, and now her mind was made up. Phoenix would come to regret his betrayal of her loyalty. She determined to give Greg Travers a call. She already knew enough to put Phoenix behind bars. The partial conversation that she had overheard when she came in today had sealed the deal. Phoenix was up to his neck in murder, harbouring international terrorists, and if what she had heard was true, complicit in a plot to bring down the UK Government.

Without warning, her door suddenly burst open. Phoenix strode in. His demeanour was angry. The tone of his voice was harsh. He marched towards her, grabbing her roughly by the wrists.

'Who was the man you were with in the Atlantic suite the other day?' His voice was accusatory and threatening.

'Just a friend I met in the bar, it was really busy; we wanted some privacy, that's all,'

'Who was it, Penelope, I want to know?'

Papandreou's reluctance to answer maddened Phoenix, whose grip on her arm tightened. A moment later, he crudely pulled her to her feet. She now stood in front of him. She looked up at his face as it towered over her, and there was a rage in his eyes that she had not seen before.

'Who was it, tell me?' insisted Phoenix.

'Why? It was just a friend, what's it got to do with you?'

The sentence had scarcely left her lips when she felt the full force of his undiluted wrath as his right hand slapped across her face, sending her tumbling backwards onto the bed. Still holding her by her right wrist, Phoenix dragged her back to her feet before slapping her again with tremendous force. Still, Papandreou refused to answer him. How dare he treat her this way? She could feel her own anger mounting with every passing moment.

Another booming blow struck her face; this time, it was a closed fist. Now she could taste blood on her lips. With the back of her left hand, she wiped away the trickle of blood from her mouth. For an instant, she looked at the blood, mortified. She had taken enough from this man. Now shaking with rage of her own, she spat a crimson globule of saliva into his face.

'Puttana! That man works for the British Security Services. Are you fucking a British spy now? Don't deny it. What did you tell him? I know you have called him.' He let go of her wrist and pushed her back onto the bed. Then leant forward, grabbed the front of her blouse with his hand, and pulled her up towards him.

'You will be sorry you met this man,' said Phoenix as he reached across to Papandreou's bedside cabinet and snatched her mobile phone away. 'You will not talk to him again, Penelope. You know what happens to people who betray me.' With that, he walked across to the window, locked it and put the key in his pocket before leaving the room.

As she lay on the bed, dabbing her split lip with a tissue and sobbing, she heard the key to her door turn. Jumping off the bed, she ran to the door and turned the handle. The door wouldn't open; she was trapped. She returned to her bed and thought about what he had said. She had never seen him so angry. He had always been possessive and jealous of her friends and admirers; they had had arguments before, sometimes heated, but he had never struck her. How had he found out about Travers? She cast her mind back and forth as she searched her memory for the answers. Sitting on the bed, looking out of the window, the fog of confusion slowly began to clear. Only one person knew she had called Travers and that he worked for MI5: Juliet, the bartender at the Atlantic. It did not take Papandreou long to put two and two together and realise that it must have been her friend Juliet's earring that had been left in the suite, and it was she who told Phoenix about Travers.

Chapter 16

Travers put the phone down; he was worried. He had tried calling Phoenix's mistress, Penelope Papandreou, several times over the previous twenty-four hours. For some reason, she wasn't picking up his calls. He had even sent a text using her own "code name" for him, Claire. As a last resort, he had called DI Beckett of the States of Jersey Police. Beckett had gone round to the Phoenix residence on a spurious pretext and asked to speak to her, only to be told that she was away. Beckett had put a watch on the airport and the ferry terminal just in case, but officially, there wasn't much he could do. She wasn't a missing person, and she wasn't a suspect. This morning, Beckett had advised that he had still been unable to contact her. Travers couldn't help but feel a pang of guilt. Even though he had thought it best not to tell her who he worked for or why he was there, he had persuaded her to trust him and to open up about her life with Phoenix.

Travers sat back in his chair and picked up his mug of hot tea. The first good slurp was always the best. It was going to be a busy day and an even busier night. It had been a struggle to convince Steph Le Sueur to agree to his plan. Fortunately, when she met Downes to discuss the proposals and her concerns, Alicia was able to assuage her anxiety. If only, because as long as Hades was at large and a threat, her life was in constant peril. With the proposal finally signed off, a suitable safe house close to St Katharine Dock was selected. The end-of-terrace property had a dense collection of trees bordering it, which would provide inviting cover for an intruder. Deery would have a man stationed in one of the trees, whilst others would be watching from the front and rear, all equipped with night vision and thermal imaging cameras. The Wing Commander had insisted on a police officer occupying the house before her request went through channels. At least then, no one in Thames House, including the traitor, would know that there was someone other than Downes there.

As Travers studied a satellite image of the area surrounding the safe house, the mobile phone on his desk rang; it was Deery.

'Hello John, how are things? I am just looking at the safe house plans. Is your man inside yet?'

'Yes, Greg, he arrived first thing this morning with enough rations to last a month. My stakeout team are getting in position now.'

'Great, I spoke to the boss earlier, she's going to advise HR as soon as I confirm that you are ready.'

'How long a stakeout are you planning for, Greg?'

'Well, she's telling HR that it's only a short interim usage as Alicia is going overseas in a few days. We want to give Hades as narrow a window as believably possible,' said Travers.

'Your girl has more balls than most of my men put together. She's basically being staked out like a bloody sacrificial goat,' said Deery with his usual bluntness.

'It's her choice, too, John, but of course, it all hangs on our in-house traitor picking up the details and getting the word out to Hades.'

Travers checked his emails shortly after 2 pm, and Le Sueur had been as good as her word. The confirming email had been sent to HR, and she had blind copied him in. With the admin done, there was nothing else they could do but follow through with the execution of the plan. The trap was now set.

With a couple of suitcases beside her, Alicia Downes stood patiently as she waited for her escort to arrive. As she wandered about by the entrance of Thames House, Downes looked at her watch. He was late. Then she heard a flurry of footsteps behind her. Turning around, she saw Travers running down the stairs towards the foyer, his coat over his arm.

'Sorry, Alicia, I got held up. One of John's men has gone down sick, he's just drafting a new man in. It's all sorted now.'

Travers looked down at the two large Samsonite suitcases and smiled at Downes.

'Alicia, you do know you are only there for a few days?' joked Travers.

'God! Only a man would say something that stupid.'

'Sorry, all the women I've known always take at least twice as much as they could possibly use.'

Travers bent over to pick up the two large bags. He lifted them both with unexpected ease; he turned to Downes.

'Yes, Greg, they are both empty. I had a call from Steph Le Sueur this morning. I dropped a few things off earlier.

It took a little over thirty minutes to cover the almost four miles to the safe house just the other side of St Katharine Dock in Wapping. Downes drove her black Audi while Travers followed her in his grey BMW. As they approached the property, Travers was pleased that he could see no obvious sign of the police surveillance team. It was essential that they remained unobserved. The two cars parked outside the house, Downes opened the boot of her car, and Travers leant over and made great play of lifting the two supposedly heavy suitcases out and placing them on the ground. Downes walked across to the front door, unlocked and opened it, and Travers followed, bringing in the suitcases. Once the door had closed, she called out to her escort. Out of one of the rooms at the rear of the house emerged Sergeant Winston Redman.

'Greg, this is Sergeant Winston Redman, he'll be keeping me company for the next few days.'

Travers walked over and shook Redman's hand. The two men studied each other. There was a tantalisingly elusive recollection of a previous meeting that neither man could immediately place.

'Where are you from, Winston?' asked Travers, who had finally given up the mental struggle to recall their prior acquaintance.

'Originally, Port Royal, Jamaica.'

'Port Royal, of course, that's it! You were with the Jamaican Constabulary; you came over for an exchange visit, I remember now. How are you? Fancy that, and now you are part of John Deery's gang?'

'Yes, sir, it's sure a long way from pounding the Kingston streets. Now I have an English wife and two great boys. I spend my evenings teaching them cricket. Sadly, I had to cut back on the rum parties, the missus disapproved.'

'Well, never mind Winston, when this is over, we'll share a jug of Jamaica's finest for old time's sake; with your wife's permission, of course.'

Downes, who had been sitting patiently by the kitchen table, finally had to remind the two men that they had a job to do first.

Travers walked back towards the front door. He turned and gave Downes a reassuring smile as he hugged her.

'Don't worry, Alicia, John's got the cavalry just around the corner, and if Drakos dares to show his face, Winston is more than capable of rearranging it for him,' said Travers, winking at the Jamaican behind her.

Redman smiled at the outlandish suggestion, although in truth, he had had his fair share of skirmishes during his former career and was quite adept at looking after himself. He stepped back out of view as Travers opened the door, said goodbye to Downes and got into his car. For a few seconds, he paused and looked back at the house through the windscreen and wondered what the night would bring. Downes stood briefly in the doorway and watched him disappear from sight, then she turned away and closed the door.

As dusk gave way to a moonless night, the house was enveloped in a shroud of darkness, illuminated only by a single light in the first-floor bedroom and later by a smaller bedside lamp. Travers sat in the control vehicle parked a short distance away. Beside him, Detective Chief Inspector Deery observed the surveillance team's night vision coverage of the house and surrounding area on a bank of monitors. The atmosphere was edgy and tense, the silence broken only by the intermittent crackle of police radios.

Travers had spoken to Downes a few minutes earlier, and everything was quiet. Winston was downstairs, and now in complete darkness. She had retired upstairs, the bedroom light now on, despite her extensive experience, the thought of being the bait in the trap was still a source of anxiety. She paced about the room like a caged cat. Picking up a newspaper supplement, Downes sat on the bed hoping to divert her racing imagination. After casually turning a few pages, she gave up and tossed the magazine aside.

Leaving the bedroom, she walked along to the landing, then down the darkened stairs to where Sergeant Redman was stationed.

'Winston? Where are you?' said Downes as she peered into the darkness.

'Over here, Alicia,' said Redman as he tapped the table in the lounge. 'You ok?'

'It's just a few nerves. I'd rather be out there doing something. Did they tell you that the man we are waiting for broke into a previous safe house and tried to kill me not long ago?'

'No shit, really? What happened?'

'He failed,' said Downes, who thought it better not to mention the fate of Ron Jackson that night.

Redman laughed 'This time we'll turn the tables on him, we'll give him a big surprise party.'

They had only met today, but Downes liked him; he was amiable with a ready wit. It helped that she had been to Jamaica many times, mostly on holiday, but recently whilst she was on an assignment working for MI6. She had always enjoyed her time there. The bond between the two was cemented when she mentioned watching the West Indies playing England at Sabina Park. From that moment on, it was as much as she could do to stop him talking cricket.

Deery regularly checked in with his teams. So far, there has been no unusual activity. The problem with stakeouts the world over is that one never knows what is going to happen. Sometimes absolutely nothing happens; everyone sits, waits, watches, and gets very bored and then after several days or weeks of inactivity, they pack up and go home. Drakos may strike tonight, tomorrow, or not at all. They just have to be ready. Deery poured a cup of hot chocolate from his thermos flask, took a sip, and gave out a sigh of satisfaction. He offered a cup to Travers, who readily accepted it as much to relieve the stress as anything else. Both men continued to stare at the monitors in front of them.

With their eyes fixed on the green images produced by the night vision cameras, it was time for Deery to check in with the three surveillance teams watching the house.

'Team one, come in, anything to report?'

'Team one here, nothing to report,' came the immediate response.

'Team two, come in, anything to report?'

'Team two here, boss, nothing to report, it's all quiet here.'

'Team three, come in, anything to report?'

'Team three here, nothing to report apart from my sore arse,'

'Williams, you just keep focused on what you've got to do. If anyone gets past you tonight, you'll have more than a few splinters in your arse to worry about, you'll have my boot in there too.'

'Yes, guvnor.'

Deery could see the look of amusement on Travers' face as he berated his subordinate.

'He's spending the night halfway up a tree. He's a good lad, I just have to remind him once in a while that I'm the only one allowed to be a cheeky bastard.'

At 1 am, Downes checked in, she was about to turn off the remaining house light. Travers informed her that the surveillance units had recently reported in, and everything was clear. However, they both knew that if Drakos was also watching the house, the last light going out might prompt him to move. The images and data received by the control van were also being relayed to Wing Commander Le Sueur in Thames House, where she was monitoring developments on her laptop. She wasn't going to risk compromising the operation by following the night's events in the Thames House situation room. Travers knew that Le Sueur had misgivings about the operation, but he was grateful for the fact that, having signed it off, she was now fully committed and supportive and would be until its conclusion.

After a few minutes stretching his legs, Deery returned to the Control Van. It was a battle of attrition; his shoulders and back were already starting to ache. The temperature had dropped, and the wind had picked up a little. As he looked at the green-tinted images on his screens, he could see the movement of the leaves as they billowed in the breeze. He checked his watch; it was now 2.15 am. He'd not had an all-night stakeout shift for years, not since he was a junior detective. It was definitely a job for one of these up-and-coming thrusting pups, not a senior Detective Chief Inspector. However, Greg was his friend, and he had promised, and that was all that needed to be said.

Deery picked up his mug of now-cold chocolate and looked down at the unappetising dregs in the bottom. He swirled them around, but it looked just as disgusting. Deery stood up, opened the door and flung them out onto the road. Sitting back down, his eye caught the briefest of movements on one of the screens, possibly a shadow moving, it was only for an instant.

'Team 1, I thought I saw something?'

'Team 1 here, sorry sir, nothing doing here, there are lots of moving shadows, the wind is playing havoc with the images, we saw a couple of foxes on the Thermal Imaging, but that's all.'

'Are you sure? Well, keep your eyes peeled.' said Deery urgently.

'Team 2?'

'Team 2 here, all quiet so far, sir.'

'Team 3 come in …Team 3 respond…Williams get your finger out of your arse and talk to me.'

There was no answer from Williams. Deery sensed something was wrong, very wrong. Williams could be a spiky character, but he was also a darn good copper.

There was no time to waste; Deery's warning was imperative. Downes hurriedly reached into her bag for a small carbon steel folding knife that she always carried and quickly moved towards the bedroom door. As her hand gripped the brass handle and opened it, she heard the sounds of an altercation. Running along the landing and down the stairs, she saw Redman wrestling with an assailant. A small single table lamp only partially illuminated the room. The intruder had his back to Downes, but she knew it was Drakos. The black-clad figure had an arm around Redman's throat, choking him. The Jamaican tried to pull the arm away with all his might, but Drakos was too strong even for him. With one mighty shove, Redman pushed backwards, sending both men tumbling across a table. Several glass ornaments flew across the room, breaking as they hit the wooden floor. The mortal struggle continued with the Greek still holding Redman by the neck like a vice as they rolled around on the floor.

Remembering the rigorous self-defence course she had been sent on before her secondment to MI6, she grabbed Drakos across the throat with one arm and supported the classic textbook strangle with the other hand behind his head and applied all the pressure she could muster. He lashed out with his free hand as he tried to break her hold, but she held on to him like grim death. Eventually, he let go of Redman, who slumped to the floor. Now turning his full attention to his intended target, Drakos rose to his feet with some difficulty, with Downes still clinging on to his head but her feet now well off the ground. He whirled around in a desperate attempt to free himself of her limpet-like embrace. She knew all too well that if he broke free, he would have the advantage. The two combatants then crashed against a large wooden bookcase. Momentarily stunned, Downes' grip loosened for a second. It was all the time her opponent needed. His right elbow jarred viciously into Downes' rib cage while his left hand grabbed her right arm and threw her over his right shoulder. She fell heavily onto the floor.

Drakos stood motionless for a few moments as he looked down at Downes' body lying in a heap on the floor. Now for the coup de grâce. He reached inside his jacket and pulled out a Glock 19. It was time to finish the job and get out. Downes quickly regained consciousness, and as her vision cleared, she could see him ominously screwing a suppressor to the end of the pistol. With a final twist, it was ready. He pulled the Glock's slide back to bring the first of the fifteen 9mm cartridges into the chamber.

As he raised his arm, he was distracted for an instant by the sound of an approaching police siren. As he turned his head slightly towards the direction of the noise, he was knocked off balance by the unexpected sweep of Redman's legs crashing into him. Drakos staggered for a moment before regaining his balance. His response was swift and final, firing twice into Redman's chest. With his last moments of life, the man from Port Royal rolled against the small coffee table, sending the lamp falling to the ground and the room into darkness once more. Drakos spun around to where Downes had been and began firing indiscriminately into the gloom. As he did so, he could now hear voices; they were the voices of police officers, rushing towards the house. There was no time to hunt for his target. He slipped out of the house, hoping to evade the oncoming policemen. Downes watched from a window and peered into the darkness as her assassin disappeared into the night.

Turning the main living room light on, Downes stood in the doorway and looked across at her fallen bodyguard. His white shirt now with an ever-increasing red stain in its centre and a dribble of blood seeping from his mouth. There would be no more evening cricket with his boys. As she cast one last look at Winston Redman, she vowed that if it was the last thing she did, she would make his killer pay for his murder.

Chapter 17

'For Christ's sake, Alicia, don't go after him on your own, John's men will be with you any second,' implored Travers on the radio as the Police's mobile control began the short journey to the safe house.

'I'm sorry, Greg, but too many people are dying. We can't risk this man slipping through our fingers again. Listen, tell John he's heading north-west on Thomas More Street towards the marina. I'll keep you posted.'

Downes maintained a discreet distance as she continued to follow the shadowy figure at a pace under a shield of darkness, fragmented only by the occasional illumination from streetlights that allowed her to track his progress.

The footsteps ahead of her suddenly stopped. Downes froze, pressing herself against the wall that ran alongside the pavement. She was thankful that she remained hidden in the darkness. Ahead, she could clearly see the tall, dark figure of Drakos standing illuminated by a single street lamp. He turned and looked back in her direction. Downes held her breath and tried to make herself as small as possible. She could see in his hand the suppressed Glock 19 that he had tried to kill her with earlier. The Greek began to walk towards her, staring into the darkness, looking for signs of movement. After taking several steps towards her, he stopped again and stared, suspicious and sensing approaching danger. After what seemed like an eternity, he turned away. Reaching the street lamp again, he walked into an alleyway and out of Downes' sight. She let out a deep sigh of relief as she stood up. Her heart was racing. Why hadn't she listened to Greg's advice?

It wasn't long before she, too, reached the street lamp that marked the entrance to the alley leading to the marina. She peered around the corner and into the short alleyway. There was a barrier across the entrance to regulate traffic, but there was no sign of the man she was pursuing. Half way down the alley was a border with tall shrubbery. As Downes approached, she heard sounds of movement in the undergrowth, leaves crunching and twigs snapping. She stopped, rooted to the spot, staring into the gloom. A moment later, a large fox emerged, clearly well-fed, with a great bushy tail. It stood for a moment, inquisitively observing its much relieved onlooker before turning away, and with an air of casual indifference disappeared into the night. Downes took another deep breath, composing herself as she watched the animal wander off and then proceeded through the alley towards the marina beyond.

Entering the south side of the St Katharine Dock Marina, Downes paused. She looked across at the spectral images on the water like so many "Flying Dutchman" gently swaying at anchor. The only thing on her mind now was Drakos, somewhere ahead. There was nothing that she could do now for Redman. Deery had wanted her to wait for support, but every minute's delay was another minute for Redman's murderer to get away. Deery had immediately scrambled a police helicopter with thermal imaging cameras from Lippitts Hill, and his own men had joined the pursuit. The marina lights gave the area a ghostly and unnerving feel in the dead of night, which only added to her sense of unease. The breeze was starting to freshen, causing the stainless steel wire rigging of the yachts to clatter against their masts in a chattering cacophony of percussive noise.

Beyond the sounds of the rigging and the rustle of leaves from the few trees dotted around the basin, Downes heard nothing, no sounds or signs of movement, nothing to suggest that Drakos was still there. There was only the sound of her rapid breathing and the continuous streams of water vapour from her mouth captured by the dock lights as she continued to recover from the chase. She continued walking westward towards the Locks and the Marina Drawbridge. Above her, she could now hear the familiar whirring of a helicopter. She looked into the night sky for the source of the noise until her eyes locked onto the green and red lights approaching from the east. Downes grabbed her radio.

'Helicopter in sight.'

'Alicia, it's Greg. Whereabouts are you now? Over.'

'Mews Street, heading South West; over', replied Downes.

'Alicia, it's John Deery here, my team are converging on the Dock area, and they should be with you in a few minutes. If you spot that bastard, I don't want you tangling with him; just stay on his tail until we close in, understand? Over and out.'

As she watched the helicopter draw closer to the Marina, her focus was abruptly interrupted by the sound of a male voice. The initial outburst was followed by a muffled cry. Downes ran towards the locks, over the basin drawbridge. Standing for a moment at the other side, she waited for a further indication as to the direction of travel. She stared into the darkness, her eyes straining for a glimpse of the person responsible for the cry. Turning to her left, towards the river, she saw what looked like a dark shape lying at the far end of the pathway close to the Timepiece Sundial sculpture. When she arrived at the scene, she discovered it to be a security guard employed by the marina. He had obviously spotted Drakos, confronted him and paid for it with his life. A single gunshot had penetrated the right eye, passed through his skull and exited through the back of the head. It was another example of his ruthless and brutal zest for slaughter. It was a shocking and grim sight. Downes took off her black jacket and placed it over the man's head.

Looking up and to her right, she could see a figure running past the Tower Hotel heading for the bridge. Downes updated the Chief Inspector on her position and the murder of the security guard. Additional police units were now joining the chase from Southwark Police Station, and a Marine Police Unit from Wapping was also in the area in case he tried to escape via the river. The Police helicopter was almost directly overhead. Drakos would soon be completely encircled. It was surely only a matter of time before an arrest would be made.

As she passed the hotel on her right and looked ahead, she could see the tall, dark figure of her assailant in front of her, climbing the steps leading to the iconic Tower Bridge. Other than the helicopter, she could see no sign of police approaching on the ground, at least on her side of the bridge. Regardless of what John Deery said, she wasn't going to let him get away this time. Looking up, she could see him already on the bridge, moving quickly away from her.

'John, he's on the bridge heading south. Where the hell are your men?' said Downes, urgently gripping her radio as she began running up the stairs leading to the Bridge.

'Alicia, he won't get far; officers are moving in to block off the Surrey side of the bridge. Hold on; my boys should be approaching you now, can you see them yet?' said Deery.

Downes reached the Tower Bridge pavement, but there was no sign of Drakos. She looked to her right along the A100 northbound, but every instinct told her that he was moving south; he was not to know that the police had already cut off his escape. Turning back to face the bridge, she moved along the pavement towards the North Tower and the double-leaf bascules.

Drakos moved swiftly across the bascules and around the South Tower, where he expected to continue along the remainder of the bridge before vanishing into the south bank metropolis and sanctuary. To his shock, his path was blocked by a number of police, including an armed response unit at the far end of the bridge. The officer in charge barked out an instruction for him to throw down his weapon and surrender. Drakos spun around and disappeared behind the South Tower, out of the Police's line of sight. Crossing the bascules and rounding the North Tower when he suddenly found himself face to face with Downes, who had now arrived from the opposite direction. Without a moment's hesitation, he drew his pistol and fired at her. The bullet whistled past Downes, ricocheting off the road and into the darkness. As he pulled the trigger a second time, he felt a heavy impact against his chest. The Glock clattered to the ground. Looking down in disbelief, he was stunned to see blood trickling from a knife wound to the centre of his chest.

The man who revelled in death and had been responsible for so many brutal and vicious murders was himself shortly to enter the underworld. He staggered backwards, both hands gripping the handle of the blade buried up to the hilt in his blood-soaked chest. Downes walked towards him as his energy and life ebbed away. Standing facing her mortally wounded nemesis, Downes' thoughts turned to Ron Jackson and Winston Redman, two brave men cut down by this psychopathic monster. Even with death moments away, his cold and heartless eyes were filled with hatred. He grimaced, staggered backwards a couple of paces and toppled off the bridge into the cold, murky waters of the River Thames. Downes rushed to the edge of the wall and peered into the dark waters. There was no sign of Drakos. If his black-hearted body had not sunk to the bottom of the river and buried itself in the mud and silt, it would be carried downstream by the strong current.

Downes sat alone on the wall beside the North Tower, lost in her thoughts. It had been a traumatic few hours with two more innocent families soon to receive the devastating news of the loss of a loved one. The only consolation she could offer was that the perpetrator had paid the ultimate price for his unspeakable crimes. As though coming out of a trance, she wiped away a tear and suddenly became conscious that she was surrounded by members of the police.

After being assessed by paramedics, Downes was taken back to Thames House, accompanied by Greg Travers and DCI Deery. The Wing Commander was there waiting for them. Le Sueur, who had been monitoring proceedings throughout the evening, was fulsome in her praise for Downes' courage. Notwithstanding the fact that their only definite suspect was now probably languishing at the bottom of the River Thames.

'Well, Detective Chief Inspector?'

'Marine Police are searching the river, and divers are already in there as well. If the body has not been carried downstream already, I'm confident we'll find it.'

'Travers?'

'Ma'am. This man, Hades or Drakos or whatever he called himself, worked for Oswaldo Phoenix, who, according to his mistress, is up to his neck in shady deals. It seems clear to me that the answer lies in Jersey. He's hiding something, ma'am, including a connection with Ali Abadi. I'd like to go back and rattle his cage a bit more.'

Le Sueur glanced down and looked at her watch, it was 03.35. It had been a long and difficult night for everyone. Nerves were frayed, and everyone was tired. She adjourned the debrief until 11 am, by which time, hopefully more information would have come to light. Deery was first out of his chair. He thanked the Wing Commander for her support, smiled and waved at the other two who were still in their seats

'See you guys tomorrow,' said Deery as he quickly left the office.

Travers and Downes slowly and wearily rose to their feet.

'Downes, as we are running out of safe houses for you, you will be pleased to hear that I have sanctioned a couple of nights at the Westminster whilst you decide what you want to do.'

'Thank you, ma'am, that's great, much appreciated,' replied Downes.

'Something amusing you, Travers?' remarked Le Sueur, whose keen eye had noticed a tickled expression encroaching onto Travers' face.

'No ma'am. Not really, I've not heard you crack a joke before, it rather took me by surprise, I didn't know you had a sense of humour,' added Travers dryly.

'I see, well, you will find jokes in short supply around here at the moment, especially in the middle of the night, so make the most of it. Alright, you two, you had better get off and get some rest. I'll see you back here at 11.00 sharp!'

Travers and Downes walked down the stairs from Le Sueur's office and straight out of the building. It was approaching 4 a.m. By the time Travers returned after accompanying Alicia to her hotel, it would be well after that.

At 10.50 the following morning, Travers finished off a second and particularly strong cup of tea. It had not been the most comfortable of nights. Tired as he was, he had found it difficult to sleep. Even two slugs of whisky from a bottle of ten-year-old Macallan hadn't tipped him into a slumberous state. As much as he envied Alicia's comfortable bed, his tired body could not command his mind to be still. There was a weight of expectation, not only from those above him but a presumption from those below that he would win through in the end. Somehow, however complex the problem, he would find the answer. He had reviewed his notes, the official files and reports, over and over again. The pieces of the jigsaw were there; he just needed to see the big picture to put the puzzle together. Behind it all, the spectre of Olga Devereux hung over him like Banquo's ghost. Had Hector's death so enraged and unhinged the woman that no horror was beyond her? Was he really the catalyst for her senseless acts of vengeance?

As 11 o'clock approached, Travers picked up his ever-expanding file and made his way up to Steph Le Sueur's office. He knocked twice on the door before opening it. Inside, Deery was deep in conversation with the Wing Commander. She looked up with a nod of acknowledgement towards Travers before resuming her discussion with the detective. Before he had time to take his seat, there was another knock on the door; it was Downes. Travers greeted her. Despite everything that had transpired only a few short hours ago, she looked refreshed, wearing a cream trouser suit with a pink scarf over a white blouse. Her blonde hair was tied back for once. Travers leant across and whispered in her ear.

'How do you do it? You look amazing,' said Travers. 'I feel lousy and I'm sure I look a lot worse than I feel.'

'Mind over matter, Greg, and the knowledge that the person who tried to kill me twice is now adding to the bio-diversity at the bottom of the river, that helps quite a lot too.'

Le Sueur opened a thin folder containing a photograph and two sheets of A4 paper. She read through the short document before handing the file across the desk to Deery.

'Police divers recovered the body of a young man about fifty yards downstream of Tower Bridge this morning. Slim build, six foot four, black jeans and jumper.'

'Ma'am, but are we absolutely sure it's him?' asked Downes.

'Yes, unless you stabbed more than one person last night, Downes, he still had your knife in his chest,' said Le Sueur sarcastically. 'He didn't have any identification on him, but fortunately, he still had his fingers. Pathology hasn't done the full post-mortem yet but they did a rush job on his fingerprints. We ran them through INTERPOL's AFIS database. We got a match and it wasn't Andreas Drakos.'

'So who is he, ma'am?' asked Downes.

'His name is Andreas Vasilakis; he was a small-time enforcer in the Greek mafia before he branched out into contract killing. He operated mostly in Europe. He went off the grid a few years ago.'

Deery examined the photograph of Vasilakis before passing it across to Travers. The picture didn't ring any bells, but the name Vasilakis certainly did and not pleasant ones.

'I know that name, Wing Commander. If it's the same family, he had a sister, Penelope. She caused me no end of grief last summer. Came to my station bold as brass posing as a Solicitor, poisoned my suspect and walked out again, as though nothing had happened.'

'Where is she now?' asked Le Sueur.

'The last time I saw her, she was suspended several feet off the ground with a rusty pole through her body. Couldn't have happened to a nicer girl,' commented Deery, who still remembered the stomach-churning sight of the young woman's body transfixed after losing control of her Ferrari Spider trying to evade arrest on one of Dorset's Purbeck country roads.

It was a significant development. Travers was also familiar with Miss Vasilakis, having remembered reading Deery's report at the time of the incident. The murdered suspect had been wanted in connection with the Devereux investigation. The fact that her brother had subsequently accepted a contract to kill Alicia simply added credence to Travers' assertion that Olga Devereux must be pulling the strings. It was a view that Le Sueur herself was now willing to accept.

'What of our traitor, ma'am, any developments? After all, this whole exercise was designed to draw Drakos out into the open and to expose our mole,' said Travers, 'Drakos or Vasilakis, as I suppose we should now call him, sneaked in under the cover of darkness, killed one of the Chief Inspector's men, then gained entry to the house, resulting in the death of Winston Redman. It was only by the grace of God that Alicia wasn't killed as well. Vasilakis wasn't just tipped off, the alarm was deactivated. He could have driven a bus in there.'

Le Sueur sympathised with Travers' growing sense of frustration. The plan, despite all its risks, had worked perfectly…in part. Yet the identity of the mole remained unknown.

'Travers, I appreciate your irritation. I have had the Director on the phone raising hell about it, and believe me, she is as annoyed as you are. Everyone who was copied in on the safe house request is under investigation without exception.'

'I'm sorry, ma'am, that's just not good enough. There is a rat in this building and it needs dealing with. We have a timeline of incidents, we should be able to easily narrow down the list of runners and riders, someone upstairs needs to get their arse in gear… apologies ma'am,' said a tetchy Travers, whose lack of sleep was exacerbating his general mood of dissatisfaction with the progress of the investigation.

The meeting went on for a further thirty minutes. However, much to his relief, Le Sueur did agree to Travers' request to return immediately to Jersey to "rattle the cage" of Oswaldo Phoenix, as he put it, and hopefully renew his contact with Phoenix's mistress Penelope Papandreou.

Chapter 18

The sky was a rich blue with barely a handful of wispy white cotton wool clouds passing across St Aubin's Bay, driven by a brisk south-westerly breeze. Three months ago, it might have been taken for a perfect summer's day, but today, there was a distinct chill in the air that no amount of sunshine could disguise. Greg Travers stood on the terrace of the Grand Hotel Jersey, looking out across the water. The tide was in with the wind whipping up the wave crests into a cavalry charge of white horses. He was grateful for the glass screens that separated the terrace from the shoreline and offered a degree of protection against the onshore winds.

The Grand was Travers' favourite hotel in St Helier. Once Wing Commander Le Sueur had agreed to his return, he wasted no time in checking that they had rooms available and with the summer season now behind them, it was not the issue it might have been even a few weeks earlier. After a tortuous few days in London, it was good to be back, and at least he had enjoyed a decent night's sleep in a comfortable bed and felt well rested; now with a full English breakfast inside him, he was ready for whatever the day had in store. As he turned and sat back in his seat to finish his morning coffee, he heard his name called. Glancing to his right, he saw the burly figure of Detective Inspector Dave Beckett striding towards him.

'Good morning, Greg, your phone call sounded urgent, what's up?'

'Hi Dave, good to see you again, well, it concerns your man Andreas Drakos. He's dead.'

'Dead?' said the shocked Detective. 'What happened?'

'He killed a MET police officer during a stakeout, but his luck ran out when one of my colleagues caught up with him.'

'That's incredible, I know people said he was a bit of an eccentric, but…'

'Well, if you think that's incredible, there's more. We fingerprinted him. Your oddball Greek wine bottle washer, called Drakos, turned out to be an active contract killer called Vasilakis. Which brings us back to Oswaldo Phoenix and your investigation into the murder of Claire Powell. If we can prove Phoenix got Vasilakis to do his wet work, we can finally put him away,' said Travers.

Beckett's murder investigation of Powell had been flat-lining for a while. The news that Phoenix's right-hand man was a killer would re-energise it completely. Phoenix had been the subject of an ongoing investigation for many months, sourced mainly from rumour and second-hand comments, but nothing had been proved, yet the cloud of suspicion remained. Beckett revealed that for months, police had suspected that Phoenix was involved in smuggling, but no evidence had been found, and multiple spot checks had proved fruitless.

'Dave, we need to fast-track this investigation. What's Phoenix up to at the moment?' asked Travers.

'He still goes to his club, but he's spending a lot of time at his winery at the moment; he has regular wine-tasting events there. There always seems to be a lot of people wandering around,' said Beckett.

'Have you been there?'

'Once or twice, it's a pretty big set-up,' said Beckett.

'Do you think he could be hiding anything there?' asked Travers. 'It might be fun to have a nose around,'

'Well, there's an open night tonight, he has them every week, sort of a PR marketing ploy to drum up local interest.'

'Oh, I'm very interested, what time is it?' said Travers.

'8 o'clock. If you like, I can pick you up and take you over there.'

'Thank you, that would be splendid. After our last meeting, it will be interesting to see if I can get under his skin again. The more I can provoke him and make him angry, the better the chances of him getting careless and making a mistake.'

The Jersey detective left with a renewed spring in his step and a new suspect to focus his attention on. Travers spent another few minutes soaking up the sea air and thinking about their conversation. The only aspect that still really worried him was the absence of news on Papandreou. Beckett still hadn't been able to find her. Polite enquiries had been palmed off by Phoenix, and her friends at the Atlantic hadn't seen her for several days. Travers pushed his seat back and rose to his feet. With no plans other than his trip to Phoenix's plant later, he had a day to relax and sharpen the mental rapier with which he intended to prod the Spaniard into indiscretion.

As he meandered back through the lobby of the hotel, Travers stopped and surveyed the array of tourist information on display. As he thumbed through the pamphlets, his eyes were drawn to one for the Jersey War Tunnels. He was well acquainted with the Channel Islands' wartime history during the German occupation, however, circumstances and a lack of time had not permitted him to visit or explore the famous tunnels until now. Only about ten minutes away by car, it would comfortably fill a couple of hours and give him plenty of time to prepare for the evening's event at the Winery. Travers took the leaflet and returned to his room.

Twenty minutes later, Travers began the short journey to Les Charrières Malorey. He found the two hours he spent exploring the Ho8 tunnels and the exhibits displayed, including the underground hospital, both humbling and thought-provoking. Over a thousand metres of tunnels, fifty metres underground all created by slave labour under the watchful eyes of their Nazi overseers. Under the circumstances, it was a remarkable feat of engineering, but it was also a salutary and sobering reminder of the cost and value of freedom.

One of the tour guides had told him that there were tunnels dotted around the island, though some had been abandoned, incomplete due to lack of resources, as the war turned against Germany. Travers returned to St Helier for a late lunch at the Pomme d'Or Hotel, where he sat by the window and watched the world go by. As he tucked into a club sandwich, his phone flashed up a notification, it was from Le Sueur. Travers considered ignoring it till he had finished his lunch, then thought better of it and, with some reluctance, opened the email.

The message from the Wing Commander was tantalizingly intriguing. The former Home Secretary, who had, to all intents and purposes, been sacked for duplicity in the original Devereux investigation, had bowed to pressure and perhaps, his conscience, and was now willing to talk to the authorities. How much he knew and whether it was of any practical value was a moot point. Travers would have loved to sit in on the interview, but he had other things on his agenda.

Travers returned to the Grand Hotel. He had barely time to take his coat off before his phone rang. This time it was Alicia.

'Hi Greg,'

'Alicia, how are you? What's new? Have you made any decision about where you are going to stay now?'

'I'm going back home to Holland Park in a couple of days, they are over there now reviewing security. Any development your end?'

'I'm going wine tasting at Phoenix's winery tonight, I'm just hoping that when it comes to the spitting out part, I remember to use the bucket rather than his face,' said Travers, who could hear Downes chuckling away at the imaginary scenario.

'I went to see the war tunnels this morning, I must say they are pretty impressive,' added Travers.

'Yes, I've seen them. They are all over the place. After the war, the Allies filled a lot of them up with German war materials left behind when they pulled out. All sorts of things were hidden away, from munitions, uniforms, and even tanks.'

'Really? That's interesting,' said Travers.

Downes confirmed the news that Travers had recently discovered regarding the former Home Secretary. The Director General had already had a conference with the MET Commissioner, who had decided to throw it into Detective Chief Inspector Deery's lap since he was already heavily involved in the investigation.

'John will really enjoy that. Roasting a crooked former Minister of State will be right up his street,' said Travers. 'I'd have a word with the Wing Commander if I were you, and see if you can sit in on it. Anyway, I'll let you know how tonight goes. I'm certain Phoenix is involved in this mess somehow, so I am just going to make myself a nuisance and poke my nose as far into his business as I can, and we'll see just how bad the smell is.'

'Alright, Greg, be careful and keep in touch,' said Downes.

After an early light Italian supper around the corner at Casa Mia, Travers walked back to his hotel room, where he dressed in a deep navy blue suit, then walked down the impressively carved wooden main staircase and across the marble lobby to the entrance, where he waited for Dave Beckett's arrival. He glanced in at the cocktail bar, which was almost empty. Travers looked at his watch. He would have liked a shot of Vodka or Gin or even a slug of Whisky before his trip, but there really wasn't time for such an indulgence, and besides, deep down, he knew that he shouldn't have anything that might take the edge off his instincts.

He turned away and walked through the revolving doors and waited outside. Five minutes later, Beckett arrived. The Phoenix Winery was only about fifteen minutes away, and it was a quick and easy trip. Beckett would drop Travers off, return to St Helier and after the event return and pick him up. During the short journey, the detective provided Travers with a rough guide to the establishment's layout.

Shortly after 7.30 pm, Beckett's car pulled into the Phoenix Winery on La Route Du Coin. There were already more than a dozen cars parked in the large car park, with more still arriving. Travers opened the door and stepped out, then leant in through the window.

'Ok Greg, I don't have to tell you, be careful, I don't want to have to come back with a flashing blue light on to rescue you. Just case the joint, have a nose around but please be discreet about it…understand?!'

'Dave, you worry too much. I'll call when we are done, alright? Now go and put your feet up for a couple of hours.'

Travers stood back and watched as the Detective pulled away and drove out of the car park and back towards St Helier.

The Winery was of a large modern design, looking less like an oblong warehouse or factory unit and more like a modern office facility. With an abundance of large glass panels providing a profusion of electric light, which flooded the courtyard. Travers followed a small group of people into the Winery through the main entrance, where they were greeted by members of Phoenix's staff, who directed them towards a reception area where they were offered a glass of sparkling wine. Travers circulated around the group of twenty to twenty-five people, all making polite small talk. Many of them seemed like regulars who treated the event as an excuse for a catch-up with old friends, along with some free wine. There was no one there that he recognised, although a number of the well-dressed young women looked vaguely familiar; maybe they belonged to the set that frequented the Atlantic Hotel. Perhaps for no other reason than that, he hoped Penelope might be there.

After approximately twenty minutes, a member of staff rang a small handbell, and the incessant nattering promptly stopped as people looked around to see what was happening. In strode Oswaldo Phoenix, dressed up like a 19th-century Spanish Caballero, including a white silk shirt with a white lace jabot under a short black waistcoat, with black trousers. He threw his hat to one of his staff standing some ten to fifteen feet away and greeted the onlookers as they applauded the flamboyant gesture. Travers, standing towards the back of the crowd, looked on with mild amusement. Phoenix spoke for little more than ten minutes, he described what the evening would entail. He then ushered the expectant audience through the building to where the giant stainless steel fermentation vats were maintained. The first-time visitors were enthralled by the process, while those for whom this was not a first visit, hung back and whispered to one another as they waited for the tour to finish and the wine tasting to begin.

It was an hour or so before the tour of the building was completed, extended by an unusually large number of questions. The group led by a vanguard of the more seasoned and enthusiastic wine tasters were taken back to the reception room, where tables had been laid out with the samples of the wines to be offered. Travers was one of the last to return, having used the time to look around as much of the layout of the building, including the number of exits, as possible, without attracting too much unwanted attention to himself.

The tasting consisted of several white, red, and rosé wines, and ended with more sparkling wine. Phoenix circulated amongst the tasters as he described the qualities of each selection. Travers, being something of a connoisseur, had to admit that they were very good. Whatever else Phoenix was mixed up in, he certainly had a flair for producing fine wine.

As Travers finished sampling a very nice red, Phoenix approached his table and stood in front of him, watching as Travers swished the wine around his palate before reluctantly spitting it out.

'Well, it is Mr Travers, isn't it? What brings you here? Here to play another game perhaps?'

'Mr Phoenix, hello again,' said Travers as he extended his hand towards his host. 'Oh, I'm partial to a glass of fine wine now and again. A friend of yours at the Atlantic Hotel told me about your winery. Penelope Papandreou, I thought perhaps she might have been here tonight.'

'No, I am afraid not. What do you think of my establishment?' said Phoenix.

'Remarkable, and the wine is quite excellent. I had no idea it was here. It's amazing the secrets you can keep hidden away these days, don't you think?' said Travers pointedly.

'Enjoy the wine, Mr Travers,' said Phoenix with a casual air of arrogant disdain as he moved away towards another table.

As Travers picked up a new glass of Rosé, he caught a glimpse of a short, stocky man in his eye line. After exchanging glances with Phoenix, he had entered a room off a corridor from the reception area. It was only fleeting, but Travers was close enough to get a pretty good view, at least of the back of the man's head. He had never seen him in the flesh before, but he had seen his photograph in a German police file. He was trouble and was going to add another worrying dimension to the investigation. Travers continued with the wine tasting and making inconsequential conversation with those closest to him while keeping his eyes trained on the doorway to the room beyond.

Another twenty-five minutes had passed, and with it the conclusion of the official tasting. Those that remained were now indulging themselves without the constraint of having to spit out the contents of their glasses. Travers continued to smile and exercise his social graces whilst maintaining his single-minded vigil.

With no sign of the man emerging from the room, Travers decided to take the initiative. Putting his glass down, he excused himself from his interlocutors and walked across the corridor as far as the entrance to the room. Pausing for a moment, he could hear nothing through the door from the room itself. With the remaining attendees still deep in conversation, he put his hand on the handle and turned it gently. The door opened, and Travers peered inside. It was a storeroom with shelves on all sides containing numerous box files and larger storage boxes. Other than that, the room was empty. There was no sign of the man he had seen entering it. Travers walked towards the far wall and put his hands on the shelves. He turned and looked around the room. There were no other doors and no windows. It seemed inconceivable that the man could have slipped out without him seeing him.

Travers backed away towards the door. As he turned, he was met by one of the winery staff standing directly in front of him.

'What are you doing in here?' said the man abruptly.

'I'm sorry, I was looking for the toilets. It's my first visit here,' said Travers apologetically.

Fortunately, the rather ill-tempered fellow accepted Travers' excuse without further questioning and escorted him back to the reception area, where the number of guests was beginning to dwindle. He looked around, but there was no sign of Phoenix. Several members of his team were already starting to clear away. Travers rang for his "carriage"

It was a little more than twenty minutes before Travers saw the familiar sight of DI Beckett's black BMW pull into the now largely deserted car park. Travers thanked the staff as he passed through the doorway and out into the courtyard. He walked towards the car, his shoes crunching on the gravel until he reached the detective's car. Placing his hand on the door handle, he paused for a moment and turned back, looking at the building. Then opened the passenger door, took his seat and closed it with a satisfying clunk. Beckett pulled away immediately while Travers drew across his seat belt as he continued to look out of his window at the winery.

'Well, Greg, how did it go?' asked Beckett.

Travers didn't respond immediately, still lost in his own thoughts. Beckett glanced across at him and called out his name again. Travers, his train of thought broken, now looked across at him.

'Dave, does the name Wilhelm Mainz mean anything to you?' asked Travers.

'Mainz? No, I can't say it does, should it?'

'Wilhelm Mainz's grandfather was a Brown Shirt in Germany in the 30s. Wilhelm's Father was a junior officer in the Einsatzgruppen, Hitler's death squads. After the war, he married, had children, including Wilhelm, but old habits die hard. When Neo-Nazi movements sprang up, the authorities didn't have far to look. The apple doesn't fall far from the tree, as the saying goes. Wilhelm Mainz was a major player. Things died down for a while, but with continuing mass immigration, they started flexing their wings again. The German Police tried to round up the ringleaders. We had a few names on our own watch list, so they sent one of my colleagues from MI6 to help out. This was a long time before I joined,' said Travers, who continued.

'There was a major operation to crack a particular cell. The Police moved in. Some arrests were made, but things got messy, and there was a firefight. As Mainz tried to escape, our man took a shot at him. He missed his head by a fraction, but the bullet removed a large chunk of Mainz's left ear.'

'…and what's the connection with Phoenix?' asked Beckett.

'Dave, whilst I was there, I'm pretty sure that I saw him, it was only for a moment, and I've not seen a recent picture of him, but he was the right age, and how many people do you know with the bottom of their left ear missing?'

'So what are you going to do now?'

'I watched Mainz go into a room, thirty minutes later I went in there, and he had gone, disappeared. There were no other doors or windows, but he had vanished into thin air. I'm sure he didn't come out. Dave, I need another look at that room. Can you get me the plans of that place and details of their alarm system?'

Fifteen minutes later, the car was nearing the end of its journey along the A2 around St Aubin's Bay before branching off towards the entrance of the Grand Hotel. Beckett pulled in and parked the car.

'I'll get to work on those plans first thing tomorrow. Anything else you need?'

'No thanks, Dave, thanks for the lift, I appreciate it. I'll talk to you tomorrow.'

Travers walked up the steps to the revolving door. Having dutifully abstained from an aperitif before his trip out to the winery, he now felt he owed himself at least one nightcap. The cocktail bar was fairly quiet with just a handful of residents enjoying a relaxing libation to end the day. Travers walked across to the bar and rested an elbow on the high wooden structure. In front of him, totting up the bill for another customer was the lovely Anabela, the senior bar manager who had looked after him and had taken great delight in making her first Vesper Martini for him.

'Hello Greg, had a good evening? What can I get you?'

'Good evening, Ana, more business than pleasure, actually, so far anyway. Have you got a Macallan single malt?'

'Single or double?'

Travers gave her the exaggeratedly puzzled look of a man who didn't expect to have to answer such a derisory question. With a knowing look, she turned away and picked up a tumbler and poured two measures of Whisky from the bottle of Macallan and handed it to Travers, who smiled and thanked her before turning away and selecting one of the tables close to the window. The evening had presented Travers with more pieces of an already complicated puzzle. The appearance of Mainz had just muddied the waters still further, not to mention incriminating Phoenix beyond mere coincidence.

Chapter 19

Deery walked away from another grilling at the hands of the MET's Assistant Commissioner. He had nothing against the AC personally, he understood perfectly well how the line of authority worked and that his was just the next set of knuckles to get rapped. The trouble was that there wasn't anyone below him, and he certainly wasn't going to take it out on his team. How do you dress up no news as good news? The death of Vasilakis was admittedly a small tick, but the AC had his own problems to deal with. A nervous Prime Minister and Home Secretary had earlier held the Commissioner's feet to the Number 10 fire, demanding answers. Not unnaturally, the buck was quickly passed down through the chain of command until it landed, as it always seemed to, in Deery's lap.

The investigation had been stagnating, which probably accounted for the dressing down. However, while progress was grinding to a halt on the mainland, he had been buoyed by news from Greg Travers in Jersey this morning. Travers may be new to fieldwork in the practical sense, but his instincts were usually right, and often they were positively uncanny. Oswaldo Phoenix, originally just a person of interest, was now firmly established as the prime suspect. The appearance of Wilhelm Mainz in Jersey would also pique the interest of the German authorities, who had long tried to run him to earth.

Deery walked into his office and stood for a few moments looking out of his window. It was another dreary day. Across the Victoria Embankment, the brown waters of the River Thames reflected the day and his mood. With a frustrated huff of resignation, he turned away from the London skyline and returned to his desk. There was a small pile of folders there, case files to be reviewed, and one large one dominating the traditional dark oak desk. He thumbed through the half dozen thin ones, two burglaries, a hit and run, two common assaults and one indecent exposure. With the AC's admonition still ringing in his ears, he shouted out through the open office door. A few moments later, his call was answered.

'Yes, boss?' said the young detective.

'You see that pile of crap over there?' said Deery looking at the bundle of relatively less important case folders on his desk. 'I've got the AC on my back at the moment over this one,' he said, holding up the much larger bombing file. 'Here, they are all yours, call it on-the-job training,' said the Chief Inspector as he tossed them into the arms of the aspiring young Police Officer.

As the Officer left the room, Deery glanced at his desktop computer. In the last half hour, six more emails had come in, the latest was from Wing Commander Le Sueur, marked "Urgent". Deery opened it immediately and read the contents. The morning had just got appreciably worse. He cupped his head in his hands for a few seconds as he looked at the screen again. The completed internal security sweep of Alicia Downes' flat in Holland Park had uncovered electronic surveillance equipment, not just anybody's, but MI5's own gear. Someone from Thames House with access to the apartment had bugged it. It was impossible to tell if it had been done before she had moved out or as a precursor to her moving back in. There was also a microphone discovered inside her phone.

Deery picked up his phone and rang Le Sueur. After twenty seconds, a slightly breathless Le Sueur answered.

'Morning, it's John Deery, have I caught you at an awkward moment?'

'Hello John, sort of. I am on my way to see the Director. You've seen my email?

'Yes, it doesn't make for good reading.'

'I had to send the Director one this morning. She's fuming and looking for someone's head to roll. I am just hoping it's not mine she's after. I'm sorry, John, I've got to dash. I will call you back later,' with that, Le Sueur hung up.

It was another two hours before the Wing Commander rang back. There had been further developments. As a result of her meeting with the Director General earlier, she had ordered a complete audit of Downes' Security Service profile and security clearance. The review had brought something up, an anomaly. Someone in Personnel had accessed her file without prior authorisation.

'Excellent, so you've got the bastard at last. What have they had to say for themselves?'

'Nothing, John, he has denied everything, completely. We're still questioning him …well, I don't know him personally. His name is Robert MacMillan. He's been with the service for over thirty years with an unblemished record. It doesn't make sense. Why throw away a whole career? He did not attempt to cover his tracks, and must have known it would be spotted.'

'I take it you are running a full check on his financials, just in case he is topping his pension pot up,' said Deery.

'Of course, but he has no history of financial impropriety. He's an archetypal thrifty Scotsman, tight as they come, according to some of his colleagues. I'm told he still owns the same suit he wore when he started. He has the security access alright, but as for motive?'

Deery agreed with the Wing Commander; it didn't add up. Why would someone with such long service and with their retirement on the horizon risk it? He didn't seem motivated by money; in boxing parlance, he was a journeyman, a solid, dependable nine-to-five kind of guy, not someone likely to be mixed up in this manner of skulduggery.

The conversation with Le Sueur had given the Chief Inspector another problem to add to the growing number he was juggling with. He had offered to help with the vetting of her suspect. A second pair of eyes wouldn't hurt, and if this man was as innocent as he claimed, it shouldn't take long to prove it. He opened the large folder sitting on his desk and began thumbing through the pages. Most of his colleagues had been brought up in the digital age, with everything on the screen instantly at the touch of a button, but for Deery, a Kindle was no substitute for a properly bound book. There was just something authentic about wading through a physical file, scribbling spidery notes on paper rather than fiddling about with "sticky notes" on a computer screen.

As he turned the pages, he came across the screwed up notepaper recovered from the bin in the bomber's flat, containing the list of initials that Travers had then succinctly pointed out were the initials of the targets. Only the last one remained, PM, the Petrie Museum of Egyptian Archaeology, which was part of the University College London. The Curator, who had been very cooperative, and all the staff, were thoroughly checked. There were no special exhibitions or high-profile visits planned, and to this point, there had been no attacks or indeed threats. They had drawn a blank on this one.

As he ruminated, a meeting reminder flashed up on his mobile phone of his date with the former Home Secretary in an hour's time. The folder would have to wait. If there was one thing he hated above all else, it was corruption in high places. According to the Right Honourable Deborah Roberts, her predecessor was now having a chronic attack of guilt, brought on, no doubt, by a recent unfavourable medical diagnosis. Perhaps he wanted to clear his conscience before his impending demise.

DI Beckett rolled out the architect's plans of the Phoenix's estate to Travers, who had arrived for a working lunch at the States HQ at La Route Du Fort. The documents included revisions and subsequent updates necessary to facilitate the granting of planning permission. Travers scrutinised the plans closely, comparing the images on the paper in front of him against his memory of the winery. He ran his finger across the plan as he retraced in his head the walk through the previous night. His finger stopped on the storeroom that Mainz had entered. Travers looked at the diagram. There was nothing to indicate another exit. He flipped the page over, looking for subsequent re-drafts.

'Is that it?' asked a frustrated Travers. 'David, Mainz went into that room, I saw him. He didn't come out, there's got to be another exit not shown on these plans,'

'No, Greg, those are the official plans signed off by the Jersey Planning and Building Control.'

'I don't buy it, there has to be another explanation. Could Phoenix have done additional building or excavation work without the Planning Department's knowledge?'

'He'd be taking a big risk, what's going on inside that head of yours?' said Beckett.

'I was just thinking about something that one of the guides told me when I went to see the War Tunnels the other day. Is it possible there could be one under his land? I understand that some of them weren't finished or were left abandoned; the records are pretty sketchy. Can you check?'

'Come on, let's go back to my office and make a few phone calls,' said Beckett. The two men rose from their table, gathered up the bundle of paperwork and walked the short distance to Beckett's office. A tunnel would certainly answer some of the questions, but first, they would have to find it.

It didn't take long for Beckett to establish the intriguing truth. Along Le Mont du Coin, the Germans built the Batterie Seydlitz, a gun battery with a tunnel system providing accommodation. However, as Beckett explained, tunnels built under private land in Jersey remained the property of the landowner, and the true extent of the tunnels remained unknown. The news reinforced Travers' belief that there must be a connection to the winery; there was no other way to explain Mainz's disappearing act. The pair spent some time discussing the options for the best course of action. Travers was acutely aware of the time factor. Le Sueur had impressed on him the need for urgency; there was no time to waste sitting around, "arses are being kicked here and don't think you are safe over there", as the Wing Commander deftly put it.

Travers badly needed to gain access to the store room at the winery. Neither of the options for entry was particularly appealing. Waiting for next week's public tasting evening at least meant potentially easier access, but a critical delay of many days. The other, an incursion, was highly risky and one that Beckett was very reluctant to endorse, given Travers' lack of experience in the field. Travers was happy to throw the problem back to Thames House. As he left Beckett's office to return to his hotel, he wished Alicia was with him. She would have no such qualms about breaking in.

The briefing room at Thames House was a hive of activity, usually the nerve centre of operations, but the mood was very different today. The Director General herself was holding court, which was always the sign that something serious was up. This time, the subject under surveillance was not a potential terrorist or a radical, it was one of their own. A senior manager with an unblemished record, but someone who had access to sensitive and personal information. Other than the fact that his security clearance had been used to access classified information on Alicia Downes and Greg Travers, he was a most unlikely traitor. In his late fifties, married with two grown-up children and living in a modest house in Wimbledon, he didn't raise any red flags, until this current crisis. Even now, it was almost impossible to believe. Checks were being run on his financial history. The results, checked and re-checked, only added to the implausibility of the situation.

The situation was ultimately resolved when it was established beyond doubt that Mr MacMillan had been recorded on security cameras attending a meeting at precisely the same time as his access codes had been used. However, far from placating the Director, the news simply re-emphasised that the true identity of the mole was still unresolved. The Director, a tall, elegant woman with a keen eye for detail, walked across to the Wing Commander's station. She didn't like loose ends, particularly when they reflected so badly on the service. She stood facing Le Sueur, her face reflecting her growing dissatisfaction. After exchanging a few short, cursory words articulating her annoyance, she left, much to the relief of everyone present. Le Sueur watched her as she left, then turned to one of her team. The two officers exchanged knowing glances at one another and smiled in a manner that British people often do when facing awkward situations. They were effectively back to square one.

The Director had made her views very clear, apprehending the mole was to be Le Sueur's top priority. It hadn't surprised anyone that MacMillan had been exonerated. He just wasn't the stuff of traitors. It did mean that someone, probably in personnel, had somehow acquired his security access codes and used them to obtain sensitive material, leaving the amiable and innocent Scotsman to "pick up the tab".

As much as Downes loved staying at the Westminster Hotel, she had hoped to return to her Holland Park home. As her mother was fond of saying, "East, West, home is best". Despite her fondness for foreign travel, there was nothing quite like waking up in your own bed surrounded by the trappings and knick-knacks that make a home uniquely special. The man who had twice tried to take her life from her was dead, and the "pest control" team had removed all the electronic bugs from her apartment, but she still felt uneasy. Like most people, Downes found the news of MacMillan's arrest problematic. She had met him on many occasions over the years, including social gatherings at the office. Whoever the real perpetrator was, it was a major faux pas to point the finger of suspicion towards a man who was certain to be cleared sooner or later.

Travers stood on the St Aubins' promenade and looked across at Elizabeth Castle. The tide was going out, leaving myriad small pools of water behind. One of the amphibious buses was trundling back from the castle, containing a handful of hardy souls that had braced the chilly day for a last wander around before it was closed for the winter. His mind was preoccupied by thoughts of Phoenix's winery; he had messaged Le Sueur earlier. Knowing how naturally risk-averse she was, he anticipated that she would veto any plans he had for breaking into the building. As he mused, his phone rang, it was the call he was waiting for.

'Good afternoon, ma'am,' said Travers. 'What's the word on the winery?'

'Good afternoon, Travers, I have spoken to the Deputy Director this morning. You are on no account to attempt to break in. It's too dangerous. If circumstances change here and an incursion is authorised by the Director, I'll let you know, but until then, proceed with your alternative option.'

'Very good, ma'am,' said Travers. It was disappointing news but hardly surprising.

Le Sueur then also updated Travers on the investigation into the personnel manager, earlier, much to Travers' consternation.

'Jock? That's crazy, ma'am. Someone has really dropped the ball if they are trying to blame him.'

As Travers wandered back to the Grand Hotel, he found it increasingly hard to understand why it was proving so impossibly difficult to unearth the elusive MI5 mole. They were clearly not infallible. If you want a patsy, you find someone with a vice or something to hide. Mac didn't qualify on either count, and therefore, it must have been a moment of opportunism rather than pre-planned. Someone who urgently needed security information about his movements and those of Alicia, or maybe it was related to the current crisis?

Travers jogged up the steps of the hotel, through the revolving door then turned left into the bar, which was almost deserted. He looked around. It was empty except for one elderly couple sitting by a table in the corner, enjoying a cream tea. Travers was pleased to see Anabela on duty again behind the bar. Some people just had a way of making one feel better, a warm smile and a kind word were sometimes all it took. Anabela just had that gift. After a brief exchange, Travers walked across to his favourite table in the corner by the window. He looked down at the thin slice of lemon peel bobbing about in the cocktail glass containing his freshly made Vesper Martini. A big conundrum needed a big drink, it was the equivalent to a Sherlock Holmes three-pipe problem and for Travers, it didn't come much more potent than the glass now in his hand.

The first sip was always the best, a powerful combination of neat Gin and Vodka with a dash of extra dry vermouth, it had a bitter and intoxicating effect. Even for someone with Travers' capacity for alcohol, it was a drink worthy of his respect. He took a second sip and then put the glass down. Taking a piece of paper from his jacket pocket, he began jotting down bullet points and ideas. Why would the mole target him and Alicia anyway? It made no sense at all unless it was part of a broader plan. The only person Travers could think of, who would have a personal axe to grind was Olga Devereux, bribery and corruption being her stock in trade after all. If she had someone on the inside, she would be well aware that she was still under investigation. In that event, she would not hesitate to take steps to derail it. Travers had already made his views known to both Le Sueur and the Director General that he believed that Devereux was behind the current threat to the Government and the recent bombing campaign.

As Travers extrapolated a range of random ideas racing through his mind, his thoughts turned to Andreas Vasilakis. He had tried to kill Alicia twice, on both occasions aided and abetted by the insider who had provided him with details of her location and deactivated the alarm system. Whilst he was an unnaturally brutal killer, he was especially known for his physical strength, first strangling his victims and then snapping their necks as an almost casual afterthought. Travers paused and took another large gulp of Martini. He looked down at the bullet points he had scribbled down until he came to the name Franz Hoffman, followed by a large question mark. Though the German Intelligence officer's killer had still not been officially confirmed, the MO strongly pointed towards Vasilakis as the man responsible. It had always puzzled Travers that Hoffman had apparently been killed by the same man who murdered Claire Powell in Jersey; it couldn't be a coincidence, but what was the connection?

In the dark recesses of his mind, the spectral image of Olga Devereux hovered once more over Travers' subconscious. She coloured his thoughts almost to the point of obsession, and yet…and yet. Travers finished his drink, turned away from his notes on the table and gazed out towards the sea for a few moments. He couldn't get her out of his head.

He stared out through the glass, vacant and without focus, blind to everything that passed his eyes. His analytical, enquiring brain was racing, searching for the thread that would tie everything together and bring order to the confusion around him. All of a sudden, his concentration was broken when he realised that his mobile phone had been ringing for several seconds. It was Alicia.

'Hello Alicia, I'm sorry I was miles away.'

'You ok, Greg? You sound like you've just woken up?'

'No such luck. I've been thinking about our turncoat, trying to reason it out. I don't know. Who is the common denominator, Alicia? Who has been around you, me, Le Sueur, and Franz Hoffman and has access to our files?'

'You heard about MacMillan then?' said Downes.

'Jock? Yes, Le Sueur told me. Ridiculous, that was never going to wash. Someone obviously got to him and set him up. It must be someone who doesn't know him very well. That must be a pretty short list.'

Travers discussed his adventures at Phoenix's winery and his disappointment that Le Sueur hadn't approved his plan to break into the establishment. Downes tried not to dampen Travers' natural enthusiasm, but couldn't hide her amusement at the thought of the still very inexperienced Travers trying to persuade the regimented "by the book" Wing Commander into allowing him to attempt to infiltrate such a potentially dangerous place on his own.

'Anyway, I'll cheer you up now. I was going on a girl's night out tonight,' said a teasing Downes.

'A girl's night out? Really, who with?' said Travers with an air of curious and mildly jealous indignation.

'Your favourite German Fräulein, Christina, and Heidi Buchan. We were going to Visconti's to celebrate Heidi's birthday, but we had to cancel because she's called in sick.'

'Well, I'm sorry to hear that. Have you spoken to her?' asked Travers.

'No, I think someone at Personnel tried to ring but got no reply.'

Perhaps it was nothing more than intuition, or simple gut instinct, that induced Travers to ring Le Sueur after speaking to Alicia. Whoever the guilty party was, they must have had access to Le Sueur's emails to Personnel regarding safe house requests, access to his and Alicia's Personnel Records, and had a connection to the death of Franz Hoffman. He had no evidence or proof, just a feeling, a suspicion, and several unanswered questions. Even though the Wing Commander had only recently taken over the duties of Section Head, she was aware of Travers' reputation amongst his colleagues for his powers of deductive reasoning, and that it was not something to be idly dismissed.

Three hours later, Travers received a reply from Le Sueur. The answers to his questions confirmed his worst suspicions. Until today, the culprit had never crossed his mind. Now it was all too apparent, he chastised himself for not seeing what was now so obvious. Everything fitted together. The results of subsequent security checks that had been immediately instigated by Le Sueur had left the Director General with no choice but to call in the Metropolitan Police, who had raided their apartment, but the bird had already flown. Unwanted clothes were strewn over the bed, and in the fireplace, a large pile of ashes still smouldered. There was no trace of the woman now suspected of being the traitor, Heidi Buchan.

Chapter 20

Travers woke with a start. Usually a good sleeper, last night he tossed and turned, unable to relax and free his mind, which still reverberated with the now-confirmed news that Heidi Buchan had betrayed them. Worse still was the fact that she had absconded, taking whatever secrets she had with her. He stretched out his arm and retrieved his watch from the bedside cabinet. Still half asleep, he struggled to read the watch face. He blinked several times in the hope that it would help him to focus. All he knew for sure was that it was daylight. He sank his head back onto the comfortable white Egyptian cotton-clad pillows for a few minutes, as he waited for his tired brain to check in for the new day. He rolled over onto his side and looked at his watch again. It was 8.10, he flung the duvet out of the way and swung his legs out until he was sitting on the bed. He hated waking up feeling more exhausted than when he went to bed.

He stood up, yawned and walked naked across the floor to the window, looking out across the bay. Yesterday's rather dreary and overcast weather had been replaced with blue skies. Even though the sun was a pale imitation of the one a month ago, it was most welcome. Travers briefly considered going down to the health club for an early morning swim in the pool, before ultimately opting to blast away the cobwebs with a cold shower in his hotel bathroom. After checking his emails and texts, he wandered down for a full English breakfast and a pot of much-needed tea. The restaurant was busy, with both the upper and lower levels well attended. A sure indication that those diners who were about to check out wanted to do so on a full stomach.

Feeling rather more alive than he had done forty-five minutes earlier, Travers returned to his room. A meeting with DI Beckett had been scheduled for 10.30 to discuss the current operation. Travers checked his phone once more for messages before casually tossing it onto the bed and going into the bathroom for a shave. As Sod's law would have it, no sooner had he covered his face with shaving gel than his phone duly rang. He stared at his reflection in the mirror, which betrayed his momentary irritation. For a second or two, he had considered ignoring it. Quickly rinsing off the thick layer of gel, he walked out into the bedroom and picked up his phone. It was Beckett.

'Morning, Dave, what's up?'

'We've got a break. We have had Phoenix's place under surveillance. One of my men spotted someone coming out of the winery; he wasn't a local. We got a picture of him, he had a hat and sunglasses on, but when we enlarged it, well, you can see for yourself.'

Travers opened the email that Beckett had sent him and tapped on the attachment. A second later, the image opened up. It was a clear head and shoulders shot of a man. Much of his face was obscured by an oversized pair of sunglasses. However, the glasses did not cover his ears. Travers could see the deformation of the left ear. It was almost certainly the Neo-Nazi Wilhelm Mainz.

'Well done, Dave, where is he going?'

'It looks like he's just going for a walk, there is not a lot around there other than country lanes, apart from La Place Hotel. Do you think he might be meeting someone there?'

'I doubt it, it's too risky. Still, it does present us with an opportunity to shake Phoenix up a little. I think you should pay him another call, Inspector. After all, a wanted man has been spotted on his property. It's another chance to search the winery, we might be able to have a look in that storeroom,' said Travers.

There was a pause in the conversation as Travers expected there would be.

'We! What do you mean by "we"? If Phoenix sees you there, the game's up. I'm sorry, Greg. This is police business, don't worry, we'll have a good poke around, I'll make sure we look in your storeroom,' said Beckett. 'By the way, I presume you've been told that your Prime Minister is paying us a short visit later today?'

'The Prime Minister, here? No I didn't, shit! What's he coming here for?'

'It's literally a flying visit. There is a two-day conference taking place about new cross-border arrangements for tackling illegal immigrants. The French are sending a delegation over. The Prime Minister is dashing over to press the flesh, fly the flag, and open the conference with some well-chosen motivating flannel, then fly out again.'

'Where is this taking place, Dave?' asked Travers, anxiously.

'Elizabeth Castle, they closed it early yesterday to get ready.'

'That doesn't leave much time for security to nail it down,' said Travers.

'Well, it's basically a civil service junket, rather than an official visit, although the Prime Minister will be met by our Chief Minister initially,' added Beckett.

Following their conversation, the face-to-face meeting they had planned was cancelled. Travers was disappointed that Beckett would not allow him to join the search of the winery. He had it planned perfectly in his head. While the Police were interviewing the blindsided Phoenix, assuming he was there, he could slip in, gain access to the storeroom, root about and then slip out unnoticed. However, he already knew enough to realise that there were also a hundred and one things that could go horribly wrong. Reluctantly, he had to admit that the Detective Inspector was, of course, right. He would have to be patient and wait.

Detective Chief Inspector Deery had heard on the grapevine that a team of officers had been called in to assist MI5. As such, he wasn't surprised when his phone rang and he heard the distinctive and familiar voice of Wing Commander Le Sueur. He had been genuinely surprised at the news concerning Heidi Buchan, having met her on several occasions. He briefly assisted in the financial investigation of Robert MacMillan until he had been cleared. Now it was Buchan's finances that he was delving into. Police had found no relevant documents at her flat. Anything that might have proved useful had probably been reduced to ashes if not removed from the scene at the time of her departure. As for Buchan herself, there was no trace. There was no evidence to suggest that she had an accomplice who had tipped her off; it was more likely that she sensed that the investigation was closing in, and it was time to get out while she could.

Deery's team spent the morning checking the entries on her bank account, savings account and credit cards for any anomalies or unusual activity before expanding the search for accounts hidden offshore or any undeclared investments. The contents of her flat had been examined, with no items of significant value found. Some pieces of jewellery had been left behind, but nothing that would suggest an income beyond her regular salary. Deery sat back in his chair and looked at the preliminary findings of the search. Something was missing; Buchan had no political affiliations and no disciplinary issues at work, so there was no axe to grind. There was just no motive, and you don't commit treason because you are bored. Somewhere down the line, there had to be a payoff. Deery rang the Wing Commander to break the news that, to date, they had found nothing out of the ordinary. He also confirmed that there was a nationwide alert out and an APW [All Ports Warning]. If she showed her face, she would be arrested on the spot.

The police continued the scrutiny of Buchan's finances, going back further and further in the hope of uncovering evidence of wrongdoing. Deery studied the details of her accounts relentlessly, but it was most discouraging. There was nothing on the statements that he hadn't seen a thousand times on other people's accounts. Then his eye was drawn to a seemingly innocuous credit to her account for one pound, presumably, it was a test payment. The reference attached to the credit was McK/Hunt. Deery's nose scented blood at last. McK/Hunt could only be the London-based accountants McKenzie and Hunt. They had been at the centre of the investigation of the William Constable murder.

Constable was an astute and very capable accountant seconded from the Treasury by MI5 earlier in the year and tasked with investigating the accountants who had been suspected of being involved in international money laundering for some time. Constable was murdered during the secondment. To the dismay of the authorities, despite circumstantial evidence, no direct proof could be brought against McKenzie and Hunt to support a successful prosecution.

This was the first real clue, but on searching Buchan's accounts, no further payments of any amount were found. The Chief Inspector was far from discouraged, though. The Constable affair had cost the lives of several of his men, and as far as he was concerned, accounts still had to be settled with McKenzie and Hunt. It was with a heightened degree of relish and determination that he contacted the firm. He would like nothing better than to see the senior partner, Graham McKenzie, in the dock. First, he needed some answers, preferably from someone less disposed to covering their arse and with more scruples than those higher up the tree.

The answers he obtained added more strands to the thread that he was weaving. The test payment found on Buchan's account was to be the precursor to regular payments from an unspecified offshore account, which was subsequently cancelled. The plot thickened considerably when it was disclosed that the originator of the aborted payments plan was none other than Richard Rackman, the former Chief of Staff to Olga Devereux at the Albatross Corporation in Poole. Before Deery could prise any further nuggets of information from the young accountant, the imposing frame of Graham McKenzie appeared.

'I do hope you are not browbeating my staff, Chief Inspector,' said the assertive and rather bombastic McKenzie, who sounded more like a retired Brigadier reliving his parade ground victories. 'I don't like that you know.'

'No, sir, not at all. Your colleague was just helping me with a routine enquiry,' said Deery through gritted teeth. He disliked the man intensely, notwithstanding the suspicions of his involvement in organised crime; he hated the man's air of arrogant superiority.

'In the future, Chief Inspector, if you have any questions, you will speak to me.'

Deery left the building chuntering. Tonight, he would dream of walking back in there and dragging the remonstrating bastard out in leg irons. In the meantime, he had another name on his radar and one that would certainly interest Alicia Downes. She had met Rackman on more than one occasion in the summer during the Constable investigation. After the arrest of his boss and the replacement of the senior management, Rackman had dropped out of sight. At least now, he had some more positive news for Steph Le Sueur.

Milton said, "They also serve who only stand and wait". It had been several hours since his call with Beckett earlier this morning, and Travers had grown tired of waiting. For Travers, no news was bad news. By 11.30, he had had enough. He was a pragmatist of great patience, but hanging around watching the world go by when he really wanted to be at the sharp end, making a difference, was proving taxing. With no word on Mainz, he decided he might as well be outside as in. Deery had spoken to him a little earlier and told him about his run-in with McKenzie and the breakthrough involving Rackman. Alicia Downes was already on the case, trying to locate his present whereabouts. All this activity only increased Travers' sense of inertia and frustration. He left the Hotel entrance and walked towards Liberation Square, which was only a few minutes away.

He sat at one of the seats there and looked around at the comings and goings. As he watched, he could see several police vans driving around. No doubt preparing to look after the coachload of very important "pencil pushers" that were arriving on the Island. He looked across at the Pomme d'Or Hotel; he always enjoyed their Café Bar Club sandwich. He stood up and began to walk towards it. As he did so, his phone rang; it was Detective Beckett.

'Hi Dave, what happened?'

'Well, it's been a busy old morning. We picked up your Jerry and notified the German authorities. I imagine there will be an extradition request landing on our desks pretty soon. He was very chatty for a German. Of course, he wasn't so happy once we told him that there was a European Arrest Warrant out for him.'

'Did he say anything? Where he had been staying?' asked Travers impatiently.

'He had been spotted coming out of the winery. We asked if he was staying with Phoenix. He claimed he didn't know who he was. Then it was just "name, rank and serial number", so to speak, after that.'

'Did you search the winery?'

'Oh yes, I am afraid we found nothing. I spent some time in your storeroom. If there is another door, I didn't find it,' said Beckett. 'Phoenix wasn't too happy about us searching his place, but we took the precaution of getting a warrant just in case.'

'Listen, Greg, there is something else you need to know. I have just had a reported sighting fitting the description of Ali Abadi at St Aubin's Harbour, but we have not been able to confirm it yet. The Harbour Master there is friends with Maria Scholefield. He spotted her talking to a tall, thin Middle Eastern man. He's not absolutely sure, but he remembered the briefing we gave the harbour masters recently when we thought Abadi might be heading our way. I've got officers over there now,' continued Beckett.

It wasn't the news that Travers wanted to hear. The arrest of Mainz was a minor success that would be greeted with delight by their German friends, but unless he had something useful to say, it would remain just that, a minor success. If the Harbour Master was correct and Abadi was on the Island, it could only mean he had unfinished business.

Travers immediately rang Le Sueur to advise her of the news. The phone rang for some time before it was eventually picked up by his former colleague and friend,

Nicky Andrew. She explained that the Wing Commander was in the briefing room watching the newsfeed from Jersey.

'Newsfeed? Of what?' asked Travers.

'The Prime Minister just arrived over there,' she said.

'Sorry, what was that, Nicky? There was a crackle on the line?'

'It's the PM, he has just touched down at the airport there. He's meeting the Chief Minister, then they are getting a Helicopter to the Castle to open the conference,' said Andrew.

All of a sudden, the pieces of the puzzle were dropping into place. Travers ran across to the edge of the Marina to get a better view of Elizabeth Castle.

'Nicky, I need to speak to the Wing Commander right away, it's very urgent,' said an insistent Travers.

Travers watched the amphibious bus as it conveyed some of the conference participants across the bay to Elizabeth Castle.

'Travers! What is it?' said Le Sueur.

'Wing Commander, why didn't you tell me that the Prime Minister was coming here?'

'I'm sorry, Travers, orders from Number Ten, it was the Home Secretary's decision, you know her views on the state of the Deery investigation and now our own internal problem. She felt it was better to leave the matter with the PM's Close Protection team and the local Jersey Police.'

'Ma'am, I am convinced there will be an attack on him today. You must get him to cancel his appearance,' Travers exclaimed.

'He can't, he is already in a meeting with the Chief Minister.'

'Ma'am, remember that list of targets John Deery discovered at the bomber's flat after the Covent Garden bomb was thwarted? I believed the initials referred to places to be targeted. Suppose the last one wasn't a place but a person, ma'am, I think the last target is the Prime Minister.'

'Is this another of your hunches, Travers, because I'll need more than that! You know how image-conscious the PM is. If he cancels this and it turns out to be a false alarm, he will feel publicly humiliated. If that happens, he will have my guts for garters, and as for you, he'll have you booked in for gender reassignment surgery before your feet touch the ground,' said Le Sueur.

'Sorry, but the man's a fool, ma'am. The PM obviously thinks he has 9 lives. By the end of today, he'll be lucky if he still has one!' said an exasperated Travers.

The possibility that Ali Abadi might be on the Island did at least give Le Sueur reason to pause and reconsider, but the Prime Minister wouldn't abort his appearance. Travers rang DI Beckett, but he was unable to provide any further information. The call left Travers feeling frustrated. He didn't have a shred of hard evidence, just instinct supported by a series of theories. He walked back along the promenade, and as he did so, the amphibious vehicle known locally as a duck pulled in after its return trip from the castle.

Two young men jumped out and opened the back of a white van that had just arrived and removed six large crates, which they began loading onto the vehicle. Intrigued, Travers asked one of the men what it was they were carrying.

'Wine mate, gallons of it,' came the reply. 'They're not going to get much done by the time they get through this lot.'

Travers watched as the other man shut the two doors at the back of the van. It was then that he noticed the name written on the doors, Phoenix Wines.

'Phoenix Wines?' queried Travers.

'Yerr he's providing all the wine and mineral water at this jamboree, he'll get some good publicity out of it, I expect.'

'Is he up there now, then?' asked Travers, whose concerns were mounting by the moment.

'I think so. He was certainly there this morning setting up. Do you know him then?'

'Yes, we had drinks a few days ago at the Winery,' said Travers.

Travers quickly called DI Beckett and obtained the necessary authorisation. Following the Inspector's immediate response, the vehicle's driver allowed Travers onto the bus for the short trip across to the Castle. The vehicle trundled off across the sand as it began its journey. Once the sea level caused the wheels to lose traction, the driver engaged the propeller and the bus, now floating, became a veritable ferry, until it reached the far side and the wheels carried the vehicle into the castle via a slipway.

Chapter 21

Travers peered out through the window as the duck passed the mid-17th-century Charles Fort on the right-hand side of the slipway. It stopped in front of the Landward Gate after two police officers flagged it down. Identification and passes were shown, and after a brief exchange of words with the driver, the amphibious bus drove on towards the King William gate, beyond which was the Green or Outer Ward. It was here that the helicopter containing the Chief Minister of Jersey and the Prime Minister was due to land. The two politicians would then walk through the 3rd Gate to the Lower Ward and finally on to the Upper Ward, the highest and most southerly part of the castle, where the conference was to take place.

As the bus continued its passage through the Lower Ward, Travers spotted a group of policemen talking together as they looked west across St Aubin's Bay. He called out to the driver, who pulled over. Slowly, the vehicle came to a stop. Thanking the men for their help, Travers jumped off the bus and walked over to where the three police officers were standing while the bus continued its passage out of sight through the Third Gate and into the Lower Ward.

Introducing himself, he was reassured to discover that two of the men were close colleagues of DI Beckett. According to one of the men, the helicopter was due to arrive on the Green in forty-five minutes. Then, the two ministers would be escorted on foot up to the Upper Ward of the castle and into the former Governor's house, which was to be the setting for the symposium.

As the dialogue with the police officers continued, a few late arrivals hurried past them, clutching their briefcases. Travers turned his head and nodded slightly, as one does when acknowledging strangers or those of short acquaintance. By their conversation, they were French; by their dress, they were bureaucrats. One of them, an impeccably dressed young woman, smiled briefly at Travers as she quickened her pace to keep up with her male colleagues.

Dressed in a smart two-piece "civil service grey" suit offset with a bright pink scarf, she had a jaunty gait that would not have been out of place on a Paris catwalk. His eyes followed her as she walked away. From her dark blonde shoulder-length hair, down her straight back and her slender, well-toned legs to her ankles, which seemed to wobble precariously with every step. Despite being married to a woman who was no slouch when it came to style, he could never understand the appeal of walking on one's toes. He had lost count of the number of times he had walked behind a woman wearing high heels and observed her feet rocking from side to side, and with every step, expecting her to turn an ankle.

Leaving the Police officers, Travers continued to walk along the pathway leading to the Third Gate and the entrance to the Lower Ward. Two more stewards greeted him at the gate and pointed the way to the Upper Ward. As he drew closer, he saw more and more people milling around, mostly chatting and enjoying the fresh autumn air. Wanting to assess the main venue before the arrival of the Prime Minister, Travers wasted no time in walking through the granite-built Iron Gate, the only entrance to the Upper Ward, which contained the oldest part of Elizabeth Castle and was the location of the old Governor's residence.

Passing through the Elizabeth Gate and another set of Police Officers, Travers walked up the wide flight of partially enclosed stone steps leading to the Lower Keep. At the top and to the right, he could see the Governor's large two-storey stone house. Usually, the top floor housed exhibitions whilst the bottom floor was given over to weddings. However, for this occasion, the whole house was to be utilised by the conference.

Travers stood in front of the substantial granite rubble-built building. Approximately eighty feet in length, with seven small windows on the upper floor and six on the ground floor, with an arched double doorway in the centre. The doors were open as both stewards and visitors passed in and out in a constant stream of human traffic. Travers stuck his head through the open doorway and glanced around at the activity inside the room. A large rectangular wooden table and chairs had been positioned in the middle of the room. On the right and left-hand sides of the room were two buffet tables. Stewards were busy putting the finishing touches to the final place settings. Some of those participating had already taken their seats and were either making international small talk or effecting introductions to their international counterparts. Despite the cursory nature of the glance, nothing seemed out of the ordinary.

Travers left the building and walked over to the battlements, and looked out over the wall at the choppy water below. He trusted his instincts, but more importantly, other people trusted them. He turned around, watching the people going in and out of the Governor's house. Nothing seemed wrong, nobody seemed out of place, with everyone going about their prescribed business. Yet his every instinct was screaming apprehension. Perhaps Dave Beckett could offer him the reassurance and the answers he needed.

Detective Inspector Beckett was at Jersey Airport when Travers called him. The Prime Minister had just finished a thirty-minute meeting with the Chief Minister and the pair were shortly to board the Augusta Westland AW109 Helicopter for the short trip to Elizabeth Castle, where they would partake of a short buffet lunch and then offer words of aspiration and appreciation to the assembled audience before returning to Jersey Airport and for the Prime Minister an immediate return to London.

'Dave, why in the world did they pick this place to have their conference? It would have been much easier to lock down a hotel,' asked Travers.

'Look around you, Greg, it's showcasing Jersey's history. This will be all over the news tonight, the executives at Visit Jersey can't believe it, the publicity is pure gold for them,' replied Beckett.

'Well, be careful what you wish for, Dave, I'm still afraid you're going to be on the news tonight, but it might be the headline and not the local news. Any word on Abadi?'

'No, nothing, he's vanished again,' replied Beckett.

'So you haven't been able to positively confirm the sighting?' said a disappointed Travers.

The brief conversation with Beckett had done nothing to relieve Travers of his uneasiness that there would be an attempt on the Prime Minister's life at some point during his visit. Just before he hung up, Beckett confirmed that the helicopter had taken off from the airport, and they would be touching down on the Green in the Outer Ward in a few minutes. He looked up into the cloudless blue sky as he listened for the sound of its approach. Two of the policemen on duty outside the Governor's house came out of the building. They had obviously also been informed that the Ministers were on their way. Travers went over to them. The three men stood and looked north across the Lower Ward to the expanse of green beyond and waited for the first sighting of the helicopter.

Five minutes later, the familiar whir of an approaching helicopter filled the air. Travers watched intently as it drew closer. It hovered for several seconds before slowly descending and landing gently on the grass of the Outer Ward. Thirty seconds later, as the rotor blades slowed, the occupants began disembarking. The Prime Minister, accompanied by his SO1 Specialist Protection Officer and Private Secretary, stepped out, immediately followed by the Chief Minister and her staff, where they were greeted by the Justice and Home Affairs Chief Officer, who was acting as host for the event. The small entourage, accompanied by two police officers, walked through the Third Gate into the Outer Ward. As the party progressed, the Chief Officer gestured towards various buildings, explaining their historical significance. Of particular interest to the Prime Minister was the evidence of German occupation during the Second World War, gun impalements, bunkers and other defensive installations, much of which remains and was being preserved for future generations.

It took a full twenty minutes before the group finally emerged from the stone steps leading from the Elizabeth Gate up to the Inner Ward. Travers observed the Prime Minister closely as he walked past him and into the Governor's house. Although he had not met him before, Travers thought the PM looked tired, as perhaps most Prime Ministers do as they suffer the daily "slings and arrows of outrageous fortune". His eyes bore the tell-tale signs of too many sleepless nights, and his complexion was pallid. He looked drained. This man had more reasons than most to be feeling the strain of office. Politics aside, Travers had some sympathy for the man. As the party went inside, the assembled audience stood and applauded. The Chief Minister and the Prime Minister walked around the large table until they reached their places. The Chief Minister officially welcomed her UK counterpart and the other attendees to Elizabeth Castle, and after a few more well-chosen words, opened the buffet before retaking their seats.

As frequently occurs at such events, there was an immediate scramble to get to the buffet tables and avoid being at the end of a lengthy queue. Travers observed the melee for a few seconds with detached amusement, then turned his focus once more to the object of his attention. The Prime Minister was engaged in an animated conversation with one of the French civil servants sitting on his left. From what Travers could deduce, the conversation was almost entirely one-sided, with the rotund Frenchman, who obviously took his love of French cuisine very seriously, gesticulating wildly with both arms as he made his point to the British Premier. The Prime Minister, to his credit, smiled benevolently as he patiently allowed the man to vent his Gallic frustrations before eventually blowing himself out as he paused to take a much-needed breath, followed by a large gulp of Oswaldo Phoenix's finest white wine.

Travers cast his eyes around the room once more. All the conference participants would have been selected and vetted before arrival, with their identification crosschecked as they entered the castle. He was prepared to take the Chief Minister and her small party on trust, which just left the stewards and the unknown factor, those who may have dodged the police to gain access to the castle. The buffet was proceeding without incident with the attendees, having now returned to the table. Two stewards maintained a roving brief, providing additional wine or water as required. Travers checked his watch; the Prime Minister was due to leave for Jersey Airport in approximately thirty minutes. He walked across to the PM's Specialist Protection Officer, who had been observing the gathering from the corner of the room, which gave him a complete field of view. They exchanged a few words, the SPO's thoughts supported the view that it was just another short unannounced engagement proceeding without alarm, and soon he would be escorting the Prime Minister back to the Airport and onward to the capital. It was a view that Travers was now having a hard time contradicting.

Opening one of the large double doors, Travers stepped outside and walked across to the battlements, where he looked over to the Outer Ward, where the helicopter waited for the signal to start up with the pilot and Police Officers close by. He looked at his watch again; time was nearly up; perhaps it was all in his mind after all. He turned and wandered around the Lower Keep for several minutes. One or two people had come out of the house for a cigarette break. Other than that and the occasional squawking of noisy seagulls, everything was normal. He waved to a young policewoman he had chatted to earlier as they descended the steps down to the Elizabeth Gate. She had revealed to him how excited she was to have been selected to take part in what was her first official visit. Travers then returned to the Governor's house. It was looking more and more as though his instincts had failed him for once.

The Prime Minister was now on his feet, doing what he did best, rallying the troops and energising those around him. Travers looked around the room, all eyes were on the speaker. Travers exchanged an acknowledging glance with the SPO, who was still standing in the corner with his hawk-like eyes watching everyone for the first sign of impropriety. Observing the room closely, everything seemed as it was when he went outside; nothing had changed. It was then that Travers noticed what he presumed was a large case of wine sitting under one of the buffet tables that he didn't remember seeing before. Walking quickly across to the Protection Officer, Travers asked when it had been brought in. The Officer reported that it was carried in by a steward about five minutes ago; he had stopped him and looked in the large box, which had been opened at one end. He pulled out one of the unopened bottles and examined it, then returned it to the box and allowed the steward to continue.

Travers thought for a moment, staring at the box nestling under the table. The buffet was effectively over; why bring in a fresh case of wine? Swiftly, he moved forward, knelt beside the large cardboard box. As the Protection Officer had done earlier, he pulled out a bottle of white wine. The seal was unbroken, he put the bottle to one side and proceeded to remove the bottle next to it. It, too, was an unopened bottle of Phoenix's white wine. He carefully removed the first six bottles. Gently and with extreme caution, he opened the top flaps of the box. As he slowly pulled the cardboard folds apart, he saw at the bottom of the far side of the box several wires connected to what appeared to be a small black box with a red LED light flashing. He waved to the SPO, who came over to where Travers was kneeling.

'We've got to get everyone out of here, now,' said Travers. 'This thing could go off anytime. If this is what I think it is, and it's detonated in this enclosed space, it will kill everyone here. The steward who brought the box in, where did he go?' demanded Travers.

With the immediate evacuation of the Chief Minister, the Prime Minister and all those in attendance underway, Travers quickly left and ran across the Lower Keep and down the wide stone steps leading to Elizabeth Gate. The lower half of the steps was enclosed in a tunnel. As Travers approached the bottom, he saw the legs of a man lying on the ground. When he reached the open gate, he saw the body of a Policeman lying face down in a pool of blood. Kneeling down, he checked for a pulse, but the man was dead. He turned him over to find that he had been shot twice in the chest. Travers looked around for signs of the assailant.

He found three nine-millimetre shell casings on the ground nearby.

If the murderer left via the Iron Gate, which led to the Lower Ward and was the only way out, he would have been faced by additional police officers, who would by this time be fully alerted to the emergency. If it had been a suicide bomber, he would have done the business in front of the PM and ensured the mission's success. No, there had to be an escape plan. As he stood up, he saw a profusion of blood spatters on the ground moving away from the body and in the opposite direction to the Iron Gate.

Travers looked around the curtain wall surrounding the yard, named after Sir Walter Ralegh, one of the former Governors of the castle. On top of the wall in the far corner, Travers saw a small stainless steel hook protruding above the line of the masonry. As he drew closer, he saw two further hooks gripping the inside of the wall and recognised instantly that it was a grappling hook. Attached to it was a nylon rope. Travers looked out over the wall towards Hermitage Rock in the distance. He could see a figure running along the stone breakwater, moving quickly away from the castle.

Without hesitation, Travers climbed over the parapet, gripping the rope tightly with both hands. It was sticky, and there was blood on his fingers, which was trickling down the strands of the rope. He began to lower himself down the wall until his feet touched the rocky and steeply sloping ground at the base of the wall. There, he found the crumpled body of a second police officer. It was the young policewoman he had met earlier. Presumably shot at the same time as her colleague at Elizabeth Gate, she had evidently been giving chase before succumbing to her wound. Rolling her over, he found a single gunshot wound to her neck, which must have nicked the artery. Travers took her bloody hand in his and squeezed it gently as he closed her eyes. She had done her duty to the very end.

He scrambled down the cliff until he reached the enormous and long concrete breakwater constructed to protect the harbour at St Helier over one hundred and fifty years ago. As he ran along the causeway, he temporarily lost sight of his quarry behind Hermitage Rock. As he approached the rock, Travers heard the distinctive sound of an outboard motor being started. Moments later, he saw the suspect emerging from behind the rock, speeding away across the bay heading west in a high-speed inflatable rubber dinghy. Travers swore under his breath as he watched the man disappear. He turned and looked back along the causeway, and the senseless murder of the aspiring young officer angered him. Travers returned his focus to the dinghy speeding away towards the other side of the bay.

DI David Beckett was already aware of the serious incident that had just taken place at Elizabeth Castle when he picked up Travers' urgent call. The dignitaries were already in the air, on their way back to the airport. He would pick Travers up at the Westpark slipway, situated almost opposite the Grand Hotel, as soon as the amphibious Ferry arrived back from the castle. A unit would be dispatched to St Aubin Harbour, where they would try to intercept the suspected assassin as they made landfall. There could now be no doubt that Phoenix was heavily involved and that the evidence was probably hidden somewhere in his winery. With or without Le Sueur's sanction, Travers was going to find out.

Chapter 22

The amphibious ferry had barely entered the water to begin its short journey back to the West Park slipway by the St Helier Esplanade when Travers' phone rang. It was a call that he had anticipated the moment the PM had been evacuated. He knew that MI5 would be monitoring events particularly closely during the current crisis, and it was only a matter of time before he had Le Sueur's voice barking instructions in his ear.

'Travers, what the hell's going on there? The Home Secretary and the Deputy PM have been blasting the Director General's ears, wanting to know what we knew about it.'

'It was Phoenix, ma'am, it had to be. The wine bottles were his, filled with some kind of liquid binary explosive. I'll bet it was PLX, that's Ali Abadi's particular cocktail of choice. He was spotted not far from here recently, it's a regular nest of vipers,' said Travers.

'Alright, Travers, the Director has authorised whatever action is necessary, but make sure you coordinate with Jersey Police, I don't want you running amok, and making matters worse, do I make myself clear?'

'Perfectly, Ma'am,' replied Travers.

It was nice to finally have official approval for something that he was now determined to do anyway. Too many people had paid the ultimate price for trying to stop Phoenix. Travers wiped the condensation from the window and peered through it as the ferry approached the beach. It wasn't a long trip, but it was too long for him as he visualised the killer's high-speed inflatable dinghy crossing the bay and making good their escape long before the police arrived. A few minutes later, the gentle rolling of the ferry through the water stopped as the wheels once more gained the traction of the sand. It would be only a few seconds longer until it reached dry land.

Travers ran across from the now stationary Ferry high on the slipway to the black BMW parked nearby. Standing beside the car, waiting for him was Beckett. As the two men got into the car, the Detective confirmed that police units had arrived on the St Aubin side of the bay. The Harbour Master of the St Aubin marina, who had been asked to look out for any approaching craft, had reported no new arrivals. It seemed obvious to Travers that the murderer would seek a secluded spot to come ashore unobserved rather than risk being spotted. It didn't take Travers long to persuade Beckett to head for the Phoenix residence and the adjoining winery.

Ten minutes later, Beckett's car approached Phoenix's house. Out of sight of the building, Beckett pulled over. They had discussed the plan en route, and despite previous reservations, the events of the day now necessitated direct action. Reluctantly, he now had no other option than to agree to Travers' proposition. Opening the passenger door, Travers stepped out of the car onto a grass verge and watched as Beckett drove on a further twenty yards until he turned into the gravel drive of Phoenix's house and out of view.

The Phoenix Winery was deserted, as it was officially closed during the afternoon. There was a solitary car in the car park. Travers watched carefully for signs of movement. The last thing he needed was to have to circumvent a locked and alarmed building. As he observed the glass-fronted foyer, a man walked through the room, opened the main door and walked out of the building and out of sight. This was the moment he had been waiting for. The door had an automatic closer, if he could just get in before the door shut again! With no sign of the other man, Travers took his chance and ran towards the glass door as it slowly began to close, stepping through and over the threshold just before the heavy door clicked shut. He looked around and, hearing nothing to suggest that there was another person close by, he pressed on.

Remembering his recent wine-tasting visit, Travers walked through the reception area to the function room where the event had taken place, though now devoid of tables and chairs. At the end of the open-ended room was the corridor containing the "magic" room where Wilhelm Mainz had seemingly vanished. Travers looked around anxiously; at any moment, he expected someone to walk around the corner and challenge him. He stood for a moment, trying to compose himself; he could feel the tension in his body. His hands were clammy, and his heart was thumping away in his chest. He thought about Alicia, how could she go through this hell time and again? If she were with him, she would just glare at him and tell him to "grow a pair and get on with it".

Walking along the corridor, he came to the storeroom. Expecting it to be locked, he was surprised when the handle easily turned and the door swung open. He stepped inside and shut the door behind him. On the three other walls were large metal storage units packed from floor to ceiling with a mix of storage boxes, box files, and wine cases. Travers began examining the walls behind the units. Somewhere, there had to be a concealed entrance. The walls on either side of the room proved to be solid. Travers stood for a moment in the centre of the room and thought. He looked at the floor and tapped it with his foot. There were no joins, cracks, or floor coverings; it was exactly what it appeared to be, rock-solid concrete from corner to corner. As his favourite fictional detective, Sherlock Holmes was fond of saying, "Once you have eliminated the impossible, whatever is left, however improbable, must be the answer". The answer to Travers' particular conundrum was now staring him in the face.

Stepping forward, he looked first at the storage unit on the left-hand side of the front wall and ran his hands down its length from top to bottom. It was a bog-standard industrially welded frame. The shelves were also welded. Travers removed some of the cases and examined the wall behind them. Stepping back, he looked at the remaining right-hand unit. As he approached it, he heard footsteps on the tiled floor in the corridor outside. He returned two of the cases of wine to the left-hand shelves and quickly moved behind the door and listened for the footsteps to pass. Holding his breath, he pressed his ear to the door but heard nothing. He froze when he noticed the door handle begin to turn. He edged back as the door opened. Looking down towards the edge of the door, he saw the protruding toes of two black shoes behind it. Travers' whole body was trembling; he could feel the perspiration forming on his brow and could not bring himself to look up. After what seemed like an eternity, the feet disappeared and the door closed. It was then locked.

Travers removed the white cotton handkerchief from the breast pocket of his suit jacket and mopped his brow. As his heart rate slowed, he returned to the right-hand storage unit of the facing wall. The answer must be there; it had to be. There were two cases of wine on the lower shelf. As he had done before, he felt along the length of the metal frame. When he checked the rear of the frame, he finally found what he was hoping for. The rear stanchions of the other frames were secured to the wall, but this one had a hinge running down its length. Travers smiled; the growing tension born of his debut incursion was suddenly replaced, at least momentarily, with self-satisfaction. Finding a small catch on the opposite side of the frame, Travers was able to swing the metal storage unit towards him, revealing the bare wall behind.

This was clearly the site of the concealed entrance. Travers ran his hands over the plaster, looking for anything that might suggest the opening mechanism. When nothing presented itself, he turned his attention to the wooden beading that ran down the walls at regular intervals. It took less than a minute for his fingers to feel the fractionally depressed section, which housed the disguised switch. Depressing it released the panel, revealing the much sought-after secret doorway. Travers stepped through to be faced by a fresh and substantial obstacle, a large locked door. In preparation for his previously aborted plan to break into the winery, Travers had acquired a set of skeleton keys, courtesy of an overnight delivery from MI5; whilst not completely infallible, it would at least give him a decent chance.

He reached into his jacket pocket and pulled out the small bunch of thin stainless steel skeleton keys. Travers looked at the door for a moment, specifically the two locks on either side of the handle, then rifling through the available options, he selected the appropriate one to try first. He delicately inserted the slim lever key into the first lock. As he pushed it further into the mechanism, Travers felt the key bypass the wards until it reached the levers. Gently, he turned the key anti-clockwise; he could feel the bolt withdraw back into the mechanism. Logically, the same key should also unlock the second. Travers took hold of the heavy-duty handle and pushed it down, praying that it wouldn't trigger an alarm. With a slight push, the door opened. Descending in front of him was a steep set of stairs leading to a narrow corridor.

Using the torchlight from his mobile phone, Travers carefully navigated the narrow stairs until he reached the bottom. The walls of the corridor were plastered, with electric light fittings overhead. At the end of the corridor was another door, this time, a solid, heavy-duty steel door. He wished he had a squad of Dave Beckett's men with him as he looked at the door and wondered what might be on the other side, but he could hear nothing through the thick steel. Travers grasped the large steel handle and pulled. The door remained resolutely closed. Once more, he reached for his set of skeletons, but this was no ordinary locked door. He tried the same key that had opened the entrance to the stairs, but to no avail. The successful second key brought about a resounding clang that anybody on the other side must have heard as the heavy bolt slid back. Taking hold of the handle once more, Travers pulled.

Standing in the open doorway, Travers directed his torchlight onto the walls, looking for a light switch. To his surprise, the switch was modern. Now illuminated by LED lighting, it was all becoming clear. The heavy steel door still bore the now-faded swastika emblem. Ahead, the tunnel was wider with additional small rooms branching off it. Unlike the old war tunnels he had visited, these were very much in use, renovated and extended by Phoenix.

Despite the signs of very recent occupation, the complex now appeared deserted. At any moment, he had expected someone to appear from one of the many small rooms that connected to the central tunnel, but nobody did. As Travers continued to move through the tunnel, he saw a great many boxes of various sizes. Opening some, he found large quantities of contraband, including class A drugs, smuggled in through Phoenix's criminal organisation, awaiting onward distribution. Strewn around the area were countless empty boxes and containers.

Progressing through the tunnel, his eye was caught by a long oblong box lying in one of the short empty passages running off the main tunnel. Partially covered by a dark canvas tarpaulin, it was the only item in the room. Travers grabbed one end of the cover and pulled it off, exposing the plain wooden box. The hinged lid was secured by a large padlock, yet there was no indication as to what the contents were. It took only a few seconds for Travers to open the padlock using one of his skeleton keys. Carefully and using both hands, he raised the lid of the box. Inside was a black blanket, which he then removed.

Inside the large vacuum storage bag was the body of Phoenix's mistress, Penelope Papandreou. Her eyes closed, her beauty undiminished. She might have been sleeping, but she wasn't. The bruising still visible around her throat testament to the manner of her passing. Travers wondered if Phoenix would have done the filthy deed himself or had one of his cronies do it. Either way, it was one more death to add to the scales of justice. Travers got his phone out and tried to ring Detective Beckett, who he thought should still be interviewing Phoenix in his house, but with the depth of the tunnel, it was impossible to obtain a signal. Travers replaced the blanket and the lid of the box and decided to continue exploring the tunnel.

As he reached the far end of the tunnel, he found several furnished rooms. Well-appointed, they resembled a good three or four-star hotel suite. Even without windows and natural light, they were spacious and comfortable. Travers walked in; the bed was roughly made up. Checking the wardrobe, he found male clothing hanging up, it was the first evidence he had come across to suggest that the complex was occupied. In the living room, Travers found an ashtray containing the remains of a large cigar. There was also an old copy of Al-Thawra, the Syrian newspaper published by the Socialist Ba'ath Party, the official mouthpiece of the Government. Travers wondered who might have been staying here.

Someone important and someone connected with Phoenix. Beckett had previously received an unconfirmed report that Ali Abadi was in town; he was just the man to prepare the Elizabeth Castle bomb and he would certainly tick all the right boxes. Travers began a thorough search of the suite. Having checked all the drawers in the living room, he returned to the bedroom to check the bedside cabinets, the chest of drawers and the wardrobe, including the clothing.

Travers' progress was brought to an abrupt halt by fast approaching footsteps. Before he had time to react, the tall, willowy figure of Ali Abadi burst into the room. The two men glared at one another for a moment. It was hard to imagine who was more shocked.

'Abadi!' growled Travers angrily as he recalled the face of the young policewoman the Syrian had murdered less than an hour ago.

'Who are you?' demanded Abadi. 'What are you doing here?' He snapped.

Had Travers had a gun, he might well have been tempted to use it there and then and end the matter. Assuming Abadi still had his, it was only a question of time before he used it. Travers reached into his inside jacket pocket, producing the simple wallet enclosing his MI5 credentials and slowly began to walk towards the Arab. If he could just get close enough, he might get the drop on his adversary.

Travers held open his wallet as he stepped closer. He had watched enough old westerns to know that when it came to the fast draw, you watch the other man's eyes. If you wait for his hand to move before you react, you're a dead man. Abadi's eyes were cold and cruel, with no room for sentiment. His attention and curiosity were focused on the small ID in Travers' hand. Then, in a flurry of frantic, spontaneous movement, Travers flicked his wallet into Abadi's face and threw himself at the Syrian. The two men collapsed to the floor, Abadi's 9mm Makarov now in his right hand. Travers grabbed his wrist with both hands and slammed it repeatedly against a table leg, causing Abadi to cry out in pain until the gun dropped onto the floor.

Ali Abadi was a far from impressive physical specimen, a tall, sinewy man whose noxious reputation and notoriety had been nurtured during the Gulf wars. Since then, he had exchanged his religious zeal for life as a salesman, a purveyor dealing in death and terror for anyone willing to pay. Having kicked the gun across the floor and out of Abadi's reach, Travers dragged him up by the collar and sat him on a high-backed upright chair. Without his pistol, the slouching murderer cut a pathetic figure. As Travers looked into his sunken, cold eyes, it sickened him that such a wretched man could have inflicted so much pain and misery on so many people. Travers glanced across at the Russian handgun lying a few feet away. He had never discharged a firearm in anger before, but as he looked down at the man in front of him, there could always be a first time. Travers demanded to know who the Arab was working for, who was his paymaster. Was it Phoenix, or was there someone else?

'Why should I tell you, Englishman?' sneered Abadi.

'You know you've upset a lot of people. Some of them are not quite as squeamish as we are; they've never heard of Human Rights. If you cooperate with us, we might be able to help you; otherwise, we may hand you over to some of our Middle Eastern allies. Who knows where you will end up? It's up to you, but you might want to do yourself a favour.'

The terrorist did not have time to answer Travers' question. A deafening bang ended the one-sided conversation as a significant part of the right side of Abadi's face disintegrated, sending bloody fragments shooting towards Travers, who turned his head away in shock at the ghastly sight. Abadi's body crashed to the floor with blood and brain matter soaking the carpet. Travers looked back at the open doorway, fleetingly, he saw Phoenix. A second later, the door was slammed shut and locked from the outside. Travers picked up Abadi's Makarov and ran to the locked door. It didn't take long to open it, but there was no sign of Phoenix.

Travers ran back along the tunnel, retracing his steps as he followed Phoenix. He couldn't see him, but he could hear both his footsteps and the sounds of objects being thrown down ahead to block or at least delay his pursuit. Despite this, he soon reached the steps leading back up to the storeroom. The door had been shut, and it took several minutes for Travers to find the catch that released the concealed door mechanism. He pushed aside the heavy metal storage unit that stood on the other side of the door. The locked door to the Winery was now wide open. As he ran through the room, there was the whiff of burning in the air.

Oswaldo Phoenix knew that the game was finally up. He had managed to avoid an encounter with Detective Beckett and his penetrating questions and the certainty of being arrested there and then. However, the incriminating contents of his safe would sink not only him but also many others and remove any possibility of a deal being done with the authorities. With the large metal bucket in his office now a mass of smouldering and burning paperwork, Phoenix rifled through his desk drawers for any additional fuel for his impromptu incinerator. As he frantically tried to destroy as much as he could, he looked out from his office door, his nemesis was approaching.

With his gun in his hand, Phoenix ran out of the office and into the winery's fermentation plant. Travers reached the office, the bucket was still smoking with the remains of the papers and other incriminating evidence that Phoenix had tried to destroy. As he neared the area, a single shot rang out, the bullet whistling past him, shattering a pane of glass behind him. Peering around the corner, he looked into the cavernous interior of the winery, dominated by a dozen giant stainless steel fermentation vats resembling vast industrial wheelie bins with gantries running above them, along with endless interconnecting pipes. Somewhere in there, Phoenix was waiting.

Travers was determined to bring his adversary out into the open; at least then, he would know where he was. On the other hand, it risked giving Phoenix a free shot. Picking the closest fermentation tank to him, Travers ran the short distance across the floor, crouching down behind the steel container, he watched for the response that must surely come. He didn't have long to wait. A second and third shot rang out, one ricocheting off the floor close to Travers' feet, the other slamming into the steel tank above his head with a resounding clang. Travers felt an unpleasant wet ooze trickling down his head. Taking his handkerchief, he gently dabbed it. It was dark red. For a moment, he was gripped by the thought that he had been shot in the head until he realised that it was only the product of the macerated red skins contained in the fermentation tank seeping out through the bullet hole in the tank.

This time, Travers had seen the muzzle flashes; Phoenix was on ground level on the opposite side of the room and was repositioning himself. Travers took out the Russian-made Makarov pistol that he had taken from Abadi and ejected the magazine. There were only three rounds left, plus one in the chamber. He flicked the safety catch down and edged forward, quietly stepping towards the other side.

There was a flurry of footsteps, Phoenix was on the move. There were no further shots fired and no sign of Phoenix. Travers decided to climb one of the ladders leading to the gantry. If nothing else, it would give him a commanding view of the area and hopefully a tactical advantage. Once on top of the metal gantry, Travers paused, crouched and waited. From his new vantage point, he could see all the fermentation tanks below. If Phoenix moved, he shouldn't be hard to spot.

It was the slightest of noises, but Travers heard it, somewhere to his left. He rose from his squatted position and, as quietly as he could, walked along the gantry peering over the railings. As he did so, he felt a heavy blow to the back of his head that momentarily stunned him. As he regained his composure, he saw the figure of Oswaldo Phoenix standing over him, gun in hand.

'Well, well, Mr Travers. I am really tired of seeing your face,' said Phoenix with a sigh.

'You murderous bastard, why did you have to kill her?'

'I didn't kill her, you did, the moment you tried to turn her against me.'

'You're finished, Phoenix, give it up now while you can,' said Travers.

'No, Mr Travers, this is one game you are not going to win,' said Phoenix as he raised his gun and pointed it at Travers.

This was only the second time that he had come face to face with his own mortality since he joined the service. The first time was when he faced Hector Devereux on the cliff top at Durdle Door, and then, he was fighting for Alicia. This time it was just mano a mano; there was no one else involved. He watched as Phoenix's finger began to tighten around the trigger.

It wasn't true what they say about one's life flashing through one's mind when facing death. At this moment, Travers had never felt more alive; the only thoughts occupying his mind were how to avoid being shot by a man standing less than two feet away. His only advantage was that he knew Phoenix was not a professional killer. If he had been, he would have finished him off straight away. He was arrogant, conceited, ruthless, callous and a murderer, but not a cold-blooded one and that might make the difference.

'Any last words, Mr Travers?' said Phoenix contemptuously as he pointed the gun at Travers' head.

'You're an idiot, Phoenix. Detective Beckett came with me. Do you really think he wouldn't have heard the gunshots? He's down there now, look.' Travers confidently asserted.

It was the oldest trick in the book, but for an instant, Phoenix was distracted; that instant was all it took. Travers kicked out with his feet, catching his opponent by surprise and knocking him off balance. As he fell, the gun fired off a final round. Travers jumped to his feet and kicked the gun out of Phoenix's hand, sending it clattering along the gantry. The two men wrestled as each tried to gain the upper hand. Finally, Travers punched him in the stomach, followed by an uppercut to the Spaniard's jaw.

As Phoenix staggered backwards, Travers grabbed him by the lapels and, pulling him quickly towards him, threw him over his hip. Phoenix landed heavily on the metal gantry, his head hitting a stanchion. Stunned and semi-conscious, he rolled across the platform until he reached the edge, then with an extravagant plop, he disappeared into the large fermentation vat below. Travers looked over the railing into the vat. There was no sign of Phoenix.

'Checkmate, I believe,' said Travers rhetorically as he looked down into the red morass, with only a few rising bubbles to mark Oswaldo Phoenix's sudden entry.

Several minutes passed. Travers climbed down the ladder from the gantry. As he reached the ground floor, he was relieved to see the Detective Inspector bustling in with several men.

'Greg! Are you alright? We heard gunshots. What's happened, where's Phoenix?'

'Dave, I'm glad to see you. What kept you? I thought you would never get here. Phoenix has been running his criminal organisation right under your nose. In the old war tunnels. Abadi was down there too until Phoenix killed him. I'm afraid I found Penelope Papandreou down there as well; she's dead, another of his victims' said Travers.

'And Phoenix?' asked Beckett.

Travers nodded towards the large stainless steel vats on the left. 'He's over there, in that one, fermenting.'

Chapter 23

It didn't take long for the news of Phoenix's death to reach London. The Director General spoke to the Home Secretary personally as soon as the head of Jersey CID telephoned her at Thames House with the confirmation. In stark contrast with their recent conversations, the Home Secretary was effusive in her praise for everyone involved in the investigation. The Prime Minister was delighted and relieved in equal measure, particularly having avoided a possible assassination attempt a few hours ago. The director promised to convey her thanks and appreciation to her team, although from his point of view, he would rather receive a more tangible token of appreciation courtesy of increased funding from the Treasury.

Greg Travers sat relaxing, looking out of the window of the Grand Hotel's cocktail bar with his third large vodka and lemonade in his hand. It had been a hell of a day; the drama was over, he had provided a full statement to the Jersey police and emailed an update to Wing Commander Le Sueur. Now it was time to kick back and relax for a few hours before the four-hour ferry trip home to Poole and a night in his own bed.

He turned and looked around the room, two middle-aged couples sitting together, tucking into a cream tea, chortling away over something they clearly found highly amusing and a young couple standing by the bar, his only companions. The bar manager, Anabela, who seemed to be permanently on duty, walked up to his table and took away his empty glasses. He would miss her when he returned to the mainland; however busy she was, she always seemed to find time to say hello and have a friendly chat.

Travers reached forward and picked up his half-empty glass of Grey Goose with Lemonade and swirled the slice of lemon round and round before finally taking a sip. As he did so, his mobile rang. It was Le Sueur. He seriously thought about ignoring the call, after all, his job was done, and his preliminary report had been filed. Whatever she wanted, it would keep for a few hours. His finger hovered over the red button for a few seconds before duty prevailed.

'Good afternoon, ma'am.'

'Good afternoon, Travers, congratulations on a job well done. I've just read your report. Putting Phoenix out of business should put a spanner in the offshore smuggling gangs' machinery, at least for a while.'

'Well, if you'll pardon the language, ma'am, the arrogant bastard got exactly what he deserved,' said Travers.

'I've had the Deputy Director on the phone this afternoon promising a commendation,' said Le Sueur. 'It wouldn't surprise me if you weren't invited to Number Ten for a few drinks after this. You've literally saved his bacon. When are you coming back?'

'Well, ma'am, unless you need me back in London straight away, I'm going to get the Ferry to Poole tonight.'

'That's fine, the PM will have to manage without you for a day, report back in 48 hours, and hopefully, we can wrap everything up. You might even bump into Miss Downes and Detective Deery tomorrow, they are down there investigating the whereabouts of Heidi Buchan.'

'Heidi? Why would she be in Poole?' asked Travers.

'We have no reason to think that she is there. Detective Deery found an entry on her bank account statement from McKenzie and Hunt relating to an aborted test payment originated by Richard Rackman, Devereux's former chief of staff. We think it might have been linked to some kind of payoff. Anyway, Rackman is still living in the area; they've gone there to question him,' replied Le Sueur.

Travers finished his drink and waved to Anabela as he left the bar and wandered back up the main staircase to his room to pack. Hopefully, the next time he stayed, it would just be a holiday. He had given some thought to staying another night in Jersey and enjoying a relaxing trip back to the UK tomorrow, but given everything that had happened and with no outstanding commitments on the island, he just wanted to get back home as soon as he could.

After packing his suitcase, Travers walked down to the concierge desk to the left of the main hall, where he thanked them for their usual exemplary service and settled the bill. It was only a short walk to the ferry terminal, but a twenty-minute walk to a ferry terminal carrying a large suitcase didn't have the same appeal as a leisurely twenty-minute stroll in the sunshine. While the concierge ordered a taxi, Travers walked across the hall to the Cocktail bar. He looked across the crowded room towards the bar, hoping to see Anabela one more time to say goodbye, but she wasn't there. Travers waited for a few moments, but she did not appear. Turning away, he looked towards the concierge, catching her eye as she put down her telephone. She called out, "Five minutes". Travers thanked her and, taking his case, stood just outside the door of the hotel entrance and waited for the taxi to arrive.

The trip to the Elizabeth Ferry Terminal took barely five minutes. Out of high season, checking in was a simple and efficient process, having purchased his ticket online this afternoon. The high-speed cruise on the Condor's Trimaran Liberation would cover the hundred or so miles to Poole in a little over four hours. Travers made himself comfortable in the Ocean Club section. The ship would cast off in thirty minutes, he calculated that, provided he could pick up a taxi on arrival in Poole, he should be home before 11 pm.

The four-hour cruise to Poole was restful and uneventful. Travers had always enjoyed sea travel. As he sat back in his luxurious leather reclining seat with a large Vodka and Lemonade in his hand, he closed his eyes and listened to the almost hypnotic rhythm of the engines. The Ocean Club Class section was unusually quiet with surprisingly few occupants. On this occasion, Travers appreciated the absence of the usual excited chatter that accompanies cross-channel ferry travel. It had been an exhausting day, and he was happy to be carried homeward across the gentle swell of the English Channel. As he looked out through the window across the water on the starboard side, everything was dark. The lights from the Channel Islands had long since receded into the night. The only other discernible sources of luminescence were from other ships that were passing in the night. Travers felt his phone in his pocket vibrate. Retrieving it, he saw that it was Alicia calling.

'Hello Alicia, I hear you are back in Poole again, how are things going?'

'Hi Greg, yes, I'm with John, we got down around lunchtime, and we're following up on a couple of leads. Do you remember Richard Rackman? Well, it looks like he's come out from the rock he has been hiding under and is making contact with several key players in the local underworld. One of the local snitches gave us a tip-off, an address here where Rackman has been living, we're going to investigate it now.'

'Le Sueur tells me that he might have been bankrolling Heidi Buchan,' said Travers.

'That's a distinct possibility, if we find him and he has been, he'll wish he'd scuttled back under his rock. What time are you coming back?'

'I'm on my way back now, on the Condor. I should be back oh, 10.15ish then disembark, clear customs and get a taxi home. I should be home before 11.'

'Alright, Greg, call me when you get in, bye for now,' said Alicia as she hung up.

As ten o'clock approached, so too did the lights from the ancient coastal port of Poole. The Liberation entered the channel approach with the Purbeck Hills on the port side and the affluent Sandbanks Peninsula on the starboard. The lights from the famous Haven Hotel, where Guglielmo Marconi developed the wireless telegraph system in the early 20th Century, shone brightly. Those still occupying the hotel's circular bar with its panoramic views across the narrow channel to Shell Bay peered out through the glass and watched the elegant vessel as it slowly sailed into the harbour. Travers left his seat and walked out to the viewing deck at the stern, where he joined several others who were happy to brave the chilly night air to watch the spectacular night time arrival. The Trimaran sailed past Brownsea Island and then straight to the Ferry Terminal. As the ship navigated the narrow, deep-water channel to its destination, Travers looked across to his right. Had it not been dark, he might even have been able to see his house from where he was.

Several taxis lined the entrance of the terminal building, attracted by the prospective business potential offered by so many new arrivals. Travers was soon on his way; in ten minutes, he should be home. Despite his recent move from Wimbledon Village, he felt at home here. The pace was not as frenetic as London, and the outstanding natural beauty that the area offered had seduced him completely during his previous visits. As much as he enjoyed the travel that work often necessitated, he couldn't wait to get back. The taxi pulled up outside his house, and the driver swiftly got out of the car and retrieved Travers' suitcase from the boot. With a cheery wave, the driver returned to his car and quickly drove off, probably to return to the ferry terminal to pick up any stragglers still making their way through customs. Travers walked up to his front door, which was immediately illuminated as the motion sensor tripped. Opening it, he put the hall light on and dropped his suitcase on the floor. He was home at last.

Travers strolled into the living room, putting his keys onto the table along with his MI5 pass. It was the first time in weeks that his mind was not fully occupied with other people's problems. Tonight, he would sleep in his own bed, and tomorrow, well, tomorrow would take care of itself without his help. Turning on a soft table lamp, Travers poured himself a Hendricks and Bitter Lemon and sat down on his sofa. Taking his first sip, all the tension of the previous few days drained away. Travers picked up his phone and rang Alicia, who was staying at a nearby hotel, to confirm his safe arrival.

'Great, I'll see you in about fifteen minutes then,' said Downes.

'Are you bringing John with you?' asked Travers.

'He's just nodded, so I think you'll need to find a couple of glasses for us and a mug of hot chocolate for John. We'll see you soon.'

'Was that nodded or nodded off?' laughed Travers 'Ok, see you both soon.'

He put the phone down on the coffee table next to him and took another large swallow of Gin. On the table was a black and white portrait of his beloved late wife,

Cassandra. It had been almost ten months now since he lost her and set in motion the dramatic roller-coaster of events that followed. Travers did not consider himself particularly spiritual, as much as he tried, it just didn't sit well with his logical and pragmatic mind. However, at their home in Wimbledon Village, there were times following her death when he was convinced he could sense her presence. He couldn't rationally explain it, but it was there nonetheless. He paused for a moment and flared his nostrils. Perhaps it was no more than auto-suggestion or wishful thinking teasing him, but he was sure that he could now detect the merest suspicion of scent in the air, maybe Coco Chanel or possibly Allure? His late wife had loved Chanel. Travers closed his eyes as he savoured the Mandarin and Sandalwood notes and the vivid emotions and memories they stirred.

The illusion was broken when he heard a slight noise behind him. He dismissed the thought that it might be Alicia and John, even the way she drives. Reluctantly, he got to his feet and turned around. Walking towards him out of the shadows was the last person he expected to see.

'Heidi? What the hell are you doing here? You must be mad! How did you get in? Everyone at MI5 and the police is looking for you, you know that,' said Travers.

'I'm sorry, I'm sorry it's you, Greg,' she said with a sincerity that Travers found difficult to accept or understand.

'Sorry! For betraying your colleagues and your country? Heidi, sorry, just doesn't cut it. Do you know how many people died as a result of your actions? There is a prison cell waiting with your name on it. You're going down, and frankly, you should consider yourself lucky that it's not six feet down!'

'No, Greg, you don't understand, I'm sorry for you, I really am,' said Buchan as she produced a small pistol from her coat pocket.

He looked at her in bemusement, a small Glock 19 in her hand. She was a fugitive civil servant, on the run. What was she doing standing in his house, pointing a gun at him? He barely knew her. She turned her head slightly over her right shoulder. Stepping out of the darkness behind her, a hooded figure approached and stood beside her before removing her shawl.

'Good evening, Greg, you have no idea how happy I am to see you again at last.'

The tension that had so swiftly drained away when he got home now hit him with the force of a flood tide. He stood motionless. The glass of gin dropped from his hand, bouncing up on the thick pile carpet before rolling over, spilling its contents. His hands clammy, his heart hammering against his chest, faster and faster with every passing second.

'Olga!' said Travers, trying not to betray through his voice the anxiety that now threatened to overwhelm him.

'Yes, Greg, I told you when we last parted that one day you would look over your shoulder and I would be there.'

'What do you want now, bloody revenge for that psychopathic son of yours?'

'A day doesn't go by that I don't think about him and what you did to him.'

As she spoke, two men quietly emerged from the kitchen behind Travers. Hearing the movement, he wheeled around just as they roughly grabbed his arms and held him in a rigid, vice-like grip.

'Tell me, Olga, it was you behind the bombings in London and the attack on the Prime Minister, wasn't it? Why, if it's me you want?'

'Of course it was, you still don't understand, do you?' said Devereux. 'You murdered my son and tried to destroy my business. That has consequences, consequences for you and everyone else, as you will find out.'

'I presume it was you bankrolling that other slimy toe rag Phoenix over in Jersey?' said Travers.

'He has useful connections I need. When I discovered that the Prime Minister would be in Jersey, it was a simple matter to arrange it. After all, who do you think financed his business operation in the Channel Islands?'

'Well, things have changed. I wouldn't count on him making any more simple arrangements for you,' said Travers.

'You think not? Everything that he now enjoys, he owes to me. Before he met me, he was nothing but a playboy and second-rate smuggler; look at him now,' said Devereux defiantly.

'I guess you haven't heard today's latest news, Olga. There was an accident at his winery today.'

'An accident?' asked Devereux.

'Your poodle, Phoenix, came to a rather sticky end,' said Travers with satisfaction.

'He's dead?'

'Yes, I think this year's vintage will have a little more body in it.'

Travers had no idea what Devereux had in store for him, other than the surety that it would be unpleasant and ultimately, probably fatal. He looked up at the ornate Victorian Skeleton clock on the mantelpiece and thought that it must be at least fifteen minutes since he had spoken to Alicia. He looked back towards his antagonist. In her sixtieth year, she was still disarmingly attractive, with her dark shoulder-length hair, highlighted with streaks of silver grey framing her flawlessly proportioned face perfectly. Even in the subdued lighting, he could see her beautiful violet eyes, encased as they were within a double row of black eyelashes, travelling up and down his body. Six months ago, when they first met, her desire for him was fuelled by corruption, manipulation, and insatiable desire; now it was fed by nothing but vengeance.

Devereux took the pistol that Buchan had been holding and whispered into her ear before kissing her on the cheek. Travers couldn't hear what she'd said. A moment later, Buchan walked towards him. Reaching him, she paused briefly, turned and looked into his eyes, then continued into the kitchen. Devereux took several steps forward until she stood directly in front of her restrained prisoner.

'Are you afraid to die, Greg? Or is it the fear of how it will happen, of suffering in pain, prolonged agonising pain?'

Devereux reached out and gently stroked Travers' right hand with her long, slender fingers. As Travers flinched, Buchan returned and stood once more at Devereux's side, her eyes downcast as though she could not bring herself to look at her former colleague.

'Ah, look what Heidi has found,' said Devereux with a sadistic gleam in her eye.

Travers shrank back as he saw the meat cleaver in Buchan's trembling hand. He wrestled an arm free from one of his captors and lashed out at the man holding his other arm. With a stomach-churning crunch, his clenched fist crashed into the man's nose, causing him to cry out, partly in pain and partly in anger. After a brief scuffle, the other man regained his hold and grabbed Travers in a bear hug that he found impossible to break. Devereux smiled at Travers' instinctive reaction as she stepped back and took the cleaver from Buchan, then pointed towards the dining table. The tall man walked slowly towards it, holding the struggling Travers in his arms, like a sack of potatoes, with his feet well clear of the ground. Then, with a violent throw pushed him hard face down against the table, doubling him over across the French polished surface.

Devereux walked across to the table and nodded to the man standing behind Travers and pinning his arms behind his back. The bruising henchman grabbed Travers' right forearm and extended it outwards across the table and held it there. Travers desperately tried to withdraw the exposed arm, but try as he might, the man held it with such force it was impossible to move. Once more, Devereux leant forward and looked into Travers' eyes, then downward to the table and caressed his exposed wrist gently with her left hand as she held the razor-sharp cleaver in her right.

'You should have stayed behind your computer screen and not interfered. Do you remember what you brought to me on Parkson? Yes, of course you do. Stimulating, isn't it, raw, unfettered terror; because you do remember, don't you, Greg. I've read your file, I know all about you, your wife, and your "long weekend" of alcohol and substance abuse. Oh yes, Miss Buchan has done more than just open a few doors. See where your so-called powers of logic, of deductive reasoning, have finally brought you. Soon you will be nobody's right-hand man,' said Olga, as she gripped Travers' forearm.

'Olga, I called you a depraved bitch when we last met…I did you an injustice. You're actually an evil, sadistic, depraved bitch. Whatever you do to me, your time is running out, you're finished.'

'We shall see.'

Chapter 24

Alicia's black Audi pulled up outside Travers Lilliput's home. She was looking forward to seeing him again. She and Detective Deery had finally caught up with Olga Devereux's former Chief of Staff, Richard Rackman, earlier in the evening. To neither's surprise, he had initially denied any knowledge; however, no one was better equipped to break down a stubbornly resistant suspect than the Detective Chief Inspector. Eventually, the cracks began to appear, and Rackman finally admitted to knowing Heidi Buchan, though he maintained that he had no recent contact and no idea of her present whereabouts.

Downes and Deery approached the front door and rang the bell. Receiving no answer, Deery looked through the windows. The hall light was on, and he was sure he could see another light deeper within the house. Having spoken to him only fifteen minutes ago, Downes had an uneasy feeling that something was wrong. Now he wasn't picking up his phone either, even though they were expected. With an anxious exchange of glances, they walked around to the rear of the property, where they found that the back door was ajar, and the lock broken; it had been forced.

Easing their way through the back door into the kitchen, there were no signs of life; it was quiet, too quiet. Deery called Travers' name several times, but there was no response. Downes was first to reach the living room, where a small red-shaded table lamp still burned. Turning on the main lights, she found Travers' shattered mobile phone and MI5 identification on the badly damaged dining table, both chopped roughly in two. After checking the other ground-floor rooms, Deery joined her at the table and looked down at the two shattered items. As he did so, she turned away and looked around the room. Immediately, she spun back, grabbing Deery's arm. There was a large red stain on the thick grey carpet. Deery looked grimly across at Downes, it was blood and still wet. Downes shuddered and shouted out Greg's name once more before running to the stairs to check the rooms on the upper floor. The Chief Inspector wasted no time in calling the local police and advising Downes not to touch anything.

Downes called Le Sueur in London. Her voice wavering with emotion as she informed the Wing Commander of their grim discovery. Le Sueur was a tough no no-nonsense ex-RAF officer; when she barked, men jumped. In the short time they had worked together, she had developed a growing respect and regard for Travers and his capabilities. Knowing the history between Travers and Devereux, without swift intervention and a lot of luck, the abduction was unlikely to end well. Le Sueur contacted the Deputy Director General with the news that Greg Travers was missing.

Downes and Deery continued to search the house but found nothing. The only crumb of comfort was that they didn't find Travers' body. So, at least for the present, his kidnappers wanted him alive, and whilst there was life, there was hope. It wasn't long before the local Crime Scene Investigating Team arrived dressed in their familiar white suits. With nothing else that Downes and the Inspector could do there, they followed up the only active thread open to them.

Chapter 25

The tyres of Downes's Audi skidded to a halt on the dark, unmade road in the Poole suburb of Parkstone. Moments later, the two black doors swung open. Downes and Detective Deery ran across the road. The thick layer of golden gravel aggregate clawed at their feet like drifting sand as they approached the unlit door in front of them. Two hours earlier, they had visited the same address, where their enquiries were firm but polite; now there was no time for such diplomatic niceties.

Deery hammered on the door, he stepped back for a moment whilst Downes went around to the rear of the property. She returned and shook her head. The Detective stepped forward again and banged on the door. As he waited, he heard two large bolts being withdrawn. The wooden door opened a few inches until a heavy metal chain restrained it. The Detective leaned forward, peered into the gloomy void and called out. His salutation was met by the sudden and startling appearance of two wide-staring eyes looking back through the subdued half-light of the unlit hallway.

'Open up, Rackman, this is DCI Deery, and it's not a social call.'

'You got a warrant, detective?' said the angry respondent.

'Rackman, you've got 5 seconds to open this door, or I'll break it down.'

As the burly policeman braced himself, the door closed, and the chain was removed. A dishevelled Richard Rackman stepped back inside and allowed Deery and Downes to enter.

'I hoped I'd seen the last of you tonight, Inspector. What do you want now?' said the former Albatross Foundation's Chief of Staff, his words slurred by an evening of alcohol abuse.

'Where is he? I want to know what's happened to Greg Travers,' demanded Deery. 'Don't jerk me around, Rackman, I'm not in the mood.'

Rackman turned away and walked across the worn carpeted lounge floor to a dark wooden drinks cabinet where he refilled a large tumbler from a half-empty bottle of cheap whisky. The stench of stale tobacco permeated the air, clinging to every surface.

'Who? I don't know what you're talking about,' said Rackman as he took a large swallow from his glass and staggered slightly as he turned to put his glass down on the nearest table.

'Don't give me that shit, Rackman. Your boss, Olga Devereux, where is she?' said Deery, trying to contain his impatience.

It soon became obvious to both Deery and Downes that Rackman was not only under the influence of half a bottle of whisky but also, after Downes found several lines of white powder concealed on a side table nearby, class-A drugs. The intoxicated and increasingly truculent suspect had fallen a long way, very quickly, since his lofty position as Chief of Staff at the Albatross organisation. In his present condition, Deery knew they would have to spend some time drying him out before they would get much out of him, but time was a luxury they didn't have.

As Deery contacted the local police, Downes' phone rang; it was Steph Le Sueur. Downes turned away from her colleague and walked towards the hall before taking the call.

'Yes, ma'am,' said Downes.

'What's the situation there?' said Le Sueur.

'Detective Deery and I are questioning Richard Rackman. I am not sure how much we'll get out of him tonight, though, he's been hitting the bottle.'

'Time is critical, Miss Downes. I've spoken to the Chief Constable there, the ferry terminal and airport are on full alert, and the Marine Patrol Unit have been notified and will be on the lookout. I have also had a call from pathology; they've tested the patch of blood you found in Travers's house; it's not his blood type. If Rackman knows anything, we need it now,' said Le Sueur.

Downes acknowledged Le Sueur's instructions and the implicit inference that, given the situation's urgency, all reasonable means should be used to persuade the former 1st Lieutenant of Olga Devereux's organisation to tell what he knows.

'That was Le Sueur, the blood we found in Greg's house isn't his.'

Deery smiled at the news as much in relief as anything else. Turning away from Downes, he looked across the room at Rackman, whose right hand, now shaking with the effects of his intoxication, tried to direct the neck of the whisky bottle into his glass once more. Deery walked across and grabbed the bottle, placing it on the sideboard.

'You've had enough, it's time to talk, now where is she?'

Rackman, red-faced and with beads of perspiration forming on his brow, tried to raise the almost empty glass to his lips as he desperately craved the last few drops of alcohol until the detective swooped and slapped the glass from his trembling grasp.

'Where is she, Rackman, and where is Travers? I want answers,' demanded Deery, shaking him by the lapels with such force that the pair almost toppled over. 'What do you think your life will be worth when she finds out you are helping us? You know how she operates better than anyone.'

'Go to hell,' was the curt reply.

Downes stepped forward and stared at Rackman. Before tonight, the last time she had seen him was at Albatross House with Olga Devereux. Then, he was a commanding figure, her Chief of Staff, second only to her eldest son, Hector. Her dramatic fall from grace had tilted his reason and plunged him into a life of depravity. In only a matter of months, alcohol and sustained drug abuse had turned his life upside down. He stood in front of her with an unkempt and straggly beard and shaking hands. As pathetic a figure as he now cut, the recollection of her torture still burned fiercely, and with Greg's fate remaining uncertain, she was not going to be messed with.

'Rackman, you know what your boss and Hector did to me? Help us bring her in, and you may have a chance at a normal life. We can give you a new identity, and you can live on the other side of the planet if you want to. On the other hand, if you don't cooperate, there'll be a press conference tomorrow morning, and we'll tell the world that you have turned King's Evidence in exchange for immunity. With what you know, how long do you think you'll last then? Think about that.'

The bedraggled man didn't reply. He looked up at Deery for a moment, then half-turned and shuffled backwards before falling into an armchair. For a minute, he sat almost motionless with his hands resting on the arms of the leather chair. Deery and Downes watched as his drug-infused brain wrestled with the dilemma that had been put to him. Even in his debilitated state, he knew that Downes was right. If Olga even suspected betrayal, he was finished. It wouldn't make any difference if he cooperated with the authorities. The merest suggestion of collaboration would be a death sentence. Slowly, he raised his head and looked up at Downes.

'I told you, I don't know where she is now. After Hector died, the only thing that she spoke about was revenge.' There was a moment's pause as Rackman let out a long sigh as he gathered his thoughts. 'Your man, Travers, I don't know him, but I know she could have had him killed anytime but that's not what she wants. For Olga, it's deeply personal, she holds him responsible for Hector's death. He has to suffer. They've been watching him for some time, Buchan told me Olga planned to snatch him when he left Jersey. I don't know where they are taking him except that it's probably outside the UK.'

'Offshore?' barked Deery 'How, by sea or air?'

'Boat, I think,' said Rackman. 'I don't know the details.'

'You'd better not be bullshitting me Rackman, or I'll bloody hang you out to dry,' said Deery as he reached for his phone.

Ten minutes later, Rackman was bundled into the back of a police car, while officers began a thorough search of his house. Deery hoped that the once efficient and organised senior manager's descent into a life of substance abuse would make him careless. The Chief Inspector and Alicia Downes returned to their car and sped away, sending a shower of gravel into the air behind them as the spinning tyres searched for traction. With no further news, they headed for the Ferry Terminal Building, where the Poole Border Force was based. Border Force Poole and the Marine Police had already been scrambled and were about to start sweeping the harbour.

Greg Travers slowly opened his eyes, everything was blurred; he could see nothing but white. As his senses slowly returned, he rolled his head to one side of the pillow that his head had been plunged into. He tried to move his arms but found them tightly bound at the wrists behind his back. Travers swung his legs to the side of the wooden single bed he had been unceremoniously thrown on earlier and sat up. He looked around at his dimly lit surroundings. A small brass nightlight on a chrome side table revealed a partially covered porthole on the opposite wall, the reverberation of a powerful engine beneath him, that he was at sea, underway, and cruising at a high rate of knots. Standing up, he walked across the small cabin until he reached the porthole. Nudging the curtain to one side with his head, he peered through the glass into the darkness. There were no lights from the shore and no moonlight. He had no idea where he was or how long he had been unconscious.

Travers flexed his aching wrists; they were sore and bleeding. The wire used to restrain him had dug deeply into his skin, and every movement hurt. He glanced around the cabin for anything that might potentially be of use. Even a pair of nail scissors might be enough. Squatting down beside a small cabinet, he managed to pull one of the doors open with his teeth, but sank to his knees in disappointment when the cupboard was empty. Not even a complimentary set of wire cutters, he mused. He returned to the bed. The last thing he remembered before waking up was the sight of Olga Devereux, holding his meat cleaver and running it deftly across his right wrist as she gazed into his eyes. He was convinced that she intended to extract her pound of flesh literally. His mind flashed back to the moment on Durdle

Door when he severed Hector's hand and sent him plunging to his death into the water below as he rescued Alicia Downes. There was no denying the fear that gripped his whole body. Olga could see it in his eyes, she revelled in the terror she instilled. Then there was a sharp blow on his head, and everything went dark. As Travers sat on the edge of the bed, he stretched his tightly bound hands once more, until the thin wire cutting into his skin caused him to wince with pain. As the discomfort subsided, it was replaced by pins and needles, he flexed his fingers to improve the circulation.

Travers looked around the small but well-presented wood-panelled cabin, but until he could free himself, there was no prospect of escape. He lay back, flat on the bed, then raised his legs towards the ceiling. With some difficulty and much wiggling, he managed to ease his bound wrists over his backside and behind his raised thighs. Drawing his knees deeply into his chest, Travers slid his arms over his feet. At least he could now see the manner of his confinement. Standing up, he walked across to one of the two small portholes and pulled the curtain back. He could see nothing, not a glimmer of moonlight to puncture the shield of darkness that concealed his passage. Travers checked his watch; it was approaching midnight. Alicia and John Deery were due at his house shortly after he was taken. Surely the authorities must have been alerted by now and a search instigated, but where were they to start looking? He could be anywhere. He turned away from the porthole and walked to the cabin door. Gently, he turned the handle, but the door was locked. Travers put his ear to it; footsteps were coming closer, and then he heard the rattle of a key being inserted into the lock of his door. He stepped back.

The door swung open, and a burly, heavy-set man walked in and roughly pushed Travers in the chest, forcing him to step backwards. Travers allowed himself the briefest of smiles as he looked at the disfigured and heavily bruised nose of the man he had punched during his forced abduction earlier. He considered a sardonic comment but, under the circumstances, thought better of it. As the man glared at him, a woman with dark auburn hair walked through the open doorway, brushing past him. It was the traitor Heidi Buchan.

'So, all the rats are on board, I see?' said Travers disdainfully.

'I'm sorry, Greg, I didn't think it would end this way.'

'Speaking of rats, is your paymaster on board too?'

'If you mean Olga, no. Mrs Devereux's gone on ahead,' said Buchan.

'Really? I'm surprised. I thought she would have wanted to be here, if only to ensure that I was properly weighted down when I was thrown over the side. Anyway, what am I doing here, and where are we heading?'

'You'll find out later,' answered Buchan, who turned to leave. Travers stepped forward as though to follow her until the guard interceded and blocked his path.

'Heidi, can you at least take this off, after all, where can I go?' said Travers, raising his tightly bound wrists towards her. She paused, and there was a momentary flash of compassion in her eyes. She looked at the guard standing beside her, his cold, menacing stare forestalled any request she may have considered. She apologised and turning away, walked out.

As she left, the disfigured guard stepped forward and punched Travers powerfully in the solar plexus. Travers grunted and dropped onto his hands and knees. Severely winded, he gasped for breath. He looked up, fighting for breath, just as the man followed up with a swinging right boot at Travers's head, sending him crashing into the corner of the room. The laughing thug smirked, then turned and left the cabin as a bloodied Travers scrambled to his feet, wiping the trickling blood from his lip with the back of his hand. He flopped back onto the small bed as his strength and wits returned. He tried to rationalise his predicament, as problematic and uncomfortable as it was, at least with Devereux not on board, he felt he was safe, for the time being at least. She would want to be in on the kill. Whilst they were at sea, he still had a chance, of sorts.

Deery paced anxiously around the Poole Harbour Control room. The Police were sweeping the harbour as they regularly did, but no unusual activity had been reported. The night had turned colder with a chilly north-easterly breeze rippling the water and the rigging of the yachts gently swaying by their moorings. There was still nothing definite on the whereabouts of Greg Travers, only the rather nebulous suggestion from a half-cut Richard Rackman that he may have been smuggled offshore. Was it true or just misdirection to give his former boss more time to evade the authorities? The frustrated detective knew full well that the harbour authorities knew their business. Apart from the harbour patrols, they had the latest marine monitoring technology, including radar, CCTV and the automatic identification system AIS 3D.

'You're absolutely sure nothing's slipped out tonight', said Deery to the duty officer.

'Yes, sir, the only ship that's left port tonight was the Ra,' said the young officer.

'The Ra, what's that?' asked Deery.

'It's a luxury cabin cruiser, a big one, over 50 meters,' came the reply. 'It's been here a week. It weighed anchor about 40 minutes ago,' he continued.

'40 minutes you say? Do you know who owns it?

The young man took a moment to check a database, while Deery hovered behind him, rattling the small change in his trouser pocket as he waited impatiently for the answer.

It didn't take long before the answer was forthcoming. The Ra was registered in the Cayman Islands two years ago and owned by a private equity company based in George Town. Deery rubbed his now furrowed brow before re-engaging in the conversation with the officer.

'So, no red flags.'

'Sorry, Chief Inspector, everything has been done by the book. Notice for departure was given 30 minutes before she sailed, we had them on our radar all the way along the Swash channel and out of the harbour,' said the Officer. 'She paused briefly in Bournemouth Bay before picking up speed and heading out into the channel.'

Deery shook his head, walked towards the window, and stared into the gloom. The answer was out there somewhere; it had to be.

Deery and Downes walked back to their car. There was still no news of Travers. The harbour patrols hadn't reported any unusual activity, and Bournemouth International Airport was locked down tight. If Rackman had lied, and Devereux was still at large, she could be anywhere in Dorset by now or even further afield. No, the more Deery thought about it, the more he was convinced that the information he had been given was true. He didn't trust Devereux's former Chief of Staff, but in this instance, he had Rackman by the "short and curlies", and Rackman knew it. The now dissolute figure had been Devereux's Mr Fix-it for years. If a whiff of his complicity got back to her, he was a dead man. The Chief Inspector sat back in his seat, if it was anyone other than Travers who had disappeared, he would be able to call on his friend, who would no doubt point out something blindingly obvious that, despite his many years of crime fighting, had escaped him.

Deery's phone rang. The local police were still questioning Rackman, who steadfastly maintained that he didn't know where Devereux was. He turned to Downes.

'Alicia, get onto the Cayman Islands Ship Registry Head Office, that luxury cabin cruiser that's just left port, the Ra. I want to know if there is a connection, anything! Get me some names, the owners and senior officers of the company and anything else you can find out about it, and quickly, Alicia. If you need to pull a few favours or strings, do it.'

'Do you think Greg may be on board her John?' asked Downes.

'Well, the harbour police and the Harbour Commissioners have drawn a blank so far. The only vessel that's left Poole Harbour tonight is the Ra. She's currently heading south into the channel. I don't know, it may just be a coincidence, but after leaving the harbour, she paused in the bay for ten minutes before getting underway again,' said Deery.

'She could have stopped to make a pickup?' said Downes pointedly.

'It's possible, but at the moment we've no evidence at all, not even a reasonable suspicion. Let's get back to the Station, get on to the Cayman Registry, and see what you can find out.'

The police station was quiet as the Chief Inspector and Downes walked through the door and approached the desk. The duty sergeant put a file he had been reading to one side and looked up as Deery presented his warrant card. With the introductions completed, the sergeant led the couple into one of the back offices where Downes sat down and booted up her laptop. Deery left her to it as he walked out of the room to discuss the ongoing interrogation of Rackman with the local detectives. On his return, he found Downes busy printing off several sheets of a report.

'Any luck, Alicia?' asked Deery.

'Fortunately, MI6 has someone onsite there, so it wasn't a problem despite the time frame. We've got the names, but what I think is more interesting is that the Cayman Islands authorities have on several occasions had cause to investigate the equity company following complaints of sharp practice,' said Downes with satisfaction that was quickly mirrored by the approving expression on Detective Deery's face.

'Well done, Alicia, now let's see if our friend Rackman knows any of these people. Check your files and see if there is any connection between these names and the Albatross organisation, any link at all,' said Deery as he took a copy of the paper containing the details from Downes and left the room.

Richard Rackman sat motionless in the interview room, beside him, the duty solicitor. It hadn't surprised anyone that he'd had waived his rights to call his own or the Albatross's former legal representatives. The last thing he wanted was to advertise to the outside world that he was being questioned by the police. He reached out and grabbed a cup of black coffee that had been provided for him. He drank most of it in one unsavoury gulp, what missed his mouth, dribbled down the front of his bewhiskered chin. Deery studied him closely; his face was flush with the effects of his substance abuse, and his eyes were puffy and bloodshot. The dishevelled beard was now home to the remnants of his coffee as well as all manner of food particles and god knows what else. It seemed impossible to believe that less than six months ago, this man had his finger on the pulse of a multi-billion-pound business empire that stretched around the globe. Deery took the folded paper from his jacket pocket and slid it across the table in front of Rackman, who peered down at it, his eyes squinting as he struggled to focus on the printed names. Deery watched his face for the slightest flicker of recognition.

'Well? Do you know any of them?' asked Deery.

'No, should I?' grunted Rackman, glancing again at the names.

Deery grimaced. It had been a couple of hours since Alicia Downes spoke to Travers on the phone to arrange a meeting following his late-night return from Jersey. When they arrived, all they found at his Lilliput house were signs of a struggle, blood stains, his shattered phone and MI5 identification. Travers had been abducted, but by whom? The only logical suspect was Olga Devereux or someone acting for her, but if she was involved, with her contacts, she could have gone anywhere and at this moment, they had no leads at all. The frustrated detective stood up and leaned across the table, then slammed his right hand down on the sheet of A4 paper with such force that the cup of coffee in front of Rackman jumped up, spilling the remains of the drink on the table. The solicitor glared at the impatient detective before reproaching him for his conduct. Deery acknowledged his overbearing approach and nodded at the legal counsel before once more turning his attention to Rackman.

'Look again! You were responsible for overseeing all the Albatross's activities and assets, weren't you? So again I ask you, do you recognise any of those names?

'I'm telling you, Inspector, I don't know any of them.'

'What about the Ra, the luxury cruiser that left Poole tonight? Is that one of hers?'

'I don't know anything about it,' said Rackman, whose mounting irritation with the detective was growing by the moment, amplified by the effects of the night's drinking.

Deery's phone began vibrating on the table. It was Alicia Downes. He paused the recording of the interview and excused himself, leaving the room, phone in hand.

'Alicia, what have you got for me?'

'A breakthrough, John, concerning the Ra. The private equity firm that owns it is a subsidiary of an American company based in Key West, Cassa Marina Holdings,' said Downes.

'I'm listening, what else? Said Deery.

'The majority shareholder and chief Executive of Cassa Marina Holdings is Christian Devereux.'

'Jesus Christ! Olga's bloody son. Well done, Alicia' said the triumphant detective.

Chapter 26

The lights were burning brightly in Thames House, the headquarters of MI5, the Security Service. Steph Le Sueur, head of Serious Crime, had returned to the Millbank building as soon as she received word from Downes that Travers had been abducted. Recruited by the Security Service after a glittering flying career in the RAF, Le Sueur's dedication to duty was absolute.

Now, with a man down, she wouldn't rest until she got him back. After thwarting the assassination attempt on the Prime Minister in Jersey, Travers's name had featured prominently in various departmental reports. Even the Home Secretary, who had crossed swords with Travers at a briefing during the recent crisis, had suggested some commendation. Le Sueur stood next to a large high-definition monitor in the Situation Room. Her dark blonde hair cascaded across her shoulders onto a white cashmere polo neck jumper. Following Downes's call, she wasted no time returning home to change out of the jumper and pale blue jeans that she had been wearing into more formal attire, but she headed immediately to Thames House.

Le Sueur watched as a succession of images was brought up onto the various screens, including the live feed from the Poole Harbour Commissioners CCTV coverage. From the Situation Room, Le Sueur and her team could coordinate the hunt for Travers in real-time. Poole traffic cameras had been unable to detect any suspicious activity around Travers's home location from the time of his abduction. However, following the request from Downes for information regarding the cruiser Ra and her ownership, the focus had now shifted. All eyes were now looking seaward, and the luxury vessel heading across the channel. As Le Sueur collated the latest batch of incoming intelligence, her mobile rang. It was Downes, she confirmed that Border Force was now in pursuit of the Ra, having despatched a cutter from Poole, and the JMSC had also launched a helicopter and were liaising with Border Force and the police. Downes continued with her report until Le Sueur was interrupted by one of her team with fresh information on the progress of the fleeing craft.

'Ma'am, the Ra has changed course and increased speed; she's now heading southwest, towards the Celtic Sea.'

'Thank you,' said Le Sueur, offering a polite smile towards her colleague, before returning to her phone call 'Did you hear that, Downes, it looked like she was heading for France. Well, the fox has decided to make a run for it. The chase is on. I've spoken to the Maritime Gendarmerie at Cherbourg, they are going to intercept the Ra from their end,' said Le Sueur.

Downes did not doubt that the authorities would apprehend the Ra at some point during the early hours of the night. Although it was a fast modern cruiser, it would be no match for the combined Border Force and French marine units approaching it, and it wouldn't be long before visual contact was made by search aircraft. Her conversation with the Wing Commander had done nothing to reassure her that there was a coherent plan to rescue Travers beyond simply stopping the Ra, assuming he was on board. At this point, whoever reached the Ra first was ordered to stop and search the vessel. The Captain and crew were hardly likely to admit to holding him on board and risk immediate arrest and the seizure of the vessel. Downes walked back to their makeshift office, where DCI Deery was deep in conversation with his colleagues.

'Any more news, Alicia?' asked Deery.

'Not much, John, the French have put to sea from Cherbourg with orders to locate and stop the Ra. What if they reach it before we do? If they go storming in at night, it could get Greg killed.'

It was a tricky problem. If the Ra knew she was being pursued by the UK authorities, it would be impossible to stop her on any pretext without giving the game away. Deery paused, his brow furrowed as he wrestled with the dilemma.

'Suppose, we send out a general distress message about a man overboard near her position, they would have to stop and conduct a search, wouldn't they?' questioned Deery.

'Oh come on, John, really? Said Downes sarcastically. 'It's pitch dark out there, and in any case, they are not going to stop or slow down to search for someone, are they? The best chance is that the Ra enters French territorial waters and they are stopped by the French for a random customs inspection. At least that's plausible, and if we are really lucky, the Ra may fall for it,' said Downes as she reached for her mobile phone.

'Who are you calling?' asked Deery.

'Wing Commander Le Sueur, I want to know what they are going to do,' replied Downes.

Deery sat at a desk in the small room at the station that had become the local nerve centre of tonight's operation. He twiddled the teaspoon, standing in a fresh mug of strong tea that had just been brought in for him. He stirred it repeatedly first anti-clockwise, then clockwise, then anti-clockwise again before putting the spoon down on the table and taking a small sip of the steaming drink. He was restless and frustrated, he felt useless. All the action was going on in the channel. What he wanted was to be on the pursuing border force ship, "cutlass in hand", preparing to board the

Ra. Instead, he was sitting in an office waiting for news. He looked at his watch for the umpteenth time, it had just passed 2 am, then stirred his mug again. The powers that be had decided that the operation would be conducted at first light. The French and UK authorities were tracking the Ra on radar as she maintained her south-westerly course. He took another swallow of tea, then stood up and walked out into the corridor. Looking out through a window, he caught sight of Downes standing outside.

'Can I join you?' asked the detective as he stepped out of the doorway into the cold night air. The moisture from his breath billowed in the frigid atmosphere, he should have brought his coat.

'Hi, John. I wish I were out there,' she said, nodding into the distance.

'Yes, me too. I hate sitting on my arse, just waiting. Shit, it's going to be a long night, and a fucking cold one.'

Downes casually glanced across at Deery and smiled. The detective, catching her eye, chuckled momentarily and apologised for his bad language.

'Sorry, Alicia, I know I shouldn't.'

Downes laughed. Industrial language didn't bother her now; she had learned to live with it. Working undercover, language and a broad vocabulary were part of her stock in trade. When the circumstances required it, she could mix it with anybody. Downes had often wondered what her old English tutor at Marlborough College would think of her choice of career. Who would have guessed that all those countless hours spent studying speech and drama and innumerable role plays would have proved to be such invaluable preparation for her working life? However, that was many years ago. Now, her mind was focused on just one thing, the Ra, moving away from home shores and suspected to be carrying with it the man who had saved her life only a few months ago. Detective Deery was right; it was going to be a long night.

Just before 8 am, the sun began to rise over the stern of the Ra as she continued on her south-westerly course passed the North-West coast of France. It was a cold, drizzly and heavily overcast day with a rising swell driven by a stiff North East wind. Even the seagulls found the weather too inclement to venture out for long, before heading south for the mainland and shelter. It had been an uncomfortable night for Greg Travers, the cabin he was in was spartanly furnished, and presumably, it had been one of the crew's cabins. Apart from his increasingly sore wrists, his chest now hurt like hell, the result of the punch from one of his captors; his ribs were tender, either bruised or possibly cracked. Added to this, the constant rumble of the engines had prevented him from even thinking of being able to sleep. The dawning of the new day also reminded him that he was still the victim of a violent abduction. Yet over eight hours had passed, and nothing had happened to suggest that the perpetrators were in the least bit concerned that the authorities were on to them.

Travers swung his legs off the single bed, stood up and walked across to one of the portholes. Looking out, all he could see were grey leaden skies as the waves continually crashed onto the ship, sending sea spray cascading over his small glass window onto the outside world. In the distance, a fully loaded container ship is heading away in the opposite direction. As he stepped away from the window, he heard footsteps, then the sound of a key being inserted into the lock of his door. A moment later, it swung open. It was Heidi Buchan, with a tray of food and a drink. At the entrance was Karl Balakin, the brutish Russian thug who had given Travers his working over earlier. With the pain every breath was causing him, Travers was not displeased to see that

Balakin was now sporting two black eyes to go with his deep purple and very broken nose. Seeing Travers's amusement at his disfigurement, he growled menacingly and stepped forward to administer another malevolent blow to his captive. Buchan stepped across and suddenly raised her arm across the Russian's chest in admonishment.

'No, Karl, wait outside please, but leave the door open,' said Buchan. He glared at Travers for a moment, then reluctantly left the couple alone and stood in the corridor, though his eyes never left the British man.

Buchan put the small tray down onto a wooden bedside table. Travers stretched out his still-bound hands to pick up the mug of hot tea, wincing as the sharp nylon bit into his severely bruised wrists. Buchan looked down sympathetically, then, glancing over her shoulder, adjusted her position slightly to block Balakin's view of Travers from the open doorway. Leaning over slightly, Buchan carefully began cutting the nylon wire until the last bloodied strands were painfully removed from Travers's wrists. Gingerly, he began flexing his hands and fingers.

'Thank you, Heidi,' said Travers. 'Are you going to tell me where we are heading now?'

'North Africa, Casablanca to be exact. We should arrive late tomorrow evening,' she whispered.

'Casablanca?' said Travers with surprise. 'Your boss must really enjoy my company. To be honest, I was expecting a very short trip down to Davy Jones's locker,' said Travers. 'Casablanca, is that where she is?'

'Yes, I think she has a very important meeting there in a few days.' Buchan furtively looked around; to her relief, Balakin was fully occupied talking to another member of the crew and appeared to have little interest in their conversation.

It had quickly become apparent to Travers that away from her confederates, Buchan was more sympathetic, not only to his immediate plight but also more willing to talk and perhaps, reveal details of Olga Devereux's plans. There was no doubting her guilt. Her betrayal had cost lives and put others at risk. At some point, there would be a reckoning, but more immediately, Travers's only thought was staying alive and extracting as much helpful information out of her as he could.

'Why on earth did you get yourself mixed up in all this?' asked Travers.

Buchan paused for a moment, her eyes downcast. Travers peered around her body to the open door. Balakin was still chatting. He looked back at Buchan as her eyes met his once more.

'My parents' business was in trouble, they owed so much money that they were about to lose everything. I tried to help, I borrowed money, then more money, until I couldn't afford the repayments and got into terrible financial trouble. I thought I would lose my job. Then, one day, I met a man who said he knew someone who would be able to help. They offered to buy my parents' business and clear my debts,' said Buchan in a hushed voice.

'And in return? All you had to do was feed them information now and again,

Is that it?'

'Yes, I never dreamed it would lead to this, but I was desperate.'

It was hard for Travers not to feel a degree of sympathy for Buchan. He knew first-hand from his own experience with Olga Devereux how easy it was for a vulnerable person to be manipulated by an expert.

'Where did you meet this person?' asked Travers.

'In the restaurant.'

'Which restaurant, what's the name?' said Travers.

'Our restaurant,' replied Buchan.

'You mean our restaurant? In Thames House? Bloody Hell! What was this person's name,' queried Travers, whose voice had now attracted the unwanted attention of his overseer in the corridor, who walked back into the room, prompting Buchan to stop talking.

'Thank you for the tea,' said Travers, as Buchan and her unwelcome chaperone left the room. Their departure was immediately followed by the rattle of a key in the mortice lock of his door. Travers sat back on the simple single bed and thought about what Buchan told him. She seemed genuinely remorseful, but what she had done could not be undone. Buchan stood accused of treason, and should she be caught, the penalty would be severe. Even turning states evidence and throwing herself at the mercy of the court might not be enough to save her.

Chapter 27

On the bridge of the Ra, the relaxed early morning mood had changed. Captain Samuels and his Navigating Officer were hunched over the Ra's radar display, whilst the First Officer was outside scanning the horizon off the port quarter with a powerful pair of Steiner Marine binoculars. Visibility was poor with grey overcast skies and a constant fret coming off the heavy seas. The horizon was no more than three miles away, but the chances of seeing a vessel at half that distance were almost zero. The first officer returned to the bridge, removing his wet coat and shaking the excess water onto the wooden floor. The Captain looked around.

'Anything?'

'No, sir, but visibility is probably no more than a thousand yards,' said the officer.

As Captain Samuels returned to study the radar screen, two men joined the officers on the Ra's bridge. Ricardo Vargas and Alec Mason, both henchmen of Mrs Devereux, were not people to be trifled with. Vargas, in particular, had a well-deserved reputation as a ruthless operator earned from his dealings in the South American drugs trade. Tall and muscular with a large scar running down his right cheek and a dark, drooping moustache that matched his hair, he bristled with restrained anger that he frequently unleashed on anyone who crossed him.

'What is it, Captain?' asked Vargas.

'We've got a contact on our radar, it's about ten miles astern, it's a French coastal patrol boat. It's been tracking us for several hours now,' said the Captain.

Vargas walked across and leaned over the shoulder of the officer watching the flickering screen as it updated.

'Could it be a coincidence?' he asked.

'It's possible, they have maintained the same position relative to us, and they have not attempted to make contact,' said Samuels.

'Do they know who we are?' asked Vargas.

'No, sir, the Automatic Identification System and transponder were switched off when we left Poole,' said Captain Samuels.

'All right, Captain, if there is any change, let me know at once,' said Vargas, who then turned and, accompanied by his associate Mason, left the bridge and returned to the luxurious lounge where Buchan joined them. So far, the trip from Poole had proved uneventful. Even the foul weather had not derailed the journey. There were no indications that the British authorities were on to them, and their French shadow could be just a routine patrol, unrelated to them. Vargus and Mason sat down as Buchan brought over two mugs of tea.

'How is our passenger today?' asked Vargas glibly.

'He's all right, no thanks to Karl. What's going to happen to him?' asked Buchan.

'My instructions are to deliver him to Olga, preferably alive... but if we have a problem with the police en route, he's not to be found on board,' said Vargas, who did not attempt to conceal a naturally cruel sneer of pleasure at the thought of disposing of their unwelcome guest.

Buchan returned to the galley and came back a few minutes later with a black coffee and rejoined the men. Apart from her relationship with Olga Devereux, something that she now bitterly regretted, she despised the people with whom she now found herself working. They were almost without exception beneath contempt. Although employed by the Devereux family, the officers and crew of the Ra treated her with respect and courtesy. As for the others, Karl Balakin was nothing more than a thug for hire, an enforcer who enjoyed violence for its own sake. Vargas was the brains, with underworld connections and numerous corrupt politicians in South America that he exploited to the hilt. Of the three, Alec Mason was the one she reviled most of all. A slimy, blue-eyed, blonde-haired narcissus, who spent most of his time preening himself in every mirror he passed. From the moment they had met, he leered at her; she could almost see him salivating at the prospect of forcing himself on her. On several occasions in the last twenty-four hours, she had to fend off his lascivious and lecherous advances. The thought of him touching her made her skin crawl. Landfall couldn't come soon enough.

Vargas and Mason sat chatting about their plans once the Ra docked in Casablanca. Buchan drank her coffee and listened to the men talk; she considered them chauvinists of the first order, with no interest in anything or anyone but themselves. She went up on deck for some fresh air. Thankfully, the drizzle had stopped, but it was the murkiest of days with little prospect of improvement; there was still a considerable swell, and even a vessel of the Ra's size found the sea heavy going. Buchan spent several minutes enjoying the bracing sea air before a large wave crashed onto the bow, sending sea spray cascading over the ship, dousing the unsuspecting Buchan with water and sending her scurrying for cover. As she closed the hatch and turned into the companionway, she bumped into Vargas, who looked at her for a moment, then burst out laughing at the sight of her drenched hair and windswept appearance.

Buchan continued down the narrow companionway towards her cabin, the rolling of the ship in the heavy seas causing her to pause and steady herself several times. Mason appeared from the opposite end of the corridor as she approached her door, grinning inanely as he walked towards her. She pressed herself against the wall and breathed in to let him pass behind her. He stopped directly behind her, putting his arms around hers, and pushing himself up against her. She hated the smell of his obnoxious and overpowering cheap aftershave as he ground himself into her. Mason's hands moved down the length of Buchan's arms until he reached her wrist, then pulled the right one behind her back and held it tight as he roughly squeezed her breast through her damp T-shirt. It was a loathsome moment with a despicable human being. She pushed back against the wall, and Mason gave ground and let go of her.

'If you ever fucking touch me again, Olga Devereux will have you chopped up and used as shark bait and don't think I won't tell her,' said Buchan angrily as she pushed him aside, opened her stateroom door, went inside and locked it. She sat on the bed, shaking, partly in rage and partly in shock, praying that her threat would be enough to keep him in check until they reached port.

As Buchan finished towelling herself down and changing her clothes, a siren sounded. She could hear the sound of running footsteps along the companionway next to her stateroom. Following the sound of the footsteps, she arrived at the bridge.

'What's happening? What's going on?' she asked urgently.

'That French patrol boat is what's happening, it's coming up fast on the port quarter,' said Vargas. 'They've ordered us to heave to and prepare to be boarded for a customs inspection, as we are in their territorial waters,' said Vargas.

'What are you going to do?' asked Buchan anxiously.

'I told you what my orders are. There is also a British Border Force cutter approaching from the North-East. We can't be caught with Travers aboard, the ship will be impounded and we'll all be arrested,' said Vargas.

'But that's murder!' said Buchan.

'It's a bit late to have a conscience, you've blood on your hands like the rest of us,'

Vargas turned away from Buchan, raised his binoculars to the window as he searched for the approaching French ship in the gloom, then addressed Samuels.

'Captain, turn to port, bring our port side to bear, then stop your engines.'

Buchan stood motionless and stared out of the window in disbelief as the drama unfolded in front of her, as Vargas gave further instructions to his co-conspirator.

'Alec, we'll dump him over the starboard side, out of sight of the Frenchies, go and get Karl, and Alec, make sure he's properly weighted, I don't want him found, understand?'

Ignoring the two men, Buchan slipped away, left the bridge, and quickly made her way down the companionway towards the crew quarters. As she descended to the lower deck, she met Belakin strolling along the corridor towards her.

'All quiet, Karl?' she asked. 'Travers isn't making a nuisance of himself?'

Belakin touched his nose. It still smarted. 'If he did, I rearrange his face permanently.'

'That's good. There's trouble, Vargas wants you on the bridge right away,' she said

The Russian nodded fleetingly, then slowly shuffled his way past Buchan and climbed the ladder leading to the upper decks. Buchan continued along the companionway until she stood in front of the locked door where Travers was being held. On a small shelf opposite the door was the key. Buchan hesitated, anxiously glanced both ways along the corridor and back to the door. After pausing again, she turned and snatched the key. Gripped by tension, her hand trembled uncontrollably as she tried to insert the key, causing a terrible rattle that she was sure could have been heard all over the ship. Eventually, the key nestled securely in the lock, and she was able to unlock and open the door. Travers, alerted by the noise, was already poised and standing in the middle of the cabin.

'Now what?' asked Travers, who was surprised to see her again so soon.

'Never mind, come on! You have to get out of here. There is a French patrol boat coming alongside soon. Vargas has ordered you to be shackled and dumped over the side before we are searched. Quickly, come on, we only have a matter of seconds,' said Buchan anxiously.

She grabbed Travers' arm and ushered him swiftly out of the cabin. On the bridge of the Ra, Balakin joined the group. Vargas was staring out of the window, and the French ship was now in sight and heading straight for them. Hearing Balakin's arrival, he put down his binoculars, muttering a Portuguese expletive under his breath, which made one of the Brazilian officer chuckle.

'Heidi said you want me,' said the Russian.

'Heidi?' said Vargas, turning with surprise towards Mason. 'Ok, listen, Karl, the French will be coming alongside, they'll be looking for Travers. You and Alec get down there. There's some heavy-gauge chain in the engine room. When we present our port side to the French, drop him over the starboard side and don't leave a fucking mess, I don't want them to find a hair of his on board, understand?'

Mason smirked malevolently, slapping the amused Belakin on the back as the two men began the short walk leading to the ladder to the lower decks and the crew quarters.

Stopping first at the engine room, Belakin located a suitable length of heavy, thick chain and a padlock. He passed it to the slightly built Mason, who struggled to lift it, causing the burly, muscular Russian to roar with laughter at Mason's weakness.

'Maybe, I take you to gym when we get to port, put some muscle on your bones,' said Belakin condescendingly.

'Fuck off, you're just a muscle-bound gorilla. There are more important things in life than that,' said Mason, running his fingers through his thickly gelled blonde hair and admiring his reflection in a sheet of polished aluminium. 'Shit! If I were as ugly as you, I'd jump off the boat too.'

The Russian sneered as he took the length of chain from Mason and easily tossed it on his shoulders. Leaving the claustrophobic confines of the engine room, the pair walked along the companionway towards the crew quarters. On reaching the door to Travers's cabin, Mason looked across to the small shelf opposite where the key to the cabin had been left. It was missing. He turned to Balakin and asked him where he had put the key. The Russian looked blankly, patting his trouser pockets as though to indicate that he didn't have it.

On leaving the cabin, Travers had shut and re-locked the door, retaining the key, a decision that would sow confusion and, hopefully, buy them crucial minutes. Mason tried the door.

'Shit! Wait here, I'll go and get the spare,' said the irritated Mason.

It wasn't long before he returned armed with the replacement key. The Ra had begun her turn to port using her bow thrusters with the main engines now stopped. Quickly, Mason unlocked the door and, to his rage, found that it was empty.

'That two-faced bitch, she must have let him out; we've got to find them,' said Mason angrily. They had five, perhaps ten minutes before the French Patrol vessel came alongside. Mason called out to Vargas and informed him of the escape. Moments later, Vargas appeared bristling with fury.

'They won't get far, start searching, I'll turn on the CCTV. Karl, get enough chain for both of them!'

Travers and Buchan squatted in the Tender Garage on the lower deck aft, behind an aluminium-hulled Zodiac tender and a pair of jet skis. They knew it wouldn't be long before they heard the footsteps of their pursuers, but for a few precious moments, they had a sanctuary and time to think. Travers looked across at his unexpected auburn-haired guardian angel, who was still shaking. He stretched out his hand and squeezed her trembling fingers.

'Don't worry, we'll make it,' he said reassuringly. 'We just have to stay out of the way until the French come aboard.'

'Couldn't we use those?' said Buchan, looking at the Jet Skis.

Travers looked at them, 'Have you ever used one?' he said.

'No, but how hard could it be?'

It would have been fun to see Vargas and his cutthroats' expression as they rode away, but the sea was far too rough to contemplate it, and Buchan looked a nervous wreck.

'By the way, thank you, Heidi, but why the change of heart? You know if they catch you, you'll be killed. You really are between the devil and the deep blue sea now.'

'I've got so much wrong in my life, made so many bad choices. More recently, becoming involved with Olga Devereux has ruined so many lives, not just my own. When Vargas said that he was going to dump you overboard, I just thought, how many more people are going to be killed before I realise what a fool I've been.'

Travers held her hand and put an arm around her shoulder as the tears began to flow down her cheeks. She sobbed with a mixture of despair and remorse. It was as though all the trauma and guilt of the last few months had finally overwhelmed her, and she had now reconciled herself to whatever punishment the UK authorities would prescribe. As he comforted her, he heard voices approaching and hatches slamming. He shook Buchan's shoulders; the wolves were at the door. At any moment, the water-tight door to the Tender Garage would swing open, and their executioners would appear. Instinctively, Travers looked around; there were very few options, a few large cupboards under the Zodiac's tarpaulin, all places that would certainly be searched. Attached to one of the walls close by were a pair of fire extinguishers. Jumping up, he grabbed the CO_2 cylinder and ran to the watertight door.

'Heidi, keep down, keep quiet and don't move,' said Travers, who waited behind the heavy door with the extinguisher now primed and ready. Standing on the balls of his feet, poised, the tension was almost unbearable. As much as he tried to control his breathing, all he could hear was his heart pounding away. His eyes strained as they focused on the steel door handle, watching for the slightest movement. A small bead of perspiration trickled down his forehead and landed with a splat on the metal canister.

Travers's eyes narrowed as footsteps sounded directly outside. A second or two later, the steel handle began to turn. Travers' body tensed, every muscle and sinew strung almost to breaking point. The heavy door swung open. The menacing figure of Karl Balakin stepped through, his eyes scouring the garage. Travers held his breath. When the burly Russian turned around, they would come face to face. Balakin took another step forward and opened the tall cupboard nearest to him. It was empty. He leaned over and tilted his head to look around the white Zodiac. Buchan, fearing discovery, shifted her position slightly, causing one of her knees to crack. Balakin grunted with satisfaction as he pulled out his large hunting knife.

'Come out,' ordered the Russian.

Buchan stood up and, pensively, slowly walked towards him.

'Where's the other one?' he snarled, gesturing with his knife for her to follow him.

'Right here!' came the reply.

Balakin turned and instantly found himself engulfed by the discharge of the CO2 extinguisher. Travers called out to Buchan, who ran behind the flaying arms of the Russian and out of the Tender Garage. With the extinguisher almost exhausted, Travers belted the disoriented man on the side of his head with the empty container, sending him sprawling to the floor.

With the Russian incapacitated, Travers stepped out of the garage, shaking and breathing heavily after the shock of the altercation. Looking along the companionway, he saw Buchan at the far end. There was no sign of Mason or Vargas. The Ra's engines remained silent as the ship manoeuvred using only her thrusters. Travers and Buchan climbed the ladder to the next deck, which would give them access to the open areas. As they peered through a stateroom window on the port side, they could now see the French Patrol Boat Maroni coming towards them through the sea mist. Travers estimated it was now no more than 1,000 meters away. They just needed to avoid apprehension for a few more minutes. Travers continued to watch as their French deliverers drew closer. His attention was suddenly broken by an urgent and insistent tug on his arm from Buchan, who had been anxiously watching for their pursuers from the edge of the doorway.

'Greg, come on! I think someone's coming,' she whispered urgently.

Travers left his vantage point and joined Buchan at the entrance of the luxurious stateroom. He, too, could now hear voices.

'It's Vargas and that sleazy shit Mason,' said Buchan.

Travers grabbed Buchan's shaking hand and led her out of the stateroom and onto the windswept deck through a hatch. As he edged further forward, he heard a sudden cry! Startled, he turned around to see the struggling Buchan, her wriggling feet off the ground, locked in a bear hug by the slimy Alec Mason. Before Travers had a chance to intervene, he felt a clubbing blow to the back of his head that brought him to his knees. Stunned, he was aware of being dragged semi-conscious through the ship until he found himself lying face down on the deck on the starboard side. As he tried to rise from his prone position, he received a painful kick to his side from the now-recovered thug Balakin, who, with retaliation on his mind, gave the Brit a second vicious kick for good measure. Travers lifted his head a little; the terrified Buchan was lying on the deck in front of him, quivering and crying, her hands tied in front of her and her feet bound by a heavy chain, secured by a padlock with several meters of unused chain still attached.

'This is how we deal with traitors,' said Vargas angrily, nodding towards Buchan.

Travers looked across at the terrified woman staring forlornly back at him, her eyes streaming with tears. He felt helpless, if only the French would arrive now and save the day, but his logical mind didn't let him believe in miracles, only ones of the man-made variety. As he thought about the watery fate that awaited them in the next few minutes, there was a call from the bridge; the Maroni was coming alongside. Vargas acknowledged the call and, with a final perfunctory word of goodbye to Travers, instructed Balakin and Mason to dispose of their unwelcome passengers quickly before the French came aboard and their secret was discovered. Vargas then left the scene and returned to the bridge to greet the French officials.

Balakin was a hulking brute of a man with a bad temper to match. Earlier in the Tender Garage, Travers had caught him by surprise, but now things were different. His only advantage was the massive adrenaline surge building up in his body from the sure knowledge that if he didn't do something quickly, he would end up as fish food at the bottom of the English Channel. The Russian stamped hard on Travers's neck, then asked Mason for a cable tie to secure

Travers's hands. Mason reached into his pocket and produced a black nylon 6/6 tie, then leaned towards Balakin, who stepped off Travers's neck, took a large stride towards his accomplice, and reached out. With his adversary slightly off balance, Travers made his move.

As the two men grappled, Mason struggled to drag Buchan towards the edge of the deck. Despite being bound hand and foot, she wriggled frantically for her life. Mason, now facing her with his arms around her back, lifted her off her feet and tried to carry her to the edge to bundle her over the side into the frigid waters. However, the weight of the chain around her ankles and his slight build made it difficult, forcing him to put her down several times before he finally reached the side of the deck. He looked around to see Balakin, red-faced with his tongue protruding from his mouth, on his knees, with Travers clinging to his back like a large octopus with his forearm across the muscular Russian's throat, gradually choking the breath and the strength out of him.

Mason sat Buchan on the side of the ship and turned to Travers with a smarmy stare.

'Let him go, or I drop the bitch. Let him go, I said!'

Travers could feel Balakin's body going limp beneath him as the Russian began to lose consciousness. He looked across at Buchan and knew he risked losing his advantage if he let go. However, if he didn't, she was finished. Reluctantly, he loosened his grip, and the Russian slumped forward, gasping for breath. Mason grinned as he took hold of Buchan and raised her to the edge. With a final heave, he flung her over the side and into the cold grey waters. As he did so, she threw her bound arms over his head and around his shoulders, the momentum carrying them both over the side. Mason screamed in terror, locked in a deadly embrace; she wouldn't die alone. The only other sound was the clatter of the length of heavy chain following them into the water and dragging them both to the bottom. Travers desperately tried to reach the end of the chain before it disappeared, but he was too late. It had gone, and so had Buchan. Travers leaned over the side and looked into the water at the stream of bubbles that was all that was left.

As he tried to absorb the horror of what had just happened, Travers heard running footsteps approaching. The cavalry, in the form of the Maritime Gendarmerie, had finally arrived. Vargas had already been arrested. As they rushed down onto the deck, two officers took hold of Balakin. To Travers's surprise, he showed no resistance and was led away towards the Maroni. One of the French officers walked across to the spot where Travers sat and introduced herself as Lieutenant Dumas. Despite a strong French enunciation, her English was excellent. There was a soft, comforting lilt to her voice, which Travers found endearing and calming. Dumas informed him that the Ra would be escorted back to Cherbourg and impounded during the Police investigation. Once he had provided a full statement to the police, he was free to return to England pending any further requests from the French authorities to appear before them. Travers thanked the young officer for her kindness as she beckoned him to follow her to the Maroni. He stood up, still unsteady on his feet, he stretched out his arm and grabbed a railing for support. After a momentary pause, he steadied himself, walked across the deck to the spot where Buchan had disappeared, and looked over the side into the grey unforgiving water. For a few seconds, he was lost in thought, thoughts of regret, and her ultimate sacrifice. The spell was broken when the Lieutenant called his name. Travers, reluctantly, turned and slowly followed her off the Ra and to freedom.

Foreword

Greg Travers has survived this encounter, but survival and victory are not always synonymous—and this victory isn't quite won just yet. As he'll soon discover, some enemies don't accept defeat. They simply regroup, recalibrate, and return with renewed purpose. The next time Travers crosses paths with the Devereux legacy, the stakes will be higher, the betrayals more intimate, and the cost of failure absolutely unthinkable.

Published in Collaboration with Noble Legacy Publishing

www.noblelegacypublishing.co.uk